Don't Fall

Michelle Lee

BLUE FORGE PRESS
Port Orchard ☸ Washington

This story is for
the girls in my life
who always have my back,
no matter how ridiculous
the situation is.
Thanks for keeping life
interesting and fun.

Don't Fall

Michelle Lee

Chapter 1

"Austin!" I yelled up the stairs for the third time. "Mom," Austin said from directly behind me, exasperated, "I'm right here."

I yelped and jumped and spun around, almost tipping over. "Stop sneaking up on me like that!" I exclaimed.

"Situational awareness, Mom," Austin repeated for about the hundredth time this week, a bored look on his face. "Why are you yelling?"

"I was only yelling because you didn't answer me. I wanted to let you know I was meeting the girls for our girl's night," I reminded him.

Austin's eyes flicked over me in that judgmental teenage way that drove me up the wall. "You should put on some makeup. It's time for you to get out and date now. I won't be around here forever to watch out for you."

"Last time I checked, it was me taking care of you." I poked my finger into his chest. *When had Austin gotten so grown up? At least grown up enough, he cared about my dating life and whether I wore makeup, I thought to myself.*

"I'm not talking about taking care of you. I know you take care of yourself, but I don't want you to climb a ladder to change a light bulb and fall off and break a bone." Austin looked like he was about to start ticking off a list of accidents I've had trying to do things around the house.

"That's enough. Is this your subtle way of telling me you aren't going to come home and help your aging mother out with manly chores?" I raised my eyebrow at my son, wondering about his sudden interest in my dating life. "Dating someone for the purpose of helping me around the house isn't cool."

He'd gotten so tall. I have no idea where that came from; Shane wasn't tall, and I certainly wasn't. Austin had my coloring, though, and honey-colored hair. He was a good-looking kid, about the only good thing that had come from my marriage to his father.

"You know that's not what I'm saying," Austin protested, looking unsure of himself now. "You aren't old. I just don't want to worry about you while I'm at college. You get these ideas in your head that you can do everything, and then you end up hurt because you tried, and that clumsy demon inside you takes over."

I snorted in laughter. "Clumsy demon? That's a new one."

"Whatever, Mom. Where are you going? Is Sasha going to be there?" Austin asked, looking interested.

Sasha was one of my oldest friends and probably the edgiest out of them. She was pixie-like in appearance, looking half her age, but she was badass. Sasha might be small but don't cross her. Black leather and lace was her style, *and* she had major skills in self-defense.

"Yes, and Hope and Lily too. We are meeting at the new martini bar that opened," I told him, watching his face for clues as to what he was thinking. "Why? What are your plans?"

"I don't have any. I asked because Sasha will make sure you get home okay," Austin hedged, looking at his feet.

I bit back a laugh. Austin asked because he had a crush on Sasha. He has since he was born. He was probably hoping she would come by so he could see what new wild outfit she was wearing now. By day, Sasha was this demure social worker, but as soon as she left work, this badass dominatrix woman came roaring out of her.

"Seriously, Mom. Go put on eyeliner or something. For a mom, you're hot. You are oblivious, but you aren't ugly. You listen to rock and metal, talk real, have sarcasm for days, and are funny. You haven't dated one person in three years." Austin pushed me back towards my bedroom.

"Oblivious?" I asked, stunned at his admission. "You just called me oblivious? What am I oblivious to?" It was the only part my brain could latch on to at his statement.

"Everything," Austin insisted. "Go do it. You deserve to have fun." He yanked my purse off my arm.

Too shocked to argue, I walked back to my bedroom, put on a bit of eyeliner, and rechecked my outfit, suddenly overcome with self-consciousness. I'd lost weight the past three years, but not in my boobs where I had wanted to. So now I had giant boobs, a smaller stomach, and full hips. The hourglass shape was there, at least.

In my opinion, I had weirdly shaped calves and big hands. My feet were large, too, for my five-foot-five height. Girly clothes didn't look right on me. My hair was wavy and a mix of light brown and dirty blond, and my eyes were hazel. My voice was my best asset. It was sultry sounding. I didn't know how to dress that up, though.

I studied myself with a critical eye and decided to stop worrying about it. I wasn't setting out to try and land a date. I was only meeting my friends for some much-needed downtime. We met once a month, all four of us together, to vent, unload, catch up, and laugh at what our lives had become. Not that we didn't see each other during the week.

"Change your shirt," Austin said, popping into my room and heading to my closet.

"Isn't it weird for you to try to make your mother attractive to men?" I asked him acidly, following him with my eyes.

"Kind of, but half my friend's dads think you're hot, so I'm going off that. Plus, you seriously do need to get back out there and live a little. Dad has," he said, suddenly timid as he went through my closet.

"Is that what this is about, Austin? You feel bad because your dad is dating?" The pieces started clicking for me. "I don't care, Austin."

I bit back the retorts about Shane's skills in bed and his penchant for masturbation and porn. Austin didn't need to know those things. I wish *I* didn't know those things. He already knew about the masturbation and porn problems, but he didn't need to know about the lacking sex life.

"It just bothers me. You're kinda awesome and here alone with me all the time and Dad's a class-A douche and dating," Austin murmured and pulled out a low-cut shirt and threw it at me. "Wear that, and put on one of your pairs of strappy shoes."

I frowned. "Do we need to have a sexuality talk?" He almost sounded like Lily. "It's okay if you're gay."

"I'm not gay, Mom. I just know what men like to see," Austin huffed, rolled his eyes and walked out of my room.

This conversation would make the girls laugh for sure. Austin had grown up way too much in the past three years; it wasn't just height. He was an adult. Austin had graduated high school, gotten into the college of his choice, held down a job, dated, made good decisions, and helped me out. He'd also developed a strong dislike for his father, which made me a little happy.

I put the shirt on and picked out strappy, flat sandals. I didn't need heels to make me fall over; it happened naturally. I rechecked myself and decided it was good enough. I went out to get Austin's approval, and he smiled and nodded.

"Much better." He returned to texting whoever he was talking to or doing on his phone. He moved it, snapped a picture of me, and then ignored me.

"If you decide to go out, leave a note, so I don't worry," I told him, pulling my purse back onto my shoulder.

"Wait, this is your phone." Austin called me back

and then slid my phone into my purse with a strange little smile on his face.

"Why were you playing with my phone?" I asked Austin suspiciously.

"Because I could, and you wouldn't," was his cryptic answer. He kissed me on the cheek and pushed me to the front door. "Don't keep Sasha waiting; she's likely to do something evil to get payback."

That was true. I still had time, but Austin had disappeared before I could question him again. Damn kid. Lucky for him, I thought he was pretty fantastic. Austin had moments of driving me batty, but he'd never done anything outright wrong or pushed me to the limits of my patience, unlike his father.

I married Shane at twenty-two and divorced him at thirty-seven. Fifteen years I spent with a man who had more passion for his right hand than he'd ever had for me. Well, to be fair, he had quite an appetite for porn too. Just not for me, it turns out. Austin found an entire room's worth of porn and his father utilizing it and his hand one day. It disgusted him so severely that Austin didn't talk to him for a month, which was traumatizing for a fifteen-year-old.

Shane didn't even have enough decency to stop to check on his son. He kept right on going, stroking and grunting away. I returned from the grocery store to find Austin crying and Shane cleaning up his sticky mess. I don't know why that had been the last straw, but it had. I hired a lawyer and filed for divorce the following week. Whatever, I had my girls, my son, a crappy job in customer service, and the house.

Fifteen years of that. I shook my head as I turned

into the parking lot. I couldn't believe someone was honestly willing to date Shane. I was even more surprised that Austin knew about it. Shane didn't make much effort to keep in touch with his son or be a father, even when we were married. It was sad. It made me a better mother, though.

Chapter 2

I should have known something was up when Austin had my phone. I walked into the bar, and Sasha could barely keep a straight face. It took me a few minutes of being tortured by them to put it together.

"If it isn't Miss independent and sarcastic but with a heart of gold," Sasha snarked as I sat down in the booth.

"Hello to you too," I answered her with a raised eyebrow. "What do I owe that greeting to?"

"You look pretty." Hope gave me a sly smile. "How's Austin?"

"Is he still breathing?" Lily asked.

Sasha burst out laughing. "Oh, my God! She doesn't even know!"

I gave Sasha a dirty look as my eyes flicked between them. "Austin is still breathing, as far as I know. Why wouldn't he be? What don't I know?"

A flurry of giggles struck the women as a waitress approached the table. "Hiya, Lena. You are even prettier in person. What can I get you?" The young waitress asked me with a flirtatious smile.

Sasha snorted and rolled her eyes. "Figures.

Round of margaritas, please," she answered, my confusion evident now. "I'll send Lena up to talk to you later. For now, she's ours."

The waitress walked away with a wink, and I looked back at my friends. "Someone going to clue me in, or do I need to guess? Was she hitting on me?"

"She was definitely hitting on you." Sasha shook her head at me. "Was Austin playing with your phone today?"

"Yeah, so spill it." I leaned forward to glare at my best friend.

Sasha pulled her phone out and did a few things, then slid it across the table, smirking. "Looks like you are on the market."

I glanced at her phone and saw myself staring back out at me. "What the hell is this?"

"An app that alerts you to single people in your area looking for love," Hope filled in helpfully.

"What?" I whispered exaggeratedly. "No way." I snatched up Sasha's phone and read the brief profile. "Don't know that I'm attractive, but I'm independent, sarcastic, have good taste in music, and a son who isn't afraid to beat a man's ass for being inappropriate with his mother," I read out loud.

Sasha burst out laughing again. "I love that kid!"

"Austin's grounded for life," I declared to the table, pushing Sasha's phone back at her. "He told me tonight that I need to start dating again because he's going off to college, and he doesn't want me to climb a ladder to change a light bulb and fall off."

Hope and Lily cracked up, laughing. "Give him credit. You've done that."

"Changing light bulbs is not a good reason to date!" I argued. "I think Austin's bothered that Shane is apparently dating. He told me that, too."

"Eeww, who would do that?" Lily growled. "He reeks of desperation."

"Shane reeks of masturbation and stale sperm," Sasha corrected and then snorted at the waitress's raised eyebrows as she set our drinks down.

"This table is so clearly the table to be waiting on tonight. Anything to eat, ladies?" Her gaze wandered back to me, and I wanted to recheck that app to see if it listed me as a lesbian.

"Nachos," I replied automatically. "Tonight is unquestionably a nacho night."

"I'm Hannah. I'll be with you all night," she purred and wrote down my order. Sasha again snorted, shook her head, and ordered a burger. Hope and Lily ordered salads.

"Seriously. Your son puts you on an app, and you have the hottest waitress in the place ready to declare her love for you as soon as you walk in. What the hell?" Sasha leaned forward. "You aren't even bi. I am, and she didn't even look twice at me! I'm hot as hell!"

"Maybe you should put yourself on that app," I snarked back at her.

"I'm on the damn app! How do you think I knew about you?" Sasha threw her hands up in the air. "It's those curves of yours. I have none of those."

"Why didn't I know you were on dating apps?" I chose not to address the curve statement.

"Because you don't listen?" Hope guessed. "I knew."

"Yep, me too," Lily joined in and gave me a bewildered look.

"I do, too, listen." It was weak because, obviously, I didn't listen to that.

"I'm on all the damn dating things, which gives me an idea now that you are out there. Let's test these sites out. Do each of the major ones for a month and compare the dates," Sasha suggested.

"No," I answered immediately. "I don't have time for that. I work and have a son."

"You have an adult son who doesn't need to be taken care of," Lily corrected. "I'm game. I could use some action."

"By action, you just want to get laid." Hope laughed and gulped her drink.

"Damn right, I do!" Lily crowed, the alcohol already hitting her empty stomach.

"Pact time." Sasha got that evil look on her face.

"We are too old for pacts," I argued again with a groan.

"You are in your prime," Sasha fired back. "We all are. We have to accept all legitimate date requests and talk about them on the podcast. No names, obviously, so we don't get in trouble, but come on, dating in our forties is not easy, and the pool is way too chlorinated."

"That seems like a good reason not to do this," I protested. "I don't think I can handle crazy. I'm not interested in women either."

"Don't knock it until you try it," Sasha scolded me, crossing her arms under her tiny breasts.

Sasha had a point. "Okay, fine. If a woman sparks

that sort of interest in me, I will go on a date with her. It hasn't happened yet, and truly, if it were going to, that waitress would have done it. She's stunning."

"Yeah, she is. I'm jealous," Sasha agreed. "She had my eye from the moment I walked in."

"To be fair, you can list yourself as straight on the sites. I think Austin didn't pay attention and mark that box," Hope clarified. "I'm curious, though. What's it like to be with a woman?"

"Are you asking about sex?" Sasha grinned. "Because that answer depends on you, sweet cheeks. If you get wild, then that's how it is. A woman knows a woman's body."

Lily burst into giggles. "That sounds like an argument for masturbation. No one knows my body better than me."

That just made me think of Shane, and I cringed. "Can I specify no porn freaks?"

"I think if you put that down, no man will respond." Hope rolled her eyes theatrically and shook her head.

Sasha was busy doing something on her phone, and my brain started to go into a dull panic mode. I called it dull because the alcohol had numbed it some by now. "I seriously can't do this. I'm not like you guys. I'm fat and ugly, divorced, with a kid and a dead-end job. I've just gotten to a place in my life where I don't hate myself. If strangers reject me, it might put me back in that bad place."

"Someone's filter came off." Sasha glanced up at me with raised eyebrows. "Sugar, how long have I known you? How long have we all known you?" Sasha's mom was from the South, and Sasha had picked up her habit of using Southern terms of endearment back in grade school.

"A long time," I muttered, drinking a large gulp from the margarita. "You all are biased. You have to be all supportive and crap because you love me and are my friends."

Sasha stood up quietly and headed to the bathroom. Hope gave me a pointed look. "Do you think we would go through with this if we thought we were just setting you up for rejection? Lena, we *all* are doing it. We all have the same shot at rejection as you."

"Maybe finding a hookup will help you regain some of your confidence," Lily said gently. "Lena, you are gorgeous."

Sasha slid back into her seat as the waitress brought the food out. Hannah once again openly flirted with me. "Hey, Hannah, do you work here full-time?" Sasha asked her.

"Sure do. Almost every night but Sunday. Why is that?" Hannah answered curiously.

"We're gonna experiment to help out Lena. We will sign up for each of the major online dating sites and a few of the apps. If we bring dates here, I'd like to know we have someone as backup close by," Sasha told her with a winning smile.

"For real?" Hannah looked over at me with a curious expression on her face.

"For real," Hope answered with a smirk, flipping her dark brown hair over her shoulder.

"Like we could give you a phrase or signal if the date is bad and you can help us get out of here. Lena here, lovely Lena, is a little lacking in the confidence department. Maybe knowing she had backup would help her a little," Sasha told Hannah, sealing my fate in this crazy scheme. "Her son is setting up her profile as we speak. He's in completely."

"That's why you left the table? You went to enlist my son?" My jaw dropped open in shock. Austin was in serious trouble.

"Austin started it by putting you on the other one. He's got a point, sugar. Your marriage was awful. I'm not sure you know what an orgasm is. You've been single and celibate for three years now; it's time. Austin is leaving for college soon, and you seriously are a walking disaster," Sasha went on. "Roll the dice and take a chance, as my grandma says."

"I'm in." Hannah gave me a considering look. "I need to spend some time with you. I won't hit on you anymore. At least I'll try not to. Give me your phone," Hannah demanded, holding out her hand.

I raised my eyebrows, but Sasha kicked me under the table, and I handed my phone over. Hannah typed something, smiled, and gave my phone back. "Okay?" I put it back in my purse, confused.

"I sent myself a text from your phone and then saved myself as a contact in yours. I'll be in touch." Hannah winked at me and returned to work.

I turned back to Sasha with a frown. "I know what an orgasm is." I felt my face heating up.

"From someone other than yourself?" Sasha fired back quickly.

"Yes," I retorted. "I dated before marrying Shane."

"Oh, my God!" Hope cried. "You haven't had an orgasm in over eighteen years?"

Totally embarrassed and not nearly drunk enough for that conversation, I ate my nachos while Lily and Hope stared at me in horror. "I didn't say that."

"You kind of did, sugar." Sasha grinned at me. "I've got your back. You are going on dates. And you will also learn what some of these lovely toys are for."

"Bullet, for sure," Lily said right away.

"I think I'm in hell right now. Are we honestly going to discuss sex toys and masturbation in a bar while my son is setting me up on some online dating site?" I was utterly flummoxed. This conversation couldn't possibly be happening. I stood up and went to the bar, Hannah rushing over to help me. "I need another margarita."

"Why are you blushing?" Hannah eyed me again. She seriously was stunning. Tall and slender, with mid-length wavy blonde hair. Bronze skin, a body that looked to be perfect, and crystalline blue eyes. She had cheekbones I hadn't seen in myself since before I was pregnant with Austin, lips that Sasha would call juicy, and a dainty, pointed chin.

"They are talking about what sex toys I need to get," I replied, my filter gone. I blushed even harder, realizing what I had just said aloud, in public, within earshot of several men who all turned to look at me.

"Mind your business," Hannah told them and leaned towards me. "I can help you out with that, too. Fingers work, but a girl needs variety. Let me get you that drink."

A man close to my age who had perked up at the

mention of sex toys moved closer to me. "I see you're trying to get back out there. Would you like to go on a date with me? I can be your guinea pig."

"Are you just hoping you can roll over and Lena will scratch your belly for you?" Hannah came back over and slid a drink across to me. "It's on your table's tab," she told me. She looked back at the guy and asked, "Is this because you heard us talking about sex toys?"

"No, though, that was an intriguing conversation. I asked because Lena popped up on my app as available and looking," the man clarified, narrowing his eyes at Hannah. "Do you have a stake in this?" He looked between us.

"She's my friend, so, yep." Hannah winked at me again.

I was in some alternate dimension right now. There was no way this was happening. Not to me. Things like this didn't happen to me. Women who looked like Hannah didn't flirt with old ladies like me, nor did men who were semi-decent looking come over and ask me out in the spur of the moment.

"Lena, isn't it?" the man persisted. "I'm Darren. Would you like to get dinner with me next week?"

"She can't on Sunday; she has plans. Any other day, she could," Hannah answered, and through the buzzing in my brain, I understood she was telling me she would be here any other day.

"Um, okay," I answered hesitantly, still unsure about this whole thing. "Monday or Tuesday about six would work. We can do it here. This place is easy for me, and I know the food is good."

"You have a date, Lena. I'll see you at six on

Tuesday." Darren smiled, and I freaked out a little but somehow managed to smile back. I hoped it was a smile, at least, and not a grimace of pain.

I flew back to my table and sat down as quickly as possible. "What is happening? Is Mercury in retrograde, or is it a full moon? Have I been drugged?"

Sasha belted out a laugh. "This is going to be so fun. I love you, sugar. Did that man just ask you out?"

"He did. Tuesday, here at six. What was I thinking?" I blurted out and gulped my drink in four swallows.

"He's not bad looking. Give it a try. Hannah will help you if you need out." Hope elbowed me in the side. "Don't take him home or go home with him."

"Have you landscaped?" Lily asked me.

I could feel my face burning, and I chugged Hope's margarita and stuffed some nachos in my mouth. "No," I finally said.

"Then, no worries, Lena won't go that route," Lily confirmed. "Just don't do it before the date."

"When was the last time you even had sex?" Hope asked.

"I don't know," I mumbled, embarrassed, "five years ago, maybe, for three minutes."

"God, he was a tool," Sasha spit out. "Look, sugar, I know how far you've come and how hard it's been for you. Austin is right that it's time to test the waters because you are on a plateau. This little experiment of ours will push you to go farther and figure out what you want and who you are."

"Truthfully, the four of us couldn't be more different, so this is perfect. Our podcast will blow up.

Maybe we'll even get sponsors and get paid to do it," Lily thought out loud. "Think about it: how many single women our age are out there facing the same daunting task we are? The podcast is to help women with issues that we face. Dating is an issue a lot of us face. It will just be less serious than it normally is, not that we can't still discuss big issues or things that come up."

"We can be their voice," Hope added, throwing her weight into it. "We aren't the only 40-year-old single ladies trying to date."

"Or a horror show that turns them off dating forever." I downed the rest of Hope's margarita. "No sex. I can't do the sex with strangers thing. I'm not sure I want to fall in love, either."

"Damn, sugar, eat." Sasha glanced worriedly at me. "I'll text Austin to get a Lyft here and come to get you when it's time to go. No sex is fine. Roll the dice, but don't fall."

"No need, I'll drive her home in her car and take a Lyft back to my place," Hannah said, coming up with another drink. "Don't worry, ladies, I won't molest her."

"She'sh m'new friend," I slurred drunkenly.

Sasha gave me an amused look. "I haven't seen you drink that much in probably three years."

"Oh," Hope said sadly. "Yeah, when you filed for divorce. This is seriously scaring you, isn't it?"

"Sure is." I stuffed some more nachos in my mouth, trying to form words correctly. "Sasha has to take me sex toy shopping."

They all burst out laughing. "Oh, sugar. You'll have one in two days; I already ordered it." Sasha grinned that sassy smile at me. "Before you argue, you will *never* turn out like Shane. Just lock your door before you use it."

"Aren't you here all night?" Lily asked an amused Hannah. "Doesn't that mean Lena has to stay until you close?"

"I'm off at eleven. One of the guys closes down. Think you can make it that long?" Hannah nudged me playfully.

"Piece of cake," I said through a mouthful of nachos. "Do you have cake?"

Chapter 3

K eys, Lena." Hannah held her hand out to me. "Okay, sweets, which car is yours?"

"The old piece of shit sitting under the streetlight." I wobbled and pointed. Flats had been the right choice.

She slipped her arm around me to keep me from falling over. "I know you're straight, but damn. You seriously hit all the right notes."

"Sloppy drunk is the right notes?" I asked, surprised at the strength this young girl had.

Hannah laughed and struggled to keep me upright. "I don't think this is normal for you, Lena. That wasn't what I was talking about anyway."

"How do you know I'm straight?" I asked stupidly. "What if I want to experiment?"

"Then you know how to find me," Hannah told me seriously. "I also know it's not you, but a girl's gotta try."

"I'm way too old for someone like you. I mean, come on, the guys were practically drooling all over you." I squinted to try to get her in focus. "You're insanely hot."

Hannah plopped me down in the passenger seat of the car, reached across me to buckle my seatbelt, and put her breasts right in my face. She smelled good. I still wasn't sexually attracted to her. I wondered what she'd do if I bit her.

"Oh my God, you're hilarious. Your face gives you away. What dirty thought were you thinking, and why didn't you act on it?" Hannah smiled at me.

"I was thinking about biting you," I confessed sheepishly.

Hannah smirked, "I bite back, sweets."

She shut the door and crossed in front of the car as my face burned once again. "Wow. I just realized how inexperienced I am. Truly sad." I shook my head and made myself dizzy. "Is biting fun?"

"Jeez. I might need to screen these men for you." Hannah adjusted the seat back and looked at me. "Do you for real not have any toys?"

"Nope. Shane was boring as hell. I had vivid fantasies play out in my head each time we had sex, but it was still rare that I got off unless I did it myself. After the divorce, I was too busy trying to put my life back together even to consider dating and making those fantasies a reality," I admitted shamefully. I blushed again, realizing how much I had confessed to a stranger.

"Your ex-husband is an idiot." Hannah shook her head. "You exude sexuality. Like, off the charts. I may lean towards women, but I date both women and men, and you had me worked up all night. Not just me but the men around the bar, too. Do you honestly believe you are fat and ugly?"

"Seriously?" I scoffed. "Look at me; look

at you."

"Why are you comparing yourself to me?" Hannah asked bluntly. "We are different body types. You aren't even giving yourself a fair chance if you are going to compare yourself to everyone else."

"Why weren't you interested in Sasha?" I turned the questions around.

"She's not my type. She's gorgeous, don't get me wrong, but I wasn't attracted to her. I go for more docile and soft. On the other hand, if you had shown even the slightest bit of interest, I would have marked you as mine from the start," Hannah purred. "Those curves beg me to touch and explore. Your huge eyes, plump lips, and petite little nose, and damn, that voice is like pure sex."

"Uh, I don't really know what to say to that." I blushed and looked out the window.

"Tell me how to get to your place." Hannah sighed. "Text me when you get the toy so I can know what it is and direct you to others. Before expecting others to worship you, you must learn how to worship yourself."

I directed Hannah to my house and invited her in while she waited for the Lyft to come and get her. Austin wandered in and almost tripped over his tongue at the sight of her. "My son, Austin."

Hannah's eyes flicked over him as they had me, and my mom side came out, but I managed to bite my tongue before I said anything. Austin was an adult. "Hannah." She held out her hand. "I'm your mom's security detail on the dates she's going on."

"Yeah." Austin shook her hand and shuffled

around nervously, "about that. Two of my friends' dads have already called."

I tipped my head back on the couch and stared at the ceiling. I didn't know what to think about any of this. "What did you say?"

"I can't answer for you, Mom. I took the message and said I'd pass it along, so that's what I'm doing," Austin told me uncomfortably.

"How do you feel about it?" I raised my head and wished I hadn't.

"A little weird. Go out with the guys, but don't sleep with them," he said quietly.

I coughed. Discussing my sex life with my son wasn't something I was planning on doing. I wasn't planning on sleeping with any of the dates. "Wasn't planning on it, Aust."

"While you are still drunk, take me to your closet and show me your clothes." Hannah held her hand out for mine. "We'll start with clothes and work on your self-image."

"She doesn't have a self-image," Austin declared. "My mom's totally awesome, though. Clumsy as hell but incredible. She can talk about pretty much anything, listens, and gives fantastic advice. Her taste in music is good, and she can cook and take care of everyone. Except herself."

I glared at my son while, at the same time, melting a little at all the sweet things he said. "I don't have time to worry about myself." My defense was pathetic.

Hannah yanked me up, making me stumble into her. "That changes now, sweets. Point the way."

"Second door on the left." Austin pointed down the hallway.

I let her drag me to my room. Once she had the door closed, I flopped on my bed. "Austin's only eighteen," I told Hannah, my mom instincts making it past the haze of alcohol.

"Old enough to make his own decisions. He looks like you; that means he's hot. If he hits on me, I'm telling you right now that I won't turn him down. I won't hurt him, but I'm not turning down a night with him either."

"I don't know that I want to know that." Hannah's honesty floored me.

"Just being honest, sweets. I wouldn't turn you down either." She came over and straddled me; she reached for my shirt and yanked it off me. "Stand up."

I was too shocked to do much else than obey her. I stood as she circled me and then instructed me to take my pants off. "How old are you?" I asked her, pulling my jeans off, surprised I was doing what she demanded.

"Old enough to know my heart and what I want and young enough to chase after it," she said, circling me again. "Woman, how in the world can you not know how delectable you are? I'm having a hard time keeping my hands to myself."

"I don't know what to do with any of that," I muttered. "Why am I standing here almost naked?"

"Because I am trying to see what I am working with to help you understand how to learn to love it. If you feel good about what you are wearing, it translates to how you carry yourself, and how you carry yourself translates to how others see you," Hannah told me, studying me.

"They aren't going to see me like this," I protested, so nervous I started shaking.

"No, that was partially for my entertainment, but now I'm so turned on I want to run my tongue over you to make you shake for a different reason." Hannah raised her eyebrow at me. "I think you are perfect. First suggestion." She stalked towards my closet and returned with lingerie. "Wear only this kind of stuff. You'll know you have it on, and you'll feel sexy."

"What about the landscaping?" I muttered, somewhat embarrassed.

"Nothing wrong with natural, but I can help with that too." She shrugged. She squatted down and ran her hand down the outside of my leg without touching me. "Yum. Okay, wear more form-fitted clothes, like tapered-leg pants, leggings, or skinny jeans. These curves demand respect." Hannah stood up and brought her hands up over my ample hips. "These, damn, I'm going to have wet dreams. Flirty skirts, dresses that tuck in here," her fingers fluttered over my waist, "and flare out here, where they drape across this curve, men will be picking themselves up off the ground."

"I don't have the figure for form-fitted anything." I struggled with the words and fear. Though the thought of Hannah's touch didn't feel awkward, or I was far drunker than I'd imagined. He wouldn't have made it down the hallway if this was a man, yet here I was with a strange woman. This situation was a weird dichotomy I was incapable of thinking about at the moment.

"Lena, you do. You have the perfect hourglass

thing going on. Your clothes are all too big, sweets. Wear shirts that show a little cleavage. You don't have to go full-on risqué but show a little. Small heels will make your legs look a little longer, though right now, I'd like to see them open," Hannah flirted heavily.

"Oh, my God. You are too much." I pushed past her and grabbed my robe off the back of the closet door. "How is it you can help me with landscaping?"

"Easy. I work part-time in a salon as a waxer. I can bring my stuff over and do whatever you want done. The more confident you feel, the less the insecurities can take over." Hannah sat on the edge of my bed. "Seriously, Lena. You are a wet dream."

"You say these things like it's easy." I sat next to her.

"It is easy. I'm not lying. I wasn't lying about your son, either. I go where the attraction takes me." She patted my leg. "Since you aren't biting even though you wanted to, I'm going there if he does."

I didn't want that picture in my head. "I don't want to know," I said again.

"Go to sleep. I'll text you tomorrow, and we can figure out when to wax." Hannah stood up to leave.

I had a feeling that I would wake up entirely humiliated by what had happened throughout the night. I didn't argue with her. I just threw my robe on the ground, pulled my bra off, and climbed between the sheets.

<h1 style="text-align:center">Chapter 4</h1>

*W*hat do I do if they want to meet somewhere other than the bar?" I shouted through the phone at Sasha.

"You pick somewhere public, calm down." Sasha remained unflappable. "You can always schedule something for Austin's day off work and have him trail you. Why are you so nervous? Aren't these his friend's dads'?"

"Yeah. I'm nervous because I haven't dated in twenty years! God, is sex different now?" I mumbled, terrified of the answer.

"If you have an orgasm, I'd say it's different. You aren't doing that anyway, relax. Just call the men back. How'd the drive home go?" Sasha switched the subject.

"Well, Hannah had me standing in my bedroom in nothing but my underwear while she told me what clothes to wear and that she would wax me. She also said she'd sleep with Austin, so I'm not sure how I feel about that," I relayed in a rush.

Sasha burst out laughing. "I like her. She's one of us now."

"Sash, I swear, the things Hannah was saying

made me almost want to sleep with her," I admitted a lot more quietly than my previous shout.

"Good. That means you heard what Hannah was saying. I knew it would take a stranger to get through to you. I'm not saying sleep with her, but listen to her. She's got that whole blunt honesty thing going for her. Especially if she had balls enough to tell you she was going after Austin when she couldn't have you." Sasha laughed again. "Did mama bear come out?"

"If I hadn't been drunk out of my mind, she would have. I tamped it down. Besides, Hannah has a point; Austin's an adult. Mostly. I'm pretty sure he's going out with her tomorrow. I got a vague 'I'll be out tomorrow but back in time for dinner' statement," I told my best friend. I was confused and conflicted about the whole thing.

"Okay, call these men back. Set up the dates for after Tuesday with the Darren guy. Let him be the first; keep all of those to the bar. We'll deal with the other requests as they come in, and I can guarantee they will be coming in. I've seen the profile Austin set up for you. We'll do our first podcast of the experiment next Sunday. We can do it here." I knew Sasha was going through her calendar. "Noon."

"What about the waxing?" It was laughable how scared I sounded. "I thought you guys said not to landscape."

"Hannah has a point about feeling good about yourself. If you are worried about sex, don't shave your legs before the date. I'd defer to Hannah on that. She seems to have you dialed in." I could hear the grin in Sasha's voice.

"Fine. If I sleep with Hannah and like it, you are in trouble," I warned her.

Sasha's rich laugh came booming through the phone. "I'll be jealous, but I'm not scared of you. The mom voice only works on Austin. Your toy is being delivered on Monday, by the way. Use it before your date. Remember, forty isn't dead, sugar. You are just entering your peak years."

I hung up and stared down at the names and numbers Austin had written down on the little notepad by the phone that hadn't worked in years. I didn't know why it was still there. I was sure going out with his friend's fathers wasn't a good idea. That was all kinds of awkward. Damn it. They had me backed into a corner, and they all knew it.

I quickly dialed the first number before I chickened out. "Hi, uh, is Todd available?"

"This is Todd." The warm, masculine voice sent a tiny little wave of desire through me.

"Hi Todd, this is Lena. My son Austin told me you called last night. I'm returning your call," I started, unsure how to proceed.

"Lena! It's so nice to hear from you! I did indeed call. I saw you pop up on a singles app and wondered if you'd like to get dinner one night this week," Todd said immediately, cutting right to the chase.

"Sure," I hesitated, insecurities flooding me again. Maybe Hannah was right; I should have worn the lacy underwear despite not going anywhere. "I'm free Thursday."

"That's perfect. Is there somewhere you'd like to go?" Todd's voice was deep and manly, and I liked it, even if I couldn't picture who he was.

"The new martini bar that opened has good food. How about there?" I suggested, feeling a little guilty knowing Hannah would be watching.

"Sounds great. Five thirty, okay with you?" I could hear him writing.

"Yeah, that should work fine," I agreed. I'd barely make it on time, but it would work.

"Fantastic! I'm looking forward to it! Thanks for calling back," Todd replied with a smile in his voice. It was kind of hard to resist.

"I'm looking forward to it too. See you then," I told Todd, smiling and hanging up.

"Which one was that?" Austin said from behind me.

"Todd." I turned. "Which one is he? Have I met him?"

"That's Patrick's dad. I think you met him once. He's a big guy with a football player-type build. Hair's kind of gray, he works as a general contractor," Austin told me. "The other one, Mike, I don't like him as much. He makes me think of those slimy guys in movies. The ones that always play a salesman of some sort. Mike is Derrick's dad. Not tall and uses a lot of hair gel, and I think Mike bleaches his teeth; they are unnaturally white."

I stifled a laugh. Mike was assuredly one I wouldn't be interested in, but in the spirit of seeing this through, I made the call and set the date up for Friday night at that martini bar. I suspected I'd use Hannah to get out of that one early.

"Okay, kid. Show me how to use the site you

signed me up for; I'll probably need to know how to edit my profile, too." I ruffled Austin's hair, making him step back and glare at me.

"You aren't going to edit it. I'll show you, though." He walked me through using the site and showed me how to look through the profiles and send messages if I wanted to. I wasn't going to go that far and told him as much. Austin showed me the people who have viewed mine and then finally showed me how to read the messages sent to me.

"By the way, Mom. About Hannah." Austin shifted around uncomfortably. "She, uh, she expressed an interest in me, and I'd be an idiot to turn her down. She also told me she came on to you and that she is bisexual."

"Whoa." I held up my hand. "Don't tell me things I don't want to hear. Yes, Hannah is, and she did come on to me, but I'm not interested. If you are, please be careful and practice safe sex."

"You don't care if I go out with her?" he seemed shocked. "She said she was your friend."

"She is, and yeah, I sort of care. But I also understand you are an adult and can make your own decisions and mistakes in the dating area. Not that Hannah is a mistake, but you need to learn what you want in your way," I huffed unhappily. "It would also be hypocritical of me to say you couldn't since I'm going on dates with your friend's fathers."

"Are you sure you aren't interested in her?" Austin folded his hands on the table as if he was suddenly the parent and I was the child.

I sat down at the table and leaned back in the

chair. "Why would you think that I am?"

"I wasn't sure because you've turned down every date ever offered, haven't shown any interest in it, and," Austin shifted again, "dad jerked off all the time. I wasn't sure if it was because you swung the other way or not."

I sighed and laughed at the same time. "That made you think I was a lesbian? We seriously need to talk about your father, I guess. As for the other, I think every female is curious to a degree about what being with another female is like; I haven't come across one yet that makes me want to try. I have seen several beautiful women and thought and voiced their beauty, but that doesn't mean I'm attracted to them. I haven't thought about the dating part much because I was trying to put my life back together."

"Mom, you have your shit together more than anyone else I know," he told me, shocked.

"Language," I reminded him. "I'm happy I appear that way to you, but it's not true. My job as your mom is to keep you safe from the bad stuff, even when the bad stuff is in me."

"What's that supposed to mean? Are you sick?" Austin sat straight up and drilled his eyes into mine.

"No, I'm not sick. My relationship with your father messed me up mentally. Sasha and the girls have repeatedly been telling me I need to love myself, and I think that's what I've been trying to do, but maybe I haven't been quite as successful at it as I thought. Your little stunt with that singles app threw me for a major loop, and all those insecurities came back in a flash." I returned his stare.

"I was trying to help." Austin slumped back down. "You don't come across as insecure."

"I think all the females in your life would strongly disagree with that," I told him gently. "They aren't wrong. I've come a long way. Hannah was blunt enough to point some things out to me, as were you, by doing what you did. Sasha fully supports you, and Lily and Hope do too."

"Did Dad abuse you?" Austin didn't look at me when he asked; it told me this was something he had thought about over the past few years.

"Physically, no. Mentally, I don't think Shane did it intentionally; the neglect set off a chain reaction in my head. Your father has an addiction. I knew he liked it when I married him, but I was naïve enough to think it was just a guy thing because all guys like it. At least that's what I thought. I had no idea he had as much as he did or had a storage shed filled with it. I refuse to go into details about my sex life with you because you don't need that trauma on top of everything else. We will simply say that your father was more interested in his hand and videos than any other form of affection, and it caused a lot of insecurities." I tried to keep it as vague as possible.

"A storage shed? On top of the stash that I found in the extra room?" Austin gaped at me.

"Yes. Your father rented one of those storage units and filled it with his addiction. If he's dating, I feel bad for the woman." I cringed. "I'm sorry you walked in on it."

"Jesus, he's fucked." Austin winced. "Sorry, Mom. I know, language."

"I'll let that one slide." I shrugged because it was true.

"You have to know it's not you, right? I mean, have you seen how many people have already messaged you? On top of Hannah's reaction? That woman is smoking hot." Austin had a dreamy look as he thought about her.

I chuckled lightly and shook my head. "I don't know it's not me, but I'm getting there. Hannah broke through the fog, and Sasha is driving it home. Your backing me into a corner helped as well. I don't suggest doing it again. I nearly grounded you for life; you have Sasha, Hope, and Lily to thank for your freedom."

"All I can say is I have never been quite as happy as I am that I take after my mother. You are the best, and all the good in me comes from you." Austin stood and kissed my cheek.

"That felt like blatant bribery," I told him with a smile. "Does that flattery come with a request?"

"Nope, that one was sincere. Dad is a useless tool and a lousy father. If I were a jerk, I'd say I got it from him." He shrugged his shoulders with no apology in his tone. "About all he was good for was supporting us financially so you could stay home and raise me."

"I'm not doing so good with that part now." Sadness crept into my voice. I felt like a dismal failure in that department. "Being so long out of the workforce didn't help me at all."

"We are clothed, with a roof over our heads and food in our bellies. I think you did just fine, Mom," Austin told me. "You need to give yourself more credit."

"What's on today's agenda?" I changed the

subject. I wasn't too comfortable with all the ego-boosting just yet.

"No plans for me. Tomorrow, Hannah is taking me on a hike somewhere early because I have to work tomorrow night. Today, I figured I could hang out with you and help out around here," he said smoothly.

"Is that so you can monitor who I talk to and decide if you need to kick some man's ass for being inappropriate with your mother?" I stood and gave him a straight look, trying to hide the laughter as he looked guilty.

"Love you, Mom," was all he said.

"I'm going to dust and vacuum," I told him, laughing.

Austin moved and made his way to the living room, where he blasted one of my playlists. Loud rock music filled the house as he started to dust. I loved that we shared the same taste in music. Honestly, I loved everything about this kid. I lucked out with him.

Chapter 5

ake sure he's gone," I demanded again.

"Austin's gone." Hannah laughed. "I heard the car pull out. Why are you nervous?"

"Because I'm about to be exposed and have hair torn out of my body in sensitive areas, and I'm sure I'm going to scream. I don't need Austin running in to see me all naked. He's my son." I twisted my hands. "Did you sleep with him?"

"Wow. I didn't think you'd ask." Startled, Hannah looked at me blankly. "No. Not yet, anyway. Why?"

"Because I have a ridiculous favor to ask, and I couldn't do it if you slept with my son," I fretted again. My hands would be in knots with as much as I twisted them.

Hannah raised both eyebrows and crossed her arms. "I'm extremely curious now."

"I'm worried I'm a bad kisser," I blurted out. "I don't know who else to ask to kiss me that would be as honest as you."

Hannah doubled over laughing and slapped her thighs. "You want me to kiss you?"

"Shit. Not now, I don't, now that you are laughing at me." I crossed my arms to keep from chewing my nails.

"I'm not laughing at you," Hannah gasped. "My immediate thought was, I wondered if I could convince you to check to see if you are bad at sex. Totally wrong, I know, and that's why I'm laughing."

Damn. "Well, now I'm wondering that!"

"You aren't doing the sex thing, so don't worry about that. The toys will help you there, though I am always willing to give you a lesson." Hannah stood back up and grinned wickedly. "Kissing, sure. I can help you out with that."

She was on me in a second flat, her lips on mine, and I froze. She was good at it, that was for damn sure. I don't know when I started to respond, but Hannah pulled back, dazed. "Did I do it wrong?" I asked, unsure why she stopped.

"A little too good at that, maybe." She licked her lips. "Damn. Lena, you do *not* have to worry about your kissing skills."

Ridiculously pleased, I dropped my robe and lay down on the bathroom counter in nothing but my bra. I'd trimmed my hair back last night, not wanting to be entirely embarrassed about how much I had let myself go.

"Wow. Doing this will be much harder than I thought it was. I'll behave, I promise." Hannah swallowed, but her eyes were hungry for me.

I can't lie; it felt damn good to have someone looking at me like that. "You might be the only confidence boost I need," I told Hanna truthfully.

"I'm going to need about three cold showers," Hannah muttered while working. "This will hurt, not gonna lie. I'll be as gentle as I can. Grip the counter so you don't clock me."

I felt the hot wax and flinched as she stretched, pulled, and manipulated my skin around. Having someone touch me like that was a little strange, but I quickly forgot about it as she tore the first strip off. "Holy shit!" I screamed.

"I know, sweets." Hannah rubbed some sort of oil onto the raw skin that felt a little nice. Until she ripped the next strip off, this process repeated way too many times. "You might walk a little funny tomorrow. Wear silk or cotton panties tomorrow, no lace."

"That was gentle?" I asked, tears streaming from my eyes.

"Yeah. The good news is you won't want sex now since it will feel a little sensitive for a couple of days." Hannah tried to find the bright side. "You'll feel sexy, though, because damn, you look good."

Heat flooded my face as I sat up and winced, pulling my robe back on. "Great. No one will ever know but you and me."

"I kinda like the sound of that." Hannah laughed. "Am I the only one to see you naked since your husband?"

"Ex-husband. Other than my gynecologist, yes, you are." No way was I putting underwear on. I slid my very loose sweatpants on and then a baggy t-shirt.

"Austin told me a little about him today. Mostly that he was a lousy dad, a perv, and didn't deserve to share the same air as you." Hannah spilled my son's secrets.

"Shane still gave me Austin, so I didn't walk away empty-handed." I frowned.

"For sure. Austin is fantastic. Now that I know what his mom kisses like, I can't wait to see what he is like," she teased me.

"This conversation is so wrong." I helped her clean up my hairy wax strips. "I'll be at the bar Tuesday, Thursday, and Friday. I have a feeling I might need to get rescued on Friday. Austin said he's slimy."

"Yuck. Those are the worst. What's our code?" Hannah followed me out of my bedroom to the kitchen, where she stowed her stuff in a bag.

"What's subtle?" I asked. I wasn't sure what wouldn't sound stupid.

"Not yelling, 'get me out of here,'" Hannah joked. "How about asking for a certain type of drink? I'm guessing if you drink, it's usually margaritas?"

"Usually. I'm not a drinker. The girls and I meet once a month and have a drink, and I usually don't even finish it. So, Friday's three margaritas was a big anomaly. Maybe if I ask for a martini?" I suggested.

"Too easy. It's a martini bar. Ask for wine. Red wine if you need to get rescued fast, white if you want to bring it to a close early," Hannah said. "I can openly flirt with the guy, and you can get mock mad or something. The guys behind the bar won't tolerate customers getting too attentive to me, so I'm not worried about me. Red for stop, white for surrender. I'll let whoever is on shift with me know in case I get busy."

"Sasha told me to use the toy before the date," I told her, a question in my voice as we went to sit in the living room.

"Not immediately before, like the day before or hours before. If you do it right before, you will be letting off some major pheromones that will draw the men to you, like bees to sugar. Take the edge off for sure by having a big orgasm the night before." Hannah waggled her eyebrows. "If you need help, I'm available."

"You can't date my son and me both. That's just sick." I wrinkled my face in disgust.

"I don't think I could choose, either. You both are pretty damn yummy." Hannah scrunched her face up. "Now that I've tasted you, I want another. I want your friendship more, though. I'll still flirt because, well, look at you, but I won't make another play for you. I'm hell on relationships. Austin made it pretty clear he wasn't looking for that, which suits me perfectly."

"Oh, God. I do not want to hear about my son's need for a booty call." I hung my head down and wished I could plug my ears.

"I wouldn't say that's what he's looking for either. I don't think you want to hear, and it's between him and me. We'll call it a mutually beneficial friendship, with the benefits expiring when he leaves for college or whenever he wants. Still, with the friendship remaining," Hannah said diplomatically.

She was correct; I didn't want to hear it. I believed that if Austin wished to gain some experience, Hannah wouldn't mess with him. I could live with that. "Good enough. Don't hurt him."

"I won't. I actually like Austin. Surprising, but there you have it, the whole truth. So now that you've kissed a girl, is the song going through your head?"

Hannah asked me with a completely straight face.

I lost it. I cracked up laughing. "It wasn't until you said that."

"It's going to be stuck in your head the rest of the night now." Hannah stretched out on the couch, happily humming the Katy Perry song. "You're welcome."

"You have a twisted-up evil side to you. I like it," I grinned. "Sasha said you are one of us now, by the way. You just got yourself four extra girlfriends."

"Sweet! I've never had a group of friends like that," she replied wistfully. "All the females hated me because they thought I posed a threat to them or because their boyfriends thought I was hot. The others I made nervous because I like women."

"I'm sorry. People are stupid. Sasha figured out she liked men and women when we were in high school, and she got ridiculed for it. Hope, Lily, and I once went to battle for her in the locker room when a group of mean girl cheerleaders ganged up on her. One of them accused Sasha of looking at her tits, and they all jumped in, calling her lesbo, shoving her against the wall, that type of thing. Despite her size, Sasha is no weakling, but there were six of them and one of her. Hope, Lily, and I walked in about mid-way through. Lily ran to get one of the teachers, and Hope and I dove right in and stood in front of Sasha. After that, we all got called lesbo's, but we didn't care. The flip side of that is the guys that Sasha dated knew she wasn't a lesbian. Sorry, that was a super long way to say you have a safe place with us." I moved to kick up my legs and winced as the newly waxed skin moved.

"Sasha might be tiny, but I wouldn't want to mess with her. She strikes me as a woman who will take you off at your knees," Hannah commented offhandedly.

"She is. She was then, too. Her dad had her in many martial arts classes when she was growing up. Sasha evolved into Krav Maga in her twenties, and she teaches a self-defense class at the recreation center with one of the female cops on the force. Sasha's also gotten attacked and marked as an easy target by some idiot in a parking lot. And a couple of her dates have tried to force sex on her; big mistakes. She made us all take the course at the rec center after that," I filled Hannah in on Sasha.

"You've been friends a long time with her, I take it?" Hannah asked curiously.

"Since grade school." I smiled fondly at the memory. "This tiny kid walked up to me and told me she would be my friend because I looked lonely. We met Hope in junior high and Lily in high school. Lots of history with us, but don't let that hold you back. If Sasha accepts you, you're in the group. Plus, you kissed me and had your hands on parts of me that they never have."

"You and Sasha never experimented?" Hannah sat up and looked at me. "That surprises me."

"It never even crossed our minds; we don't see each other like that. We're sisters more than anything else. You should kiss Lily and Hope. I'd say kiss Sasha, but that might lead her on since she is already attracted to you. Lily and Hope always ask questions about what it's like to be with a woman. Just plant one on them the next time you see them. Sasha will pee herself, laughing," I giggled. "They would be the ones to start singing about kissing a girl. I guarantee it."

"Challenge accepted. Sure, I shouldn't kiss Sasha too? She could be fun," Hannah mused.

"I'm sure she would be, but in my eyes, that would kind of mess with her emotions a bit. I'm not okay with that," I replied warily. "If you want to include Sasha, talk to her about it first so she knows why."

"What's the story with Hope and Lily?" Hannah seemed to be taking mental notes, which was promising.

"Hope never married and was in a couple of long-term relationships, but both fizzled out. I think Hope hasn't found what makes her tick yet. In my eyes, she stuck with them because it was comfortable and easy, even though she wasn't honestly happy. Lily was married for about five years, and hers ended when her ex tripped and fell penis-first into the vagina of someone he worked with; tragic accident. More tragic that Sasha didn't castrate him." I gave her the short answers.

"Okay, good to know. What's the podcast Austin mentioned?"

"That's Sasha's baby. We get together and do it with her about every other week. Usually, we talk about an issue that affects females, like the Me Too movement, unfair pay, sexual pressure, or whatever is on her mind that week. She collects thoughts and issues that come up in her work, and we talk them out. Most of the followers are females, and she's trying to help others. Adding the dating thing was her idea. She makes me do it because she said my voice records well," I added wryly.

"I can hear that. There's a lot more to Sasha than meets the eye. Well, I'm guessing that goes for all of them. Don't talk about our red and white wine thing on the podcast. It will spread if you do, and your dates might hear about it. Don't mention me or the restaurant by name either, or they will insist you meet other places," Hannah advised.

"I talked to Sasha about that. I can't always meet at the bar. She suggested that I go to places where Austin could follow me. I'm not sure how I feel about that either. A part of me wants to do it on my own, kind of prove to myself that I can. Then there's the other side that says, are you kidding? People are crazy!" I looked over to see what Hannah thought about it.

"Do what you feel is right," she said softly. "Trusting yourself is a big part of being comfortable with yourself. You know, the whole confidence thing and all."

Chapter 6

Waxed, wearing sexy lingerie, a tiny amount of makeup and clothes that weren't baggy on me made me feel good but also self-conscious. Because people were looking at me, and I was complete shit at translating those looks.

I kept my head down and headed into the building, which meant I could watch where I was walking and not trip over any imaginary cracks that would send me sprawling out and get everyone looking at me differently.

Except keeping my head down made me walk right into someone. "Oh, excuse me, I'm so sorry," I apologized before looking up to see Rowan, one of the lawyers on the twelfth floor.

"Lena! You are just who I was hoping to run into this morning!" he blushed hotly. "I mean, sorry, not like that." He was apologizing to me for running into him. Men like him were rare. Rowan was charming, extremely handsome, and, for a lawyer, totally shy.

When I first started for the company I worked for here, after my divorce, I had thought that he had been trying to ask me out, but it hadn't materialized. I would have said yes, too. We became friends instead, and I still had a crush on him.

"Hi, Rowan. You shouldn't be apologizing; it should be me. I'm the one that ran into you. Why were you hoping to run into me?" I blurted out uncomfortably. I put my hand on his arm to steady myself so I didn't fall over.

He blushed again but covered my hand with his. "I saw you were on the market for dates and was hoping I could get one with you?" he said fast. His face was red but hopeful.

Rowan Carson was asking *me* out. "I, uh, yeah, sure," I stuttered out. Maybe I was in a parallel universe or something.

"Really?" he sounded relieved. "I've wanted to ask you that for almost three years." I did stumble then and almost took both of us down. "Are you okay?" Rowan asked me, steadying me.

"I'm a hopeless klutz. Are you sure you want to go out with me? Could be disastrous for you," I replied, chagrined.

"I've never been more sure. How about I make us dinner? I don't usually invite people over, but I just got a new puppy, and I don't want to leave him alone too long," Rowan offered. "Saturday?"

"Sure," I repeated stupidly, still stunned he'd been wanting to ask me out. "Here's my number." I fumbled for a piece of paper and wrote my cell number down. "Text me the address and the time, and if you want me to bring anything."

Rowan smiled, put it in his pocket, and walked me in the elevator. "Thanks, Lena. You look amazing, by the way."

I was about half a second away from announcing I'd been waxed and was no longer hairy because my brain short-circuited at the compliment, and I didn't know what to say. I bit my tongue hard and then smiled back at Rowan. "Thank you," I murmured, hoping that blood wasn't dripping out of my mouth like some deranged vampire.

Four dates in one week. What had my life become? I stepped off the elevator on my floor and almost ran to my little cubicle, frantically digging through my purse for my phone only to have it go off and be in my pocket.

I pulled it out to see an unfamiliar number and opened the text. It was from Rowan, making sure I had his contact information. I swear my stomach fluttered like I was in high school and about to go on my first actual date; this was sad.

I texted Sasha. *The cute lawyer I always talk to just asked me over for dinner on Saturday.*

Whoa. No shit? Sasha replied immediately.

Yeah. After I crashed into Rowan because I was looking at the ground while I walked. Then, I almost made us fall when he said he'd wanted to ask me out for nearly three years.

You are a hazard. Tell me you said yes; I could almost hear Sasha laughing.

I'm not stupid. Yeah, I said yes. I think I stuttered out a sure, I wrote back.

I love you, but you are a mess. Go work. We'll talk later, Sasha replied.

I think I floated through the rest of the day in a

shocked haze about Rowan. He was tall, successful, handsome, charismatic, shy, intelligent, had a sense of humor, smelled divine, and had a puppy. The puppy cinched the bow on the package.

His hair was dark brown and cut shorter on the sides than the top, which had that super sexy, just-out-of-bed, tousled look that I loved so much. His facial hair was a shaped stubble that made me want to rub my cheeks on it. His lips were full and ripe looking, and his eyes were this rich and decadent brown, sinful chocolate color.

I was so lost in thought about Rowan I almost crashed into him again as I left the building. "Lena, are you okay?" his deep timbre voice tickled my ears.

I laughed. "I swear, I didn't just learn how to walk today." I felt a flush creeping up my neck. This man would run for the hills if I weren't careful.

"I don't mind catching you." Rowan smiled easily, keeping his hand on my arm until he was sure I wouldn't fall again. "Can I ask an embarrassing question? Meaning it's my embarrassment, not yours."

"I guess?" I had no idea what he considered embarrassing.

"How many men am I competing with?" Rowan quietly asked, and I wasn't sure I heard him right.

"Competing with; for what?" I blurted out, stupefied.

"You," he continued in a quiet tone.

"Me?" I squeaked in surprise. "You aren't competing with anyone."

"No one has asked you out?" Rowan sounded incredulous now.

"Oh, you mean dates? I have one Tuesday, Thursday, and Friday. Then you on Saturday. I wouldn't consider any of those guys competition. I'm meeting them all at a bar where I know the bartender, so she can rescue me if needed. That's how much faith I have in these dates," I told him and then wished I hadn't. I sounded like an alcoholic who was playing the field.

Rowan chuckled gently. "I'm the only one you aren't meeting at the bar?"

"Correct." I shrugged helplessly, unsure how to take any of this.

"I feel better about my chances now. You don't strike me as a drinker." He walked with me to my car.

"I'm not. I'm also nervous about going on dates, so it seemed like a safe place since I have backup without actually showing up with backup." I chose to go the honest route. I was so over my head that I couldn't make it worse with honesty.

"Smart. I wasn't trying to be nosy; I just wanted to clarify my interest. I'm not great at that." Rowan stood next to me as I unlocked my car. "It's been a while since I dated."

I laughed, finding that hard to believe. "You and me both."

"Have a good evening, Lena. See you tomorrow." Rowan's soft smile turned my insides to goo as he closed my car door after I got in. I felt tempted to break my sex rule for him.

I waved and smiled as I pulled out of the lot and headed home. Thankfully, the drive was quick today, and when I walked in, I saw the box on the counter and said a small prayer of thanks that it was a plain box and not one that advertised sex toys. I doubt I could face Austin if that had been the case.

I saw a note Austin had left for me near the phone. "Got called into work. Will be off at nine. I'll eat at work. Love you."

I guess that meant I had the house to myself until nine-thirty. The priority was the special delivery. I opened the box, pulled out the inner package containing my new toy and studied the alien-looking thing. It looked like a penis with a horn on the back of it and antennae on the front. I felt like I needed a sex-for-dummies book.

Shane had been a one-trick pony, two if you counted the constant self-gratification. I hoped this thing came with directions. I pulled the plastic wrap off the outer box and studied the contents a little closer. Oh my, Sasha was naughty. I was getting a better picture of how it worked.

I brought it up to my bedroom and returned to the kitchen to find something to eat for dinner. I settled on a salad since that was easy. I turned the music on and pulled out the laptop to check the dating site for messages as I ate.

There were several with varying degrees of interest and creepiness. I replied to a couple of them, opening the lines of communication to see if there was anything there. A few of them were drop-dead gorgeous, and I was suspicious they were fake accounts.

My phone rang with a video chat request, and I glanced down to see Hope, Lily, and Sasha on a group chat and answered, turning the music down.

"Hey, ladies," I answered after swallowing the crouton I'd been crunching.

"I have two dates," Lily crowed in excitement.

"I have one," Hope chimed in.

"I have a stalker," Sasha added wryly.

"I have a toy." I blushed. "And dates."

"Oh! It came in? Which one is it?" Hope asked excitedly.

"Have you used it yet?" Lily butted in before I could answer. Sasha just laughed.

"I haven't even been home for an hour and just finished eating dinner. No, I haven't used it yet," I replied, grabbing my plate and phone to put my plate in the dishwasher.

"I got her the one with the pincers on it," Sasha informed them.

"Looks like an alien penis. A purple alien penis, no less." I laughed nervously.

"That's for out-of-this-world pleasure," Hope joked, making Lily laugh.

"Aren't you the clever one," Sasha purred. "Now, it's up to one of you to send her one of your choices."

"Oh! Me! I'll do it," Hope volunteered. "I know just what to pick, too. It's my favorite."

"With all these toys, who needs a man?" I asked curiously.

"You can use them with the man for an even better time." Lily smiled slowly, her eyes getting that mischievous look.

"You all have a variety of toys, then? I mean, I knew Sasha did. She's like a dominatrix or something." I closed the dishwasher. They all nodded their response to me. "I'm the lone holdout on sex toys, then?"

"Sex toys and orgasms." Sasha winked. "With the toys, you'll catch up on the orgasms, and then you'll know what a man should be able to do to you. Or a woman if you get adventurous."

I blushed, then rolled my eyes. "You all have dates, and Sasha has a stalker. Sounds promising."

"Tell us about the lawyer!" Lily demanded.

"The cute one you see every day?" Hope turned away from whatever she was doing and looked back into the phone's camera.

"Yep. Rowan. He asked me out after I crashed into him this morning. Then, as I left work, I did it again. He asked me who he was competing with," I told them, unable to stop the grin from splitting my face.

"He likes you." Sasha leaned back in her chair. "That's a good start."

"I'd seriously consider breaking the no-sex thing for him," I told them. "He's that yummy."

"Not on the first date," Hope advised.

"You're no fun," Lily responded to that. "I'd do it. It's not like he's a total stranger."

"You're easy; naturally, you'd do it," Sasha let loose. "Our little Lena isn't quite to that level yet. I'm with Hope. There's no sex on any first date, but I'm okay if you do it after a couple. You are the only one with the no-sex rule. I mean, hell, I would have taken Hannah up on her offer. Roll the dice."

I burst out laughing. "No big surprise there."

"Your next toy will be there by Friday," Hope interrupted.

"My life has taken a drastic turn," I mumbled with a shake of my head.

"It's good for you," Sasha promised. "Okay, I need to prepare for court tomorrow. Got to give a statement about a kid and need to re-read the notes. Talking about sex toys and dates isn't putting me in the right frame of mind for that."

"Probably more fun," Lily snorted.

"Probably?" Hope asked. "I'm sure it's more fun."

"I'm with Sasha on this. If I am going to use this toy, I'd rather do it before Austin gets home from work." I glanced at my watch.

"Good idea," Lily responded with a laugh.

"Especially after walking in on his dad," Hope added with a frown. "Poor kid."

"I do have enough sense to lock my bedroom door and mask the sound." I sighed.

"Sugar, go, do you. The rest of you queens, I'm out. Have fun." Sasha winked, and then her image disappeared.

"Talk to you later," I told Hope and Lily, and we signed off after saying goodbye.

It looked like I was about to try out this new toy. I was intrigued, excited, and nervous. I went to my room, locked the door, checked it three times, and played some music again. I took the toy from the box and washed it in the bathroom.

"Okay, alien penis, wow me," I said to it, feeling slightly foolish as I rinsed it off. It was larger than Shane had been, but he had nothing to brag about in that department. "Sadly, I don't even know if this represents the average size," I said to my empty room.

I turned it on to see if it had battery power, and

at the gentle humming sound, I sat down on my bed and stared at it for a few seconds before turning it off. "Is it weird that I am scared of a toy? God, Lena, how sheltered can you possibly be that you haven't used a vibrator by the age of forty? How weird is it that you are talking to a vibrator in your empty bedroom?"

I turned it off, stood up to pull my pants off, and arranged the bed pillows, so I felt sort of propped against the headboard. I laughed at the absurdity of the situation and my fear. I wasn't Shane; it was ridiculous for me to feel like I was.

I grabbed the toy, and without thinking, I rammed it in and instantly regretted it. A little lube would have been excellent. I arranged the pincers, got it situated after the burning sensation eased, and turned it on. Not used to the sensation, it was a jolt, and my head slammed back into the headboard with a hard thwack as the feeling washed through me. Thank God it was a padded headboard.

I didn't even know I was humming until the song that had been on ended, and my voice filled the empty space. Within a matter of maybe ninety seconds, the lube was no longer an issue, and my first toy-induced orgasm was looming extremely close. When I shifted my hips, it hit hard, and unintelligible sounds came out of my mouth. I could have been summoning demons for all I knew.

I broke a nail; I gripped the comforter so hard. Wave after wave of that beautiful vibration kept rolling through me until I was so sensitive that I was about to cry. I yanked my hand off the comforter and fumbled around until I hit the power button, only to have the vibration change, and another orgasm tore through me. I cursed myself between groans that I hadn't read the instructions.

Tears were now leaking out of my eyes while other fluids leaked out from different areas of my body, and I frantically tried to turn the thing off. After another orgasm and four more button pushes, it finally shut down, and I was a mess. I felt amazing, but I was a mess. I now fully understood why all my friends had toys. I simultaneously cursed Shane's existence and his insecurities for not letting me have any.

When I finally stopped shaking, I tried to pull the toy out to find that my body had clamped down so hard on it that I couldn't. Hysterical laughter bubbled out of me, causing more ripples of pleasure to run through me with the object firmly planted inside me. I tried again, but my body wanted the alien penis inside me, or my muscles were so unused to the feeling that they wouldn't relax. I didn't know what was going on.

I was keenly aware that every move I made caused the object to rub up against some spot inside me that Shane had been unaware of all these years, and holy shit, it was a spot I wanted to mark on a map for any future sexual experiences with a live man.

I tried to hold still and reached for my phone, my brain cells clearly not working as I dialed Hannah's number. It rang a few times before she answered.

"Heya, sweets, what's going on?" her voice came through the line, a small amount of background noise joining it.

"I can't believe I just called you," were the first words out of my mouth. "I got my toy today, just used it, and it's stuck."

There was a pause; the background noise dimmed, then a quiet, "Come again?"

"I can't come anymore! I think I'm going to pass out!" I exclaimed, starting to panic.

The sound of laughter floated across the airwaves. "I need a picture of this, or I'm going to believe this is a prank." Hannah giggled.

"Hannah! I'm serious!" I cried. "I can't get it out of me! I'm *not* taking a picture either!"

"It's seriously stuck inside you? Did you use it right?" Hannah asked, sounding like she was trying to suppress laughter. "I'm guessing you don't want me to come and pull it out of you, though the offer is there."

"I have no idea why I called you," I said again. "How do I get it out?"

"I can guarantee you this is going to be the best phone call I get all week." Hannah laughed again. "Relax your muscles, sweets. Try thinking of peeing," she suggested.

"I swear to God, if I pee on the bed, we are never talking again," I snapped.

"Would you rather wet the bed or walk around tomorrow with a dildo stuck in you?" Hannah's question was unfair. "At least tell me if you got off?"

"Yeah, several times. I didn't know there were different levels, and it just wouldn't turn off," I mumbled, totally embarrassed. These were things women my age should know and I was clueless.

"I'm sorry." Hannah laughed heartily now. "This is fucking hilarious. Some man is going to be beyond happy with you. I'm so jealous of that future man right now. Oh, Lena, I might be half in love with you."

"Not helping," I growled. "This is going to hurt, isn't it? I shoved the damn thing in with no lube and practically screamed it hurt so bad."

"Oh no," Hannah sobered up. "Yeah, sorry, sweets. It's probably going to hurt a little. Warm the engine up next time." My panic subsided a bit at the sound of sympathy in her voice, and I tried again quickly before losing courage and managed to dislodge the toy with an audible pop and a slight whimper of pain.

"Shit," I muttered with relief. "Damn, I need to wash my bedding."

"You okay now?" Hannah asked softly.

"Yes. Sorry to bother you. I'm humiliated right now and so glad you can't see me," I said bluntly.

"No worries. That's what friends are for, those utterly horrifying moments of brutal embarrassment that plague us for the rest of our lives only to be brought up repeatedly at the worst times. I've got your back, sweets." Hannah laughed again. "This call has given me the strength to get through the rest of my night, no matter how many slimy assholes hit on me."

"Glad I could be of service," I grumbled, but I could also see the humor in the whole thing now that I'd dislodged the stuck toy from me.

"By the way, if you don't tell the others, I will. That is too funny not to share," Hannah said as the noise around her reappeared.

"They'll find out. Sasha always seems to know when I've done something stupid," I admitted sheepishly.

"Clean up extra good; you might have torn some

tissue," Hannah warned. "Go pee."

"Yes, Mom," I muttered and hung up. I found it a little amusing that my legs were as rubbery as they were. One toy brought on more orgasms than fifteen years of marriage had. What a sad statement that was about my marriage.

Chapter 7

I locked eyes with Hannah, who couldn't stop smirking at me, and I fidgeted uneasily, waiting for my date to show up. Maybe if I were lucky, he would ghost me, and I could run and hide. I still couldn't believe I had called Hannah last night for help.

I glanced at my watch for the hundredth time and tried patiently to wait for Darren to show up. He was my trial run date. Honestly, I considered Mike and Todd to be trial runs, too. Rowan would be my real date. I was looking forward to that one.

"Will you relax?" Hannah's voice in my ear made me jump. I hadn't even seen her come over here.

"Between you staring and smirking and waiting for a date I didn't want, I'm a little nervous," I told her. "I can hear you laughing in your head."

"Come on; you don't see the humor in that?" Hannah set the menus on the table and tried to hide a smile.

I barely refrained from laughing. "No, I see it

now. I didn't feel that way when I called you, obviously."

"I almost peed myself laughing after we hung up." Hannah crossed her arms. "Matt thought I was crazy because, at odd moments, I would just burst out laughing."

"Great, that's not embarrassing at all," I mumbled. "Shit, Darren's here. I was hoping he'd ghost me."

"He wants in your pants. No way was he ghosting," Hannah said quietly and took a professional posture. "What can I get you to drink?" she asked as Darren smiled and slid into the booth across from me.

"Martini, dirty," Darren said immediately. His face twisted into what I can only imagine he thought was sexy but instead made him look like he was in pain.

"Got it," Hannah said evenly and looked at me, "and for you?"

"Iced tea for now, please," I said with a smile. Hannah nodded and went back behind the bar. "Hello, Darren, how are you?"

"I'm great now that I'm here. How are you?" Darren asked, and I wondered if he remembered my name.

"Not bad," I answered as he stared intently at me. It was kind of an intense, creepy stare, like he was trying to read my mind. Thankfully, Hannah returned with the drinks and asked if we were ready to order.

"Not yet. I haven't even looked at the menu," Darren answered rudely, which sealed the deal for me. I hated it when people were rude to servers for simply doing their job. "I just got here."

Hannah nodded curtly, and I hoped somewhere

in there that meant she planned on spitting on his food. "I'll give you a few minutes then," she replied and walked back to the bar and glared across the room at him.

I pointedly opened my menu without saying anything and looked it over as if I didn't know what I wanted. I was going to intentionally ask Hannah what the special was and what she recommended, only to keep her here longer and piss Darren off. I didn't even feel bad about it.

"It's a bar. Probably the only good thing here is the burger. Did you eat last time?" Darren tried to make conversation with me.

"We did. The food was great. My friends had salads, one had a burger, and I had nachos. All were good." I closed the menu and set it on the table, a cue for Hannah to return. Darren placed his down, too, and Hannah started walking towards us.

"Ready?" she asked.

"Could you tell me about the specials?" I asked her, biting my lip to keep from smiling. It made Hannah's eyes focus on my mouth, and she raised her eyebrow at me. I released it immediately, remembering that some men took that as a sexual cue.

"The chef did a marvelous chicken ravioli in a pesto sauce," Hannah recited. "There's also a clam chowder that's fantastic."

"The ravioli sounds great," I gushed. "I'll have that." I smiled politely at her, hoping she could read my mind and spit in his food.

"Burger, medium rare, fries, and a side salad with blue cheese dressing on the side," Darren ordered, his eyes watching my lips. Damn. I needed to be more aware of what I was doing. At least from this vantage point, I could see Hannah without turning my head and looking for her.

She disappeared into the kitchen and then came back out and watched us while she served drinks. She also said something to the other bartender that caused him to look over at us and frown. He said something back to Hannah, and she stiffened, her eyes widening. Whatever it was, it wasn't good news. It also distracted me from listening to whatever Darren was rambling about nonstop.

Mom skills came into play then, with the automatic nodding and making the appropriate noises when necessary until he stopped talking and was looking at me. I tuned back in to see his expectant face looking at me. Crap, I had no idea what he said. I knew I didn't like him, so I didn't care what my response was.

"Do you remember my name?" I smiled at Darren. The immediate question caught him off guard, and he paled slightly. "It's okay if you don't. I was just curious since you haven't said it. We only talked for less than a minute on Friday."

"That's true, we did, but your name was on the single's app," Darren said quickly. "You are right, though; it did slip my mind. I'm sorry."

"No worries," I assured him. "What do you do, Darren?"

"I work in marketing for a sporting goods company," he told me, looking smug.

"Sounds interesting." I folded my hands on the table before me and tried to keep my attention on Darren.

"It is sometimes. Others, it's pandering to the creative whims of people who don't know what they are talking about," came Darren's arrogant answer.

I hated small talk; this was going to be painful. "To play devil's advocate, creativity is different for different people. It's subjective to the person viewing it."

"Very true," Darren said, sounding surprised I had a brain. "You are gorgeous; did you know that?" The subject change was deliberate; I wondered why. Perhaps he was hiding something.

"Thank you," I replied graciously. How long had Darren been talking? Was the food ready yet? It didn't take that long to cook a burger.

"What made you decide to jump back in the dating pool?" he continued to make conversation.

"It wasn't my decision; my son decided it was time, and my friends boarded the bandwagon with him," I shrugged.

"I see," Darren said slowly. "How old is your son?"

"Eighteen," I told him, glancing around the bar. A group of three women sitting across the bar next to a window kept looking at me. "He's a great kid."

"I'm assuming that means you were married?" he pushed for more information.

"I was. How about yourself?" I asked politely.

"Never got on that train. Thankful for it at times, too. Marriage seems like a headache," Darren said arrogantly, confirming his pig status.

"I know several people who are happily married.

Nothing is perfect, and everything worth it takes effort to make it worth it." I spied Hannah, heading our way with plates, and let out a small sigh of relief.

"Would you care for wine with your dinner?" she asked me, her tone slightly off. That was a warning of some sort, the wine being our code and all. Only, I didn't know how to decode the signal.

"If she wanted wine, she would have asked for it," Darren snapped at Hannah, sparking my temper.

"Chill, she's just doing her job." I let my anger cool my tone as Hannah walked away.

"Isn't she your friend?" Darren asked out of the blue. "Didn't she say that when we met?"

"She did say that, though I met her for the first time that night, too," I told him, trying to disavow his rising idea that we were ganging up on him. It was written all over his face. "It was my first time here."

"So, it's some woman solidarity thing?" Darren sneered.

"I think what that was was a waitress doing her job," I corrected Darren. It didn't take long for his asshole side to surface. I didn't say anything else and just ate my dinner. It was guys like this that had kept me from even being remotely interested in the dating scene. I'd rather do my taxes than this.

Darren excused himself to use the restroom, and Hannah came flying over. "He's married!" she whispered urgently. "He was here with his wife on Sunday, and the other bartender told me."

Fury sparked in my veins, and I shooed her away. I wonder if he even noticed the group of women across the bar that had been watching us. My guess was it was either a friend of his wife or his wife. Either way, I wouldn't be surprised to get a visit from them. It gave me a possible excuse to throw my drink in his face, which, right about now, sounded like a whole lot more fun than sitting here with him.

Darren stopped at the bar on his way back and ordered another drink from the male bartender, making it a point to avoid Hannah. I rolled my eyes at this; he was beyond ridiculous. When Hannah caught my eye, I pointed to my iced tea, and she nodded.

She brought the tea over before Darren returned. "It's electric. Throw it in his face." It was like she had read my mind. "He asked you out because he heard us talking about the toys, thinking it made you an easy mark. That's what Matt said."

"Asshole," I mumbled. "Go before Darren comes back. Thanks for the drink." I pushed my plate at her so it looked like she was clearing the table.

Darren walked back as Hannah left and eyed the empty table in front of me. "You must have been hungry to eat all that so fast."

"I was hungry, but it wasn't fast. I didn't get up to go to the bathroom and stop at the bar to order another drink. I finished my dinner," I calmly said, even though I didn't feel it.

"Have you had a lot of dates set up since you joined the singles app?" Darren shifted the conversation as he started eating his remaining dinner.

"I have four this week," I said off-handedly.

Darren choked a little on his burger, his eyes widening. "You have four dates this week? Wow, busy lady."

"Three more that I'm talking to from an online dating website that will probably turn to dates," I went on, ignoring the shocked look on his face.

"Certainly a lot of playing the field going on in your life," was his response. He hadn't noticed the woman come up behind him, and I kept my eyes on him to not give it away. I wanted to watch whatever was about to play out.

I hadn't expected him to run his foot up my leg. That made me yelp and jump, my knee slamming into the underside of the table, jostling it enough to move his plate, which bumped into his martini, knocking it over into his lap.

As his crotch became soaked, the woman said, "Seems to me like you are playing the field."

Before the shock of his wet crotch set in, he jumped at the sound of her voice, and his plate of food joined the spilled martini. It was too perfect. I grabbed my new iced tea and flung it in his face, the glass slipping out of my hand and thunking him in the head.

"Married?" I yelled. "That's a pretty douchebag move to pull, Darren. I wouldn't have known without the bartender filling me in."

"Darren?" the woman laughed. "He told you his name was Darren? It's not. His name is Clive. Smile for the camera, Clive." She pulled out her phone and snapped a picture with me, smiling and waving for extra effect.

Darren/Clive shot to his feet, his food falling off his lap, eyes red from the alcohol's sting. He certainly wasn't happy. "What the hell?" he shouted. "You are not a good date."

"Oh, ouch." I smiled. "Like you are? You asked me out because you thought I'd be easy since you eavesdropped on a conversation about sex toys. Then, like a true idiot, you brought your wife here a couple of days ago and now are seen with me. Pure genius."

"He's never been smart." The woman snorted.

"I'm truly sorry if you are married to him." I looked at the woman.

"Oh, I'm not. My sister is. I don't imagine for much longer. She's been suspecting him for years." The woman gloated and walked away.

The male bartender had leaped over the bar and came over to ask if I was okay. "Her?" Darren/Clive shouted. "Why wouldn't she be okay? I'm standing here soaked!"

"Your skeevy ass deserved it," the bartender told him. He looked back at me and gave me a polite smile. "Your dinner is comped."

"Damn right, it's comped." Darren/Clive took an aggressive step towards the bartender.

"Hers, not yours. I've called the cops already; we'll press charges if you don't pay. I can probably convince her to press sexual harassment charges as well," the bartender stood his ground. "You can also consider yourself banned from coming here again."

"Like I'd want to. This place has the worst service ever," Darren/Clive grumbled but withered at the cold face the bartender presented. He handed his credit card over.

"If you'd join me, please. I'd rather not leave you alone with *Clive*." The bartender held his hand out for me to take, and he helped me out of the booth. I winced at the pain in my knee when I stood, then promptly stepped on a piece of ice, and my legs flew out from under me, crashing right into Darren/Clive, who now fell flat on his back on the floor.

The bartender quickly helped me up, put his arm around my back for support, and brought me to the bar, sitting me on one of the stools while he handed the card to Hannah to run for dinner and drink charges.

"Thanks, Matt," Hannah said softly.

"Matt. That's your name?" I asked him, rubbing my knee. "Yes, thank you."

"I'm going to get you some ice for your knee. Are you okay?" Matt asked sincerely. "You had to have hit that table pretty hard to get it to move like that."

"I'll be fine," I answered him. "It scared me when he suddenly ran his foot up my leg."

Hannah handed Matt back the card and started laughing. "You weren't kidding when you said you were a klutz."

Matt returned to give the card back to Darren/Clive and then escorted him out, none too kindly, and came back in, walking around the bar this time instead of super-manning it. "He doesn't have your phone number, does he?" Matt asked me.

"No, thank God." I breathed an exaggerated sigh of relief. "Did you really call the cops?"

"Nope." Matt grinned. "I know his type; they always fold in the face of confrontation." He grabbed a bucket and went to clean up the mess on the floor so no one else fell.

"Well, that was a complete disaster," I said casually to Hannah.

"Yeah, it was a circus. I feel bad for making you take that date. Let's not accept any more from a bar," she suggested, her face twisted up in a frown.

"The ones I get online aren't much better." I grimaced. "I'm going home now. Jerk made my knee hurt."

Chapter 8

Austin hovered the next couple of days, worried I was hurt or upset. It was both sweet and frustrating. "I'm fine, Austin," I told him Thursday morning before I left for work. "Don't forget, I'm meeting Todd after work today."

"He's nothing like that other douche," Austin insisted. "Mike is tomorrow, right?"

"Yeah." I wasn't too excited about that one.

"He might be a little like the douche," Austin warned.

"Sasha is going to be there Friday with a date, and I think Hope is too. I won't be alone on Friday," I reassured him. "Stop worrying, kid."

"Can't help it, parent," Austin fired back, then kissed my cheek. "Have a good day at work, Mom." He handed me a brown paper bag, "I made lunch for you too."

"You're the best, Austin." I hugged him and darted out the door before I was late.

I had to admit that Hannah was right about wearing sexy underwear. I felt better about myself when I wore them, and it gave me a little more self-confidence when I talked with Rowan. He had met me in the lobby each morning since he asked me out. I rather liked that.

I'd told him about the disastrous date yesterday, and when I walked in this morning, his first question was about how my knee felt. Rowan was dangerous in that I genuinely liked him—a lot.

"How's the knee today?" Rowan asked me as I came into the building.

"Tender, but it will be fine, thanks for asking." I smiled warmly. "How are you?"

His look set off a chain reaction inside that made me want to fling myself at him. "I'm great. Starting my morning in the best way possible." He put his hand on the small of my back and escorted me to the elevator. "You have another one tonight, don't you? A date that is."

"I do," I said, surprised Rowan remembered. "I don't think this one will be anything like Tuesday's. The ones tonight and tomorrow night are with the dads of my son's friends."

"From my perspective, hearing about what went wrong can only help me know what not to do." Rowan grinned. "You look beautiful today, by the way."

That was another thing this man said to me every morning since he asked me out. He complimented me every day. I didn't think Rowan needed pointers on making a date better; he was fantastic already.

"Thank you." I flushed. "So do you. Handsome, I mean." I tried to backtrack, flustered.

Rowan chuckled. "I'll take it. I can't wait until Saturday," he reminded me as if I could forget.

"Me too," I said shyly. "Have a good day,

Rowan." I stepped off the elevator and turned to wave. The sight of his smile was what got me through the busy and hectic day. I was a few minutes late on leaving, and when I got to the elevator, I found him standing there leaning against the wall, waiting for me.

Chivalry wasn't dead. Not with Rowan around. "Hi, Lena. How was your day?" he asked as I stopped before him.

"Hectic," I answered automatically. "How was yours?"

"Mine was filled with lawyers and meetings. Figured I'd end the day with the vision of you to make it all better," Rowan replied smoothly.

"You made mine better," I said quietly, fighting the urge to touch him. He made me want to cancel all my dates and focus on him. That was scary to me.

"You have my number, right? If this date goes badly, you can text me, and I'll find a reason to sue him for you." Rowan settled his hand on my back again as we rode the elevator down.

"That's something to keep in mind." I laughed. I didn't even know what kind of lawyer he was.

"I'm at your service, my lady." Rowan gave me a slight bow. His face was slightly flushed, which was adorable.

He'd been less shy around me this week, but I still caught glimpses of it. "Perfect gentleman," I told him. I was one hundred percent certain I'd have to use a toy before my date with him. The one Hope had ordered was supposed to be delivered today.

On a whim, as Rowan walked me to my car, I turned and hugged him. He embraced me back and then gave me a curious look. "Don't take this as a complaint because it's certainly not one, but what was that for?"

"For being you," I replied, the feel of his body imprinted on my brain. Rowan had gotten under my skin, and now I wanted him in every naughty way I could think of, which was substantially more imaginative now.

"That may be the nicest thing anyone has ever said to me," Rowan told me, the look in his eyes unreadable but the heat between us very noticeable. "Be safe tonight."

I waggled my fingers at him as he closed the car door, ensuring I was safe from parking lot bogeymen. I'm sure I was smiling like an idiot, but Rowan had that effect on me. I was glad it had taken him three years to ask me out. If he had done it right after my divorce, I was sure I would have used him as a rebound.

It scared me to admit I wanted more than that with him. I pulled out of the parking lot and headed to the bar. I wouldn't be early like I was last time. I was also at a disadvantage since I couldn't remember what Todd looked like other than the broad description Austin had given me. I remembered that he had a sexy voice.

When I walked in, Hannah gave me a wink and a slight nod in Todd's direction. He must have said he was meeting someone here because Todd didn't look like he was someone who was waiting for a date. I took a step, and the knee I had smacked into a table decided to stop working, and I fell right on my ass in front of everyone.

I glanced up to see Hannah shaking her head and trying not to laugh, and who I assumed was Todd making a beeline for me. "Are you okay?" he asked, helping me up. It was the voice I remembered.

"Embarrassed, but okay." I steadied myself. "Sadly, this is nothing new for me. I'm guessing you are Todd? Hell of an introduction, right?"

Todd smiled and walked next to me back to the table he had been sitting at waiting for me. "Yes. We've only met once, so don't feel bad if you don't remember me."

I hadn't, but good. "Lena." I held out my hand, and he shook it gently. "That little episode is why Austin put me on that app. He said I need to find someone to help around the house in case I do something like that and hurt myself."

Todd laughed at that. "Austin put you on the app? He's still alive, right?"

"He did, and yes. It was a little extreme, but his heart was in the right place. My friends and I decided to each do it and compare notes on what it's like to date in your forties," I over-explained.

"I'm an experiment?" he asked, a friendly smile on his face.

"No, it's a real date, but I will talk about you." I winked. Todd didn't give me any creeper vibes, and he was attractive to boot. Tall, broad, with an angular face, clean-shaven, dark hair and eyes, a warm smile, and a relaxed personality.

"I feel like I know you. Patrick has talked about you so much," Todd opened the conversation. "I know you like rock music and are a good cook. Austin is a good kid; you are divorced and good-looking."

A little startled, I smiled hesitantly. "I don't know much about you other than you are Patrick's dad, and I think Austin said you work as a general contractor?"

"Yep. Sure do. I'm divorced as well. My ex-wife decided she no longer liked men, and I'm unsure if I drove her to it. We share custody of Patrick, and I own my own company. I work a lot and haven't had extra time to get back out on the dating scene. I've gone on a few but found I wasn't interested," Todd said smoothly.

"Are you that bad that you seriously think you could drive your wife into lesbianism?" I couldn't help but ask. It was probably the wrong comment to focus on.

"I don't think so, but she says it sometimes when she's angry." Todd shrugged.

Hannah appeared to take our drink orders and drop off menus. I settled on a salad, wanting something fresh, and Todd ordered a steak. The conversation with him was comfortable and relaxed. Todd was intelligent and well-read, which I genuinely liked.

By the end of the date, we had covered several topics, and he had offered to be my handyman if I needed help with something so I didn't fall and break myself. No strings attached, he made sure to say. When he asked me out for a second date, I agreed.

I wasn't anywhere near as attracted to Todd as I was to Rowan, but I had fun and enjoyed the conversation. Hopefully, Austin wouldn't be upset about a second date. We set up a time for the following weekend, a lunch date this time, and he gave me a small hug before we parted ways.

Hannah stopped me as I came out of the bathroom. "He wasn't bad looking, and it looks like you had fun," she poked me.

"He was fun. We made another date for the

following weekend. I can't say I was hugely attracted to him, but he was comfortable and easy to be around," I told Hannah with a shrug. "I kept comparing Todd to Rowan, which was entirely unfair."

"You seriously like this Rowan guy, don't you?" Hannah leaned on the bar.

"God help me, I do," I muttered. I told Hannah how Rowan met me each morning and walked me to my car each evening. I filled her in on the conversations we had and how, when I hugged him, I wanted to strip his clothes off and lick him.

Hannah laughed. "You've got it bad. Hopefully, it works out with Rowan. Just don't be the type of woman who leads a guy on. If you don't feel it with Todd, let him know. Todd knows you have other dates, right?"

"He does. I do like him, just not how I like Rowan," I tried to clarify. "I wouldn't lead him on. Plus, I want to see how Austin feels about me going out with Todd again. Tomorrow is the one I am not looking forward to."

"Think it will be as bad as Tuesday?" Hannah asked, frowning. "Matt's also on schedule, so you've got both of us. Oh, and really? I can't believe you fell walking in the door."

"Hey, my knee gave out," I tried to defend myself and laughed. "What a way to start a date!"

"No dull moments with you, that's for sure," Hannah joked. She hugged me and returned to work, laughing and shaking her head.

I went home, got ready for bed, and slept surprisingly well. I didn't dress up as I had for the other dates, keeping it to jeans and a somewhat dressy shirt for work since it was casual Friday.

Once again, my heart stuttered madly in my chest when I saw Rowan waiting for me. I could get used to this. His smile was just for me, even though several women were cutting looks towards him.

"Good morning, Lena. You look wonderful this morning." Rowan held his arm out for me, and I hooked mine through it. Our walk slowed as we approached the building. It felt romantic.

"Rowan, you are spoiling me." I moved a little closer to him.

"You deserve to be spoiled. I don't see it that way, to be honest. I'm acting like a gentleman. Spoiling you would be taking you on vacation to Europe or a cruise through a tropical location, feeding you breakfast in bed, and showering you with trinkets," Rowan said dreamily. He'd put thought into those things to rattle them off so quickly.

My breath caught at his words, and suddenly, I wanted all of it, but only with him. "Wow," was the only literate thing I could say. I got so lost in his words that I walked right into the glass door and bounced off it. Super smooth.

"Lena, are you alright?" Rowan sounded alarmed.

"Humiliated but physically fine." I blushed. Someone should wrap caution tape around me.

Rowan ran his hands over my face and down to my shoulders, and I shuddered. "Are you sure? You're shaking."

"Because when you touch me, I get all tingly," I blurted out without thinking. *Oh my God.* This man would run screaming in the opposite direction if I didn't get a hold of myself.

Rowan blushed, but his smile made me want to rip my clothes off. "Lena, my day can't possibly get any better now. How was your date last night?"

"What?" I asked, all flustered. "Oh, um, it was good. He asked me out again."

"Damn. Guess I have competition after all," Rowan mumbled. "Time to step up my game."

I have no idea if he meant to say that out loud, but I was glad my mouth stayed shut for once. I had no idea what blunt truths would get aired if I had tried to talk. I merely walked with Rowan, standing closer than I probably should have, but when another woman looked him up and down, I couldn't help it.

His hand was warm on my lower back, almost resting on my hip as if Rowan had a claim on me. I didn't care either. Shane had *never* acted that way about me. Shane hadn't ever said the romantic things that Rowan did or given me one of those smiles that made me wet. *Why on earth had I married that man?*

Those were all reactions that someone you would marry should elicit from you. I found myself leaning into Rowan when the elevator dinged for my floor, and I didn't want to move. I had to force myself into motion and smiled back at him.

Using my best sexy voice, I called over my shoulder, "Have a good day, Rowan."

Chapter 9

I swear to God, Sash, I'm about to fall on my knees and ask him to marry me," I told Sasha. I was on my break and had to call her.

"Please don't." Sasha laughed. "At least go out with Rowan once. So you agreed to another date with Todd? That sounds promising."

"Does it? I compared Todd mentally to Rowan the entire time," I confessed. "He's nice and attractive, but I think he's more Lily's type. To me, he feels like a friend."

"Lily?" Sasha asked, surprised. "Was he a jock type?"

"Kind of built like that, but also intelligent," I supplied.

"Ah," Sasha drawled out. "You going to try to hook them up then? Don't give the guy false hope with you."

"Funny, Hannah said the same thing. I won't. I was thinking about bringing Lily up on our next date," I told her.

"You're a heartbreaker, sugar. I knew you had it in you," Sasha said, pleased by that. "I gotta run. My next appointment is here. Watch out for those invisible doors. Or tell building management the cleaning crew is doing a good job."

I groaned and hung up, returning to my desk to finish the day. Once again, I found Rowan waiting outside the elevator on my floor. I felt the embarrassment of the morning flood my cheeks, and he shook his head at me.

"Don't be embarrassed," Rowan said quietly. "It's exactly those things that endear you to me." He handed me a piece of chocolate. "If your date is going to be as bad as you think it is, I figured you could use something sweet."

"Because you aren't enough?" came flying out of my mouth. This awkward bluntness was why I was still single. I popped the chocolate in my mouth and groaned at the rich flavor that exploded across my tongue. "Damn, that's good."

There was a dazed expression on Rowan's face. "Next time, I'm bringing more of those," he whispered.

"Rowan," I said when I stopped being pornographic with the sounds I was making from the excellent chocolate, "if you hadn't seen me on that singles app, would you ever have asked me out?"

"Yes," Rowan said hoarsely. "I believe I would have gotten there. I am woefully inept at all things romantically inclined and with women."

"I find that extremely hard to believe when almost everything you've done has been off-the-scale romantic with me," I replied honestly. "I'm not judging; we've all got baggage and insecurities. Women don't hold a monopoly on that. I just have to pinch myself to make sure you are real, and this is happening."

"Maybe you bring it out of me," was Rowan's shy response.

"You aren't as bad at this as you think," I told him as we approached my car.

"I want to be a better me for you." Rowan's eyes shone as he looked down into mine. I was a goner. To keep myself in check, I hugged him again and sighed a little as he hugged me back tight. "See you tomorrow night." He released me and smiled.

Oh, man. If I weren't careful, I would fall head over heels in love with Rowan. I didn't know if I was ready for that. I didn't even know if I believed in happily ever after. Rowan, for damn sure, made me want to. He waited until I was in the car with the door closed before taking his hand off the top of my car and letting me pull out. Rowan Carson was indeed a very dangerous man.

Now I had to go on this date with Mike with all my hormones revved up from Rowan. I saw Sasha's car when I pulled into the lot; I was happy she was there. When I walked in, I scanned the room for her and was surprised to note that her date was with a guy. Sasha caught my eye and gave me a slight wink.

I headed to the bar to check in with Hannah, who gave me a quiet wolf whistle. "Girl, you look like sex. Did you get laid?"

Taken aback, I gave her a crazy look. "No, I just came from work!"

"Oh, it's the lawyer. You were just with him, weren't you?" Hannah smirked. "The pheromones coming off you are potent!"

That was *not* what I wanted to hear. "Damn.

How do I make that go away? Austin told me this guy was probably going to be like the douche guy."

"You can't make them go away." Hannah laughed. "It's just you. Every guy in here noticed you walk in. You drinking tonight?"

"Maybe one margarita, don't make it strong. I might need something to make it through this." I glanced around the bar again. "I don't think he's here yet." I quickly told her about my day and more about Rowan.

"I hate to admit it, but Rowan sounds amazing," Hannah said with a touch of jealousy. "You, for real, walked right into a door?"

"I did." I shook my head and rolled my eyes. "I'm a train wreck."

Hannah giggled in response. "Not even close, but it makes me want to stalk you to see the shit happen. A slimy-looking guy just walked in, betting that's your date since his eyes are on your ass. Don't turn around." Hannah started making a drink. "Sasha spotted him too. That girl misses nothing."

I snorted quietly. "Nope, Sasha doesn't."

"Incoming," Hannah whispered. She finished making the margarita and set it in front of me. "There you go!" Hannah said louder. I saw her gesture to Matt, who looked up at me, then looked behind me and back to what he was doing.

"Lena?" I heard a man's voice say.

I turned around. "Mike?" I asked, a fake smile plastered on my face.

"In the flesh." Mike smirked and violated my personal space to press himself against me in a hug. I was trapped; the bar was behind me, and I had nowhere to go. I didn't hug back either, hoping he'd get the hint. That was clearly wishful thinking.

Hannah cleared her throat. "Can I get you something to drink?"

"Scotch," Mike said over my shoulder, still hugging me. It was awkward. He finally let go, and I moved swiftly out of range and off to the side where I could back up if he did it again.

I feared looking at Sasha; I knew she'd see the distress and intervene. Instead, I headed to a table close to the bar where I'd be in sight of Hannah and Sasha. Austin had been right; Mike's teeth were way too bleached, and he had used an inordinate amount of hair gel. He also had a fake tan.

"Derrick speaks highly of you, Lena. I can see why," Mike's slimy voice said from too close behind me. I quickly slid into a booth and set my purse next to me. Mike slid across from me and leaned into the corner, stretching his legs across the booth seat. At this point, I was ready to order red wine. Derrick obviously got his manners and looks from his mother.

Mike immediately started talking, and I tuned out. I didn't even pretend to listen, and when Matt came to drop off the menus, I buried my face in it, even though I almost had the thing memorized now. Mike ordered another scotch, and I ordered tacos. I hated letting the menu go.

"Tell me about yourself, doll face," Mike interrupted me, staring at nothing and daydreaming about being lost in space with no oxygen or spacesuit.

"Not a lot to tell," I said hesitatingly. "Divorced,

working, raising Austin."

That small sentence sent him off on another long-winded diatribe about the woes of being a single parent and having no help from the other. From what I gathered, he only had Derrick every other weekend; I had no idea why he was complaining. I think he just liked the sound of his voice. I tried to make myself have an open mind and I found a brick wall instead. There wasn't anything authentic or genuine to find common ground with.

Matt finally brought out my tacos, only to have Mike try to steal one. "What?" Mike asked, offended when I pulled my plate back. "You aren't going to share?"

"Hell, no," I snapped. "If you are hungry, you should have ordered some food. Never steal a taco from a hungry woman."

I don't know what I said to put that look on Mike's face, but it was scary and predatory. I almost stood on the bench to scream for red wine. "I already ate, and I'm saving room for dessert." Mike's smarmy voice made me lose my appetite.

I forced down half of my dinner and downed my drink in minutes flat. When I pushed my plate away, Mike attacked what was left of my food like he was starving and ate while continuously licking his lips. The sounds were atrocious. There was something seriously wrong with this guy.

"Excuse me, I need to use the restroom." I slid out of the booth and beelined for the bathroom. I locked myself in a stall and checked my phone, seeing a text from Austin.

"Watch out. Derrick texted me and said his dad is drunk and that's never good."

I wish I would have seen that earlier. I stuffed my phone back in my pocket and flushed the toilet. Taking another moment, I sat there in the relative quiet for a few minutes, then stood and went to wash my hands. I stepped back into the hallway and someone immediately slammed me against the wall. It was Mike.

My head cracked painfully against the bricks, making my vision swim. But it was the hot, stinky mouth that was crushing mine that made me want to throw up. I tried to push Mike away, but he had me pinned well. When Mike finally moved his mouth and grabbed my boob hard enough to make me yelp. I cried out, "Matt!"

I hoped Matt heard me because if Mike date-raped me in the hallway of a bar, there would be hell to pay. Mike slammed his mouth back onto mine, and I struggled to break free, finally stomping on his foot when he shifted to try and dry hump me into the wall more.

"What the fuck?" Mike yelled, which did bring Matt running.

"Help!" I shouted and sank to the floor as Matt shoved Mike off me. Hannah and Sasha came running right after Matt.

"Motherfucker!" Sasha yelled and launched at Mike, Matt catching her mid-air.

"I've got this. Take your friend out there and make sure she's okay." Matt redirected Sasha to me.

Hannah and Sasha helped me stand, and when Matt saw the blood on the brick from my head, he instructed Hannah to call the police. I wasn't going to argue. All I did was break down in tears. Hannah led me to the office instead of back out into the public eye and left Sasha with me while she operated the bar since Matt kept Mike blocked in the hallway until the police arrived.

When Hannah returned to check on us, I looked up at her, seeing double. "I'd like some red wine, please."

Hannah let out a shaky laugh. "Jesus, Lena. Are you okay?"

"My head hurts, and I think he bruised my boob," I muttered. "This tops one of the worst dates ever. Sasha, go back to your date."

"I'll go back to tell him to go home," Sasha agreed and marched out the door. She came back in a few minutes later with my purse in hand. "The cops are here. Once they finish, I'll drive you home. Hannah will return your car and spend the night, or Austin can take her home."

"God, Sash, I was so scared. I couldn't move." I detested the way I started shaking. A female officer took my statement, took some pictures, and said I was free to go after I repeated that I didn't want to go to the hospital. Matt came in to walk us both out, saw us safely into Sasha's car, and took my car keys to give to Hannah.

When I got home, Austin flew out the front door in tears and clung to me. I let my sweet boy help me inside, and he helped Sasha clean the back of my head up. He brought me some ibuprofen and hovered until Sasha ordered him to sit in the living room.

"I want to go to bed, Sasha. No, honestly, I want to shower and get the icky feeling off me, then go to bed," I revised.

"I know, sugar. Let me help you, or at least stand by until you are out of the shower," Sasha insisted. I didn't argue. After a scorching and steamy shower, brushing my teeth about fifteen times, and almost swallowing mouthwash, I curled up in bed and cried.

"Want me to stay with you?" Sasha offered, lying next to me and stroking my hair.

"No. Make sure Austin is okay, please," I said through my tears.

"Goes without saying, sugar. Call me in the morning," Sasha said firmly, kissed me on my forehead, and left me alone.

Austin came in less than an hour later and curled up with me, and I didn't have the heart to send him away. If I was honest with myself, I probably needed his closeness. He stayed with me until I fell asleep.

Chapter 10

I woke up with bodies on either side of me. Austin was in front of me, and when I turned my head, I saw Hannah behind me. The gesture brought tears to my eyes. They stayed to take care of me and make sure I was okay. I smelled coffee and breakfast, too, which meant Sasha was here.

My movements woke up Austin. "Mom, are you okay?" he asked worriedly.

"I'm fine, honey. Angry, embarrassed, and a little sore, but nothing that would hinder me. Sasha would kick my ass if that were the case," I told my son truthfully.

"Sasha told me she almost kicked Mike's ass. Derrick wants to come over and apologize today. He tried to stop his dad from going out; he'd been sober for a while, but he punched Derrick and left anyway. I didn't know any of that. Only that Derrick doesn't like his dad much and that he was divorced. I would have told you not to go if I knew any of that stuff. I'm so sorry, Mom," Austin fretted and teared up again as he rambled out his apology.

I held my arms out, and he willingly moved to

hug me. "I don't blame you, Aust, don't think that. I don't blame Derrick, either. Mike is an adult, and he chose to make the choices he did. It got stopped before it went too far, and I'm extremely grateful for Hannah's co-worker and Hannah. Now, we have to move past it. It was scary, without a doubt, but it could have been worse."

Those were brave words that I wasn't so sure I believed. That little event had put a brand-new fear in me, one that was growing roots pretty rapidly, too.

"He was crying, Mom, Derrick was." Austin was a lot more shaken up by this than he was letting on.

"You can call Derrick and tell him to come over before three. Anytime. I'll be here, but remember, I still have a date tonight," I reminded him.

"You're going to go out again?" Austin sat up, dumbfounded. "After that?"

"Rowan isn't like that, Aust. I can say that with full certainty. I also really like him. You're gonna have to trust me, kid." I grabbed his chin and saw the bruises on my arms in the process. I tried to fight back a wince, but he saw it.

"Mom, I don't want to go away to college anymore." Austin's voice shook.

"We'll talk about this later, I promise. Get up and get dressed. I think Sasha is cooking breakfast. Knowing her, if we don't show up down there soon, she will storm the room like an out-of-control tsunami." I tried to smile.

Austin gave me a ghost of a smile. "A tsunami is never in control. Sasha's just as worried as I am."

"I know. Go get dressed, and I'll be right behind you," I promised my son. "I'm kind of trapped now and need to pee."

Austin flew off the bed and helped me climb out. I was a lot stiffer than I thought I would be. Once he made sure I was okay, he left the room, and I headed to the bathroom. I knew Hannah wasn't sleeping; I'd heard her breathing change.

When I returned, Hannah was sitting up, looking a little rough. "Do you mind if I use the bathroom?" she asked quietly.

"You know I don't. Go do your business and then come say what you need to say," I told Hannah as I headed into the closet. I managed to tug a sports bra on by the time she came back out.

"Let me see your back," Hannah said softly, and I turned. "You'll be sore for a couple of days."

"I didn't feel any of this last night," I murmured, surprised by what she had shown me by moving the mirror.

"Adrenaline." Hannah leaned back on the door frame. "Don't brush this under the rug, Lena. It has lasting effects."

"I know. Sasha went through it. I'm guessing by your reaction that you did, too," I said softly.

"I did. It's also shaken Austin up like you wouldn't believe." Hannah dropped her head. "I wanted to murder the asshole. I don't know what would have happened if Matt hadn't been there."

"I'll take care of Austin. I owe Matt a huge debt, and you. Thanks for having my back." I reached out and hugged her. "How long will it take for the bruising here to go away?" I pointed to my lips.

Hannah shrugged. "A couple of days, maybe? I'm

not sure. My advice is to be upfront with your lawyer tonight. Tell him what happened, so if something scares you, he knows it's not him. I know you like this guy; if he knows, it helps him understand."

It was good advice that I would probably follow. The bruises were visible, and I knew Rowan would notice. Hell, everyone would see. "Makeup will help, right?"

"It will help with the coloring, but your lips are still quite swollen like Botox has gone horribly wrong," Hannah said candidly.

I pulled on some sweats because that was all I had the energy for. "Come on. Sasha will storm up here if we aren't down there soon."

"I know. Sasha loves you," Hannah said with a smile. "I hope to have a friend like her someday."

"You do. You have four of us now," Sasha said from the doorway. "Come eat breakfast." Sasha's eyes roamed over my face, her expression worried.

"I'm okay, Sash." I tried to ease her mind.

"No, you aren't, sugar, don't lie to me. I can see it in your eyes," Sasha said sadly. "You will be. We'll make sure of it. Did you stay all night?" she asked Hannah.

"Yeah. Austin was pretty upset and freaking out. I'll have him take me home after we eat so I can shower and change. I still have a shift tonight," Hannah answered, following us out of the bedroom to the kitchen.

There they all were: my best friends and son. Ready to fawn all over me and make sure I'm okay. Sasha was right; I wasn't as okay as I wanted to think, and I needed their love. When I broke down in tears again, they were there. When Austin flipped out, they were there to talk him back down, too. Together, we talked through Austin's leaving for college, listened to his fears individually, and worked out answers.

The girls all left at lunchtime, and Lily took Hannah home. Austin had Derrick come over, and Austin and I talked through it all with him. The poor kid had one hell of a black eye, and he divulged the abuse his mother went through while his dad had been drinking. He'd been sober, or so Derrick had thought, until last night.

The boys were an emotional wreck, both taking on guilt where they shouldn't be, and Derrick worried he would turn out like his dad. It took a lot of talking to help Derrick see that since he was concerned about it, he would be working extra hard to ensure that didn't happen. I was exhausted by the time he left.

Austin started getting ready for work, and I bathed before my date with Rowan. I hoped the Epsom salts and hot water would ease the pain in my back a bit. I gingerly pulled the sports bra off and honestly looked at my breast for the first time since Mike had grabbed it.

The fingerprint bruises were bright and vivid against the pale flesh there, and they made me sick to my stomach because it brought back the memory of Mike grabbing and touching me. I took a few more pictures, twisted to see my back, and tried to get some photos of that, too. Then, I took a few of the ones around my arms.

I know the police took them last night, but I doubt they looked like they do now. Shane was an awful husband. I can't even say he is a good man, but he never once raised a hand against me. For that, I was thankful. The whole experience gave me an inside look at how Sasha felt when she went through it.

I got in the bath and started to shave my legs and found bruises there as well. I grabbed my phone, took a couple of pictures of those, and continued. The Epsom salts did help a little, but I took more ibuprofen when I got out of the bath.

I went all out, pampering myself with the comforts that made me happy. I applied lotion to my whole body and even decided to wear a complete set of sexy underwear in hopes that the confidence would come back.

I carefully applied makeup to try and hide the bruises around my mouth and on my lips, but I'm not so sure I did a bang-up job. Botox gone wrong, indeed. There wasn't much I could do about it. I went through my closet and found a cute outfit to wear. One that wasn't too big, like Hannah had pointed out, and it hugged my curves. I wore a pair of flats so I wouldn't trip, and as an afterthought, I grabbed a sweater I could wear over the top to hide the bruises on my arms.

Chapter 11

$\mathcal{L}$ ena! I'm so glad you are here." Rowan threw open his door. His face lit with a warm smile, and my insides melted. I should have worn ugly underwear.

"Did you think I wouldn't come?" I asked, stepping inside.

"Insecurities are hard to beat back sometimes," Rowan said, narrowing his eyes on my face. After a few seconds of scrutiny, he asked, "Are you okay?" His voice was so soft and kind that it completely undid me.

My stupid fat lips quivered, and tears spilled out of my eyes. I was happy I hadn't put mascara on. "I'm fine," I lied.

"I admit to being bad with women, but the tears are kind of a flashing sign that you aren't fine." Rowan drew me into the living room and settled me on the couch, handing me a box of tissues. He sat on the coffee table in front of me, his eyes filled with concern.

Hannah was right. I needed to tell him. I wiped the tears with the tissue, wiped the makeup off my face and pulled my sweater off. Rowan's eyes missed nothing, and his expression shuttered fast.

"My date last night didn't go very well," I said,

my voice cracking.

Rowan stood up. "Hold that thought." He strode from the room, and I set my sweater on the arm of the couch, dropping my purse on the floor. My keys were still in my hand, so I put them in my sweater pocket. That way, I didn't lose them, and my phone was in my pants pocket.

Rowan came back in, and the sound of scurrying paws accompanied him. He had a pad of paper, a pen, and a bottle of water. Rowan handed me the drink, and the puppy that followed him flung itself against the couch, trying to jump up.

I reached down and lifted it, the sweet little animal nuzzling into me and soothing the aches in my heart. "This is Demon." Rowan smiled at the wiggling puppy. "Aptly named, I assure you. He was the runt of a bunch that got rescued. The vet says he's mostly pit bull, with something else mixed in."

"He's the cutest Demon ever," I cooed at the puppy. He settled immediately into my lap, much to Rowan's amazement.

"That's a first. Okay, back to serious. I want you to give me the case number the police assigned you, and call the station and have me listed as your lawyer," Rowan said gently. "Then, I'd like you to walk me through everything."

"Rowan," I started to say, then shut my mouth when he moved closer and knelt before me.

"Please accept this. I deplore violence against women. Seeing these bruises on you, much less, hurts me deep inside. I know this is our first date, but I've also had feelings for you for three years. I can only do my best to ensure this doesn't happen to anyone else and help give you peace of mind. I do things like this pro bono for a local women's shelter, so I'm no stranger to it. It would mean so much to me if you let me help." Rowan feathered his hand over my cheek.

"You have feelings for me?" I asked, shocked at the admission.

"I do," he confirmed, his eyes locked on mine.

I spilled everything. I sang like the cliched canary. I told Rowan every grisly detail from when I left work to when I showed up at his house. I answered all his questions and gave him the names he asked for and the phone numbers. I held nothing back, including our little experiment and why I was on that date in the first place.

"Is that why you said yes to a date with me?" Rowan asked me after I finished.

"No. I said yes to you because I've been attracted to you as long as you have me." I gave Rowan the truth. "I would have said yes whenever you asked me. That also scares me because you make me want to fall and I don't know I'm ready for that."

"How long is the experiment?" Rowan asked me with a slight smile on his face.

"Three months," I said, confused about where this was going.

"I want you to keep dating, go out with whoever strikes a chord with you, have fun, and learn you are ready. Just promise to work me into the schedule. I want you to be entirely sure of me before we take anything to the next level," Rowan told me. "With that in mind, it doesn't mean I won't do my best to show you that you are ready and I'm worthy of you. I don't want you scared."

I was speechless. One-on-one like this, Rowan was far less shy than he was in our shared work building. I still saw it, but he was the same person. That person I saw every morning before work and after wasn't a ruse. I wanted him more than ever.

"Okay." I exhaled the word. I leaned forward and brushed my bruised lips over Rowan's perfect ones. I'd play this his way if getting to be with him was the outcome. "Kissing is still level one."

A slow smile spread across his perfect face. "I can live with that. You look beautiful, by the way." Rowan pulled back and stood, picking up Demon from my lap and laying him on a doggie bed I'd missed. "Come to the kitchen."

His house was about the same size as mine but without the teenage boy touches. His color scheme was a soft grey with accents of various colors. The kitchen was stainless steel and granite in dark tones, dark mahogany-type wood, and an oversized island.

"I thought we could eat here." He pulled out a tall chair at the island. "I have wine if you'd like?"

"I'm fine with water." I sat in the chair. "Can I help with anything?"

"Call the number on the card the officer gave you and leave a message that I am your lawyer, and all questions or information needs to come through me. I'm going to fill out a protection order, which they should have done last night, and I'll get that filed right away," Rowan explained as he pulled out plates. "If this guy violates the order, I'll go after him with everything I have to get him put away since it sounds like he has a history of this."

I stood up and went to dig through my purse for the card and did as Rowan instructed me. I'd take any help I could get to make this unsafe feeling go away. I *had* noticed that I didn't feel it around Rowan, but I was pretty sure I couldn't get away with gluing myself to him all day, every day. Even if I wanted to, and I most assuredly did.

I returned to the kitchen with the card, and Rowan took a photo of it with his phone and resumed doing what he was doing. "What is that smell?" I took a deep breath in. "It smells fantastic."

"I know Mexican is your favorite, so I made pulled beef enchiladas," he told me.

"How do you know Mexican is my favorite?" I asked, stupidly happy that Rowan knew that.

"Three years of watching you sit on that bench out in the courtyard eating lunch when you go get it, wishing I was sitting next to you. I'm observant when the subject interests me," Rowan said patiently. "Every time you get lunch, it's from a Mexican restaurant. I also know your favorite color is green, you love rock music, you are intelligent, you like to read, and you go out of your way to make people feel good. I sound like a stalker."

Wow. Rowan knew more about me than my ex-husband did. "Do you have flaws?" I blurted out.

Rowan laughed a deep laugh, "More than I care to admit on a first date. I'm painfully shy and introverted; my imagination is sorely lacking sometimes. I overthink almost everything and have difficulty letting people in."

"I don't see those as flaws, Rowan," I

said quietly.

"That's because you tend to see the best in people from what I've observed," he countered.

"Not true," I argued. "I'm not stupid enough to try and argue with a lawyer, though. I will say I see flaws plenty and often overlook things that I shouldn't because of my baggage."

"We have time to get to know each other, Lena." Rowan looked up from pulling the rest of the dinner items out. "As much as I'd like to be a caveman and stake my claim, I won't. At least not yet. I want you to see this experiment through because, if anything, it's a great learning experience about others and yourself."

"Speaking of a learning experience, I'm ashamed to say I don't even know what kind of lawyer you are," I told him, blushing.

Rowan pushed the food across the island, grabbed a salad from the fridge, and a couple of salad dressing bottles; he slid them across the counter before sitting next to me. "Contract law. Our firm handles business contracts. But on the side, so they can claim pro bono work, I do the cases for the women's shelter, from estate planning, divorce, child support, parenting plans, restraining orders, and pretty much anything they need. I just made partner this year, which was a huge step for me. I got to hire an assistant and a paralegal."

"Wow! I bet you had them lining up to interview with you. Is she pretty? Your assistant?" I blushed furiously, shocked that those words came out of my mouth.

"He. I hired men to avoid situations where a significant other might feel threatened," Rowan said carefully. "They were also the best qualified for the jobs. I may add a female paralegal to make some women feel more comfortable, but for now, this works. Were you jealous?" He smiled wide, and his eyes sparkled.

"Maybe." I reached for an enchilada to hide my embarrassment. "If we are honest here, look at you! You're gorgeous, successful, kind, intelligent, funny, and sweet; you are the whole package. What woman wouldn't want to throw themselves at you or take a job working for you just to get close to you?"

Rowan shrugged, his eyes on mine. "There's only one woman I want. Only one that I look at with romantic interest and longing."

Me? I hoped it was me, at least. I tried to make myself ask the question, but what came out was, "I haven't had sex in years."

Rowan choked a little and gave me an odd look. "Is that a proposition?"

It probably was, but I didn't say that either. "A warning, perhaps. You might find yourself a little disappointed."

"Highly unlikely," Rowan chuckled. "We are still at level one, and I'm doing my best to remain there until your experiment is over. However, level one can be fun too, Lena."

"I swear to God, the moment I get around you, the worst things possible come out of my mouth. You should just stick something in there to keep me quiet," I said, frustrated. At Rowan's choking sound, I realized what I had just said and almost fell off my chair. "For example, that sentence."

"I may be fully in love with you by the time you

leave tonight." Rowan laughed and reached out to steady me.

I decided to stop talking and shove food in my mouth. It was a wise choice because it was delicious and I moaned. "This is so good," I praised Rowan.

"Thank you. I'm so happy you like it," Rowan said, and I suddenly didn't want to date anyone but him. It hit me that fast and hard. I sincerely liked this man. I was, in fact, inching towards that impossible other "L" word. Not lust; I was already in that one. I didn't want to fall.

I kept quiet and just ate because I was genuinely afraid of what would come out of my mouth, with those thoughts racing around my head. When I finished, I slid my plate away before I became tempted to overstuff myself and end up scaring Rowan away with a Mexican food fart. Given how things had been for me lately, it wasn't out of the realm of possibilities.

"I'll do the dishes," I offered, standing up. "It's only fair since you cooked."

"Nonsense." Rowan stood as well. "How about we do them together?"

My phone chirped with the sound of a text message. "Sorry, I forgot to silence it." I reached into my pocket to do so and saw the message from Sasha requesting the photos I took of the bruises today. I quickly sent them but didn't ask why. I also let her know the date with Rowan was fantastic and that my phone was getting silenced. I slid it back into my pocket.

"Everything okay?" Rowan asked.

"Yeah. Sasha asked for the pictures I had taken today of my bruises, so I quickly sent them. It's silenced now," I assured him.

"No need to silence it. Your friends are probably worried about you after last night," Rowan said gently. "By the way, I'm sending you home with this enchilada for your son."

Stunned, I stared at Rowan blankly for a moment. "You are sending me home with leftovers for Austin? Why?"

"He needs to eat too. That's why I made an extra one."

I wanted to throw myself at him. "I don't want to date anyone else," I blurted out once again.

Rowan slowed his movements. "Meaning you don't want to go out with me again?" He packaged up the enchilada and looked at me.

"Meaning, I only want to go out with you," I clarified.

"No, Lena. I meant what I said. I want you to finish your three months; I just want to be included. We can make a standing date every week if you'd like, but I want you to go out with others too. You're worth taking the time to do things right with." Rowan rinsed off a plate and handed it to me.

"I have a no-sex rule," I said. I loaded the plate into the dishwasher. "I won't be sleeping with anyone I go out with, but damn, I want to break it with you."

Rowan grinned at me. "We will spend each of our dates getting to know more about each other. By the time we are ready to take this to level two, if that happens, I hope you know there won't be anyone else for me. I mean, there already isn't, but at level two, we are exclusive."

"You can have that now," I protested.

"I need to earn it, Lena." Rowan leaned forward and tenderly brushed his lips across my forehead.

"Fine, every Saturday belongs to you then," I retorted stubbornly, wishing it had been my mouth he'd kissed.

"You have a deal. I'm a lawyer. That's a binding contract."

I laughed then. We finished the dishes, fed Demon, and then went out to Rowan's backyard so Demon could run around and do his business. He was adorable, with gray fur, white paws, and a little cow patch of white on his side with those big brown puppy eyes.

"Pick dog-friendly places to have dates. We can't leave this little guy behind," I reminded him. "He's welcome at my house, too; we are currently animal-free unless you count Austin."

"Aside from reading, what are your hobbies?" Rowan scooped up Demon and brought us back into the house.

"Oh, no. I'm not giving you that information, so you can tailor dates to what I like. If you want something real with me, it has to be a give and take; that means I must do things you like, too. I know some women believe it's all about their man pleasing them all the time, but I'm not one of those women. I like to do new things and go on adventures, just as much as I like to sit quietly and read or blast music throughout the house and be goofy with Austin."

Rowan put his hands up in surrender. "Fair enough. How about you tell me about your family then?"

He led us back to the couch, had me take my shoes off, and then put my feet in his lap while he rubbed them.

My mind blanked out; it felt so good. "Damn, Rowan, I don't even remember what you asked me," I said with a groan.

"Tell me about your family," Rowan requested again, his face lit with happiness.

"Oh, yeah. Um, I was born and raised here, an only child. My parents moved to Arizona a couple of years ago. Austin usually goes down there for a week during the summer to hang out with them. They are both retired, and my dad likes to take Austin to cool places. I think this year he's going to take Austin to some caves somewhere down there," I mumbled. "He's going the first week in September. College starts mid-month for him. What about you?"

"Hmm, I have two brothers, both of whom live on the East Coast. My parents are retired as well and live in Florida. My father was a lawyer, a criminal one, and my mother worked for a bank. I'm a middle kid who tried the hardest to get noticed but always fell short. It drove my dad up the wall that I was shy and introverted. I got a full-ride scholarship on my basketball skills and decided on law, trying to gain my dad's approval, but since I didn't choose criminal law, I fell short again. It's hard to believe it took me all those years to learn just to be happy with myself."

"Don't feel bad. I haven't quite learned that yet," I said, feeling sad. "Having brothers should have been fun, right?"

"Sometimes, yeah. We were hell-raisers when we were all together. We aren't very close anymore; our family wasn't like that. My dad was always busy with a case. My mom was always busy at work or with one of her charities. We were alone a lot, and therefore in trouble a lot. We were close enough to call each other when we needed help to escape whatever mess we created, but the distance has kept us from being more united." Rowan switched to the other foot. "I call them when I miss them."

"I always wanted a brother, but my mom said I was a handful enough for her. I had Sasha, then we added Lily and Hope, and now Hannah. For sure, Sasha and I were always in trouble. I'm close to my parents but also glad for the distance. My dad liked to hover; he was the helicopter parent, not my mom. You have magic fingers." I groaned when he hit a tense spot on my arch.

"This was something I learned because of basketball. Later, I took it upon myself to learn more about reflexology. Some of these spots I'm hitting should help the pain in your back and head," Rowan replied gently.

"How did you know they were hurting?" I asked, curious.

"Your posture was stiff while we were eating, and you've touched the back of your head a couple of times, and it made your eyes squint a little. I'd offer a backrub, but it will just hurt if the bruises are fresh." Rowan cleared his throat. "I'll also need you to send me those pictures you sent Sasha for the file I'll start."

I pulled out my phone and texted them without a second thought, only to realize as I put my phone away that one of them was an obvious shot of my boob. Damn. "I think I just sexted you," I joked.

Rowan gave me a startled look. "Excuse me?"

"One of the pictures is my breast." I blushed. "Oh, damn. Pretty sure my ass is showing in the one of my back too." I covered my eyes, embarrassed.

Rowan shifted, then tugged on my hands. I dropped them but kept my eyes closed. His mouth settled gently on my bruised lips, the kiss tender and sweet, and heat pooled between my thighs as I ran my hands up his back and into his hair.

I parted my lips, and his tongue swept across my bottom lip. I swear I almost had an orgasm. Jeez, Rowan was good at this. Not wanting to be left out, I explored his mouth with mine until I was ready to tear my clothes off.

Rowan pulled back, panting slightly, his eyes foggy with need, and I'm sure that mine were showing pure animal lust. I wanted more, a lot more. In nineteen years, he was my first kiss from a man other than Shane. All I got from Shane was a peck on the lips. He had thought kissing was dirty and spread germs. The train wreck of Mike last night didn't count as a kiss.

I moved and straddled Rowan's lap, his arms coming around my lower back as I sunk into his juicy lips again. My body was on fire, and there was a building crescendo inside of me that as the groan ripped out of me, I realized it *was* an orgasm. Holy shit. Rowan gave me an orgasm from kissing.

He pulled back and rested his forehead against mine. "We are about to bypass all levels and go straight to marriage if we keep doing this," Rowan warned.

A giggle built up and then escaped my lips. "I have never had that happen before." I giggled again.

Rowan gave me a confused look. "You've never been kissed?"

"Not like that! I've never come from one either," I confessed and then realized what I just admitted. Oh my God, I needed to leave. I stood up from his lap and noticed the bulge I'd been sitting on; I wanted to unwrap it.

"Wait; what?" Rowan smiled slowly. "Did you just say what I think you did?"

"I was hoping you didn't hear that." I grabbed for my sweater and pulled it on to try and hide the fact that my nipples were poking out of the lacy holes of my bra. "I think you are right; if we don't stop now, we won't. At least I won't."

Rowan stood and took my hand, placing it over his heart, which was thudding as hard as mine. "This has been the best date of my life."

I swooned. "Jesus. I'm forty, not a damn virgin teenager!" I had hoped that was just a thought in my head, but nope. I'd said it out loud.

"If it makes you feel better, I feel the same way." Rowan chuckled.

There was going to be a toy in my immediate future. I fumbled around, looking for my shoes, only to find them soaking wet and in complete tatters, with a pleased Demon sitting behind them. Another laugh bubbled up inside me.

Rowan looked mortified. "Did you have to live up to your name?" he chastised the puppy.

"I can drive home barefoot." I tried to staunch the laugh. Rowan's face was beet red, and he didn't see the same humor I had.

"I'm so sorry, Lena." Rowan followed me to the front door as I fished the keys out of my pocket.

"Don't worry so much about it," I told him and stood on the tips of my bare toes to kiss him again. "He's a puppy, and I know better than to leave my shoes on the floor like that." I added another kiss that I fell into again, the magic of Rowan setting all my nerves on fire.

He groaned this time, his fingers tangling in my hair on either side of my head. I was going to start a countdown calendar when I got home to when this stupid dating experiment was over, and I could ride this man right into every sexual fantasy I'd ever had.

I pulled away with a whimper. "See you Monday?"

Rowan nodded, running a shaking hand through his hair. "Probably text you later, too."

"Goodnight, Rowan. Thank you for an amazing evening." I backed up, stepping on a sharp rock and cussing quietly.

In less than a second, Rowan was out the door and telling me to climb on his back. He looked so upset that I didn't argue. He gave me a piggyback ride to my car so I didn't step on any more rocks.

"Goodnight, Lena," Rowan murmured, giving me a whisper of a kiss on my lips, then a firmer one on my forehead.

Chapter 12

With a start, I realized my purse was sitting on the floor next to Rowan's couch. My head became clearer after a night of debauchery with myself and my new toy. Damn it; I'd just have to drive without a license and hope like hell I didn't get pulled over.

Sasha's house was in the opposite direction of Rowan's, and I was already running late due to sleeping in. "Austin! I'm heading to Sasha's. Make sure your laundry gets done so I can do mine when I return."

"Got it. Have fun." Austin rounded the corner from the kitchen. He looked my face over, still wincing even though it was better than it had been yesterday, and kissed me on the cheek.

"See you soon." I grabbed my keys and exited the front door. Sasha hated tardiness and would find some way to embarrass the hell out of me if I was late. I already had enough embarrassing ammunition for this week's episode. Thank God no one could see my face. They could only hear my voice, and Sasha assigned us numbers to identify ourselves.

The week had been a roller coaster of emotions, and whoever listened was guaranteed at least one laugh at my expense—probably more. When I pulled up at Sasha's house, I had three minutes to spare and flew through the door.

Sasha narrowed her eyes at me. "Barely on time, but you made it."

Hannah smirked from her seat on the couch. "I don't even have a car, and I was on time."

"Behave, that's because I picked you up." Lily swatted at her playfully. Lily and Hope examined my face and clucked their disapproval at the still visible bruises. "Take your shirt off and let us see your back," she ordered me.

Arguing wasn't an option; I would have done the same to them had the roles been reversed. I pulled it off and let them examine me; Sasha's face was set in stone, giving no expression. That was dangerous. "Show me the goods," she told me quietly.

"Do we need to do this? I sent you the picture," I answered back. Something flickered in her eyes, and I quickly realized it was tears. I threw my arms around her and hugged her tight. "I'm fine. You, Matt, and Hannah saved me."

"I haven't slept since it happened," Sasha whispered in my ear, brokenly.

"Then we talk it out like we always do. How about we introduce the experiment, then start with that and end on the rest for a lighter note? We can include phone numbers and suggestions at the end for people to call. I know you already know them all," I told her, pushing her back to look at her face.

Sasha nodded and swiped angrily at her face. "Sorry, Hannah, this is a bit of a rough introduction to our group."

Hannah waved it off. "I can fix that." She winked at me and turned to Lily, planting a big kiss smack on her lips. Before Hope could react, Hannah moved to her and did the same with a bit more oomph behind it. She then turned to Sasha and raised her eyebrows, and at Sasha's nod, she gave Sasha a scorching hot kiss.

"Well, damn," Lily breathed out. "Now, there's a different type of tension."

"You left out Lena," Hope pointed out.

"No, she didn't. I asked Hannah to kiss me to see if I was a bad kisser when she came over to wax me. It turns out I got skills," I said happily.

"Yeah, she does," Hannah agreed. "There wasn't a toy that existed to take away that tension she left me in."

Sasha burst out laughing. "That doesn't surprise me in the slightest. The asking for the kiss does, but not that she's good at it."

I sat down, glad that Hannah had broken past the awkward moment that had been brewing. "Let's do this so you can learn about my date last night."

Sasha had the recording equipment set up already, gave Hannah a brief description of the podcast and how we would play it, and told her that she should refer to herself as number five. "I went alphabetically with the rest of us; Hope is one, Lena two, Lily three, and me four."

Sasha flipped on the machine. "Hey, all you beautiful people, the quartet is back, and we've added a new one to make us a quintet. Welcome number five." We all said hello to her. "Disturbing the Peace is bringing you a new episode, where we will talk about an experiment we are doing. We will first call out some horrible behavior after we explain it. Number two, why don't you start since it all began with you?"

"All right then, ladies, you'll have to fill in the parts I missed. Last Friday, before I left home to meet you all for drinks and meet number five for the first time, my son started talking about his father and me living alone. We all know I'm klutzy, and he used that as an excuse for me to start dating since he is leaving for college. I blew it off as I always do and went to get ready. Unbeknownst to me, the tricky devil had used my phone and added me on a singles app," I started.

"Yeah, he did." Hannah giggled. "She popped up on my phone the minute she was close, and it didn't say Two was straight, so, in my eyes, she was fair game. I started hitting on her almost immediately."

Sasha laughed at that. "God, it was hilarious too. Poor Two had no idea what was going on. People all over that bar were looking at her, and she was oblivious to it all. We clued her in and then decided to make an experiment out of it. We all agreed to join the dating apps, the three big ones, and a couple of the smaller local apps and talk about our dates here on this platform to give you all an idea of what dating in your forties looks like from four different women. We are all rolling the dice, so to speak."

"For ninety days, approximately," Lily added. "We are going to give each major online dating site a month. Which is looking a little generous right now if you ask me."

"We've all had dates this past week, except five,

who is watching from the sidelines and helping out Two, which is its own story." Hope giggled. "Oh, and now I've finally kissed a girl."

Hannah and Sasha immediately started singing the Katy Perry song while we rolled our eyes. "She actually kissed all of us," Lily amended. "Five, that is. She kind of tasted like cotton candy."

I snorted and then cleared my throat. "Before we get into the dates, we will veer to my third date to start because we want to get an important message out there."

Sasha broke back in, her voice a little shaky. "Critical, for anyone, any age. Two, take over."

Hannah reached out and rubbed Sasha's back as I gave her a worried look. "This is pretty serious, and it's affected Four badly. Well, myself, too, really. For my third experiment date, I'm going to call this guy Douche. It's apt. He's the father of one of my son's friends. When I set the date up, he gave me a slimy feeling. Then my son told me that he was a slimy sort of guy. I went into this date knowing that. But it was also at a public place, a bar, where I knew the male bartender. It also happened that Four was there on a date as well. I got there before him and had already established a security code with the bartender. I didn't like Douche the moment he started talking. I told myself to stick it out and just not show any interest. Leading him on was the last thing I wanted to do since he was already checking out my ass when he walked into the bar."

"He seriously was," Sasha agreed. "I didn't even talk to him and I didn't like him."

"It took me a bit to notice that he was already

drunk when he arrived. I ordered a margarita but asked the bartender to keep the alcohol light. Douche was drinking scotch. He didn't order dinner, just more drinks, and I ordered food. When it arrived, he tried to steal some of it, which pissed me off. He was gross. Fake tan, way too bleached teeth, and so much hair product I don't think any of his hair moved at all; just yuck. He talked non-stop about himself, and I flat-out stopped responding. I wasn't even looking at him or giving him any attention. It didn't deter him at all."

"She's not kidding," Sasha broke in. "Two always is polite. Unfailingly polite. She was flat-out, staring vacantly out the window. When I saw that, I laughed, confusing my date, which was pitifully boring. Cute, but dull."

I smiled. "Douche made me lose my appetite for tacos. That's unheard of."

"Seriously?" Lily asked. "Tacos are like your go-to food."

"Seriously. When I pushed my plate away, Douche dove into my food like he hadn't eaten in a week. I got up to go to the bathroom. I locked myself in the stall to get away from him. I checked my phone and saw that I had missed a text from my son warning me that this guy was drunk. But as Four said, I'm polite, so I usually silence my phone when I arrive to meet people somewhere, so I never heard it. Lesson learned there. I stayed in there for as long as socially acceptable."

"By that, she means she was in there about five minutes. In that time, Douche had devoured the rest of Two's food and downed two more drinks," Sasha filled in for me. "In that span of forty minutes, he had drunk five glasses of scotch."

Lily and Hope winced, and Hannah kept her face bland. "When I walked out, I was immediately slammed into the wall behind me. A brick wall," I added. "My head hit hard enough for my vision to blur and my ears to ring. Douche had managed to pin me against the wall. He had my hands trapped, pressing all his weight into me, his knees digging into my legs to hold them in place. I want to say what he did was a kiss, but it was more like punching his lips into mine. Hard enough, in fact, to split and bruise them. Visibly bruised; my lips are blue and purple. They cut into my teeth. He did that a couple of times before he came up for air, and I yelled for help. When Douche let go and grabbed my boob, I was able to move a leg and stomp on his foot. That made him yell out, which got the bartender's attention."

"It got my attention, too," Sasha said quietly. "I ran so fast; I just launched myself into the air, ready to beat his ass down because I knew what he was going to do. I also knew Two didn't want it. I've been in that situation, and I know how she felt. I saw the shock setting in, the fear, grabbing hold of her."

"Rape is no joking matter," I said bluntly. "I've never been physically attacked like that before. Needless to say, I don't want it to happen again, either. The bartender moved me to a safe place while they called the cops. It was surreal to have a stranger taking photos of my breast and forming bruises that didn't even have time to color yet. By then, the fear had settled in my mind. I didn't feel safe."

"Please, if anyone goes through something like that, call for help," Hope begged.

"If you are in an abusive relationship, get out. I know it sounds easy, and it's anything but easy, but just leave. You don't deserve it," Lily spoke softly.

"No one does," Sasha reminded them. "At the end of this episode, I'll list numbers to call for people who need them. We wanted to get this out there. That could have ended so much worse than it did. Two could have been raped or beaten, or both. If a person doesn't feel right to you, trust your instincts. If you are on a date, make sure it's public, check in when you get there, and work out a code to text someone who knows where you are. I can't stress enough how important it is to be aware and to trust your instincts."

"It's not always strangers who are the ones that will attack either," Hope pointed out. "Situational awareness is so important. So is a basic understanding of self-defense."

"Flight or fight is real," Sasha said. "Backed into a corner like that, fight. Don't let the fear take over, fight. Fight for yourself. If you aren't trapped, then run, get help."

There was a moment of silence, and then I said, "Now that *that* is out of the way. Let's move on to the amusing parts. The ladies decided that since my marriage seriously sucked in the sex department and denied years of orgasms and toys, they would order me some toys. Understand, I've never had toys before."

Hannah started laughing. "That's how she got her first date. The dirtbag, which will be his name, overheard us talking about them and promptly asked her out. Me, trying to be helpful and nudge her to get back out there, accepted on her behalf. Lesson learned; I will not be doing that again."

"Turns out Dirtbag was only interested in the sex. Not only that but he was also married. The bartender remembered that he had brought his wife in a couple of days before the date. On top of that," I cried, "his wife's sister was in the bar!"

Lily and Hope burst out laughing. "You've got to be kidding me. Dirtbag had some major karma coming at him that night."

"He felt up Two, making her knee jerk into the table, spilling his drink in his lap. Then his food spilled there when the sister-in-law came up. She took a picture of them together, threatened him, and the cheating coward took off like a bat out of hell," Hannah described.

Sasha, Lily, and Hope were cracking up. "What Five failed to mention is me using the toy. Oh my God," I laughed, "I am so bad at this stuff it's crazy. It arrived Monday, and Five and Four both told me to use it before the date. Here I am Monday night, getting romantic with myself, and honestly, the purple alien penis worked and quickly. But I didn't read the directions on how to operate it. I had no idea there were different levels of intensity. So after my second O, I hit the power button, thinking it would turn off. It got stronger, and the rhythm changed. By the time I got the damn thing shut off, I was so sensitive I was crying and lying in a wet bed."

Hannah was laughing so hard now she was crying. "Oh God, she called me in a complete panic while I was at work because she couldn't get it out!"

Hope and Lily, having not heard this part yet,

howled in laughter. "It's funny now, but it wasn't then," I defended myself. "I thought I was going to have to walk around with this purple alien penis inside me, hoping the damn thing wouldn't turn on. It was a full-blown panic time."

"Hands down, the best phone call of my life." Hannah wiped her face. "I mean, I'm standing there, listening to a hot woman I hit on tell me she couldn't get her toy out of her va-jay-jay. While at work. I had to go outside because damn, what the hell do you say to that?"

Sasha was grinning like the Cheshire cat. "Yeah, that would have been the call to get."

Hannah started laughing hard again. "I heard it come out with a pop when she finally got it out. Oh my God. I looked insane for the rest of my shift because I couldn't stop laughing."

Hope and Lily had tears streaming down their faces. "Only you, Two, only you." Hope gasped. "The only safe sex to have is with yourself unless you are Two!"

Lily took the time to talk about her date and how all the guy wanted to do was take selfies with her and then texted to ask for boob pictures. Hope talked about hers, where the guy spent the entire date talking himself up for her to find out he lives with his parents.

"Oh boy, that would have been good to know at the start," Hannah chirped. "Big red flag there."

Sasha talked about her boring date and then brought it back to me. "You had a whopping four dates, and we've only heard about two. What about the others?"

"The second date was fun. This man was nice, smart, funny, and entirely not my type, but I agreed to a second date anyway. He's truthfully your type Three. I'm hoping to set you up with him." I looked at her.

"My type?" she echoed. "Like what?"

"Successful, muscles, tall, handsome, funny, smart, jock type," I described.

"Oh, I'm in," she said immediately. "Isn't that everyone's type?"

"That was ridiculously easy," Sasha laughed. "I thought you'd put up a little more fight than that. Two's type is specific in her mind."

"Why fight? The responses I'm getting are awful. Two already vetted him for me. Now I get the fun part; she's the one with the no-sex rule, not me." Lily grinned.

"No joke, you need to vet one for me now." Hope raised her eyebrows. "It's like the dredges of society are responding to my profile. Send nudes; I want to know what I'm getting, one of them said. He was fifty-two!"

"Wow," Hannah said. "Sad. Why do they think that's acceptable?"

"That's what I want to know," Sasha agreed. "I had so many like that, too."

"I did too," I added. "I deleted those."

"Now, dish on the last date." Lily leaned forward. "This is the one we've been waiting to hear."

I sighed dramatically. "I want to end the experiment altogether and just focus on him. I was ready to break my no-sex rule, too. He's a dream come true, and I seriously like him. I mean, really like him. Close to falling head over heels for him type of like."

"That good?" Sasha asked, her tone solemn.

"Better than that good. This man is so much more than I thought he was. I fessed up about the experiment, and he told me he wanted me to keep doing it because he wanted to be sure I'm ready for the next level with him when it was over. He said it's a great way to learn about myself and what I want. He also said we could have a standing date throughout to get to know each other slowly." I sighed dreamily again.

"Holy shit," Hope swore. "Where can I find one of him?"

"No joke," Lily agreed. "What did he say about the bruises? Those are kind of hard to miss."

"He studied my face and asked me to tell him, and I started crying. I told him everything, every horrible detail. He wrote down things, took names and numbers, had me call the police station, and tell them all questions were to go through him because he's my lawyer. He's filing a protection order, and he just took care of me," I described.

They all went silent. "I'm with you," Sasha finally said, "he's the one. End the experiment and mark that man somehow so no other women get near him."

"Right?" I exclaimed. "He knows my favorite food is Mexican, which he made for dinner. Oh, the hilarious part: his puppy ate my shoes. I had to drive home barefoot. Utterly worth it."

I filled them in on all the little details that added up to so much, and by the end, they were demanding me to marry Rowan without saying his name. They all fell silent again when I told them about the O from kissing.

"I can see that," Hannah said softly. "I mean,

damn, you almost gave me one."

Sasha laughed and shoved her playfully. "Down, girl. She's spoken for now."

"Here's what's scary, am I ready for him? I know he wants me to continue this to find the answer, just like I know he's not a fling. After the ex, I swore off men, yet a few seconds in this man's presence, and I'm ready to break every rule I set for myself," I said, looking for advice.

"You've what, crashed into him twice, literally? Walked into a glass door, fell, almost fell out of a chair, cried in front of him, fed his puppy your shoes," Sasha started listing off.

"Don't forget I debauched myself thoroughly after getting home last night because I was so worked up and forgot my purse at his house," I added to her growing list.

Hope and Hannah started laughing. "He hasn't run," Hope pointed out.

"Does that make him crazy?" I asked them. "I mean, jeez, I'm a walking hazard."

"I think it means he's crazy for you," Sasha said softly. "He did more for you on one date than your ex did your entire marriage."

"Do what he suggests," Lily advised. "Finish the experiment, even if you don't want to, and keep getting to know him. Ask the hard questions and don't be afraid to take that first step into the unknown."

"Three is right; just go with it and stop doubting yourself." Sasha leaned forward to pat my knee. "You rolled and got doubles right off the bat with him. I know you don't want to fall, but maybe you should."

"I think that you already learned some pretty good lessons in this first week," Hope volunteered, seeing the look on my face. "I think we all did. Dating isn't easy, especially for a woman in her forties. We all got through the first week, maybe in Two's case, a little bruised up and unsteady on her feet, but we survived. And we all got to kiss a hot younger woman in the process."

Hannah laughed again. "Anytime I can be of assistance, just pucker up."

"As always, leave comments, ask questions, or reach out for help. Here are the numbers I promised you." Sasha recited off several phone numbers, and we all said goodbye. Once the equipment got shut off, they all turned to me.

"What?" I asked.

"Are you in love with Rowan?" Sasha asked first, a twinkle in her eye.

"I'm not sure, but I think it's headed that way. As much as I try to stop it, he gets in somehow." I sighed melodramatically, "Am I pathetic?"

Lily laughed at me. "In some ways, sure. In others, you are a complete badass. Don't overthink this, Lena. It sounds like he truly likes and respects you. Respect is the key. Shane never respected you. Neither did the other dates, except the one you want to fix me up with."

"Lil's right," Sasha prodded me. "Rowan has shown nothing but respect. Go with it, sugar." She messed with something on her phone, "Okay, the episode is up."

Chapter 13

I pulled up the driveway at home and waited for the garage door to open before pulling in. I had the rest of the day to decompress; I had chores to do still and dinner to figure out. When I entered the house, Austin sat at the kitchen table, eating an enchilada.

Wait. "Where did you get that?"

"Get what?" Austin looked up guiltily.

"The enchilada?" I raised my eyebrow at him.

"Rowan brought your purse back." Austin looked back at the food guiltily and shoveled more into his face.

Suspicion grew the more Austin tried to avoid conversation. "That was nice of Rowan. Now tell me why you are acting like that. Did you say something rude to him?"

"No. I actually like Rowan. His puppy is super cute." Austin quickly took another bite.

"Spill it, Aust. You are acting guilty."

"I'm serious, Mom. I like Rowan. He's perfect for you, and I might be young and inexperienced in life, but he's totally into you. I'm talking long-term here. He told me he would be your lawyer and get a protection order for you, which, after talking with Derrick a little bit ago, is probably a good idea. He said his dad is unhinged, which scares me. Rowan also told me that he wants you to continue what you and your friends are doing, and he told me why. He gave me a few pointers on how to help make sure you stay safe. He talked with me about college, told me about himself," Austin rambled.

I was a little surprised, but not much. "None of that would make you act that way. What else?"

"I swear, Mom's are like natural lie detectors," Austin mumbled. "I might have mentioned the podcast." He was forbidden to listen to it for a good reason.

That was it. That was the guilty look right there. Oh, God. I was going to die of embarrassment if Rowan listened to it. I don't think there was anything in there he didn't know except the sex toy part. My face burned red. "Oh, jeez."

"I seriously wanted not to like Rowan, but I do. I mean, like, I *really* wanted to be a rude teenager and be all stupid about it. He's one of those real types. Rowan didn't talk down to me like I was an idiot, and he brought me food. He said he made extra so I could have some. Rowan didn't even know me! He's the one, Mom. Don't screw this up." Austin went back to eating while I stared at my son like he was possessed.

"Is your laundry done?" I jammed my hands on my hips and scowled.

"I know you want to yell at me, but you can't find a reason," Austin snickered. "It's funny. Yes, my laundry's finished."

Defeated, I slumped down into a chair. "Is Rowan going to listen to it?"

"The podcast? Probably. Did you talk about him on there?" Austin correctly guessed.

"We did. We talked about each date." I rested my head on the table. "You like Rowan then?"

"Yeah. Rowan's pretty shy for a lawyer, but he asks smart questions. Huh, I guess that makes sense," Austin said to himself. "He wasn't awkward with me and skipped the small talk, too. He didn't try to impress me and offered himself up for any questions I had."

"I like him, too," I admitted. I was sad I missed him stopping by.

"Don't forget to check your messages on the online site," Austin reminded me. "I've already logged in and removed the psychos. Go ahead and get mad at me for butting in, but after Thursday, you can't say you blame me."

"I truly don't want to date any of them." I lifted my head, not caring that Austin had logged in.

"I know. I can see your side and Rowan's. Go out with at least one a week. He's right in that it will help you, and if Rowan's the one, it will become obvious and help combat that fear I can see in your face." Austin's words were soft but hard to hear.

"You see too much, kid." I stood up and went to start my laundry. On a whim, I texted Rowan, thanking him for returning my purse and feeding Austin.

Austin is a great kid, Rowan wrote back. *You're welcome. I'm glad Demon didn't eat it.*

Austin thinks you are pretty awesome, too, I responded.

I think level two will be a lot of fun, was his following text.

Oh, God. Rowan listened to the podcast. I was so happy that no one could see me turning the color of a cherry tomato. After listening to that, I was also giddy that he still wanted to go to level two with me. And he was flirting with me!

I'm a little embarrassed you listened to that, I wrote back.

Don't be; this is a fantastic podcast. I've listened to several now. You women tackle some big topics.

That we did. We usually followed Sasha's lead on it since it was her baby, and we often addressed the issues from a female standpoint to try to help other women. We had a few male subscribers, but they were primarily women.

One question. Purple alien penis? Rowan asked. I about died when I read that. All I could do was take a picture and send it back.

Will you be disappointed if mine doesn't look like that? Rowan asked.

I burst out laughing. *I'd be worried if it did. We can skip the experiment and go right to level two if you'd like. I'd be happy to give you my honest opinion.* I held my breath, shocked that I was brave enough to send that.

You're worth waiting for, Lena. I read his words probably six times, my heart beating madly against my ribs. I didn't know what to say, so I returned a heart emoji to him.

I stood in my bedroom, trying to picture Rowan and realized I couldn't. I'd lived in this house with Shane, and he used to share this room with me. Not this bed, since I'd gotten a new one, but this room. For the first time since my divorce, I wished I had been the one that had moved.

There wasn't anything wrong with the room. The décor was all me, soft yellow and blue colors that soothed me. My brain knew that even though Shane had never seen the new décor, he had still spent many years inside these four walls.

I returned to the kitchen, pulled out my laptop, logged into the dating site, read through the messages, and looked at the profiles of the ones who had sent them. Two of the ones I had responded to during the week had written back, asking if I'd like to meet up.

With Rowan's wish that I continue in mind, I suggested the martini bar with dates and times to both men. Then, I responded to several other messages that didn't seem too scary. The two men I had offered a date to responded before I logged off, one guy requesting that I go to a work party with him instead of meeting at the bar. He said it was still a public place and I could meet him there. I accepted both and added them to my calendar.

With that completed, I also added Rowan to every Saturday until the end of time. Austin walked back in, and seeing I was looking at my calendar, he let me know which days he was working and suggested that I put a physical schedule on the fridge that listed my dates, where they were, and what time and their names.

I knew he was worried about me, and I was a little concerned, too, so I printed a blank calendar and did precisely that, and he said he'd add the days he was working as well. That way, if he were at work, I would know to check in with someone else. I hugged him hard.

"You have grown up to be amazing, Austin," I

told him, proud of who he was becoming.

Austin smiled shyly, wrote Hannah's name on a couple of Sundays, and then filled in each Saturday with Rowan's name in big letters. "Rowan, I'm not worried about; he'd cut off his limbs before hurting you, I am sure of that."

On that, we agreed. "What do you want for dinner tonight?"

"Burgers," Austin answered automatically. "I'll grill them," he offered. "Oh! You can make that pasta salad I like so much. That would be easy for me to take to work too to eat on my breaks. I don't have to cook that."

"Deal. That means we need to go to the store. Want to go?" I asked, grabbing my purse.

"Yep. I'll drive." Austin snatched the keys from my hand, making me roll my eyes. "Dad called earlier and told me he mailed my tuition check."

"He better have," I mumbled.

"He asked about you, too. I played nice since he paid for my college, but I wanted to tell him to f-off," Austin told me as we pulled out of the garage. "I think he saw you on that dating app I put on your phone."

"Great," I drawled out. "I never even thought about that."

"I didn't either, sorry," he apologized, looking chagrined.

My phone chirped, and I pulled it out to see a text from Lily telling me I'd have a new toy on Tuesday. I stifled a laugh and sent her a thumbs-up emoji, telling her I was in the car with Austin on my way to the grocery store.

"I hope you find a group of friends like I have," I told Austin, sliding the phone back into my pocket. "They make life so much better."

"I have a couple. Remember the twins?" Austin glanced at me quickly before turning back to the road.

"You still talk to them?" I'm not sure why that surprised me; they had been inseparable while still living in the area.

"All the time. We're tight. The twins are going to UCLA, too," Austin informed me.

"Crap, did you already tell me this, and I'm an awful mom that hasn't paid attention?" I tried to recall all our conversations about college but was drawing a blank.

"No, I hadn't told you yet." Austin laughed. "We'll be trying to room together. Dad tried to get me to change my mind about biology again. I haven't decided what aspect of biology interests me the most, but I know I love biology. It's a close tie with environmental sciences. Neither of them he likes."

"He doesn't get a say," I said vehemently. "He needs to shut up and pay the bill. It's your choice because it's your future. He can support you, or I'll kick him in the balls. He's not even paying the full way; you got a scholarship for the sciences."

"I know. Dad won't deter me; I just wanted to warn you in case he calls. I doubt he will, but just in case." Austin parked and got out, waiting for me at the back of the car. "Divide and conquer or together?"

"Together, I haven't gotten to see much of you this week, and I'm feeling like an absentee mother." I hooked my arm through his.

"I'm an adult, and you are the farthest thing possible from a bad or absent mother." Austin rested his head on my shoulder. I suddenly wished for the days when he was little again and he loved cuddling up on my lap to hear a story or watch a movie. I missed him needing me.

"What am I going to do when you're gone?" I asked him as he grabbed a cart.

"You are going to live your life for you, take care of you and listen to my whiny phone calls about homework and having to do my own cooking," Austin joked. He turned serious then. "Really, Mom. It's time for you to learn you while I learn me. We do it together, but apart."

Tears filled my eyes with how astute he was. "Austin, you are wise beyond your years and so sweet. I'm going to miss you needing your mom."

"I'll always need you, you're Mom," he protested. "I just need to stand on my own two feet and try to be as strong and good as you are."

Like an idiot, I stood in the middle of a grocery store aisle, crying because my son was grown up. "You are better than me, Austin. You are the best thing I've ever done. Let's do this before I mentally break down in the pasta aisle."

Chapter 14

When I rolled into the parking lot at work on Monday, I saw Rowan waiting, and my heart soared. Even though I was blushing like crazy because he now knew I played with toys after our date to relieve myself of the tension. I needed to get a grip on myself—without the toy.

Rowan's face had a slightly teasing smile as he waited for me to get out of the car, and when I did, he boxed me right up against it and planted a smoldering kiss on me in front of everyone. I whimpered when he pulled away.

"Good morning, Lena." His voice was husky.

"Wow," I breathed out, trying to focus my eyes. "That was quite the hello."

"One of many," Rowan promised. "I never promised to make it easy for other guys to date you."

I glanced up at him and smiled. "Ah, the sneaky contract lawyer surfaces."

Rowan caressed my face lightly. "I do want you to go on dates with other people, but after tasting you, I can't sit idly by and just watch. I'm also declaring myself unavailable."

"You are?" I whispered.

He lowered his head to a breath away from mine."I am." Rowan brushed his lips over mine with a feather touch before he put his arm around me.

"That was a tease," I told him, aching for more.

His smug smile had me grinning right back at him. "I know. It was intentional. After listening to your voice and hearing what you said, level two was all I could think about for the rest of the day. It was pure torture."

"Then you'll be happy to hear I have two dates lined up this week." I glanced at him to see his reaction.

It was a grimace. "I waited for three years; I can wait a few more months. I already told you, you're worth it."

"Do you ever get rattled?" I stabbed the elevator button with frustration.

"Why would you think I don't?" a V-shape appeared between his eyebrows as Rowan frowned. "Wait, did you say that just to get a reaction?"

"No, I seriously do have two dates this week. You are just so calm about it. I know we aren't exclusive, but if you told me you had a date with another woman, I'd probably lose my mind," I answered.

"I was quite upset when you told me what happened on your date. As a matter of fact, I had tears in my eyes, and if I hadn't walked away for a moment, I probably would have lost *my* mind," Rowan said into my ear.

"You have some excellent control." I stepped into the empty elevator, my mind scattered, unsure which direction to go.

"What good would it have done for you to see me upset when you were already upset yourself? Me adding to it wouldn't have made you feel better, and more than anything, I wanted you to have fun and forget that bastards like that exist." Rowan pulled me close to him and kissed my forehead.

It made sense. If I had seen Rowan get emotional, I would have wanted to console him. He held on to me a moment longer after the door opened, in plain view of the people outside the elevator, then released me with a promise to see me after work.

A little dazed, I walked to my desk, ignoring the blatant stares of my co-workers. A couple of the women looked almost hostile. I put my purse in my drawer, pulled my phone out, and texted Rowan.

I think the female masses received your message about being unavailable.

A few moments later, I got a return text. *If it makes you feel better, I've gotten a few nasty looks myself, which makes me happy.*

I was forty; I shouldn't want to giggle like a middle school girl. Rowan Carson had staked a public claim on me. *Me.* A divorced, frumpy mother of a teenager, unknown anybody. I shook my head; I needed to stop those thoughts. Those were the ones that got Austin and my friends mad at me.

Work was a blur until lunchtime, when I bolted out to the courtyard to eat my lunch and call Sasha. I brought her up to speed on Rowan and again felt like that middle school kid.

I told her about the people that commented on my face and the still visible bruises. That one was a bit tough for me because I didn't want to fan the gossip mill's flames, but I also didn't want to sweep assault under the rug. When we hung up, I finished my lunch and stood up to throw my garbage away.

One of the women I work with was approaching me, a guarded look on her face. "You know it's against company policy to date co-workers?"

"I do. Why?" I frowned.

"One of the salespeople is talking about going out with you," she replied, slouching down on the bench I had been sitting on seconds before.

"You shouldn't believe everything you hear. I'm not going out with anyone from the office," I declared hotly.

"Did you truly get those bruises from a date?" she altered the conversation to a different path.

"I did. It wasn't pleasant." I slowly sat beside the woman. "Did something similar happen to you?"

She nodded guardedly. "I was drugged, then brought back out to an ally and was being undressed when a person in the ally saw and intervened. I've been too scared to try again."

"I don't blame you. I'm pretty scared, too. Have safety plans in place if you do it," I suggested quietly. "Meet at public places, get there early and talk to a bartender or security to let them know. Text someone the location of where you will be, check in when you get there, and decide when to leave. Never leave a drink unattended. Small things like that help you gain a sense of security back."

"Thanks," she sighed. "Watch out for Cory."

"That's who's talking? I wouldn't date him even if

we worked for separate companies. He's a player and not a good one," I laughed harshly.

"Are you seeing that lawyer?" she finally asked, curious.

"We just started," I admitted reluctantly, and then he magically appeared.

"Good afternoon, ladies," Rowan said smoothly. He placed his hand on my back and handed me a piece of chocolate. "I saw you down here and wanted to bring you another since you enjoyed it so much last time."

His shy tone was back, but the look in his eyes wasn't. Of course, he was only looking at me. "Thank you, Rowan."

"You're welcome." He ran his hand down my cheek. "See you after work."

I hoped for another kiss, but his shy smile told me it wasn't happening. "Have a good rest of your day." I smiled back at him.

"I could have been dancing on this bench naked, and he wouldn't have noticed me. Hold on to him." My co-worker stood. "Thanks for listening to me."

"Anytime," I replied. I hadn't done anything to help the woman whose name I couldn't remember. I followed her back in, and we rode the elevator up, going our separate ways when we reached our floor. Not long after, the salesman Cory she had mentioned walked up to my desk.

"Hey, Lena. I saw you are entering the dating world again. How about we get a couple of drinks after work one night, and I can help you?" he leaned against my cubicle wall.

"No, thanks. It's against company policy, and I'm booked up and started seeing someone," I politely refused.

"No one has to know," he pushed. His arrogance knew no bounds.

"A little late for that now since your voice carries, and you are asking me while we are at work, surrounded by people," I pointed out. I pitied any woman who went out with this guy.

"Well, I'd say that whoever you are seeing isn't doing an outstanding job if they leave your lips like that." Cory smirked. He crossed his arms arrogantly over his chest.

"That happens to be from an attack that happened while I was on a date. It is not from who I have started seeing." I felt my temper begin to rise, which wasn't good.

"Cory!" Another co-worker, Marty, popped her head over the cubicle wall. "That's inappropriate. Leave Lena alone; you heard her answer."

"Jealous I never asked you, Marty?" Cory sneered at her.

"Hardly." Marty snorted.

Thankfully my phone rang with a customer, and I turned my back to him. I shot her a quick thank you e-mail and returned to work, keeping my head down and my voice low. I didn't particularly appreciate how I found myself in the spotlight now. I was uncomfortable for the rest of the afternoon.

When it came time to leave, I couldn't get out of there fast enough. I hoped to do it unimpeded, too. I made it halfway there before I heard Cory coming up behind me, calling out my name. I rolled my eyes; this guy didn't know when to give up. I ignored him and kept walking toward the elevator, knowing that Rowan would be there waiting for me.

He was. Unfortunately, Cory had caught up with me, his hand grasping my arm to get my attention in the same place that Mike had pinned me and left bruises. A hiss escaped my lips at the flare of pain, and my temper quickly followed, channeling Sasha.

"What is your issue? Don't put your hands on a woman unless she asks you to!" I snarled at him, anger coloring my words.

"I just want to talk with you. Give a guy a chance." Cory didn't let go and didn't seem to understand my disinterest.

"I'm not interested, Cory," I repeated, louder this time, trying to yank my arm free. *What was it with men like that putting their hands on people? When had that become socially acceptable?*

"I believe the lady has made herself clear," Rowan's smooth voice spoke from behind me.

"Let go, Cory," I demanded, trying to keep my voice level.

He released my arm, and Rowan lifted my sleeve to look at the red skin he'd left next to the already present bruises. "Are you okay, Lena?" he asked, touching my sore arm gently.

"When men begin to realize that no means no, I'll be great. Cory, if you even think of doing something like that again, I'll take it straight to HR, have my lawyer get involved, and make sure that you understand that it's unacceptable and I won't tolerate it," I spat out. It would have made Sasha proud.

Rowan stayed silent, thank goodness. Or I probably would have snapped at him, too. I wasn't in the mood for macho posturing, the pissing games of testosterone, and whose dick was bigger. I didn't honestly believe Rowan was like that, and the fact that he didn't throw his weight around as the aforementioned lawyer made him even more desirable.

"We could have had something good, Lena." Cory's eyes flicked over Rowan coolly.

"You are dead wrong there," I said, moving towards the elevator. "I'm pretty sure you don't know the first thing about what a woman wants. If you have nothing to say about work during work hours, stay away."

Rowan held the elevator doors open for me while I finished my sentence and walked in behind me, his hand moving to my back once the doors closed. I stepped closer to him but said nothing until we were out in the parking lot, away from ears that would spread gossip.

"I'm sorry," I apologized. "Thank you for not jumping in. I appreciated you letting me handle it. I was serious, though; if Cory does it again, I'll go to HR and tell them you are my lawyer, and he's sexually harassing me."

"As your lawyer, I'd advise you to do it now. As a suitor, I'll let you use your judgment and not overstep my bounds," Rowan replied. "As your friend, I wanted to punch him in the mouth."

I let out a little laugh at his wording. "A suitor?

So formal."

"You bring it out in me." Rowan smiled at me. He walked me to my car, and we leaned against the side of it. "When are your dates?"

"There's this one guy I promised all my Saturdays to; he's hot. Of these other two, one is on Friday, some work party he needs a date for; I almost feel like an escort for that one. The other one is Wednesday, at the bar." I smiled flirtatiously. I hoped I didn't look like a killer clown since I was still on edge.

"Hot?" he blushed slightly. I loved it. "How do you know he's not crazy?"

"I don't really. I mean, this guy uses words like suitor and lets me fight my own battles. He's like a mythological creature," I said with a straight face. "Like the tooth fairy."

"I'm genuine, and I play the long game, the one for keeps," Rowan answered with just as straight of a face. My heart fluttered so wildly that I thought it was going to burst through my rib cage. "Tooth fairy?"

A thought hit me then, randomly. "Shoot. Todd! I set up a lunch date with him on Saturday. I can't believe I forgot about that. Can we make our date for later in the afternoon or evening? I'm hoping to be able to set him up with one of my friends."

"Of course," he agreed readily, not in the slightest upset that I had a date with another man before our date.

"I promise, no more Saturday dates unless they are with you," I hastily added, wondering if I could get out of it without hurting Todd's feelings.

"Lena." Rowan reached out and lifted my chin

with his thumb. "We've made no commitments yet. I want you to see this through. In that time, we'll get to know each other," he reminded me. "You'll get to know my flaws, and maybe you'll change your mind about wanting to take this to the next level."

"Doubtful." I raised my eyebrows. "Regardless, my Saturdays are yours after this."

His deeply dreamy eyes held a message I couldn't decipher, but he riveted them on me. "Why the tooth fairy?"

I laughed. "Because it's what popped into my head for a mythological creature."

"Out of everything? Not a dragon? Or a wizard? Even Santa?" Rowan held back a smile.

"Did I offend you?" I stopped laughing for a moment.

"No." He smiled finally. "It was pretty funny." He slid his arm around me. "Does that mean you are free tonight?"

"It does. Are you asking me on a date?" I asked coyly, fluttering my eyelashes.

"I believe I'm inviting myself to your house with the promise to bring pizza and a puppy. I think hanging out with you and Austin sounds nice," he said thoughtfully.

I grabbed my phone from my pocket and texted Austin to see if he minded and, if he didn't, what sounded appetizing to him. When I got the answering text, I looked up at Rowan with a grin. "Austin is good with it, and he said he wants pizza without me telling him you offered that."

"It's a boy thing." Rowan shrugged casually,

then dipped his head to mine, kissing me softly. "Then, Demon and I will see you within an hour."

"I'll go hide all my shoes." I shot him an evil smile over my shoulder and climbed in the car. His closeness was distracting.

Chapter 15

Once again, I had beat my date to the bar. Hannah nodded to a table in the corner for me, and I went there, waiting until she came over with a couple of menus.

"This guy didn't give you the heebie-jeebies, did he?" she asked with a small smile.

"No, but it's hard to be interested when I am only interested in Rowan," I admitted sheepishly.

"Austin likes him." Hannah leaned against the wall.

"Did he say why?" I turned to look at her, sitting sideways in the booth.

"Rowan was straight with Austin. He didn't pump Austin for information about you. Instead, Rowan asked Austin about himself, his interests, and his goals. He offered up himself for interrogation and answered every question Austin asked. According to Austin, Rowan is one of the most genuine people he has ever met," Hannah readily told me.

"Sounds about right," I agreed. "Do you think I need to continue this experiment?"

"That's a little harder to answer. Each date you

go on, you seem to slip a little more into yourself and gain confidence. I think that's priceless. On the other hand, I don't believe you will find a better match for you than Rowan. I understand his reasoning, but I also understand yours. I do love seeing you get more self-assured. It's incredibly sexy." Hannah winked at me.

It said something that I was getting used to Hannah's flirting. My gaze shifted to the man walking up behind her, and she noted it. She stood straight and asked what I would like to drink. I knew it was my date; the picture looked the same as the one on the profile, though it obviously was a photo from when he was younger than he is now.

"Lena?" he asked tentatively.

"Yep. Hi, Andy." I held out my hand, and he shook it. He ordered a beer, and Hannah walked away.

"You look exactly like your picture," Andy said, as if it was unheard of that people used recent photos.

"I hope so. My son took it a couple of weeks ago." I smiled to try to take the sarcasm out of my tone.

"Well, you know how people photoshop and use fake photos all the time," Andy said quickly. I was adult enough not to point out that was what he had done, but just barely. I was forty, not brain-dead.

"If I remember right, you are a school teacher?" I asked. Andy was my age but looked older. Mostly balding, soft in the middle, not very tall. He was nondescript when it came right down to it, but I was also looking through Rowan tinted lenses. Right now, all other men paled in comparison.

Andy's eyes were kind. His eyes spoke to me, which was why I agreed to this date. They were this crystalline blue color that reminded me of Hannah, and it was like looking at the pages of an open book. I might not be interested in Andy, but I saw his loneliness and need to connect with someone.

"I do. I teach eighth-grade math," Andy responded with a smile. I didn't miss the look he shot directly at my chest, as if my answers were going to come from there.

I bit back a groan; I hated math. "Must be challenging working with teenagers every day." I thought about asking Hannah to make that iced tea electric again.

"It has its rewards. Some students are very difficult, and others make my day worth it. I love seeing them able to connect the dots and find the logic in a problem and work out how to solve it," he prattled on.

"I can see how that would feel great," I admitted. Hannah returned with the drinks and asked if we were ready to order food. "Mac and cheese," I told her immediately.

Her chuckle was audible, but I don't think Andy caught it. "Burger for me, please, well done."

"Tell me more about yourself, Andy," I forced my voice to sound cheery. His eyes wandered to my chest again. "You know they don't talk, right?"

Startled, his eyes flew up to mine. "I apologize. I'm not honestly looking for a relationship. Asking you out was kind of a test for myself to see if I could muster up the nerve to meet an attractive woman and converse. It seems I'm failing."

"You aren't failing. You are having a conversation." I sighed. "Just try to do it without staring at my boobs."

"Can I ask why you agreed to a date with me? From what I can see, you shouldn't have a shortage of men wanting to spend time with you." He took a sip of his beer.

"You have expressive eyes, and you weren't a creep asking me to send nude photos," I answered truthfully.

"That bar doesn't appear to be set very high," Andy said glumly.

"I'm here, aren't I?" I replied. "Bad break up?" I guessed.

"Yeah. About six months ago. My confidence has suffered a bit," Andy confessed, picking at his beer bottle's label.

"Relax, you aren't doing badly, except the talking to my boobs thing. You spoke with passion when you talked about your students. That's great. It shows confidence and intelligence, both qualities that I think women look for," I explained.

"Why did you look like you were on a trip to space then?" Andy bluntly asked me.

"Math isn't my thing. I picked up on the passion you had for it, and I found that attractive."

"Fair enough, I suppose."

Gee, I am so glad he approved of my impression. "What hobbies do you have?" I attempted to keep the conversation going. I understood where Andy was coming from, and I did want to help him.

"Is this genuine interest or a pity question?" Andy fired off. Whoever had left him had hurt him pretty badly.

"Genuine interest. I'm not looking for a relationship either, Andy. There is someone I just started seeing, and he insists I see others for the time being. I wouldn't have agreed to meet with you tonight if there wasn't a genuine interest in who you are as a person," I answered patiently.

"Sex is off the table then?" His cautious question threw me for a loop.

"I didn't know it was on the table, to begin with," I said slowly. "To be clear, sex is not an option."

Andy smiled then, and his eyes sparkled. "It makes me feel a little better. Astronomy. I love the stars, their science, their mysticism, and their endless possibilities."

I pointed to him and grinned. "Right there, Andy. There's the real you coming through; do that on other dates, and you'll have her won over."

"What did I do?" confusion clouded his face.

"You were you. That was an honest answer with no hidden agenda or need to impress. It was just you talking about something you are passionate about other than math. Talk more about the stars. I love them too." I smiled genuinely.

He relaxed, and we spent hours talking about constellations, the legends behind them, and even their composition and life span. It was a great conversation and made me very glad that I accepted the date. We said our goodbyes, and when Andy left, I blew a kiss to Hannah since she was busy with customers and went home. I managed not to fall and injure myself the entire date.

Chapter 16

Friday after work, I checked myself about three times before giving up and video-calling Hope to ask her if I looked okay for a date at an office party with a stranger. I wore a pantsuit outfit with a low-cut shirt to give it a sexy and elegant feel instead of a work feel.

"I can't believe you are asking me. You should be asking Sasha or your new man. I think you look great in everything you wear. I will say that the low-cut thing works for you." Hope grinned wickedly.

"You are such a pain. I can't call Sasha; she's on a date. And it feels weird to call Rowan and ask him if I look good for a date I'm not going on with him." I shot her an impatient look.

"It's his idea for you to continue this. Make him suffer." Hope prodded me. "Take a selfie and send it to him, see if he thinks it's appropriate. Just shut up and do it."

"Why aren't you on a date tonight?" I stood in front of the mirror, got a selfie, and then sent it to Rowan, asking if I looked okay for an office party with a strange man.

"I will be on one, but it's not for another couple

of hours." She flipped her hair over her shoulder. "Did you do what I told you to do?"

"Jeez, yes. Now Rowan's texting back," I told her and snatched up my phone.

"Read it out loud!" Hope shrieked excitedly.

"He asked if I was kidding and said he felt tempted to follow me," I told her.

"Told you." Hope laughed. "You are meeting with the Todd guy tomorrow, right? The one you are going to try to hook up with Lily?"

"Yeah. Lunch at a fish shack," I confirmed as I checked my ass in the mirror to see if it looked too big.

"Okay. See you Sunday, my place this time," Hope told me. "I gotta go get ready myself. I'm going to take a bath first and get all nice and smelly, so this guy wants to feel me up. He's a biker and hot."

"Right up your alley." I laughed. "Go easy on him."

"Not a chance in hell. Have fun tonight." Hope signed off, and I looked down at my phone.

Does that mean it's okay or not? I texted back.

It's unbelievably sexy, and I'm utterly jealous right now, was Rowan's immediate reply.

We can skip all this, and I can wear nothing for our date tomorrow, I suggested.

I just cursed and scared an old lady in the grocery store. Wearing nothing isn't taking it slow, and as much as I want to say yes to that, we are going to a nice restaurant tomorrow, and clothes are required.

What about Demon? I wrote back.

Austin offered to puppy-sit, he replied.

Wish I was with you tonight. I hesitated before I

hit send, but it was the truth.

Me too, Lena. I find myself wishing that a lot. Have fun, regardless.

Damn it; this was driving me nuts. I was a little angry with Rowan for insisting I continue dating others, even if I understood the reasoning behind it. Maybe there was something to Hope's telling me to make him suffer. I sent out a quick text to Hannah asking for her help before my date with Rowan tomorrow.

Satisfied with my plan, I headed downstairs and asked Austin if I looked okay. He assured me I did, kissed me on the cheek, and I left for my date with Stanley. I pulled up to the office building address he sent me and parked in the garage under a light. I didn't get out until I was positive I was alone.

I walked into the building and saw someone sitting on a bench outside the elevators. That had to be Stanley. At least, I hoped it was. He was sitting in a shadow, and I couldn't see his face. I genuinely did feel like I was a hired escort for this. It was a little unnerving.

The man heard me approaching and looked up, a hopeful look on his face. "Lena?" he asked.

"Stanley, I presume?" I held out my hand, and he shook it quickly, then tucked it under his arm.

"I was worried you wouldn't show up," Stanley admitted, leading me to the corner of the lobby.

"Why would you think that? I told you I'd be here." There was something in his intonation that I needed to pay attention to, and I listened harder.

"It's kind of a weird first date scenario," Stanley said with a shrug. His voice was soft-spoken, and there was a lilt of something to it that my brain struggled to identify. He let go of me and circled me. "You look, fa-nom-in-all!" he enunciated every syllable.

My eyebrows raised slightly. There was something more going on here than a simple date. "Thank you." I accepted Stanley's compliment and gave him a quick once over.

He had a touch of Asian ancestry in him, I was sure. He was a good-looking man, very well-dressed, and other than his drawing out of phenomenal, he was well-spoken with a soft voice. His hands had been very smooth, and his touch was gentle. He had no bad vibe, but I was sure something else was going on here.

"I just got promoted to a new position last month, and this party is one where we are supposed to bring our significant others," he explained. "I am fresh out of a relationship and back on the market, and to be frank, terrified of showing up alone."

"I'm not trying to be rude by asking this, but what else aren't you telling me?" I put a couple more steps of distance between us.

"You are more perceptive than I thought you'd be," Stanley said, that lilt coming into play again. "I'm gay."

"That's what that is!" I crowed, then cringed, realizing I'd said that out loud.

He gave me a wry smile. "The management here is very anti-gay, very much an old boys club type of people. They don't know, and I refused to bring the man I had been dating with me; thus, the relationship ended. He also works here but is open about his sexuality and has been passed over for countless promotions."

"So, I'm here to pose as your date so you don't

look gay?" I frowned. "They can't discriminate against you because of that."

"Legally, no. How am I going to prove that's what is happening? I need time to establish myself in this role and gain a bit more experience before I market myself for other companies to get away from that type of attitude," Stanley whined.

"What makes you think this will be believable?" I asked incredulously.

"They'll be so focused on your assets that they won't pay attention to the fact that we aren't all cuddly and well acquainted. I promise I won't touch you inappropriately, but I will hold your hand or put your arm in mine," Stanley quickly said as if I hadn't just heard him refer to my boobs as assets.

"Unbelievable," I murmured. "At least I get food out of this, right?"

"Oh yes, the party's catered and has an open bar." He looked me over again, adjusted my jacket, and then led me to the elevator.

"Why didn't you just hire an escort? A professional date, not a hooker," I clarified.

"Well, that costs money, and you are real." He jabbed the button for the top floor.

"Better yet, just announce your sexuality and be done with it. Stop living a lie," I admonished Stanley. "I quite seriously feel like a cheap whore right now."

"I'm sorry," Stanley apologized. "That wasn't my intent. You are a beautiful woman, and kindness shines out of your eyes. You are perhaps someone I'd like to start a friendship with, and when I contacted you, that was my initial thought. Because really, I need more friends."

"You should have started with that," I muttered darkly. *When had kindness become a weakness to prey on instead of admirable?* I wondered.

"I didn't lie to you, Lena. I told you in the message that I needed a work party date. Only, I didn't tell you I was gay," Stanley defended himself.

"I get it. I know. I'll play my part and do what you need me to do, but I'm still mad at you for not being completely honest upfront." I hooked my arm through Stanley's as the elevator reached the top.

"I understand. Thank you for helping me," Stanley said quietly as the doors slipped open to reveal a party in full swing. At least my outfit matched. It was similar to what I saw many other women wearing.

Stanley led me towards a specific group, which I assumed was the people he wanted to think we were dating. I plastered a fake smile on my face and hoped I didn't look like a clown. I shouldn't have worried because each of these older men fastened their eyes on my chest. I could have been sporting a neon green mohawk with ornamental penises hanging from the ends, and they wouldn't have noticed.

"Gentlemen, I'd like to introduce my date, Lena," Stanley said, the lilt mostly vanished from his voice. "Lena, this is our company's owner, president, and vice president," Stanley said graciously, listing their names that I didn't listen to in the slightest.

"How did you manage to land such a beauty?" the one I thought was the vice president asked, leering at me. My instinct was to kick him in the balls and run. Instead, I kept the fake smile on my face and nodded to accept the compliment, such as it was.

"We just started seeing each other this week," Stanley said smoothly. I should have known he'd be good at lying, having to hide his sexuality all the time. It wasn't a lie, more of a half-truth. Having to speak that way so frequently must get tiring and depressing.

The more I thought about it, the angrier I became on Stanley's behalf. His sexuality had nothing to do with the way he did his job. It drove me insane that people still acted that way. I found myself biting my tongue to keep from saying anything. Given that, I decided that drinking alcohol would probably be a terrible idea.

Stanley dragged me through the rounds of introductions, the women looking me up and down as if I competed with them, the men speaking to my boobs. By the time we reached the food table, I'd worked myself up into a snit over it all.

"Are you okay?" Stanley whispered into my ear.

"No. I'm angry that you must hide who you are and that these people are judgmental. The men keep talking to my boobs, and the women look at me as if they can't wait to tear me apart after I walk away," I griped. Shallow was the look these people went for.

"I never really noticed it quite as much before until now," Stanley agreed. "Well, the hiding who I am, I did, but not how critical they are of others or how condescending to women they are." He filled his plate with some food. "I mean, I knew they'd look at your chest, but not that they'd talk to it."

"You need to find a new job. Pronto. I'd leave here suicidal every day if I had to work here," I continued. "Wait, you aren't, are you?" I paused to look at him carefully.

"Suicidal? No. Depressed absolutely." Stanley grabbed some cutlery for us both. "Do you want a drink?"

"Water, only. Alcohol would be a horrible idea as the carefully placed filter I have on would come right off if I drank," I warned him.

Stanley gave a little brittle laugh. "Who knows? Maybe that would be the push I need to change my life. I'll bring you water in a bottle so you can see it's not been tampered with."

Now, *that* was something I could appreciate. Stanley wasn't a bad guy, and I hoped he found a place that would accept him as he was. Not this masqueraded man who had to modulate his voice to get a deserved promotion or keep his job.

I stuffed a carrot in my mouth and glanced around the room casually. My eyes lingered on a lone figure standing by the windows. I'd seen the guy look at us several times; his face was seemingly tight with anger or other unhappy emotions.

"Is that your ex?" I quietly asked as Stanley came back, nodding over to the guy.

He looked at me, startled. "How would you know that?"

"He keeps looking at us with what I am guessing is anger." I spoke in a low tone so my voice wouldn't carry.

"I don't know why. He's the one who dumped me," Stanley muttered. "Ignore him."

"Done. You don't seem very happy." I took a bite

of my chicken and watched Stanley's face morph into a grimace before he schooled it back.

"I'm not, but that's not your problem." He stabbed his chicken a bit too hard.

"Got it. How old are you, Stanley?" I asked, changing the subject.

"Forty-four, why?" his tone lost its hard edge.

"Just making conversation, as one would do on a date, you know," I shot back at him. "I'm going to go out on a ledge here and guess that dating at this age isn't any easier for you than it is for me."

"True statement. I'm not sure if I ever found it easy, though. Was it ever easy for you?" the hint of lilt returned. I was starting to see that it only appeared when Stanley felt comfortable.

"I married early. In my teens, I didn't have any issues with it. My best friend is bi-sexual, but she prefers the company of women more than men, and she hasn't ever had an issue with it either. Until now, that is. Maybe we are just too jaded to fall for the shit anymore," I babbled, just to talk and keep Stanley from stiffening up again.

"That is true, as well. We've gone through enough at this point to know what we want and don't want. I guess for women, it might be a little different, especially seeing how those men acted towards you. It's become apparent harassment is just as much of an issue as being gay is. At least a gay male," he quickly clarified.

"I'm sorry that you are dealing with that. I've seen it with my friend, but not quite to the degree you experience it. I don't understand the difference. If people can accept two women together, why can't they accept two men? It doesn't make sense to me," I continued with the conversation and noticed Stanley's pinched expression. "Sorry, I'll change the subject again."

"It's okay," he said softly. "Same-sex relationships have been happening since the bible, between Greek gods, it's throughout history. I don't understand why people have an issue with it at all. Nowhere does it say that I expect someone else to feel the same because I find men attractive. We can wax poetic about this for hours and still not find a good answer. It's a constant source of irritation with me."

"An environment accepting of who you are will help with that. Just think about it. It's not okay for these assholes to treat anyone the way they are." I patted his hand. "Now, I want some of the cheesecake I spotted. That sounds like divine goodness to me."

Stanley laughed heartily. "I can easily agree with that. Bring me back a piece?"

"You got yourself a deal, sweet cheeks." I winked at Stanley and made my way to the food table again. I grabbed two plates, and with a piece of cheesecake on each one, I turned and found one of the old guys in my face.

"Excuse me," I said and tried to side-step him, but he stepped with me, his eyes probing my cleavage. I rolled my eyes so hard I was surprised they didn't make noise. "Hey, my eyes are up here, thanks."

"I didn't want to appreciate your eyes," he answered bluntly and tried stepping closer to me.

Instinctively, I backed up and crashed into a waiter, who dropped the tray of dirty dishes he was carrying to help try and steady me. Instead, my cheesecake plates went flying. The waiter and I crashed onto the floor on top of the broken dishes. The waiter landed on me as he pivoted to try and right both of us. Lucky for him, not quite as fortunate for me.

Every eye in the room was on us, then on Stanley, as he let out a shrill, girlish squeal and ran over to us. "Might want to tone that down a bit," I warned him quietly as he frantically pulled me to my feet.

Pain lanced into my hip as I took a step, and the waiter's face paled drastically. "Miss, you're hurt." He pushed to his feet and pointed to my hip, which now had a piece of the broken dish sticking out of it.

I yanked the damn thing out and whirled to face the old guy. "If you had stayed out of my personal space, this wouldn't have happened. You can expect to hear from my lawyer," I snapped at him.

Stanley gasped and widened his eyes as he took in the bloody piece of ceramic in my hand and quickly grabbed a napkin to hold to the tear in my pants. "Let's go clean this up," he said dramatically, the lilt of his voice quite evident.

"The firm will pay for any medical costs associated with this," a woman said, shooting a nasty glance back at the man. "Do you need help getting to the restroom?"

"No, Stanley can help me," I said, trying to keep myself from lashing out. This little mishap hadn't been my fault. However, not watching where I was walking while injured was. I tripped over the tray the waiter had dropped and sprawled face-first on the ground with a loud oomph, smacking my chin on the ground.

"Oh dear," Stanley cried, helping me up once again. "This just keeps getting worse."

"Get my purse, please," I requested quietly. Stanley ran over to the table, grabbed my purse, and escorted me to the restroom. Any semblance of manners I had went straight out the window when I sat on the countertop.

Stanley started laughing a maniacal laugh that made me pause when I started to pull down the waistband of my pants. I looked at him with a question in my eyes as he doubled over. "The cheesecake hit him right in the face! The plate bounced off his head! The entire company saw it!"

"Who was the woman?" I asked, fighting back the giggle that threatened to erupt. "I wish I had seen the plate bounce off his head; it would have made this more bearable."

"HR!" he crowed, slapping at his knees. When his breathing was under control, he righted himself, grabbed some paper towels, and got them wet. "I am sorry you got hurt."

"That part wasn't so fun," I agreed. "The girly scream you let out was a little bit of a giveaway as to your nature." I finally gave up trying to tug my pants down and just undid them and pulled them down from my hips. There was a good-sized gash there that was dripping blood down my leg.

"Oh, that looks like it needs stitches." Stanley sobered up quickly, seeing the wound. "Let me grab a first aid kit and see if we can get it bandaged up enough to keep you from bleeding all over."

Stanley darted back out of the bathroom, and I

grabbed my purse, pulling out my cell phone. I texted Austin that I fell and would head to the ER to see if I needed stitches and might be a little late in getting home. A slew of texts came back almost immediately, and I tried to answer them all so that Austin wouldn't freak out.

Stanley came back in, and together, we got enough gauze taped to me to staunch the flow. The lump under my ripped pants wasn't flattering. "The HR lady gave me this." He handed me a card with policy information and relevant insurance information. "She said to give this to the ER and tell them all bills should come here and to her attention. She also said to have your lawyer contact her."

Crap. I'd forgotten I'd thrown that out. "That was a bluff," I said meekly.

"Follow through on it." Stanley stood firm. "Get a lawyer."

Like magic, my phone rang, and Rowan's name appeared. "Hang on, let me get this," I told Stanley and answered my phone. "Hey," I said softly.

"You are going to the ER?" Rowan asked urgently. "Which one? I'll meet you there. Are you okay? Can you drive? Do you want me to come and get you?"

"Whoa, slow down. I'm fine. I probably need stitches; I fell on some glass. I'm pretty sure I can drive myself. I'm in the city, so I'll go to whichever is closest. I also threatened someone with a lawyer," I added.

I heard Rowan's breathing change. "Something happened to make you fall, didn't it?"

"Does Austin have your number? Is that how you knew?" I asked him suddenly, narrowing my eyes.

"He does." Rowan hesitated. "Austin texted me right after you told him you were going to the ER."

"We'll talk about it later," I sighed. "The pain is a little distracting, so I'm going to head to the ER now. Thank you for checking on me."

"Go to TG. I'll meet you there," Rowan insisted. I didn't argue, just quietly agreed.

"I took an Uber, so I'll drive your car wherever you want me to," Stanley said as I hung up. "I'll just send for a ride from there. I don't think you should drive alone."

The absurdity of the entire situation hit me all at once, and I started laughing. "Fine. I'm not going to argue anymore. I can't believe this is what my life has become right now."

Chapter 17

Twelve stitches and one tetanus shot later, and I was finally released to go home. Rowan was hovering at my side despite me having yelled at him for doing so. He'd brought Austin with him, and Austin had driven my car home, leaving me in Rowan's hands, who grilled Stanley at least three times on what had happened.

At some point during the second grilling, I'd lost my temper with both of them. Stanley couldn't withstand my anger and took off like he got fired out of a cannon. On the other hand, Rowan didn't even flinch at my verbal outburst—more points on his scorecard in the win column.

Once in his car, Rowan turned to face me and kissed me sweetly. "I have no idea how you find yourself in these situations, but I'm glad it's not worse. I'll make sure that the company also takes care of your medical bills."

"Should I put you on retainer?" I feebly joked. The pain medication they gave me made me a bit loopy.

"Already paid for with that kiss," he said softly.

"Isn't that prostitution?" I queried.

Rowan chuckled and shook his head at me.

"Your sense of humor amidst all this is something admirable."

"I think it's likely to drive you crazy is more apt," I replied with a smile. "You've never talked to my boobs."

Rowan sputtered and gave me an incredulous look. "Do they speak?"

That was the final straw; I broke down into half-laughter, half-crying. "You'd think they do with how people have stared at them! Are you sure you want me to continue this experiment?" I wiped my face and shook my head. "I mean, come on. I'm clumsy, but this has crossed a bizarre line into an episode of some hidden camera show."

"I seriously rethought it tonight," Rowan admitted solemnly. "I do think you should see it through. The confidence that's coming out of you is pretty amazing. If you see yourself as I see you, and it's the result of calamitous dates, it's worth it. You're so special, Lena."

"You better take me home before we move straight to the sex in the car of an ER parking lot stage," I replied dryly. "Thanks for rescuing me."

"Sorry for annoying you," he returned.

"No apology necessary for that." I looked out the window as we pulled out of the parking lot. "I'm sure it will happen again as you insist on this path of disaster dates."

"What about a compromise?" Rowan asked while we waited at a stoplight.

"Are you lawyering me?" I raised my eyebrows at him. I wasn't sure I had enough mental capabilities to handle that.

"No, I'm offering an alternate suggestion to ease my suffering." Rowan blushed. "Totally selfish on my part."

"You have my attention." I went to turn in my seat and hissed as a bolt of pain cut into my hip.

"Stay still," he commanded me gently. "What if you do this for another month, and then we stay at this infernal level one until the experiment is over, but we only see each other?"

"Interesting," I drawled. "I'll discuss this with my entourage and get back to you with an answer."

Rowan smiled slowly, and my belly got the tingles. "Fair enough. Do you want me to stop at a pharmacy and fill the prescription of pain medication they gave you?"

"No, I won't take them."

"I'd rather you have them and not take them than need them and not have them," Rowan countered my statement.

"Arguing with a lawyer doesn't do any good." I shook my head futilely.

"Not true. If that were the case, there would never be a winner in any lawsuit." He grinned.

"Correction, arguing with a lawyer when you aren't one doesn't do any good," I revised it.

"I listen to you," Rowan said softly, pulling into a drugstore. "I'm just erring on the side of caution because I don't want you to hurt. If you felt strongly about it, I would do as you wish and not argue."

Pain pills made my lips loose. "Do you know how long it's been since someone took care of me like this?"

"A long time, if that question was any indication." He took off his seatbelt. "Do you want to come in with me?"

"I have to since my name is on that prescription." I opened my door and almost fell out. "Oops."

"Nope." Rowan flew out of the car and pushed me back in gently. "Drive through it is."

"This might be one time I won't argue with you. I think I'm battered enough today." I sank back into Rowan's comfortable leather seat.

"Words I hate and cherish both," he mumbled as he climbed back in the car. "I'll need your insurance card and ID." He patiently waited while I dug through my wallet and handed them over. He put it all in the slide-out drawer, and we waited until the pharmacist came over the speaker and said fifteen minutes.

"I didn't want to like you," I told Rowan, laying my head back and closing my eyes. "I wanted it to be some lust thing only. Emotions scare me now. Yet, I want more than anything just to curl up next to you and fall asleep. I never cuddled with my ex-husband. Ever. I don't even know what cuddling with a man who isn't my son feels like."

"Lena, tonight, you will know what cuddling feels like; I will lay with you until you fall asleep. After I watch you take one of these damn pills, so at least, I have the peace of mind to know you aren't going to be awake and in pain the rest of the night," Rowan promised.

"See? That's why you scare me so much." My loose tongue returned with a vengeance. "No one has ever done anything like that for me. My friends have, but no one I was in a relationship with like this. God, you just drive home how awful of a husband Shane was. Even worse, I'm terrified that when I have sex again, I'm going to find out it *is* me, and that's why he never wanted to have sex."

Too late, I realized what I had admitted. I wasn't sure what the look on Rowan's face meant. "I don't know what your marriage was like, but instinctually, I know that if there was a physical intimacy problem, it's not you."

"How could you possibly know that?" I asked, closing my eyes in embarrassment.

"The way you kiss me." Rowan's hand feathered a touch down my face.

While we sat there waiting for the pain pills to get filled, I blurted out the truth of what my marriage had been. My face burned in shame the entire time; all the details about only achieving orgasm with my fingers, the ban on toys, the infrequency, the complete neglect, and finally, Shane's masturbation and porn fetish.

"Lena, it's not you. If it was, do you think all these men would have asked you out, hit on you, been wildly inappropriate and taken liberties they should get arrested for taking? You are sensual, passionate, and beautiful," Rowan told me. "I'm sorry, but he is evidently an idiot."

"He is," I agreed with a shaky laugh. Thankfully, the pharmacist saved me further embarrassment when he shoved the drawer back out with a spot for money. I handed over my card silently, and when Rowan gave it to me, I pushed it into my purse along with the pills.

Rowan drove me home in comfortable silence, his mere presence comforting. That was the first significant clue I was in way over my head with this man. I was falling hard for him. There was a chance I'd already fallen, but I wasn't ready to admit it. Some part of me was still waiting to wake up.

"Wait," Rowan instructed me kindly. "Let me help you out," he told me as he turned the ignition off.

I did. I waited because it felt damn good to get treated like this, like I mattered. I also didn't want to fall on my face again; that hurt. Rowan opened the car door, pulled me out as gently as possible, and supported me until my legs were less wobbly. He kept his arm around my waist as he led me to the front door, which Austin had already opened.

"Jesus, sweets, you have some seriously shitty luck on dates," I heard Hannah call out.

"Why aren't you at work?" I asked Hannah before I even got in the door.

"I'm off at eleven, and it's midnight. Austin asked if I wanted to watch a movie with him, and then he came to pick me up." She looked me over as Rowan led me in. Then she gave him a complete once over and then hummed her approval. "He'll do."

"Hannah," I warned her, shaking my head.

"Can you help Lena to her bedroom?" Rowan asked Hannah. "I'd like to talk to Austin for a minute."

"Sure thing," Hannah said happily, putting her arm around me. "He's hot," she said in my ear. "Definitely a keeper."

"Shut up," I hissed at her. "Rowan's going to cuddle with me. Did you know I've never cuddled before? With a man, that is."

"I didn't know, but from what Austin has told me, it was a safe assumption to make," Hannah's tone changed slightly. "Let's get you changed up into bedclothes then. I'm guessing that man is out there telling Austin his plans on cuddling to make sure he knows you aren't being taken advantage of."

I'd thought the same thing, too. It was just who Rowan was. "He makes me want happily ever after."

"Pretty sure he'd give it to you, too." Hannah pulled my shirt off and saw the bruises. "Damn. These look miserable."

"They feel like it too. I seriously fell on my face," I giggled insanely. "In front of everyone."

"Austin told me the story. I only laughed a little. What do you want to wear?" Hannah asked.

"T-shirt. I have a huge and baggy one in there somewhere. It's dark gray and has an outline of mountains on it," I tried to remember. I pulled my pants off while leaning against the wall and threw them on the floor. "Those are garbage now."

Hannah looked at my hip, clucked her tongue, and then unsnapped my bra before I knew what she was doing. "I've gotten good at that." She winked at me. She pulled the shirt down over my head and then knelt to look closer at my hip and the forming bruises down my leg. "That's going to suck tomorrow."

"It sucks now." I hobbled over to the bed, somewhat unsteady.

"Easy," Hannah cautioned, lending her arm. I held on to it while I flung the covers back and collapsed on the bed.

"Knock, knock," Rowan said from the doorway. "Can I come in?"

Hannah quickly moved out of the way and smirked at me. "You're in good hands. I'm going to go watch that movie now."

"Where's Demon?" I asked as Rowan perched on the edge of the bed.

"Asleep on the couch like he owns it." Rowan smiled. "Legs under the covers." He moved them gently until he could cover me. Once he tucked me in, he moved to the other side of the bed, lay down next to me, and held out his arm.

I wasn't sure what to do at first. "Roll onto your side, into me," Rowan said gently.

I did, and he settled his arm under my head and wrapped it around my back. "Well, this is nice." I breathed in the scent of Rowan.

"Shoot. Sit up for a minute. You need to take a pill," Rowan reminded me. He got up and went to grab some water and the pills I had thrown in my purse. He brought them back and watched me take them. Then Rowan resumed his position, and I snuggled into him.

My hand rested on his chest, and he stroked the back of my hand, lulling me into a feeling of contentment. "Damn," I mumbled. "I fell."

Rowan's breath caught for a moment, and then he stroked my hand and arm. "I promise to show you all the things you missed and shouldn't have," he softly said as I drifted off to sleep.

Chapter 18

I woke up stiff, very sore, and alone. For the first time I can remember, I wished I hadn't been alone. Rowan had cuddled me until I fell asleep. I wasn't sure how to feel about that. On the one hand, I loved every bit of it. On the other hand, I was worried I was losing my independence. This relationship was going to take some getting used to on my part.

I sat up, groaning, and saw a note on my nightstand. *"Take some ibuprofen, at least. Thank you for allowing me to take care of you. I know it wasn't easy for you. See you tonight, Rowan."*

I smiled and took the ibuprofen he had left for me. He understood me. Maybe this wouldn't be as complex as I thought it was. I slowly got out of bed and stretched a little, wincing at the movement.

"Hey, Mom. How do you feel?" Austin asked from my doorway.

"I imagine if a punching bag had feelings, it would be similar to this," I groaned again. "I'm going to take a hot shower."

"Good. I'm going to make breakfast," Austin declared.

"Nothing heavy, please," I begged as I made my way to the shower. The hot water felt so divine I wanted to stay there. I needed to eat something, get ready for the lunch date with Todd and try to figure out how I would set him up with one of my best friends.

Picking out an outfit was a little more challenging; pants irritated the stitches, so I was stuck finding a loose skirt or wearing sweats. Wearing sweats would undoubtedly convey the message of not being interested, while a skirt might give off a flirting vibe.

For now, I put on the sweats and went to eat the oatmeal that Austin had made. After I took my first bite, he started peppering me with questions about everything that had happened. I gave him the rundown and finished eating while he digested the information.

"Rowan told me about the compromise he made on the experiment. I think you should take it, if not quit altogether. He's great, Mom. Even Hannah thinks so. You've gotten hurt twice now; both times were serious." Austin thumped the table to drive his point home.

"My choice was to stop the experiment altogether. I made that clear to Rowan; he is the one who wants me to continue, and I'm starting to understand why. The dates are making me feel comfortable in my skin. They give me some confidence; at the very least, I am learning about others and myself. You don't need to lecture me, Austin. I think I've fallen, tripped, or something on each one of the dates," I confided.

He didn't say anything in return for that. He finished his oatmeal and gave me a crooked grin. "The plate bounced off his head?"

"That's what Stanley said. I wish I would have seen that part." I stood up and grabbed the empty bowls. "You and Rowan sure talk a lot."

Austin flushed. "Sorry, Mom. I grilled him a lot when I first met him, and since then, he has kept me in the loop and asked for my opinions. I'm not trying to interfere. I know I'm inexperienced and young and all that shit, but can I say something about him?"

"Language," I reminded him. "What?"

"I'm eighteen; I can swear." Austin smirked. "Being an adult and all. Anyway, from what I can see, I think he's in love with you. Hannah thinks so, too."

"What qualifies you to think that?" I finished loading the dishwasher and crossed my arms, staring at him. "That's not an accusatory question; I genuinely want to know your thoughts."

Austin relaxed and thought about his answer. "There's something in the way he looks at you and the way he talks to you. I never saw Dad be that way with you, and I thought Dad loved you. Rowan's soft even when he puts his arm out to walk with you. He worries about you; as you can see from last night, he's willing to take care of you and make sure you are okay. Dad never took care of you."

He was right. Rowan did all of that and more. "How would you feel if I told you I was falling in love with him?"

"Happy. I know Rowan would keep you safe. He wouldn't ignore or use you to feed him and keep the house clean. I think it's kind of early to know if that's what it is or not, but Rowan did tell me that he's had strong feelings for you since he first saw you, and they've only grown as he has gotten to know more about you," Austin admitted.

"I agree with you, Aust," I finally said. "I just want to take my time with it. Rowan is amazing; there's no arguing that. I'm just not sure I'm ready for the kind of commitment I know he wants. Your dad soured me on marriage, and it's going to take me a bit to want that again."

"Don't shut Rowan out," Austin warned. "Do what you need to do, but don't shut him out. He's sensitive when it comes to you. I seriously thought he was going to cry last night when he picked me up after hearing you were hurt."

"I don't plan on shutting him out, Austin. I also don't need you pressuring me to act a certain way because you like him and want to make sure I'm taken care of while you are at college." I pushed away from the counter and winced as the sweats brushed against my hip's sensitive skin.

"Did you take something?" Austin stood up fast. "Hannah said you were all bruised up."

"I am, and I did. Stop fussing." I moved to grab my computer and sat back down at the table. I decided to check the messages on the dating site, with Austin still hovering.

"Some of those guys are flat-out creepy," Austin muttered, seeing what I was doing.

"Tell me about it," I agreed, deleting the ones like that immediately. I responded to a few that asked me questions about myself; some of the prepicked questions that took the guesswork out of it for men who didn't know what to ask.

I read through those who wrote their own messages and weeded the crazies out of those. I realized there were far more of the crazy than those genuinely looking for a meaningful relationship. It was sad to see the lengths people would go to scam someone or prey on the vulnerable.

With my responses sent and no requests for dates, I was relieved. "Okay, smart kid, here's a question for you. How do I mention that I think Lily would be a good match for Todd?"

Austin frowned and drummed his fingers on the table. "She kind of is, isn't she? Is this your way of letting him down easy?"

"No, not really. Todd's a very nice guy, and I had a great time with him, but there wasn't a romantic spark. Hanging out with him as a friend would be fun, but nothing more. I think, for the most part, Todd would hit it off great with Lily," I mused.

Maybe the only kink in that would be Lily's kink. Her sexual appetite might not match Todd's, and I wouldn't know what his even were since we didn't talk about that. I sure wouldn't have made a second date with him if we had.

"Todd's one of those guys that likes it straight. Be honest with him. Maybe set up a double date to help ease the whole blind date thing," Austin suggested candidly.

"Honesty is always good." I closed up the computer and put it back in the carry bag. "Glad that was the first thing you said. As your mother, I can only hope that you follow it."

"What time do you need to leave to meet him?"

Austin got up and pushed the chairs under the table.

"A couple of hours from now. Why?" I glanced over at him.

"If we work together, we can knock out the chores, so neither of us has to do them tomorrow." Austin moved over and hugged me. "I already dusted this morning. The bathrooms and vacuuming are left. Oh, and laundry."

Surprised, I felt his head. "No, you don't feel sick."

Laughing, he pushed me away. "I just wanted to help, so you aren't doing so much and don't hurt yourself anymore. I'll do the bathrooms and vacuum. You do the laundry."

"Thank you, Austin," I said gratefully. "I did something right with you."

We cleaned the house, and I went to get ready to meet Todd. I changed into the skirt and pulled my hair back. I kept it simple without looking like a bum, in my opinion. I kissed Austin on the cheek and headed out. I moved a little slower than usual and tried to take care not to kiss the ground again.

The café Todd had picked wasn't far from where I lived, and I got there right on time, pulling into the parking lot as Todd was getting out of his car. Much like my first date with him, I started by meeting the ground I had been working on avoiding. I had swung my car door open and held on to it while exiting the car. Between the bruises and the stitches in the one hip, it gave out, and I went tumbling to the ground in a fantastic display of arms and limbs flying with my skirt bunching up around my hips. At least I'd worn pretty underwear.

"Oh my God, Lena! You are all bruised up!" Todd said, rushing over to help me up. "Are you okay?" He got me to my feet, and I was rapidly smoothing my skirt back down.

"I think the universe is mad at me," I mumbled, embarrassed beyond belief. "I have yet to have a date where something disastrous hasn't happened."

"Maybe the universe is trying to tell you these are the wrong guys?" Todd suggested gently.

We sat down at a table, and I sighed. "I truly wanted to talk to you about that."

"Me too, but you go first." Todd patted my arm.

"I started seeing someone that I genuinely enjoy, and I think that you and I are better off as friends." I just got straight to the point.

"I think so, too," Todd said with a big smile and a sigh of relief.

"Oh, good!" I exclaimed. "In that case, I have a friend who I think would be a great match for you if you are interested."

"Really?" he sounded surprised and a bit skeptical.

"Really." I dug in my purse for my phone and pulled up the pictures on it until I found Lily. "This is her." I showed him the picture.

"She's gorgeous. She's not going to want to hang out with me." Todd sounded sad. "She's way out of my league."

"That's nonsense. Lily doesn't think that way, and you shouldn't either. You are exactly her type. If you are interested, I'll give her your phone number," I offered.

Todd hesitated briefly. "Sure, I'd like that. What's her name? Wait, you just said it, didn't you?"

"Lily. She's been one of my best friends for years. We met in high school," I told him. I quickly texted Lily, said that Todd was interested, sent her his phone number, and slid my phone back into my purse.

"What's her story?" Todd asked, but before I could answer, the waiter appeared, took our drink order, and asked if we were ready to order lunch. I ordered a sandwich since I wasn't that hungry. Todd gave his order and then turned back to me.

"I'll give you the basics, but you should ask Lily for the rest. She has no kids but is divorced. She was married for five years. Two others and I are her best friends, and she's like an aunt to Austin." I wasn't comfortable giving more information than that.

"What does Lily do for a living?" Todd asked.

"Interior design," I supplied, knowing he'd be interested. "Lily has a great eye for it. She can look at a space and see the possibilities that exist."

"Sold," Todd said with another smile. "Tell me about these disasters that keep happening to you."

With a whole lot of embarrassment, I told Todd. He got angry on my behalf in the right spots and laughed at the others. Being around him was effortless, and he made a great friend, and I shared that with him. He told me that we should go on a double date if things work out with him and Lily.

Before I knew it, we had talked away another two hours, and Todd's phone going off interrupted us. "Damn, I'm sorry, Lena. There's a problem on a job site, and they need me to come by."

"Don't apologize. I wasn't aware of the time either." I pulled my phone out to see several missed texts from Lily and Austin and one from Sasha.

Todd paid for lunch and walked me out to my car, probably to make sure I didn't fall again, and then he thanked me and promised to be in touch. That had been easier than I thought it would be, aside from the whole showing him my underwear part.

I texted Austin that I was on my way home and then sent texts to Lily and Sasha, promising I'd call them when I returned home. Austin met me out in the driveway, looking worried.

"What took so long?" he asked as soon as I opened the car door.

"We were having a good time taking, that's all. Why are you so worried?" I gently extracted myself.

"Why wouldn't I be? Look what's happened on your other dates?" Austin snapped and then realized his tone wasn't one he should be using. "Sorry, Mom. You were in the hospital last night. Sasha ripped me a new asshole for letting you go out today."

"Between the two of you, this whole dating thing was your idea!" I let the frustration color my words.

"Hey! It led to Rowan asking you out," Austin protested weakly.

"I know which I'm happy about; what I'm not happy about is you two trying to dictate everything. I was at lunch with Todd; you already knew nothing had happened with him, and he was safe. I'm the adult; you are the kid," I snapped at him.

"Mom, I'm not a kid anymore." Austin followed

me in.

"You are to me. You're my kid, you will always be my kid, and I will always be your mom. Those roles don't change." I threw my purse on the table and sat down wearily in the living room chair. "How did Sasha find out anyway?"

"I think Hannah told her." Austin slumped down on the couch.

"Here's what I want you to do: take me off the app on the phone and off the site I'm on now. Add me on whichever is next and only sign me up for a month. That's it. I'm not doing any more after that. If you need to discuss this with Sasha, feel free." I pushed myself out of my chair and tossed him my phone.

Austin nodded meekly at me and went to the kitchen to do what I had asked. I moved over to the couch, turned my music on, and lay down. When he brought my phone back to me, he didn't say anything; he just handed it over and went to his room. I texted Lily back and told her I was home but was lying down for a bit and to call or text Todd.

Chapter 19

I was exhausted when I pulled up to Hope's house. I didn't want to go in; I didn't want to do the podcast. I just wanted to go back to bed—preferably a bed with Rowan in it, which wasn't happening either.

I climbed out of the car and headed inside, Sasha meeting me at the door. "I'm so sorry, sugar."

"For what?" I asked her, blinking slowly.

"Making you do all this." She bit her lip and looked ready to cry.

"Don't Sash, I know how to say no to you. I agreed, reluctantly, but I agreed. None of this is your fault. Are you going to let me in now?" I told her.

Sasha pulled the door open and followed me in. Hannah stood up and looked me up and down and then frowned. I shook my head at her, and she sat back down slowly. Lily bounced up and threw her arms around me, completely missing the tension.

"I called Todd! We have a date tonight," she crowed exuberantly.

"Great news," I told her. "I think you'll like Todd."

Hope glanced between us, and once Lily let me

go, she asked, "Why do you look totally wiped out?"

"Had another disaster date on Friday with some fallout," I said quietly. "I'd kill for a back massage."

"Why didn't you say so?" Hannah asked. "I'd have come over and done that for you."

"Because I'm mad at you for spilling to Sasha before I could explain it." My blunt words stilled both Sasha and Hannah and now Lily and Hope stared at me in open curiosity.

"I'm sorry," Hannah apologized. "I'll still help you, though; if it makes you feel better, you can yell at me the whole time."

"Listen up, ladies." I got right down to it. "I'm out of this after another four weeks. I had Austin pull me off the phone app, take me off the online site I was on, and list me on whichever one he and this dictator here decided on. If anyone responds, I will do no more than one date a week and focus my energy on Rowan. After the four weeks, I'll still be in the platonic stage of kissing only with Rowan until Austin heads to school."

Hope narrowed her eyes at Sasha before looking back at me. "Were you hurt?"

"Sure was. Rowan is now heading up two cases for me, and I spent Friday night in the emergency room. I'll explain it all during the podcast because I don't think I'll have the energy to review everything twice. I'm just exhausted." I slumped back in the chair. "Hannah, you can come home with me and do the massage and then do whatever with Austin. He'll make sure you get home."

"Deal," Hannah agreed, watching me carefully.

Sasha dropped to the floor before me and put

her head in my lap. "Sugar, I'm so sorry," she repeated.

"I know, Sash. It's not your fault, and I don't blame you. I'm just taking the reins back of my life. That's all, stop feeling guilty. I'm not mad. I know you love me and you are just concerned. This deal was Rowan's compromise to the whole experiment. Four more weeks." I bent to kiss the back of her head. "The rest of you can continue on the online sites, and I'll talk about my dates with Rowan after the four weeks."

Sasha nodded, got the equipment ready to record, and then did the intro. Hope jumped in and said she would start things off. "One here, I had one date this week, and the guy was great. Surprisingly enough. This guy was funny and smart after scraping the bottom of the barrel with the others. Both things that I love in a date."

"What did you guys do?" Lily asked to keep the conversation going.

"We met at a park and took a walk before going to dinner, then he took me to a standup comedy show, and after, we went and got ice cream. It was fantastic! He's a computer programmer, so we didn't talk much about work stuff, which was good because I would have looked like an idiot trying to follow that. He's not a whole lot taller than me, which means I didn't have to stretch to kiss him, and I did kiss him." Hope grinned.

"Was it as good as Two's kiss?" Sasha joked.

"Close, but not quite. We were in public, but the man's got a talented tongue." Hope giggled. "I'm going to go out with him again."

"That's awesome!" I exclaimed and clapped.

Lily spoke up next. "I didn't go on any dates, but

I have one set up now, thanks to Two. One of the guys she went out with last week. I'm totally looking forward to it, too. So next week, I'll have info to share with everyone."

"Oh! That's great!" Hope clapped again. "How did the initial conversation with him go?"

"So good." Lily sighed dreamily. "He's incredibly easy to talk to, down to earth, not rude or condescending, and funny too! Dreamy voice."

"He does have an excellent voice," I agreed. "Easy on the eyes, too. Quick to help when you fall on your ass in front of him as well."

Lily laughed heartily. "Hoping that doesn't happen with me."

"Has it ever happened to you?" Sasha fired off.

"No, thankfully, that is purely a Two thing." Lily winked at me. "Thanks for the hookup, Two."

"You're welcome, Three." I winked back at her.

"I had a date as well," Sasha said. "This time, a woman, and I must say, she was just as bad as the men."

"Seriously?" Hannah broke in, shocked.

"Seriously." Sasha nodded. "We met for dinner, and the entire time before the waitress took our drink order, she talked about my body. Don't get me wrong, this woman had a good one, too, but I can talk about things other than how my date looked. She was downright lewd, too. However, she didn't cross any boundary lines physically with me. Verbally, there were zero lines; she was everywhere and quite clear in letting me know she was interested in nothing more than a hookup."

"Damn." I shrugged. "What did you do?"

"What do you think I did?" Sasha grinned wickedly.

"I think you slept with her," I answered casually.

"Sure did. The woman was hot, but that was out of the norm for me. I wouldn't ordinarily sleep with someone that fast. Wait, before Two throws her argument in, I wouldn't sleep with someone that fast that I met that way," Sasha clarified. "Her conversation had me going, though; it was like she could read my mind on the things I liked, and she stroked those enough to get a fire lit in me. The sex wasn't disappointing either. She backed up her talk, and I think we used every toy I owned."

Hannah let out a low whistle. "Now that sounds fun."

"It was. It was nice how my date let me know upfront that sex was all the woman was looking for. There wasn't this pony show and trying to impress me. This woman is a serial dater. I wouldn't have agreed if she hadn't stoked the flames she lit," Sasha went on. "What about you, Five?"

"The person I am seeing, I didn't meet online, and while they are dates, it's more of an educational thing." She glanced at me. She was talking about Austin. I groaned. "I won't say any more than that."

"Thank God," I murmured. Lily laughed. "I had a couple of dates with the lawyer from last week, and one date with the guy I sent to Three, and then a total disaster on Friday. What do you want first?"

"My guy, do that one first," Lily said. "That way, I can get to know more about him."

"We met for lunch, and right off the bat, we

decided to tell each other that we would make better friends than anything else. It took the strain of it all right off me, and we once again talked for hours. That is, of course, after I fell trying to get out of my car." I paused for dramatic effect.

"You fell getting out of the car?" Sasha asked, stupefied.

"Sure did. I wore a skirt that went right up to my hips and flashed the poor guy my underwear; flashed everyone within view of my car, actually. Thankfully, I have been taking Five's advice and wearing nice underwear, or that could have been a lot more embarrassing than it was." I shrugged casually. Sadly, it was getting to be routine.

Hannah laughed lightly. "Oh, man. What did he do?"

"Exactly what a gentleman would do. He ran over to help me up and said nothing about the underwear but told me maybe the universe was trying to tell me I was dating the wrong guys." I blushed.

"He might be on to something," Hannah interrupted. "With the lawyer, you've fallen into him, right?"

"Among other things. I crashed into him twice and walked into a glass door once. Slipped, and he caught me; his puppy ate my shoes and I almost fell out of his chair," I started to list off.

"Think about it," Hannah insisted. "Every time you are with him, you are somehow being pushed into his arms, except the puppy thing. Maybe the universe was telling you not to leave that time."

"Holy shit, she's right," Hope burst into the

conversation. "It's a sign."

"Several signs," Sasha agreed in a quieter voice.

"To play devil's advocate, it could be a coincidence because Two is a natural klutz," Lily remarked.

"Can't argue that." I nodded my agreement. "The dates with the lawyer were great. He brought his puppy over and hung out with my son and me, bringing dinner. Last night, he took me out to a nice restaurant, and we danced without me awkwardly landing on the floor. I would have had to go into hiding if I had."

"He's pretty fantastic," Hannah said.

"You met him?" Lily swung to face Hannah.

Hannah raised her eyebrow at me. "Yeah, she did," I said. "That brings me to the disaster date. I met this guy at his office for a work party. Something felt off about the whole thing. Nothing against the man whatsoever; he was nice, attractive, and completely gay. It was a sham date. He asked me to go with him to hide the fact that he was gay from the executives, who are all total dickwads. Luckily, I found this out as we rode up the elevator, not while inside the party."

"He has to hide being gay? But discrimination against that is illegal," Hope butted in.

"Happens more than you think," Sasha opined sadly.

"He described them as a good old boys club," I told them. Then, I launched into the rest of the party's details, ending when I returned home. There was a moment of silence where Hope, Lily, and Sasha gaped at me, and Hannah looked between them and me.

"Show me," Sasha demanded. "Let's let

everyone hear our reaction."

"Because your voice isn't reaction enough?" I returned. I stood anyway and pulled my sweats down so they could see my hip and the bruises lining that side of my body.

"Jesus!" Lily exclaimed. She reached for me, but Hope smacked her hand down.

"Don't touch, that looks painful," Hope admonished her.

"When she got home, her lawyer took care of her," Hannah continued the story. "I was there. I got Two to her room and into a shirt to sleep in; then he came in and cuddled with her until she fell asleep. It was the sweetest thing ever."

Once again, Sasha was speechless. Hope's eyes brightened. "He stayed until you fell asleep?"

"He did. It was amazing. No one has ever taken care of me like that before other than you ladies," I sighed.

"He cuddled you?" Sasha finally said. I nodded at her. She knew I'd never had a man do that before. She knew what it meant to me. "Marry him."

I laughed delightedly. "Might be a bit premature for that. The man is a dream come true, though."

"Oh my God," Hope's eyes got big, "you've fallen for him!"

I couldn't say anything. I couldn't deny it because the women would know I was lying, and I couldn't admit it because I knew Rowan would be listening after Sasha uploaded it. Sasha nodded at me. "What's in the box, Two?"

"Oh!" I blushed brightly. "Uh, this is the toy that

Three ordered me, and I have no idea what it is or how to use it! It didn't come with directions."

Hannah's face puckered into a repressed laugh. "Open it then, and show us."

Lily was snickering, trying to hold back laughter as she knew what it was, and she could have saved me the embarrassment of pulling it out, but she kept it to herself. I opened the box and pulled out this string of metal spheres attached to a piece of black rope.

Hannah busted out laughing, and Sasha lowered her face to try to hide that she was laughing, but I knew she was. Hope, it took a minute for her to figure it out. "Ben wa balls? Is that what those are? Didn't you say what you got her was your favorite? That's your favorite?" Hope peppered Lily with questions.

"Ben wa balls?" I echoed. "What do you do with those?"

Hannah was about to fall on the floor; she laughed so hard. "Three, I think I just fell in love with you," she gasped.

"At least someone appreciates what I was trying to do here." Lily giggled. "You insert those into your, whatever word you are comfortable with, your va-jay-jay, and hold them in. Don't let them slip out. It's like kegel exercises, but if you keep them in, they move around and bump into that spot inside you that makes your toes curl, and it feels so damn good. You can also lube them up and stick them in your rear, and when you use the purple alien penis, it adds more sensation. I suggest trying both."

"What if they get stuck up there?" I asked bluntly.

Sasha coughed, again, trying to hide a laugh. "That's what the string is for, you to pull out, like a tampon."

"You guys are evil," I muttered. "Sending me things I don't even know what they are."

"Does that mean it's my turn next?" Hope asked, her eyes twinkling. Hannah nodded at her, wiping the tears from her eyes. "I got you, girl." Hope grinned at me and pulled out her phone.

"For sure, try them," Sasha advised, swallowing another laugh.

"I'm going to be a sad disappointment for the man who sleeps with me next if I don't know these things," I said quietly.

"Not even close, sweets." Hannah sobered up and shot a look at me.

"She's right." Sasha glared at me. "You are filled with passion and curiosity. He will eat it up and be blown right out of the water."

"Oh, speaking of that, what if I'm not good at that either?" I asked suddenly. It was too late, realizing that Rowan would most likely be hearing this.

"I got you," Lily assured me. "We'll discuss what exactly to do if you decide to go down on him. You better make sure he returns the favor and that he's better than the toys."

I blushed furiously, and seeing my discomfort, Sasha changed the subject. "You mentioned that you are pulling back on the experiment, right Two?"

"Yes, I am giving it another four weeks, and if the lawyer is still interested in me and not running in the other direction, I'm going to focus on growing things there," I said, grateful for the switch.

"I think that's a great idea," Hannah replied. "There's something there worth pursuing."

I wondered if it would still be the case after he heard all this. Sasha signed off on the podcast, and then once it was ready, she uploaded it and then looked at me. "How are you, really?"

How was I? I didn't know the answer to that. "Part of me says I've already learned quite a bit about myself, and then, in cases like this," I held up the ben wa balls, "I'm completely stumped. Friday's disaster didn't scare me as the attack did, but it affected Austin and Rowan."

"It did," Hannah said quickly. "Still want that back massage?"

"More than anything," I breathed out. "I'm so stiff and sore it's ridiculous. By the way, thank you for not spilling details on what you are educating Austin on."

Sasha laughed at me. "It doesn't take a genius to figure that out."

"No," I pushed her away from me, "but I don't need the details either."

"Are we good, sugar?" Sasha asked me solemnly.

"Yeah, Sash, we were never bad. I wasn't hiding it from you; it wasn't the same as the attack. I only got hurt because the asshole crowded me. Then, the second falling over was my clumsiness. Truly. Hannah only knew because Austin told her, and she was there when I got home," I pulled her in for a hug.

Sasha got teary again and then looked at Hannah. "Take care of her. Please."

"Goes without saying," Hannah agreed readily. She winked at Sasha. "I can take care of you too."

That made Sasha belly laugh. "Oh honey, I'm too much for you."

"I'd normally agree with that statement, but really, I think you've met your match in her Sash," I laughed at the expression on Sasha's face. "Really."

Chapter 20

$\mathcal{I}$ debated the intelligence of wearing these ben wa balls to work since I wasn't in a BDSM movie, but if it became too much, I could always go to the bathroom and take them out. Hannah convinced me to try them after making me watch the movie. Now, driving to work and hitting bumps in the road, making things move, I found concentrating hard.

I was flushed and incredibly turned on by the time I got to work. Seeing Rowan standing next to his car didn't help either. Oh God, and he was smiling that smile. The one that made me want to climb him. I swear she did this to me on purpose.

I got out of the car slowly, doing my damn hardest not to groan as they shifted inside me, hitting that exact spot Lily said they would. I barely had my car door closed before Rowan was before me, dipping his head for a kiss that almost had me a puddle of goo.

"Good morning, Lena. You have a glow about you today." He brushed his lips against mine again.

I laughed, which turned quickly into a groan, and I blushed wildly. "Thank you," I said quietly.

Rowan stilled, and a stunned look came over his

face. "Holy shit. Are you wearing them?" he whispered into my ear, moving his body closer to mine.

"I swear, if you touch me, I'm going to come right here in the parking lot," I blurted out.

Rowan's breathing changed. Apparently, the man could get ruffled. "The rest of my day is going to be extremely uncomfortable. Why on earth are you wearing them to work?"

"Hannah told me it would be a good experiment for me," I muttered, my body shuddering as the damn balls moved inside me again. "Now, I think it was some sort of plot to see if I could embarrass myself even more than I already have."

Rowan groaned low in his throat, an animalistic sound. "Never think that I wouldn't be satisfied by you. I feel so tempted to change my mind about not moving this to the next level that I won't be able to concentrate on anything else today, but the fact that you have those in you and how much I wish it were me."

Oh no, a jolt of pleasure at Rowan's words hit me so hard that I almost dropped and instead collapsed into Rowan, my body quaking as an orgasm hit me. Hannah was going to pay for this. All I could do was moan as Rowan held me and blocked me from view.

Rowan cursed under his breath. "I'm walking you to your desk and putting on the biggest display of PDA any of them have ever seen."

I laughed and then groaned again. "Not sure I can keep these things in, though maybe it's just because I'm near you this is happening."

"Not helping," Rowan growled as he walked me to the elevator. "You are perfect, Lena. So perfect."

Thankfully, we were in the elevator alone. "I think you have us confused. You've given me two happy endings without even doing anything. Abstinence has never been so hard."

Rowan chuckled with a frustrated sound. "Pretty accurate statement there. I need a cold shower." He laughed to lighten the mood. "I don't think I have ever had a conversation like this before without blushing or feeling awkward. You have quite an effect on me."

"Ditto," I told him weakly as the elevator opened. True to his word, he walked me to my desk, left me panting after the kiss he gave me, and promised to come to get me after work. I almost laughed at the stiff way he was walking when he left.

"Lena," Marty hissed from her cubicle. "Are you seeing him?"

"Really? Do you think that's how I kiss people I'm not dating?" I hissed back at the nosy woman. I grabbed my phone out of my purse, put it on silent, and then texted Hannah, letting her know that payback would be severe.

My phone buzzed with a text. *I know what stone feels like now.*

I almost laughed out loud. *Is this sexting?* I sent to Rowan.

Almost immediately, my phone buzzed again. *No, I would tell you I want to remove the lucky toy with my teeth and replace it with my tongue.*

Heat flared through me, and I almost groaned again as my body tightened. *Thanks for the clarification. It almost gave me another happy ending. This conversation is level one and a half.*

Sorry. You have me in a state, Rowan replied.

Don't apologize; I'm wearing you down. I smiled as I hit send.

There were a few minutes of phone silence, and I settled in to work with as little movement as possible. After several phone calls and solving problems for people who couldn't figure out how to solve them independently, my phone buzzed again.

I volunteer at the women's shelter tonight, so dinner tomorrow night? Move in with me in September? Rowan wrote.

I gasped. Those damn metal balls moved again, and I stifled a groan. I had no idea if Rowan was kidding or not. *Well, that's unquestionably jumping some levels there.*

I'll wear you down, was his response.

Rowan would, too. I'd do it now if I thought I could get away with it, just to get to sleep with him. I had very little resistance when it came to this man. *But will you wear me down before I wear you down?*

Good question, Rowan answered. *I don't have an answer for that one.*

My phone rang again, and I had lost complete focus at that point. By lunch, I beelined for the bathroom to take the ben wa balls out. I was a mess. Halfway tense from trying not to move and halfway mush from moving and having that pleasure spot hit too many times.

I was biting my lips so hard, pulling them out, that I made it bleed. I used toilet paper to clean the infernal toy up as much as possible and stuffed it in my pocket. My legs were wobbly as I walked to the breakroom and dropped into a chair.

I fished my phone out of my other pocket and texted Rowan. *Dinner tomorrow, my place. I'll cook for you this time.*

Phew. I thought I scared you away. Sounds good, but you don't have to cook for me. I can bring dinner.

Why would you scare me away? Are you afraid of my cooking? I smiled, knowing he wasn't. He just wanted to wait on me.

Nothing about you scares me except the thought of losing you. I was worried my comment went too far, Rowan replied.

I no longer had any questions about whether I was falling for him. I had already plummeted. Hard. *Nope, didn't go too far. It only made me plot harder on how to wear you down first.*

I watched the dots roll across my screen that told me he was typing. They blinked on, then disappeared so often I started laughing, drawing the attention of the others in the room. I took a bite out of my apple to smother it.

No mere mortal man can hold out against the sweet agony of temptation, which is you. Time to bust out my superhero cape.

I almost choked on my apple. *Oh God, please wear tights and a cape. PLEASE! It would almost be like seeing you naked.*

There was silence for another few minutes, the dots appearing every so often on my screen. *You're killing me. See you soon.*

I grinned like a loon and sent a quick text to Sasha asking for help in getting revenge on Hannah for convincing me to wear those damn balls today. I got back a laughing emoji. After finishing my apple, I returned to my desk and found a few of the chocolates that Rowan liked to give me. The sneaky man played dirty.

I did not doubt that this man would wear me down before I would wear him down. I sent a group text to the girls asking if they wanted to come for dinner tomorrow night and meet Rowan. If he could handle the lot of them all at once, I'd give in and tell him I had feelings for him.

Once they confirmed yes, except for Hannah, who had to work, I told Austin the plans. I didn't let Rowan know because I knew how shy he was, and I wanted him to appear natural, not on guard. Maybe it was unfair to him, but he hadn't been ruffled once by all this other stuff. The emergency room trip being the exception to that.

Chapter 21

The girls got there before Rowan did, and they anxiously sat on the couch. Austin merely shook his head and sat on the chair to watch. "You ladies are kinda evil, ganging up on him like this. He's cool."

"We aren't ganging up on him, Aust," I scolded him. "I want them to meet Rowan because I think he's important."

"About time." Austin sighed and rolled his eyes.

Sasha laughed at his response. "It's been two weeks, kid. Give your mom a break."

"Remember, Rowan's shy. Go easy on him," I told them as I heard a car door shut. I waited until he knocked and then moved to open the door, and my jaw dropped open.

Rowan stood there in Superman tights and a cape, with his hands on his hips, grinning at me while Demon tried to barrel into the house. At the gasp of Lily, his head swiveled, and he immediately started to blush, seeing all the women.

Oh no. I threw myself at Rowan and closed the door behind me to give him a minute. "I can't believe you did this." I grasped his face and smattered it with kisses. "Can I tell you something I wasn't planning on saying?"

"Uh, you mean that you invited the cast of your show over to meet me?" Rowan asked, flustered.

"Besides that," I waved them off. I knew the women were in the window watching.

"I wore you down, and you are moving in with me in September?" he guessed, a small smile playing on his lips.

I laughed and wrapped my arms around Rowan. "No, but are you going to keep guessing?"

"I'd rather you tell me and put me out of my misery so I can change into my sweats." He tipped his head down to kiss the end of my nose.

"I realized yesterday that I have fallen hard for you," I admitted quietly. "This just sealed the deal."

Rowan's breathing faltered. "Please tell me you aren't joking."

"I'm not joking," I told him with sincerity.

"I'll admit, I didn't think it would happen. I mean, three years, and you never indicated you even noticed I was a man. I've been in love with you this whole time." Rowan reached behind him and pulled the cape over both of us, blocking their view. "All it took was a cape and tights?"

"Oh, I knew you were a man. I knew you were a man so far out of my league that I didn't allow myself to even fantasize about you. Kiss me, please," I begged. "I just bared my heart, and I'm scared."

"I promise to protect it with everything I am," Rowan said quietly and kissed me so thoroughly I forgot we had an audience. "I also promise that when you look back on our relationship, you won't ever wonder if I loved you because I will make sure you always know it. That doesn't mean I'm giving in on the next level, though." He smiled against my lips.

"Superheroes aren't supposed to be evil," I quipped and stepped away from him. "Time to prove your strength, man of steel."

I opened the door and stepped back in, Rowan following, looking a little sheepish. "Ladies, this is Rowan."

"Rowan, from what I can see, you have big balls," Sasha joked. "You've got my vote."

Austin groaned and shook his head. "This is my cue to go check on dinner. Come on, Demon. This crap is an adult conversation we don't need to hear."

I pushed Rowan to the hall. "Go change. They don't get to see it if I don't." Rowan fled down the hallway, the cape flapping behind him.

"Okay, what was that about?" Hope asked after she heard the door shut.

I pulled out my phone, brought up the string of text messages, and showed them. All three were grinning at me when Rowan returned, this time in his sweats but still looking just as hot.

"Let the ambush begin," he said shyly, sitting in the chair. He pointed at Sasha. "Number Four? Which means, Sasha?"

"Very good." Sasha smiled and nodded. "You listen?"

"I do now." Rowan chuckled. He looked over at Lily. "Number Three? Lily?"

"What gave it away?" she asked.

"The voice, for starters, and I recognize all of you from the personality descriptions Lena has given me. That leaves Hope as Number One. Nice to meet you all," Rowan said smoothly.

Sasha got up and moved in front of him, leaning over to hug him. "Thanks for taking care of my girl. Speaks volumes about who you are."

"Aside from being brave enough to show up here wearing tights and a cape," Lily snickered. "That's a whole different level of taking care of her."

Rowan blushed again, then looked at Sasha. "It was my pleasure. I'd do anything for her."

"Including showing up dressed as Superman." Hope laughed. "Best dinner date ever."

"Lesson learned to check with Austin before showing up to dinner here," Rowan joked.

"Sorry, Rowan, I like you, man. But Sasha can be pretty scary. I wouldn't cross her," Austin said as he returned. "Actually, Hannah is just as scary, but Sasha has known me longer."

Demon ran from person to person; he was excited about everyone willing to lavish attention on him. "You might want to make sure that your purses are out of reach and that no shoes are lying around," Rowan warned.

They all picked their purses up off the ground and handed them to me to stick in the closet. Afterward, I checked on the dinner and returned in time to hear Rowan talking to Austin.

"I have a friend in L.A. with whom I went to school; he works in the bio-med research field. I told him about you and that your interest in study was similar, and he said to pass on his name so you could contact him with any questions. He also said he might be able to find you an internship somewhere once you decide which field," Rowan was telling him and handed Austin a card.

"Seriously?" Austin stared down at the card, then back up at Rowan. "This is amazing!"

Sasha walked up next to me and slid her arm around my waist. "Marry him," she said in my ear. "Move in with him in September and do what you have to do to marry that man. Rowan is perfect for you."

"I'm starting to think that," I agreed softly. "This seriously is who Rowan is, too. He's not doing this to impress anyone. But the whole moving-in thing is premature, don't you think?"

"I'd be willing to make a sizable bet that man is already planning the wedding ceremony," Sasha whispered.

"Oh, stop." I pushed her gently.

"Sugar, Rowan's so far removed from Shane they aren't even on the same planet in the same universe. This man is in love with you. And if what I'm seeing is correct, he has been for a while. Rowan looks at you like you are a priceless treasure. I mean, I think you are, but it's nice to see someone else thinks so, too." Sasha gave me a look that let me know she was serious.

"I told him I fell for him, Sash," I admitted quietly.

Sasha laughed, tipping her head back. "No wonder Rowan came in and faced us wearing that! You made him feel like Superman, sugar."

I looked back at the two men in my life, Austin sitting on the floor with Demon in his lap, talking animatedly with the man who professed his love. How different my life was now than three weeks ago, much less three years.

"You deserve happiness, Lena, don't fight it." Sasha bumped me. "I'm happy we got to meet Rowan. Did Hannah mention that she asked me out on a date?"

"What?" Stunned, I faced her. "No, she didn't."

"I told her I'd be interested, but only after she finished with Austin. She's teaching him to be a lady pleaser." Sasha grinned at me evilly.

"Don't tell me!" I covered my ears.

Sasha pulled my hands down. "Listen to me. Austin knows the score between them; it isn't love, and he views her as a friend. Hannah told me Austin told her he was so worried he'd become his dad and had no experience. He wanted someone trustworthy to teach him how to treat a woman so that no one he was with would ever have to feel how you felt with his dad."

Tears flooded my eyes. My baby was grown up. "Are you serious?"

"Yeah. Dead serious. Austin's even talked to me about it, and no matter how much I tell him he isn't like his father at all, he still worries. He saw way more of how you were affected than you think he did, and it left a mark on him. Lena," she tipped my chin up, "it's not bad. Austin's doing everything he can to ensure he doesn't ever act like that."

"Cover for me," I whispered roughly and fled to my room to cry in private so Austin didn't see. A few minutes later, there was a gentle tap on the door, and Rowan walked in.

"Did I push you too far?" he sat on the floor in

front of me.

I wiped my face on my shirt, confused. "What? No."

Some of the worries eased out of his face. "What's wrong, Lena?" Rowan reached forward and took my hands in his. I pulled them back and crawled up to him.

"Will you hold me for a minute?" I asked meekly.

"I'll hold you for a lifetime if you want." Rowan opened his arms and invited me in. "What happened?" he kissed my head as I cried into his chest.

"Sometimes, I think I've failed my son." I sobbed. My fear bubbled out of me.

Rowan stroked my hair and my back. "In what regard? Austin is an incredible young man." I spilled out what Sasha had told me, and Rowan chuckled lightly. "Sweetheart, that isn't a failure on your part. Some things a son can't ask a mother for guidance. The simple fact that he wants to make sure no one ever suffers as you did means you did a wonderful job raising him. He idolizes you."

"Isn't he using Hannah?" I asked through the slowing tears.

"No. It's mutual. Austin might have a small crush on her, but they seem to be friends more than anything else. He gains sexual experience, and she gets pleased," Rowan carefully worded. "When you started working in my building, was that right after your divorce?"

I nodded. "I needed a job, and it was entry-level. I'd refused alimony and agreed to a small amount of support for Austin but took the house since there was no mortgage. I needed an income to pay the bills. Why?"

"The first time I saw you, I was struck dumb. You were everything I had no idea I wanted. At the same time, I also saw the pain in you, and I wanted badly to take it from you. Being awkward and shy kept me from making a fool of myself, but I couldn't stay away. Stupid small talk was all I could manage for the first few months, and then you started asking more direct questions. It opened the door for me to ask you out, but I still couldn't because the fear of rejection was way too high, and you still carried a cloud of hurt." Rowan shifted and leaned against the bed, pulling me with him.

"You saw the damage?" I asked, horrified. I thought I had hidden it well.

"Yes, I saw it. I'm not sure others did, but it was obvious to me. I didn't know what caused it, but over the last three years, I've seen you shed much of it like a butterfly coming out of its cocoon. I purposely timed my schedule so I would see you every day. I wanted you to notice me. I put myself on that stupid dating app, hoping to see you there. When I finally did, I knew it was my one shot. I have never been more terrified in my life, but I took the chance. I was less shy around you than anyone else I have ever met. This is how I see it: if Austin knew how much you suffered over what had happened in your marriage, if he pushed you into this, and if he's doing this with Hannah to make sure he never repeats the mistakes of his father, then that makes you one hell of an excellent mother. He saw you push through it, grow, and give him everything he could ever need."

I had no idea what to say to that. "You timed your schedule around me?"

Rowan laughed and nuzzled my head. "I sure did.

I also noticed you paid zero attention to any male, and that's how I got through it. You weren't ignoring me; you were ignoring all the men. In every conversation I had with you, I cataloged every valuable piece of information I could to learn about you. It took me about a year to realize I was head over heels in love with you. Then it was just waiting for the right opportunity to come up."

"I never saw it," I told him, amazed. "You were always friendly and polite. A warm smile to start my day. If I'd had a hint of that, I would have asked you out. Even though you were a stalker."

"I guess I was. It just means it wasn't our time yet. We're here now, and we will be exclusive in a month. I won't have to stalk you, and I won't be giving in to the demands of my body until Austin goes to school," he said playfully.

"We'll see." I smiled at Rowan. "Thanks for coming in to talk me down."

"Lena, I'm holding out because I want you to see that you're it for me. You aren't there yet, but you are closer, and I won't stop trying to prove it to you. Even once you see it, I will prove it every day of my life," Rowan promised solemnly.

"I should just start packing now, then?" I half-joked.

"Yep." Rowan kissed me deeply, and his phone rang before I could strategically place my hands. He broke off the kiss and glanced at his phone, his face breaking into a smile as he stood up and pulled me up with him. "I've got to get this."

I pushed him out the door before I threw his

phone out the window and tried to get him out of his clothes. I checked my face and ran a cold washcloth over it before leaving my room in time to see Rowan grinning when he hung up.

"Good news?" I asked, fishing for information.

"Possibly." He followed me down the hallway. We found Austin setting the table and Sasha pulling the broccoli from the fridge.

Sasha glanced at me critically, looking for signs of distress. I smiled and shook my head at her. "I've got this, sit down. Or go turn on some music. Watch the volume, though. I think I had it on loud last time," I warned her.

She laughed at my warning. "When do you ever have it on quiet?"

"Never." Austin laughed with her. "Mom rocks it every time."

"Remember the concerts?" Lily joined in the conversation.

"Oh, my God!" Hope cried. "I've never seen Lena that wild before."

I started to blush, knowing that all sorts of embarrassing memories were about to pour out of their mouths. I busied myself with finishing dinner when the music turned on at what was considered a reasonable volume.

"How many concerts did you go to, Mom?" Austin asked curiously.

"Hundreds," I answered automatically.

"Hundreds," Austin repeated, "all before you were twenty-two."

"I went to a few after then, when I was pregnant

with you. That's how I credit you with good taste in music." I grinned, cutting up the broccoli.

"She didn't go into the mosh pits then," Sasha joked. "I mean, she tried, but a security guard picked her up and carried her off. Lily had to crowd surf even to find her. She experienced her first group groping."

"Hey," I protested, "I got to meet the band. Even got my belly signed."

"I have that picture somewhere," Hope remembered suddenly.

"Shane put you on lockdown after that," Lily said, then saw the reaction that happened on Austin's face and grimaced.

"Do you all listen to the same music?" Rowan stepped in smoothly to help ease past it.

"For the most part," Hope answered. "Lily has a broader range."

"By that, Hope means I listen to more than rock," Lily explained.

"Mom does, too," Austin argued and frowned as if I were being insulted.

"Your mom listens to songs that pack a punch and carry a strong message. She might listen to some rap, but it's not rapping about blunts and hoes," Lily told him.

"Lil's not insulting me, Aust. I've got a lot of genres on there. It just happens that most of it is rock," I said gently. "You've heard them all."

Austin's face cleared. "You honestly went into a mosh pit with me in your belly?"

"Oh, she did." Sasha stepped in close to him. "I don't think it was intentional, but once she was in, she was in until we saw a couple of security guards bust through the crowd and carry her out. She was furious. Her belly was sticking straight up, too, with you kicking away as if you were mad that she stopped her crazy jumping around."

"I wasn't in any danger," I told them sourly. "A group of guys around me were keeping the crowd away from me. They had a circle around me."

Rowan laughed at my description. "I can see it. What would you all say if I told you I just got six tickets to see the group that's playing on the speakers right now?"

I paused what I was doing and looked up at Rowan. "Are you serious?"

Austin jumped up and down. "Really?"

"Really. Would you all like to go see this group live?" Rowan asked.

Sasha looked at me and smiled slowly. "Told you so," she whispered to me.

"Yes!" Austin yelled.

"Take Hannah instead of me," Lily told Rowan. "It's not my thing anymore; she'd have way more fun than I would."

"This is Mom's favorite group!" Austin fist-bumped Rowan.

"Comes with backstage passes," Rowan added, and Austin about fainted. I almost dropped the pan of broccoli.

"That's like an engagement ring," Sasha said out loud. "Damn, sure, I'm in."

Austin turned his eyes to me, pleading. "Mom, are we going to go?"

"Wouldn't miss it for anything," I said quickly,

setting the broccoli down and throwing myself at Rowan. "I don't know how you managed that, but wow." I hugged him tightly.

"I think that's worthy of a kiss." Lily smirked.

"Oh jeez," Austin turned his back, "go ahead." I heard the smile in his voice, though.

I yanked Rowan's head down and planted a big kiss on him. "Thank you."

The rest of the night the girls filled Rowan and Austin's heads with stories of my antics at concerts. And otherwise embarrassing stories that the ladies pulled out of the recesses of their minds. Austin was howling in laughter, and Rowan was listening intently with a giant smile on his face.

Chapter 22

*W*ell, damn. I had a message. I had to admit that it was pleasant with no dates this week other than with Rowan. It was a whole lot fewer mishaps, too. I read the message several times and then responded, choosing my words carefully, as I agreed to meet for dinner one night next week. This guy had been clear in his intentions that he didn't want to meet at a bar because he didn't drink.

He wanted to meet in the next city over at an outdoor restaurant. That part wasn't the problem; it was summer, warm, and didn't get dark until late. My concern was the way he had worded the didn't drink part. It made me believe he was a recovering alcoholic, which made me think of Mike.

I glanced at my watch. Rowan was supposed to be coming over to chill with me, Austin was at work, Sasha was on a date, and so was Lily. I hadn't talked to Hope. I'd wait and see what Rowan thought about it. He was by far the most sensible of all of us, and he also had a stake in the whole thing.

The toy Hope had ordered for me arrived, and thankfully, this one was pretty self-explanatory. A bullet.

It is not much larger than one that would go in a big pistol and is pretty easy to operate. It also came with a separate remote control. I had thought I would use it before Rowan got here, but the scenes from that movie where some kid found the remote to a vibrator and made the main character have orgasms at a business dinner flew through my head. My luck, Demon would grab the remote, and the same thing would happen.

I stowed the toy inside my nightstand with the others and made sure it had a charge. I would probably need it by the time Rowan left. At least I had learned my sex drive wasn't dead. Shane had only put it in hibernation. I made it back downstairs right as Rowan knocked on the door.

I opened it to a rambunctious Demon who sped through the house looking for Austin with his leash trailing after him. I laughed and took the bag of groceries from Rowan. "I can see who matters most to Demon."

"Good evening, beautiful." Rowan dipped his head to kiss me as he pushed the door shut with his foot. "I got everything on your list, plus ice cream, because I craved it."

"Yum." I turned towards the kitchen. "I had a message on the new site today. I agreed to the date, but I have concerns. Will you look at it and let me know what you think?" I asked him. "By the way, only three weeks left of this nonsense."

"Seven weeks until you move in with me." Rowan grinned at the reminder. "Are you still logged into the site?"

"Yeah, it's still there. I'm going to start dinner," I

told Rowan. "Demon!" I called the puppy, who came racing into the kitchen like his tail was on fire. "Want a cookie?" I laughed as he danced around me, his tongue hanging out of his mouth. I tossed a cookie to him, and he caught it midair and then raced back into the living room to bark at it. "I love this dog."

"Good," Rowan called out, "because he'll be your dog, too, when you move in."

"I haven't agreed to that," I said back to him.

"Not yet, but you will." Rowan laughed. "Demon would be heartbroken if you didn't."

I pulled out the pans I needed and got to work making nachos, which is what my craving was for, other than steamy nights with Rowan. I was just finishing cooking the meat and assembling things on the tray when Rowan returned.

"The message is slightly concerning; I'll give you that. Are you worried because of the attack that happened to you?" Rowan asked astutely.

"Yeah. I'm trying hard not to categorize this guy in the same group as Mike, but I'm finding it difficult," I told him, feeling a little guilty.

"Understandable. Park within sight of the café, and don't have this man walk you to your car," Rowan suggested. "If you're anxious, don't go on the date."

"Let me ask you this: how do you get past it when you are nervous about something, or scared?" I slid the nachos in the oven and turned to look at him.

"Is this a getting to know me question, or are you asking for advice on facing your fears?" Rowan asked, his lawyer mind surfacing.

"Both. I'm interested in what you do and what

your advice might be." I set the timer on the oven and then focused on Rowan. I loved how he thought, how intelligent he was, how patient, and how he asked direct questions.

"Okay." Rowan drummed his fingers on the counter, "what I do," he mused. "I might not be the best person to ask this question. I was terrified to ask you out, and it took me three years. Let me think."

"Regardless of the time it took you to do it, you still did it," I reminded him gently.

"I know. For this instance, I went slow in a dating type of fear or relationship type because I was already in love with you. I faced it but at a snail's pace. I talked to you, listened to each little piece of information you doled out, applied the knowledge, and kept going. I think I use the same principle in terms of other situations, like life or death or job-related. I face it and pick it apart until it's not quite so big. I haven't had many life-and-death situations. Regarding the snap decisions, that fight or flight response, I almost always choose fight," Rowan generalized his answer.

"So you think I should just face this fear," I summarized. "Go on the date, and not let the fear consume me and hold me back."

"Yes and no." Rowan frowned a little. "You have to trust your instincts. Your gut is usually always right. If there is something about a person that tells you to stay away, then stay away. In this instance, I think you should go on the date, if only to face that fear. However, leave if your instincts rear up when you meet this guy and you don't feel right. You still faced it by going, but you trust yourself enough to keep yourself safe."

"What if my instincts tell me I should only be dating you?" I smiled at him.

Rowan grinned back. "They'd be right, but the timing is off by three weeks."

"I'll admit that these experiences have helped me in some ways. I've gotten a better grip on what it's like for people looking for love. I've learned just how dangerous things can be and better understood what prejudices still exist that shouldn't exist. I've gained a small amount of confidence and learned what I do and don't want in a relationship," I confessed.

"You've gained more than a small amount of confidence," Rowan corrected. "Those things you just listed are why I want you to continue for the next three weeks."

"I'm beginning to think that you want me to continue so that these awful dates make you look like Prince Charming," I joked.

Rowan laughed and kissed me. "I never thought about that. Pretty devious. I think I'd have to be the one to pick out your dates for that to be true. It's a pretty big gamble to take on my part because there are bound to be some nice guys in the mix."

I giggled. "Todd was nice. I set him up with Lily. Hope has found one that has promise. Sasha, I'm not sure she's truly looking, but something is brewing with Hannah and her."

"Hannah has a crush on you, doesn't she?" Rowan asked carefully.

"Attraction, I don't know about a crush. I don't want Hannah to hurt Sasha, though. She initially said Sasha wasn't her type," I recalled.

"Maybe the more she gets to know Sasha, the more she likes her," Rowan countered my statement.

"I hope that's the case." I grabbed three bowls and set them on the counter to transfer the sour cream, salsa, and guacamole. When I filled them, Rowan brought them out to the living room, where we would eat and watch one of the Marvel movies.

I pulled the nachos out while Rowan grabbed a couple of plates, napkins, and drinks. It was eerie how natural it all felt. We flowed well together, and I wondered if he was serious about the moving-in thing.

As I set the tray of nachos down, Rowan kissed my cheek. "We make a good team."

Flustered, I sat down, Demon lying between our feet in case we dropped something. "What's the plan for our date tomorrow?"

"Wear outdoorsy clothes. We're going to take a little road trip to one of my favorite places, so wear supportive shoes, hiking boots, or tennis shoes," Rowan told me.

"You are a brave man." I nodded my head to him respectfully.

Rowan laughed easily. "Trust yourself, Lena." He tapped my nose, "It was your idea to incorporate things that interest me into our dates."

"It was, and I love that you are." I swallowed the lump in my throat. "I can't wait to see it." I clicked the movie that he had set up for us.

Chapter 23

*H*oly crap, it was early. I was barely awake and was finishing up a note to Austin to let him know I'd be gone all day on a date with Rowan that was outdoors-related and probably had no cell phone reception. I'd gotten that much out of Rowan after an intense make-out session.

I packed an extra set of clothes into a backpack I'd found in the back of my closet. I knew myself. I chose to wear a pair of leggings and a t-shirt, with a sweatshirt over the top. I pulled my hair up, put some thick socks on, and donned the barely worn hiking boots that had been sitting in my closet for a couple of years.

I got a text from Rowan saying he was in the driveway but didn't want to wake Austin up by knocking. I grabbed my backpack and went to the door to find him standing on the porch, waiting for me. Damn, he looked good.

"Good morning, beautiful." He leaned over to kiss me and took my backpack from me. "I have coffee for you in the car."

"Caffeine," I breathed out with a happy sigh. "This is a good look for you." I gestured at Rowan as he walked me to the car. "Do we need to let Demon out to pee before we go?"

"I just did that before I texted you. Hop in, my lady." He held the door for me.

Demon was in the backseat, happily gnawing on a bone. "Bribery?" I asked as Rowan got in.

"You know it. I didn't want Demon to eat our food, so I gave him something to distract himself with." Rowan leaned forward and pulled out a bag that smelled of heavenly baked treats. "Wasn't sure what you preferred, so I got a variety."

I looked in the bag to see scones, pastries, bagels, and muffins. "Oh, man," I groaned. "You know how to treat a lady."

"Not really." He chuckled. "But, I do know you. I've seen you with a couple of different things in the mornings, and I know this is a lot earlier than you are used to being up. We've got about a two-and-half-hour drive, so you'll have time to fuel up."

"Fuel up? Are we doing some sort of aggressive hike?" I asked, worried.

"There is a hike, but I wouldn't consider it aggressive," Rowan soothed me. "I wouldn't take Demon along for something aggressive; he's still very much a puppy."

"Is this what you like to do? Go for hikes?" I pulled out a muffin, unwrapped it, and gave it to him before pulling out one for myself.

"It's one of the things I like to do. I find it soothing, but I don't have much experience doing it, so I stick to popular spots where if something were to happen, I'm likely to encounter people who can help me.

Do you not like being outdoors?" Rowan thought to ask before taking a big bite of his muffin.

"I like it. It just doesn't like me. Have you ever hiked with a walking disaster before?" I bit into my muffin and groaned at the soft, deliciousness.

Rowan chuckled lightly at my responses. "You aren't as bad as you think you are."

"I have no idea how you can possibly think that after all you have seen," I snorted, "and heard."

"Are you afraid of heights?" Rowan asked, changing the subject.

"I think that it depends on the situation. In some instances, absolutely. In others, for example, I can walk over a super-high bridge and not freak out or stand on a dam and look down and be okay. Climbing a ladder or going up on a roof would probably present some issues," I thought aloud. "I'd skydive, but it would scare the hell out of me."

Rowan openly laughed at that. "You have such an adventurous spirit. I love it. I'd say what I like best about being outdoors is exploring, seeing new places, and learning about things. Hiking tends to bring me to some of those places, so it's a necessary evil. I don't hike for the sake of hiking; I hike to get to the place I want to explore."

We finished our muffins, and I sipped my coffee before it cooled too much. "Do you like spooky stuff?" I asked him, thinking about places we could explore. He doesn't always have to be the one to plan our dates.

"You mean like horror movies and books?" he glanced at me questioningly.

"Kind of; anything, really. Like haunted houses,

or ghost towns, Halloween, spooky legends?" I tried to think.

"Love it all. When I was little, we went camping often, and we used to sit around the campfire and try to out-scare each other. Then we'd be up all night, too scared to sleep." Rowan smiled fondly at the memories.

"You and your brothers?" I giggled at the image in my head.

"Yep. With my parents gone a lot and always busy, we had lots of time to play out in the woods, make forts, camp, and find trouble where trouble didn't exist to begin with; it was how we amused ourselves. Sometimes, friends and one of their parents, usually a dad, would accompany us. We kind of had a reputation as wild kids," Rowan shared freely.

"I think the farthest Sasha and I ever got with that was camping in the backyard." I laughed. "We were wild in different ways."

Rowan laughed heartily and grinned at me. "I gathered that from the dinner conversation the other night. That wild girl is still in you. I see her pop up now and then."

"Marriage and a baby smothered her." My tone fell flat. "I don't regret Austin. There are several times I have wished that I hadn't married Shane. Austin and I would be a lot different if I had just been a single mother. It was not even two months of being married when I first wished I hadn't married him. Then I got pregnant and tried to make the best of it."

"Lena, you are damn amazing. Don't shortchange yourself. Austin is a great kid; not a kid, but you know what I mean. He has your fire and passion, a love of learning; there's so much of you in him, and it's obvious."

"Thank you for that, Rowan," I replied meekly, blushing. "I'm so nervous about having him gone and excited for him simultaneously. I'm not quite ready for the empty nest, and I think it will make me a blubbery mess."

"I hope you'll let me help with that." Rowan took my hand. "You'll have me. I know you think I'm joking about moving in with me, but I'm not. I won't push you on it; that's not who I am. I hope that you'll consider it as our relationship progresses. I know what I want and have the patience to wait for you to figure out what you want."

I could only squeeze his hand in reply; he utterly disarmed me. I needed to focus on the long game with Rowan; that's what he was after. Did I want that with him, or was I content to be alone? I know that laying in bed with him was probably the best feeling ever, and we didn't even have sex.

What if all these feelings I had for this man were tied up in sex somehow? What if I slept with him, had phenomenal sex, and then felt like I accomplished what I set out to do and no longer needed Rowan? It would crush him, and I didn't want to do that to Rowan. He went out of his way to take care of me.

"Are you sitting there, overthinking?" Rowan broke into my thoughts.

"You know I am," I replied with a small laugh.

"Are you doing the what-if game?" he asked.

"I'm going to start thinking you can read my mind." I glanced at him.

"It's not a fair game, remember that. You only ask yourself what-ifs for all the bad situations when you play it. When you do it again, ask, what if I get everything I want? What if it works?" Rowan said gently.

"Sounds like you've played this game quite a bit, too." I stroked my thumb over his hand.

"For three years, all my questions were of worst-case scenarios. Then I asked you for a date, despite the question of whether Lena says no. Then it became what if she says yes? What if I get to be happy? What if I make her happy? Those questions were so much more fun to answer."

"What if I hurt you?" I asked the one that bothered me the most.

"What if you don't?" Rowan countered. "That's an unfair question. We *will* hurt each other. We are human; we make mistakes, and that happens in relationships. We talk it out and go from there. I won't discount the things you think or say, nor will I neglect you and not ask your thoughts or feelings. If we go into this, we are equal partners, Lena. Always, and in everything, including housework, cooking, planning adventures, or vacations."

"You make it sound so easy," I mumbled, a little overwhelmed.

"It's not. It takes work on both our parts, which is why I insist on going slow. That's why I want you to go on dates for the next three weeks and then see what it feels like to date me exclusively without sex. If we can make it work without the sex, adding sex can only make it better," Rowan reasoned with sound logic.

"Aren't you worried we won't be compatible

sexually? I'm not experienced, and I'm sure you are," I asked before I could chicken out.

"That concern isn't even a blip on my radar, sweetheart. I know all I need to know from how you kiss me, from the way you willingly try out the toys and openly talk about it with your friends. I would never be disappointed in that aspect of our life. That promise is one I can easily make," Rowan assured me with a firm but gentle voice.

"What if I snore?" I asked, a small smile tugging at my lips.

"You do." Rowan looked over and smiled at me. "It's cute, too. You also mold yourself to me, and when I stroke your arm or your back, you let out these tiny sighs that made me never want to leave your side."

Well, shit. I needed to talk to Austin about moving now. I wanted that. I desired what he described more than anything. I didn't need a marriage license to move in with him. I wanted those languid moments where we were both so at peace that it was just soft caresses and sighs, our bodies intertwined and relaxed with sleep. Even if it wasn't true, I craved waking up with Rowan calling me beautiful.

Thankfully, Demon chose that moment to crawl up into the front seat and plop down on my lap. I scratched his head, and he fell asleep, making me grin with his puppy snores. I still held Rowan's hand with my other, and he raised it to kiss the back of mine.

"Hypothetically speaking, if I did move in with you, what would we do with my house?" I asked him.

"We'd have to talk to Austin about that. My initial suggestion would be to put the house's title in

Austin's name. It would give him collateral if he wanted to take out a loan, or he could outright sell and use the money for whatever he needed. If he wanted to keep it, because it's his childhood home, he'd always have a place to live if he didn't want to stay with us. Those were my first thoughts. My second thought was just to sell it. It's where you lived with your ex-husband, right?" Rowan asked me.

"Yes. Austin has always lived there," I told him. Fear and excitement mixed in my blood. "I'm not sure if there is something in the divorce papers about selling it."

"I can look those over for you if you decide to go that route." Rowan kissed the back of my hand again. "Does that mean you would consider living with me an option?"

"I'll keep an open mind. But it also means I'd need to have a girl's night out with my ladies and get drunk and talk about it drunkenly so they can all point out the areas I'm acting stupid in and then take me back home and pack me up and drop me off on your doorstep like a door prize. That would be after, of course, talking with Austin," I said with a chuckle.

Rowan laughed at the scenario described. "Let's get through these next three weeks, then our time, and see how you feel."

"Are you lawyering me?" I hesitated. I didn't want manipulation to decide my life choices. "I mean, by trying to convince me to see it your way?"

"Not at all," he replied softly. "The last thing I want you to do is jump into it and then regret it. I could sit here and point out financial gains, time-saving ways to share chores, not being alone, sexy time, and logical reasons that it would be smart, which would be lawyering you. Please do it because you want to; you want to be with me, not for any other reason. I know you are the last face I want to see before my eyes close and the first one I want to see when my eyes open."

"You're killing me slowly here," I said weakly. The picture Rowan painted was a dream; if I were honest, I saw the same things he did. It was the next natural step since I knew I loved him.

"Not trying to." He chuckled. "No curiosity about where we are going?"

"North, I know that much." I looked out the windows, my mind still spinning. "There's lots of stuff up this direction. Are you going to tell me?"

"It's in the North Cascades." Rowan gave me a hint.

"Then, I have no idea. I know there is a ton of stuff up there. It's probably all beautiful, too. I've been through there but never stopped anywhere," I told Rowan.

"It's a tourist spot. That's why we are going early like this. Our end destination is Diablo Lake," Rowan told me, giving in.

"Diablo? We are going to a lake named after a devil?" I asked, surprised. "With a puppy named Demon? What could possibly go wrong with my clumsiness there?"

Rowan let out a belly laugh. "Relax, Lena. It's gorgeous, and you are going to love it."

"I trust you," I told him. We fell silent for a while, still holding hands. While Demon slept the drive away, I was taking in the scenery and oohing and aahing over it. We pulled into an already crowded campground and found a spot to park. Rowan displayed a parking pass on his dashboard.

"We'll do the hike first. Give ourselves a chance to stretch out," Rowan said while Demon danced around, realizing he got to hop out of the car now. Rowan took his leash and got him out of the car while I slowly got out and looked around.

Chapter 24

I stared at the sign at the trailhead. "Thunder knob? Whoa, it's all uphill Rowan." I shot a look at him. "I thought you said it wasn't aggressive."

"It's not. It's an easy trail of switchbacks up. It's not very steep, either. The view is incredible. Leave everything here in the trunk. I've got my cell phone for pictures and a backpack with water and protein bars, along with some Demon treats," Rowan said calmly.

We had to tromp through people's camping spots to get to the start of the trail and cross a log over a little creek. I was sure I would fall in, but I made it across safely. Rowan took the lead for the first part of the trail, and I have to say it went by pretty quickly, mostly because I was watching his fine ass the whole time. *He was right; it was an incredible view;* I snickered to myself.

When Rowan caught me, he laughed, said it was his turn for the excellent view, and made me go before him. I wasn't very fast and caught my foot on some roots a couple of times, almost pitching forward into the dirt. Magically, it never happened.

When we finally reached the top, it was all rock, and we were very high. We were so high up that I was a little dizzy, considering no railing kept me from pitching right over the edge. It didn't help that it was windy too.

I clutched at Rowan's hand to steady myself. The water was an aqua-blue color that sparkled in the sunlight with the dramatic views of the mountainous area surrounding the lake. "Holy shit! The color of that water is amazing!"

"Worth it, right?" Rowan said in my ear. "I mean, the view of the last half was more than worth it and gave me a bit of difficulty walking. I should reevaluate calling it an easy hike."

I snickered at his innuendo. "Are you acting naughty?"

"I'm trying very hard not to be naughty," Rowan reworded my statement. "I used to think I'd be able to be a priest easily; the celibacy thing wasn't that difficult. Then I met you and realized I could never be celibate with someone like you."

I wrapped my arms around his neck and kissed him. "You were made for sex."

"I was made for sex with *you*." He punctuated his words with a kiss. "In seven weeks. The longest seven weeks of my entire life, mind you."

"Would you still sleep with me?" I whispered in his ear.

He growled some sexy sound that rumbled up through his throat. "Let's sit down and get a picture of that view."

"Whoa, you mean over there, where it drops off several hundreds of feet?" I kept myself rooted in place.

"Trust me, Lena, I've got you," Rowan soothed me and led me to the edge. Every time Demon got too close, I freaked out and called him back. Rowan chuckled and said, "He's fine. He won't go over the edge."

Rowan sat me down with my back facing the water, then dropped his backpack and sat beside me. Demon sprawled across both our laps and Rowan took a few selfies. Then he left Demon on me and got a few of me alone. Once satisfied, he turned me so I faced the water and sat back down next to me.

"Beautiful, isn't it?" he whispered.

"It is. I thought water that color only existed in the tropics," I breathed out, suddenly very glad that he had chosen to do this today. "Thanks for bringing me here."

"You like it?" Rowan asked, hopefully.

"I do. I'd be down for things like this. I'm not sure I could do much more steepness, but this was good. The height is a little daunting, at least this close to the edge. Back there, I was better mentally, but it's also exhilarating knowing I'm this close to the edge and not screaming like a bratty child who got told they couldn't have ice cream," I told him with a soft smile. "You did good, Rowan. It's perfect."

"Lena, I'm so madly in love with you," Rowan breathed out, blushing. "I know it's early to say that, but I am. Having you here with me makes it much more obvious to me. Please don't say it back. Not with three weeks left of other people. It was enough to know you said you fell for me."

I cupped his cheek, rubbing my palm against his stubble. "Most certainly, I have. I'll leave it there for now."

Rowan dug around in his pack and brought out a

bowl for Demon and some water. He filled Demon's bowl, who guzzled it down and then gave Demon a treat. He pulled out our bag of baked goods, handed me water, and let me pick something from the selection of goodies.

We sat there in peace, taking in the view and eating. It wasn't peaceful for long as a group of teenagers made it to the top and were joking around about falling off, and it freaked me out and made Demon go nuts. We gathered up our gear, and Rowan carefully helped me stand, got me away from the edge, and headed back down.

We encountered many more people then, and we stopped to take pictures on the way down of us lying on the benches in silly poses. Demon joined in on the fun, pouncing all over us with his big puppy smile and oversized paws.

To my utter surprise, we made it back down the trail and to the parking lot with no significant catastrophe, and I'd had a fantastic time outdoors. I grabbed Rowan in another hug. "Thank you!"

His smile was dreamy. "Let's go head over that way. I think there are some spots where we can get to the shore."

It was like Demon understood what Rowan was saying, and with puppy energy and enthusiasm, he bounded in that direction, yanking the leash I'd been holding right out of my hand. Luckily, Rowan was fast and caught it before he got too far.

"Rambunctious devil," I said, smiling affectionately.

We found a rocky beach with only a few people

around, which was better than where we had been, where at least twenty people were. Rowan set his backpack down and lowered himself to a log sitting there. "Join me." He patted the trunk next to him.

I sat down slowly, and Rowan wrapped an arm around my shoulders, pulling me into him. I slid my own around his waist and just savored the feel of it. A date like this was something I'd never experienced before. It was refreshing and invigorating. It was a breath of fresh air, literally, that gave me a different outlook on things.

"Did you truly have fun today?" Rowan asked in my ear.

I rested my head on him and savored the feeling. "I genuinely did. I couldn't be happier, Rowan. This type of thing is a complete first for me, and I got to share it with you."

"That makes me very happy." Rowan brushed a kiss over my lips.

"Hey, excuse me." A young female came over with a camera strapped around her neck. "I'm a photography hopeful and need to practice portraits. If I promise to e-mail you all the pictures I take, can I use you guys to practice?"

Rowan whipped his wallet from the backpack and pulled out a business card. "Sure. The e-mail address is on the bottom."

"This is so cool, thank you!" she gushed. "Go stand by the water. I'd like to see if I can get the mountains behind you while the sun hits the water in that position right now—so much color," she added, her mind clearly on the scenery.

I shrugged and got up, and we went and stood

by the water. Demon was having none of the sitting still for a photo thing, so Rowan stood on his leash instead of having our arms yanked everywhere. "What do you want us to do?" Rowan asked the girl.

"Just be you. What would you normally do, standing there with the woman you love?" the girl moved around and was snapping pictures.

Rowan gazed deep into my eyes and spoke softly to me. "I'd be doing exactly this, memorizing how you look standing here. Maybe kissing you." He bent to brush his lips across mine.

"God, you are so romantic," I whispered, my hands reaching behind his neck to pull him back to me. I got lost in his kiss. The sound of the gentle lapping of the lake on the rocks, the fresh air, and the scent of Rowan wrapping around me; I could die happy here.

Neither of us noticed Demon running in circles around us, wrapping the leash around our legs. At least we didn't see it until we broke apart and tried to take a step. Huge mistake. Rowan tripped first but righted himself. It toppled me and with our legs bound, I went down, pulling Rowan on top of me right into the frigid turquoise water with Demon barking excitedly at this new game.

The landing was hard for me since I brought Rowan down on top of me. He was frantically trying to undo the leash from our legs so he could get us out of the water. Demon thought the game was the best since dog cookies and jumped on Rowan's back, shoving me down into the water. The puppy jumped off and bit at my floating hair like it was a toy. The girl, on the other hand, was laughing her ass off.

"I got the entire thing on photo!" she crowed.

"Fantastic." I tried to wipe my hair out of my face, only to have Demon fling himself at me and knock me right back into the water. Sputtering, I pushed myself back up as he trounced through the water like it was the most excellent adventure in the world.

A hysterical laugh bubbled out of my mouth, causing Rowan to glance over at me as he finally freed himself and was working on getting me released. "Are you hurt?"

"I have no idea. I'm so cold that I'm numb." I laughed. "My powers of calamity have grown; I took you down with me this time!"

Rowan chuckled faintly, not as amused as me. "Sweetheart, that was Demon that did that, not you." He stood up quickly and pulled me up, trying to check me over. "I want every one of those pictures e-mailed to me and then deleted and not shown to another soul, or I'll sue you for defamation of character."

She stopped laughing then and nodded meekly at Rowan. "Yes, sir."

"Calm down, Rowan," I said quietly, hanging on to Demon's leash as he jumped everywhere like springs were strapped to his paws.

"Sit down, Lena." Rowan instructed me worriedly. "I'm going to run back to the car and grab some towels and clothes; your teeth are chattering."

"No, I'll go with you. There were bathrooms across the parking lot from your car, and the cold water has made me need to pee now," I told him. I was a walking disaster, not a damsel in distress.

"I want to check to see if you are hurt." He

looked worried.

"You can come in with me then," I promised. I just needed to start moving before I froze. That is one beautiful but cold lake.

Rowan looked back at the cowed girl. "I'd better see an e-mail within twenty-four hours."

"Yes, sir," she repeated timidly under the power of his lawyer's voice. She was scared of the legal threat but obviously wanted to laugh again.

"I'll look over the photos and contact you to see if you need any of them for an assignment you are working on; I'm sure there are some you can use," I told her gently. "Rowan's just trying to protect me."

Her face relaxed slightly. "He is a lawyer, though."

"He is. He won't sue you if I permit you to use them," I promised the cowed photographer. She was just a young kid.

She nodded gratefully. "By the way, I think you are bleeding."

Rowan cursed softly. "Come on, let's get back so I can check."

We started trudging back through the woods toward the parking lot, my body getting stiff as we moved, muscles beginning to protest. "Please tell me you found humor in that," I told Rowan. Honestly, it was hilarious, bleeding aside.

"Once I see you are okay, I am sure I will laugh hysterically, but only after I can see that my landing on you didn't break you." He glanced me over again. He was truly worried he'd injured me further.

"Hands down, best date ever, Rowan." I grinned,

trying to keep my chattering teeth quiet. "Notice that I still managed to fall into you? Maybe they are right; all my accidents with you are the universe throwing us together. It just used Demon to do it this time."

Rowan finally laughed, his pinched frown disappearing. "How could we not notice that leash?"

I bent over laughing because how could I not? "If you sucked at kissing, I probably would have noticed!" I stood back up. "Just find a hot spring next time. That is one cold-ass lake. It was like an unexpected polar bear plunge."

"Glaciers feed it," Rowan said with a small laugh. "It's still early in the season too."

We returned to the car, and Rowan grabbed the towels and my bag and hauled it to the bathroom. He took us both into the women's and down to the wheelchair-accessible stall, closing the door behind us and wrapping Demon's leash to the post.

Rowan draped a towel over my shoulders, knelt to undo my shoes, and pulled off my socks. "I'm going to wait outside the door while you pee." He blushed. "Then let me back in so I can look you over."

"You just want to cop a feel," I teased him, shivering.

"That too." He gave me a half-smile and stepped out the door. I heard a woman exclaim loudly at seeing him in there. "My girlfriend fell, and she's in there. I'm waiting for her to finish so I can look her over to make sure she isn't hurt," Rowan explained hurriedly.

There wasn't a response, so I assumed she was okay with it. I did my business, flushed, and stood back up, kicking the pants off. "I'm ready," I called out.

Rowan came back in and stopped in his tracks, his gaze landing on my naked lower half. His blush deepened. "You are damn beautiful." He bit his lip and shook himself. "You're bleeding, she was right. It's your hip, Lena. Does it hurt? I think that some stitches might have broken." Rowan grabbed his backpack and pulled out a small first aid kit.

"I'm numb. I feel sore and stiff but no pain," I told him honestly.

"There are seriously so many dirty thoughts in my head right now that I don't know what I'm doing," Rowan grumbled. His hands were shaking, but he got the gauze over my hip, and I held it there for him to tape down. Then he secured a band-aid over it.

He quickly checked over the rest of my legs, planting kisses on my thighs that made me want to make his dirty thoughts a reality. Rowan pulled out my underwear and helped me into them while he audibly gulped, then got me in my pants, socks, and shoes.

"This is so backward," I joked, not embarrassed in the least. "You should be taking me out of my clothes, not putting me in them."

"Oh, believe me, my brain is saying the same thing. Both of them," Rowan muttered. "Bruises are forming, sweetheart. I'm so sorry." He stood up and pushed my sopping wet and stringy hair out of my face, kissing me sweetly. "I know some bruises will appear on your torso or back because I am certain my elbow hit you. Did you, by any chance, bring an extra bra?"

I laughed at his question. "No. It didn't even cross my mind, but it will now." I pulled my sweatshirt and t-shirt off while Rowan bit his lip, his eyes hungry on me. "My shoulder is a bit sore. Can you unhook it? We can hang it on a hand dryer for a bit."

Rowan growled his agreement and unhooked the bra, slipping it off my shoulders, wrapped the towel around me and went back out to hang it off a hand dryer. He came back in flushed. "I never really imagined my first time seeing you naked would be like this, with me looking for injuries."

"It's not surprising at all." I laughed again.

"Maybe you should hold your hands over your nipples to save some mystery." Rowan blushed even redder than he already was. I had to admit I was enjoying his discomfort.

"Nope. You are the one holding out on me. Plus, you were just at eye level with my crotch. I think we are beyond the mystery stage," I quipped. "Wait, I think you need to get dry before you look for any more injuries on me. Strip," I demanded with a wicked smile. "Give me something to think about when I practice with those toys the ladies are adamant about."

Rowan grinned and stepped out quickly to restart the hand dryer. He came back in, pulling his shirt over his head. My jaw dropped. "Wow!" My hands let go of the towel, Rowan swiftly catching it before it fell. He started drying his chest off while I drooled.

He was soft in the middle around his belly button, but he was still built and hot as hell. "Nope, not cold anymore," I mumbled distractedly. "That's a fantastic tattoo." I reached out and ran my fingers over the massive dragon on Rowan's side, spilling on his back and front.

He said nothing, but his eyes were hooded as I

traced the tattoo. When Rowan bent to take his shoes and socks off, I dragged my fingers over the ink on his back. He stood up and pushed his pants down, and once again, my jaw dropped.

"As you can see, your touch has a bit of an effect on me," Rowan whispered roughly. "Not to mention the state of your undress."

"Your state is having an equal reaction on me," I fired back. "Better cover that before I do," I warned him. Heat roared through me at the sight of him naked. "You are a masterpiece, Rowan."

Rowan pulled a pair of sweats out of his backpack and donned them as quickly as possible, yanking on dry socks and shoes. "I need to go restart the dryer." He ran back out and came back in again. "Let me check your ribs, please."

"No broken ribs or I wouldn't have been able to get my shirt off," I assured him.

His fingers were on my skin, gently going over my one tattoo, which Shane never even knew about because he didn't bother looking at me. "Maya Angelou?" Rowan asked quietly.

I gaped, astonished he'd guessed so quickly. "How could you know that?"

"It's an open birdcage, sweetheart. I know your marriage made you feel like a caged bird," Rowan said softly. He pushed on my ribs a little, testing them, and turned me, gasping slightly. "Found where my elbow hit. You're going to have a big bruise there." His touch whispered across my back under my shoulder blade. "Probably why your shoulder hurts as well." He cursed under his breath.

"Hey, Rowan. I'm fine. I promise. It's not the first time I've had a bruise; come on. Look at my recent dating history," I reminded him, starting to shiver again.

He leaned forward and brushed his lips over it. "Despite all that, this is from me, and I'm struggling with it. What did you bring for a dry shirt?"

"Just a t-shirt. One that I certainly have to wear a bra with," I said as an afterthought. My boobs were way too big to go braless.

He held the towel up to cover me and returned to check my bra. "It's still damp, but I have an extra sweatshirt you can wear over your t-shirt in the car." He returned, and I dropped the towel, pressing my upper body to his and kissed him.

I almost swooned when Rowan wrapped his arms around me and returned it, backing me into the wall so I could feel the entire length of him pressed up against me. When he broke it off, he leaned his forehead into mine. "Seven weeks," he reminded us both.

"Fine, we can still kiss naked. That's only level one and a half. Like sexting," I argued, frustrated.

Rowan laughed, startling Demon, who started bouncing around again. "Turn around. Let me help you get this on." He turned me, and I settled my ass right over the very hard part of him he was trying so hard to hide from me. I wiggled my hips a little, making him curse again. "You don't play fair."

"Not when I know what I want," I agreed readily. When Rowan fastened the bra, and it settled against the spot he said he had hit, I sucked in a quick breath of air and wondered if I had any ibuprofen in my purse.

Rowan cursed again. "I know that hurt you."

"You've sure turned into a potty mouth today," I chided him, hoping he'd let it go. "Cussing, tattoos, wild naked kisses, what's next?"

He knew what I was doing exactly and raised an eyebrow at me. "You'll find out in seven weeks what's next." Rowan bent down to grab my dry shirt and pulled it over my head. "Stick your head under the dryer to try to dry your hair a little," he suggested, digging around in his pack for his shirt and pulling it on.

Rowan gathered the wet clothes and stuck them in a plastic sack he pulled out, tying it closed and following me out of the stall to the sinks. He lifted Demon, washed him up as best as possible, and then held him under a dryer next to me. I couldn't help it; I started laughing again.

Chapter 25

I pulled up to Lily's house five minutes early. That should give me points. I was stiff and sore today, but waking up in Rowan's arms was pure heaven. At the same time, it was also pure torture because I wanted to hop on and take him for a ride, and he was determined to make it the seven weeks.

When I walked in, Lily threw herself at me. "Thank you, thank you, thank you!" she crooned.

"What did I do now?" I asked, hugging her back and wincing.

"Todd is wonderful!" she said happily. "I had two dates with him this week!" She pulled me into the living room, where the rest of my friends sat waiting for us. Lily's furniture was all the overstuffed variety, in white and light beiges. I was always afraid to sit in here, but once I did, I didn't want to get up because it was so comfortable.

"Okay, before we begin, for real? Rowan scored tickets to the hottest concert around?" Hannah asked me. "Austin said Lily didn't want to go and that I could go in her place?"

"Sure did." Lily grinned. "You're welcome."

"Backstage passes, too." I smiled at Hannah.

"Oh damn, Rowan's a keeper. I seriously get to go to this?" Hannah gasped as the reality sank in.

"Yep," Lily answered, winking at Sasha. "I gave up my ticket."

Oh no. Lily was trying to play matchmaker with Sasha and Hannah while she was sort of seeing Austin. I caught Sasha's eye, and she mouthed that she would talk to me later. Satisfied with that, I just smiled at them.

"It should be a lot of fun," I said. "I'm looking forward to it."

"Austin was totally stoked," Hannah gushed, getting excited about going.

"He about fell on the ground when Rowan told him backstage passes were a part of it." Hope laughed. "It'll be cool for him to see his mom in one of her natural elements."

I burst out laughing. "Concerts aren't a natural element!"

"They were for you!" Lily threw in.

I snuggled back into the comfy chair, kicking my shoes off and pulling my legs under me. "Let's get this started," I prodded Sasha.

Sasha got the recording started and did the intro. "Who wants to go first?"

"I'll go," Hope volunteered. "One here. I had two dates this week. Both were very nice, though one was a little eccentric, I'd say. I had a second date with the guy I saw last week, and things are pretty groovy with him. I did get a slight indication that he might like a little kink in the bedroom, which I am good with."

"Wait, how did that come up?" Hannah asked, a

gleam in her eye.

Hope giggled before responding. "I was talking about that meme that you guys keep sending me about the handcuffs and safe word with the cops, and he told me that his cuffs had lining."

Hannah hooted, and Lily snorted. "How did you feel about that?" Sasha asked, keeping her face straight.

"I almost asked him to show me!" Hope laughed. "I haven't done that before, but I'd try it."

"Ask him if he has a spreader bar and uses that with the cuffs, too," Lily quipped, a smile lighting her eyes.

"I'm learning way too much detail about your sex lives," I muttered, blushing.

Hope winked at me. "The second guy, I wasn't sure how to take. Very nice, good looking, can converse about current topics and answer intelligently. With social things, though, he seems to be awkward. I wasn't quite sure if it was something I was putting out there or if it was just him, for example, after dinner. We were walking down the street, and I asked if he wanted to get coffee. He agreed quickly, pushing me up against the building and kissing me as if that's what coffee meant."

Sasha snorted. "How did you say coffee? Did you say it with a come hither, big boy tone?"

"I don't have one of those tones. That's all Two, not me. I just asked if the guy wanted to get a coffee. Does that mean I asked to have his tongue shoved down my throat?" Hope asked Hannah.

"You are asking me?" Hannah's eyebrows raised.

"You're younger than all of us; I wondered if coffee was some new slang for publicly making out,"

Hope asked seriously.

"No, coffee still means that dark drink that so many people need simply to survive," Hannah told her.

Hope shrugged. "Okay. He was a good kisser, but it was still awkward, and I didn't know what to do about it. Especially when we walked into a coffee shop after that, and he said he didn't drink coffee."

I snickered at the absurdity. "That sounds like something that would happen to me."

"Right? That's what I thought, too, and then I wondered if that was assault. But since I didn't mind the kiss, I guessed it wasn't." Hope shrugged again.

"When we turned forty, did all the men our age revert back to teenagers trying to get lucky for the first time?" Sasha asked. "Except for Two's lawyer, he's pretty much a dream come true."

"The guy I'm seeing that Two set me up with is a dream, too," Lily defended Todd. "I went out with him twice this week. He's incredibly handsome and has all these muscles everywhere. Chiseled face and gorgeous smile; oh man, his voice is sexy too. He was all for dirty phone talk the other night."

I would have never guessed that of Todd, and I smothered a laugh. "I'm so glad that's working out for you," I told her sincerely.

"You all know I like the kink, and I'm trying to figure out if he does or is open to it. I haven't quite been able to read him on that yet. Should I just come right out and ask him?" Lily asked us.

"Are you at the sex stage already?" Hannah asked her.

"I want to be!" Lily declared.

We all laughed at her expression. "Be straight with the man then," Sasha suggested. "At least you'd know what to expect going into it. We aren't kids. We are women, know what we like, and have experience and shouldn't be afraid of that."

"Good point," Lily agreed.

"I had two dates this week," Sasha told us, a sidelong look at Hannah. "Seems I'm going to be in the same boat as Two. Going to be no sex and getting to know her as I go through with other dates through the experiment of dating."

"You had sex on your last date," Hope frowned. "Was this a different person?"

"Yes, this one I have more interest in and would like to see if it will pan out, and she's also seeing someone else as well," Sasha hedged.

I got it. Why didn't Lily and Hope understand she was talking about Hannah? I almost said something, but Sasha shook her head at me.

"Well, glad I'm not in the celibate boat alone. Though it's not my choice," I retorted with a huff. "Suffer with me, Four."

Sasha sighed dramatically. "Yeah, I'm not used to not getting my way. Will be different, that's for sure." Hannah snorted but didn't say anything. "The other date, that one was a man, and he said he was a nature nut and loves hiking. He asked if I wanted to go on a morning hike with him yesterday."

"Tell me you didn't go," Hope demanded, her voice worried.

"I met him there." Sasha shrugged. "It was a little more remote than I would have liked, but you know me, I was armed. This guy didn't even look like he had taken more than ten steps in his entire life. This guy was definitely using a fake profile, and he had a major creep factor written all over him. He didn't dress for hiking, and I'm not kidding you; he pulled up in one of those vans from the eighties that your parents warned you about as kids to stay away from."

"Holy shit, you're serious?" I blurted out, stunned.

"Oh yeah. Dead serious," Sasha told us. "There's certainly a downside to dating online or using one of these services. I understand that they help match based on the criteria you entered, but there is also the element of people who lie flat-out. This date was clearly one of those times. I gave the date information to Five; I told her when I was leaving, the location and time, what I was wearing, and how long I expected it to take."

"Thank God for that," I butted in again. "You didn't do the hike, did you?"

"Damn straight, I did!" Sasha declared. "He didn't. I kept my car between us, and as soon as I saw him step out of the van, I knew he was up to something. After about five minutes of him trying to get me to get into the van with him to share a cup of coffee before we got started, he said, I pulled out my gun and told him to get the fuck out of there before I called the cops and had him arrested for attempted abduction."

We all gasped. "Then you went on the hike anyway," I filled in the rest, shaking my head.

"Sure did, sugar. That man wouldn't have been able to keep up with me, and he knew I was armed. He wasn't about to follow me. I halfway expected him to try to disable my car in some way, but after I pulled the gun on him, he took off. The hike was great; I needed the exercise and fresh air."

"Four checked in before I expected her to, so I didn't need to call out search and rescue," Hannah supplied.

Hope looked like she wanted to say something angry but held back. "What about you, Five? Did you have a date?"

"I did. I taught my date the fine art of seduction and how to make a woman feel special properly." She winked at me, and I cringed.

I guess the upside to this thing Hannah had going with Austin is that he learned how to treat a woman. Ugh, it wasn't something I wanted to think about in detail. "I had no new dates this week, only the lawyer."

"You say that like it's a bad thing." Lily smirked.

"Oh, no, definitely not bad." I smiled, remembering how much fun I had.

"You know that might have something to do with the wording on your profile," Hannah informed me.

"It doesn't say the same thing the other one did?" I asked, wondering what Austin had done.

"Essentially, the same things are there," Sasha grinned, "but it also said if you are looking for a hookup, phone sex, or nude photos, don't bother."

Hope snorted and grinned widely. "Oh, yeah, that's one way to weed them out."

I laughed at Austin's audacity. "That's what I get for having my son set up my profile. Not that I'm complaining. I did get one guy asking me some questions, and then he requested a meetup. I have concerns about it, but after talking with the lawyer, he said I should go."

"What concerns?" Sasha was quick to ask.

"He's a recovering alcoholic, I believe. He wants to meet in a different town, and at an outdoor café. The concerns for me are the recovering alcoholic and a different location. It's not one I'm familiar with, and the guy that attacked me was a recovering alcoholic. I know I can't lump them all into one group, but it made me feel nervous," I told them. "I agreed to the date, and it's this week."

"He was right to urge you to go," Hannah defended Rowan. "You shouldn't be afraid to get to know someone because they have something in common with an asshole. If we lived our lives that way, no one would be talking to anyone."

"She has a point," Sasha agreed. "Just make sure your safety is covered."

"I will. Now for the date that I did have," I chuckled, knowing it would elicit reactions. "I, too, went on a hike. It was beautiful, romantic, fun, and more physical than I'm used to, but I did it!" I told them with a smile.

"No way. You went on a hike?" Lily asked, dumbfounded, her hands smacking down on the soft arms of the chair.

"You didn't break anything either," Hope added.

"Thanks for the vote of confidence." I gave them a quirky smile and shook my head.

"They bring up valid points." Sasha laughed and shrugged innocently.

"Three, please grab your laptop," I told Lily. "I

have pictures to show you; your reactions don't need eyesight to be understood by the listeners."

Lily hopped up, grabbed her laptop, and then sat back down with the rest of the women crowding around her as I handed her a thumb drive.

"When we finished, we were walking along the shore of the lake, and this young lady was there taking pictures. She said she was trying to learn photography and wanted to use us as subjects. Neither of us saw a problem with that, so we agreed. She positioned us several times, then told us to be natural. Now, look at the pictures," I told them, holding back my laughter.

When Rowan got them last night, we laughed so hard we cried. She honestly had gotten frame-by-frame photos of the fall in the lake. Our expressions were downright hilarious. They were going to love this.

"Oh, how sweet!" Lily exclaimed as the first couple of pictures went by. "You two are so cute together."

I stood and looked, seeing she had the pictures on a slide show. I sat back down and waited as they oohed and aahed over those first regular shots. I heard Sasha let out a little laugh, and soon, they were all howling as my graceful dive into the cold lake played out in front of them. Their laughter as they tried to describe what they were looking at became interspersed with cackling, snorting, and tears.

When the laughter calmed down some, I told them, "At least that wasn't me this time."

"How could you not notice the leash?" Hannah bubbled up in laughter again.

"Did you see that kiss?" Hope asked. "I probably

wouldn't have noticed either."

"I swear to God, I want all these framed." Sasha laughed. "This is so one hundred percent you."

Lily turned the computer, "I just saved this one, and I'm printing it." It was captured right as both Rowan and I hit the water, the splash up around us, and our faces frozen in complete shock with Demon mid-jump at us as if we were playing a game.

They all broke out laughing again, and I couldn't blame them. "Despite that, my lawyer still wants to be with me." I giggled. "He helped me undress in the women's bathroom, checked me over for injuries, saw me naked, and didn't run screaming and took care of me. I insisted he strip as well because you can see he is just as wet as I am, and oh man, that is one sexy man."

"You weren't disappointed with what you saw then?" Sasha twisted her lips into a wicked smile as she gave me a smirk.

"Not even a hint of disappointment, and I completely forgot about the cold water. I even got my lawyer to stay the night with me, though he didn't give in to sex. I have to say, waking up with him was pretty terrific. Knowing he would be there all night, falling asleep was great, too. I'm so gone on him." I sighed dreamily.

"Yeah, you are." Lily turned the computer again, the one of our hot kisses before the dunk in the cold lake displayed.

"Save all those, Three, then e-mail them to me." Sasha broke out in laughter again.

"You're awful," I admonished her lightly. "By the way, One, that toy was fantastic. It made me quite vocal."

Sasha and Hannah laughed. Lily thought a moment. "Now, use several of them at the same time. If you do it while he spends the night again, I bet he'd give in."

I blushed bright red at that thought, making them all laugh again. "On that note, we'll sign off until next week when Two reveals what new level our dating wonder has taken dating disasters to," Sasha ended the recording. A few minutes later, she confirmed the upload.

"Aren't you worried that Rowan will get upset you talk about him?" Hope asked.

"No. Rowan loves it. He thinks it's a great way to learn more about me." I shrugged, "I was embarrassed at first because of all the sex toy talk. But he's alluded to things over text and, every once in a while, in conversation. I haven't revealed anything I wouldn't say to him if he asked."

"Does he know you were going to show us these pictures?" Lily asked with a grin.

"Rowan's the one that put them on the drive for me and made sure I had it when I left. We laughed so hard last night. Oh, and hot damn, he has a giant tattoo of a dragon over his side that made my mouth water," I told them.

"I've got a feeling that sex with Rowan is going to change your view on life," Sasha said with a laugh.

Chapter 26

After several more texts to Rowan, I looked at the café where I was meeting Jason for dinner. It didn't look impressive, and the signs on the windows told me they served alcohol, so I'm not sure why he chose this place.

I slowly got out of the car and made my way inside, noting that next to the outdoor seating area was a small park where many people gathered. Lush green mounds of grass and carefully landscaped shrubs and trees dotted the lawn as more people crowded in. I wondered what was going on over there. It looked more exciting than this café.

I walked inside, expecting the interior to be as it was: somewhat trendy with a European flair, as Lily called it. Pictures of the London Bridge, the Eiffel Tower, the Leaning Tower of Pisa, and some of the victory day in France from World War II graced the walls. It wasn't bad; it was only clichéd and played out.

A sign at the front said to wait to be seated, so I stood there until a waitress noticed me. "Hi, I'm supposed to be meeting Jason here," I told her when she walked up.

"Certainly. Jason's sitting out on the patio in the back. Follow me," she replied, not friendly, but not unfriendly either. More in the manner that told me she didn't care if I was here to spend money or not. We got held up by a person on crutches trying to get out of their seat.

I would have thought that, being in the hospitality industry, the hostess would have offered to help, but no. She stood there with an irritated expression while this man plainly had difficulty getting to his feet.

"Excuse me." I moved around the waitress, "would you like some help?"

Relief spread across his face. "Please. I can leverage myself up if you could lend me a hand," he said gratefully.

I held my hand out for him and braced myself while he pulled himself up. I held him steady until he got his crutches situated under him. "Do you need help getting outside?" I asked.

"I don't want to trouble you or hold you up," he replied, frowning at the hostess.

"No trouble at all. I'd hope that someone would help me if I were in your situation and saw me struggling," I offered pointedly. The hostess either didn't care or didn't understand that she should have helped the man.

"Then I graciously accept. It's hard getting in and out of my car," he said with a small smile.

"If you could please tell Jason that I will be with him in a moment, I'll find my way back there after I assist this gentleman," I told the hostess, my tone changing to slightly cold and clipped.

She huffed but moved past us out to the patio. "Good help is hard to find these days," the man said as I followed and held the door open for him.

"I'm not sure what she's doing could be considered help," I remarked caustically. "Which car is yours?"

"The red one." He nodded to my left. I saw it about four cars down from the door. I followed behind him, and when we got to the car, he fumbled with his keys and unlocked the door. I held his elbow, steadying him while he got the crutches inside, and then helped him lower down into the car.

"Are you okay?" I asked when he grunted painfully.

"Yes, I just need to lift my leg in. It doesn't bend too easily," the man explained. I bent over and helped him, and when he was all in the car, he gave me a genuine smile, albeit a sad one. "Thank you so much."

"You are very welcome." I returned his smile. "I hope the rest of your evening is pleasant."

"I'm going to go over to the park and sit with my windows down a bit. I should be able to see the show and hear the music at least." He nodded to where the people had all gathered.

"What's going on over there?" I asked curiously.

"There's a belly dancer tonight and some steel drums afterward. Something new the city is doing during the summer months, displaying local performers," he told me. "Thanks again."

"Enjoy." I smiled, waving him off. I went back inside, ignoring the hostess, and went to the patio.

There was only one table where a single man was sitting, and he resembled the photo on the profile, so I headed his way. He stood up as I got close.

"Lena?" he asked politely.

"Correct. Hi, Jason." I held my hand out to him.

He moved to pull out my chair for me, which was nice. I saw people filming the dancing in the park with their cell phones as I went to sit down, so I moved fast, not wanting to block their view. Jason went to push my chair into the table as I sat.

Suddenly, I was flying backward, the tops of my knees slamming into the table's underside, which made it tip, spilling whatever was on it. I didn't care about that. I found myself hitting the ground with a loud oomph among the sound of breaking glass. My legs went straight up in the air and over my head as I somersaulted backward from the fall's momentum. My loose skirt fluttered up to my hips, proudly displaying my purple lace underwear as I let out some weird squeal sound that sounded like a pig getting stung by a jellyfish.

Several people gasped, and Jason stood there staring blankly at me as if he didn't understand what had just happened. To be honest, I didn't either. I found a young waiter looking down at me, asking if I was okay.

I pushed my skirt back down and tried to slide around to get up as gracefully as possible, gasping and wheezing from the air getting knocked out of me. Graceful was a long shot after that little show. The waiter slid his arms under my armpits and heaved me up. "Are you okay, ma'am?" he repeated.

I found myself surrounded by wait staff and what I assumed to be the manager of this little café.

"What happened?" I asked, somewhat stunned, the air returning to my lungs as my face burned in humiliation.

"The grate, ma'am," someone said, pointing down to the ground. Jason had pushed my chair in over a drainage grate on the patio. The chair's back legs had gone right into the holes when I sat down. "Your elbows are bleeding. Please allow me to get a bandage for you." He scurried off back inside the café while the others righted and moved the table away to solid ground.

No one was paying attention to the belly dancer now, I noted. The focus was centered squarely on me and the entertainment I provided. Fantastic. I smothered a laugh, then decided just to let it loose. There is no one else I know alive that this would have happened to on a date, or ever.

The manager returned with some wet napkins, helped me clean my elbows, and then bandaged them. "I'm so sorry. That placement is something we should have thought about. Your meal will be on the house tonight," he assured me, his face blanching.

I wasn't going to protest, and as I sat back down at the table, on cement this time, I finally looked at Jason seriously. He hadn't said anything since it happened, nor had he tried to help me. All bad marks against him, not that it mattered since I wasn't interested. But jeez, your date just fell, you can't even help her up?

Jason shook slightly as one of the other patrons approached me with her cell phone. "I got that on video since I was recording the dancing. Would you like me to send it to you in case you have some injuries?" she asked.

"Please, yes," I told her, holding back a laugh. I wasn't going to have injuries other than to my pride, but Sasha would laugh her ass off at this debacle. I gave her my e-mail address, and she assured me it went through before returning to her table.

"Let's try that again, shall we? Hi, Jason. I'm Lena." I held out my hand, and he stared at it blankly. Oopsy, it was a bit dirty and had a smear of blood on it. I wiped it on the wet napkin, cleaned it off, and then held it back to him.

He shook it this time but still hadn't spoken. Not even to ask if I was okay. Rude. One of the servers returned and set a drink in front of me. "Margarita, ma'am, on the house." He bowed a little, and I saw the smile playing on his lips.

"It's okay to laugh; God knows I'm going to," I told him quietly with an unladylike snicker. He let out a small chuckle and then hurried away before he got in trouble.

"That's alcohol," Jason said bluntly. His face was a mix of longing and horror.

I was over it. "No, shit. The waiter just said it was a margarita." I picked it up and took a big swallow. "After that show I just put on, no thanks to you, I need it."

Jason shot to his feet, panicked. "I can't be around that." He looked downright terrified and sounded like he got caught with his dick in his hand during prayer time among monks. It wasn't like the alcohol was going to jump out of my glass and right down his throat. I understood the addiction part of it, but if he didn't think he could be around it without temptation, he shouldn't have asked for a date or at least made a date for somewhere that didn't serve alcohol.

Once again, people were looking. Jason, balls to the wall, ran to the small fence that bordered the patio, leaped over it like a criminal fleeing a K9 unit and tore off down the street like the hounds of Hell were after him. Oh man, I guess I didn't need to worry about inappropriateness with my date. I no longer had one.

I couldn't help it; I started cracking up laughing. I didn't even care that people stared at me with fascinated pity. I set my head down on the table and laughed maniacally. "Ma'am, are you sure you are okay?" the waiter was back.

I looked up, unable to stop laughing. "My date just took off! He hopped the fence like the hounds of Hell were after him, and he had raw meat in his pockets, and Satan hadn't fed them in a month. All because he's a recovering alcoholic and you brought me a margarita. After he pushed my chair in, making me fall in a hole and saw my underwear!"

The waiter knelt before me, his shoulders shaking as he tried to hide the laughter. "I'm truly sorry; he's an ass. Please don't report me for saying that. I know you said I could laugh, and I'm trying very hard to be professional here, but that was probably the funniest thing I have seen this year. I hope I don't get fired." He looked nervously over his shoulder back at the café.

I tried to stem my laughter and maintain some composure but that ship sailed when I sat in the chair. "Your customer filmed the entire thing." Giggles bubbled out of me again. "Oh my God. I didn't even want to come on this date."

The waiter, his name tag said Luke, snorted a little. "At least you get a free dinner out of it; take advantage of it. The manager is so worried you will sue us. He's about ready to offer you his child."

I wiped my eyes with a final giggle. "What's good then?"

"I'd get the ravioli, a side salad with the house vinaigrette, the breadbasket, and then order the death by chocolate cake," Luke advised.

"Do it. No more alcohol, though. I gotta drive home. Iced tea or water, or both." I giggled again. "Fuck my life."

"I'll get your order started for you." Luke stood up and touched my shoulder. "Seriously, don't worry about that guy. Enjoy your food, watch the dance over there, and keep that attitude. I'm young, but your attitude about this is pretty sexy." He gave me a wry smile. "I'm not joking."

"Thank you, Luke." I patted his hand and laughed again. "At least I wore good underwear."

Luke let out a loud laugh, then tried to smother it again. "I'll be right back with your iced tea."

It looked like I was on a date with myself tonight. I fought back another round of giggles and looked over at the park. From here, I got a good view of the belly dancer on the small stage. I watched her dance until Luke came back with my iced tea.

"The manager asked if you'd like to take a duplicate order home perhaps to have for lunch tomorrow," Luke informed me. "I'd do it."

"Sure." I grinned at him. "Please tell me others

are laughing and not freaking out."

"Oh, they're laughing, and now that they know you are cool about it, don't be surprised to find your to-go bag filled with goodies." Luke smirked and sauntered back inside the café.

It was a pleasant evening, and I went home with so much food that Austin would have dinner, and we'd both have lunch.

Chapter 27

"How was your date?" Rowan asked as I got out of my car the following day. His eyes immediately zeroed in on my bandaged elbows. "What happened?"

I started laughing insanely again. "It's just something you have to see to understand," I told Rowan, trying to get my laughter under control. I had shown Austin when I got home, and we both laughed until we cried and then he bolted for the bathroom before he peed himself.

I pulled out my phone and opened the e-mail, handing it to Rowan. "Watch that."

He looked concerned but leaned against my car, one arm over my shoulders while watching. I watched his face go from confused to shock to abject fascination to laughing. I wiped my eyes again, my stomach muscles sore from how much I had laughed over this.

"I have no words," Rowan finally said, his voice full of mirth. "How did it go after that?"

I filled him in on the disappearing act and all the free food. "Want lunch today?" I patted the bag in my hand. "I showed Austin when I got home, and he almost wet his pants. It was so unreal."

Rowan shook his head, still chuckling. "Only you, Lena; only you. Come up to my office at lunch. We can heat it and eat in privacy."

"I haven't shown the ladies yet. I want to see their faces, like we did with the photos," I told him with a smile. "Words would never be able to describe this accurately."

"You're right on that." Rowan shook his head as he walked us inside. "Are you going to wait until Sunday to tell them?"

"I think so. Hannah might find out earlier because of Austin, but I'll ask her to keep it quiet. I didn't send the e-mail to him, so he can't show her." I stabbed the button for my floor. "What time do you want to have lunch?"

"Whenever you show up." Rowan kissed me until the elevator stopped, then evilly pushed me out. "See you soon, sweetheart."

My phone chimed with a text as I got to my desk, and I saw a message from Hannah.

You are due for a waxing touch-up. What's your schedule like this week?

You just want to see the video; I can see through you. I wrote back.

Damn right, I do, but I also have you on my calendar for a touch-up. That was real. I'm off tomorrow.

Then, tomorrow after work, I agreed.

The day flew by. Lunch with Rowan was amazing, and then the rest of the day passed in a blur. Austin had to work that night, so I was alone and answering messages I had gotten on the dating site.

Only one appeared to be genuine. I answered,

asking questions of my own, and then finally decided to go to bed. The next day was a repeat of the one before lunch in Rowan's office again, and then back to work and home.

I had just gotten out of my work clothes when I heard Sasha's voice calling to me, which was quickly followed by the rest of them. Hannah had set me up, damn her. I pulled my sweats up and went to confront them. "I thought I was getting waxed?" I rested my hands on my hips and used my mother tone with her.

"Oh, you are sweets. I told Sasha I was coming here, and then she decided to ambush you because I wouldn't spill anything else." Hannah grinned.

I cocked my eyebrow at Sasha. "Really?"

"Can you blame me? She said Austin cried; he laughed so hard. Whatever happened has to be classic, Lena, and I want to know," Sasha challenged me.

"Hannah, do the mirror thing you did with your phone," I told her, relenting and handing her my phone. She turned on the TV, set it up for me, and returned the phone. "This is worthy of a big screen."

Hope and Lily sat eagerly on the couch while Hannah took a chair and Sasha stood beside me. "Play it then." She elbowed me.

"You are taking up all my good stuff that I was going to share on Sunday," I retorted snarkily.

"You can still tell it, but whatever this is, it has to be good." Sasha crossed her arms and waited while the attachment opened and started to play.

The house filled with the sounds of hyenas, braying donkeys, pig snorts, and giant monkeys as they all succumbed to the sight presented to them. Sasha and

Lily fell to the floor; they could not hold themselves up from laughing so hard. Hannah and Hope were both clutching at their bellies with tears streaming down their faces.

That was what Austin was presented with when he walked in. He immediately burst into hysterical laughter, knees bent, pointing at Hannah. "Didn't I tell you?" he guffawed.

"Oh my God," Sasha gasped. "That lady is so putting that up on YouTube. Holy shit, I have to pee." Austin laughed harder as Sasha ran down the hallway. I couldn't even feel offended because it was seriously the funniest thing ever.

"Please tell me you showed that to Rowan." Austin couldn't stop laughing.

"I did," I told him. "At least he didn't wet his pants and made sure I was okay."

"You knocked the table over," Lily huffed, trying to stand up. "Oh. My. God. That glass flew like it got catapulted and soaked the people behind you! They looked like they saw Bigfoot stomping towards them with a chainsaw in his hand!"

"Totally!" Hannah joined her. "She looks offended that you fell! Thank God you had the sense to wear decent underwear. But on this big screen, you can totally see that you need to be waxed again," she howled.

Austin sobered up at that and ran out of the room. "You are awful," I told her, trying not to laugh. "Just for that, you guys get to explain the video on Sunday."

"I can't believe that ape just stood there and

stared at you like that. The guy never said anything or moved at all," Hope said when she caught her breath. "What did Rowan say?"

"He is starting to believe the universe is telling me not to date anyone other than him." I smirked. "He still won't change his mind."

Sasha returned and collapsed in my arms, laughing again. "You seriously can't make this stuff up." Her shoulders started shaking with her giggles. "Sugar, I love you, but holy shit. I think the sight of you lying there with your legs up over your head as you tried to breathe and exposed yourself got seared into my memory. Definitely one of the top ten of all time."

I filled them in on the rest of the date, and by the time I finished, we were weak from laughing so much. "Makes me wish I could go on the dating site and leave a review on the jerks profile like people do for books." Hope snorted. "Leaves date laying on the ground with her underwear showing and hops a fence to flee at the sight of a margarita."

"How to banish a demon date," Lily retorted.

"Reviews wouldn't be a good thing." Sasha gulped air between laughs. "Can you imagine what Lena's would say?"

"Hey!" I protested. "Not all of them were my fault, and Rowan still likes me. In fact, he was going to send a letter to that café to have them change the grate out there so chair legs didn't fit through it. That's negligence on their part!"

"I swear, sugar, you can keep that man employed for years if you keep having dates like that." Sasha belted out another laugh.

"Behave, or I won't share the rest of that death-by-chocolate cake they sent me home with," I threatened. Twenty minutes later, Rowan and Demon showed up with pizza, Austin having texted him. It brought another fresh round of laughter as they watched it again on the TV and stuffed their faces with pizza.

Hannah took me to my room and got me waxed again. This time, it only elicited a few pained yelps from me. "At least you have a fantastic ass," Hannah tried to reassure me as she broke down in laughter again.

"I don't think that helps." I scowled at her. "I seriously laughed about it, though. Those poor waiters were trying so hard to be professional. If that had been me working and witnessing that, I would have lost my shit."

"Sweets, if that had happened in front of me, I would have been fired on the spot. I would have laughed so hard. I mean, once I realized the person was okay, of course." She giggled. "Life with you in it will never be dull."

Chapter 28

I went a week with no dates from anyone other than Rowan. The one guy was still messaging me but hadn't requested a meet-up. He would be out of luck if he didn't before the next two weeks were up. I didn't mind at all, and I wasn't going to push either. I was completely content with just Rowan and had far fewer mishaps—something he had noticed.

Hi, handsome, I texted Rowan. *I hope you didn't plan a date for Saturday.*

Are you dumping me? Came Rowan's reply.

I laughed, making my co-workers look at me. *Ridiculous question. You haven't slept with me yet.*

After about a minute, all I saw was the dots flashing across my screen, and I knew he was trying to figure out if I was serious. I took pity on him and sent another text.

I figured it was my turn to plan a date for you.

That was mean, he replied. *I couldn't figure out how to respond to that.*

I know. The dots on my screen were a dead giveaway. You know I have zero interest in kicking you to the curb even after you sleep with me.

I can honestly say I've never wanted to spank someone until now.

I snorted. Would that need increase or decrease if I told you I wore a red thong today?

Do me a favor and don't fall backward out of any chairs and show anyone else.

Well played, I texted back, trying to hold in the laughter. *Austin would like to have you over for dinner tomorrow as well.*

Austin, huh? Not you?

Are you offering yourself as the main course? I couldn't help it.

Rowan replied, *I'd be delighted to come over for dinner with Austin. See you after work, sweetheart.*

This man made me smile. Austin and I had finally talked about what would happen after he left for college. We'd gone and gotten tacos and sat outside in a park and talked until the sun went down. It wasn't just me that dreaded it; the change scared him, too.

Austin had come clean on all the mixed feelings he had been having. He had brought up Rowan and a possible future between him and I. Austin had suggested asking Rowan to move in, and then it was my turn to come clean and tell him that Rowan asked me to move in with him after Austin moved out.

Austin had initially taken it wrong, thinking Rowan didn't want him to be a part of it and that Austin would lose his place with me. It took me a few minutes to help him understand that wasn't the case and that there would always be a room for Austin if we went through with it.

We both cried and then drowned our fears in

tacos again. Austin had suggested dinner with Rowan, where he could talk it out the same way he and I were doing, and then he'd asked me what I wanted. I had to think about that for a moment. I valued my independence, but I'd be lying if I said I didn't want something with Rowan.

It turns out, Austin was hoping I'd want something with Rowan as well. We discussed the relationship we each had with Rowan in great detail, leaving out the sexual part of it because there wasn't one. Austin had told me that he had so much respect for Rowan, and while he may have pushed me into dating because he didn't want me to be alone, Austin was ecstatic that it had brought Rowan to me and hoped that Rowan had long-term goals.

It had been one of our better talks, and when I suggested that we might need to have a similar conversation with Rowan, he'd been all over it. I could only relay what Rowan and I had discussed, and some of the questions that Austin had asked me were things that Rowan himself needed to answer.

"Boss is coming. Look sharp," Marty's voice came over the cubicle wall. It wasn't like I was doing anything wrong. My phone wasn't visible; it was in my pocket, and my work caught up.

"Lena, can I see you in my office, please?" a voice came from behind me. Shit. Jerry was my immediate boss.

"Sure," I stood up and followed him, not making eye contact with anyone else.

Jerry closed the door behind me. "Sit, please." He gestured to one of the crappy green plastic chairs in front of his desk, and I perched on the end of it.

"What's going on?" I asked, folding my hands in my lap to keep them from fidgeting.

"First, I'd like to say that you've been a model employee. You never call in, you are never late, your work is impeccable and on time, and you don't cause issues," Jerry started.

"Thank you," I replied, not seeing where this was going.

"I understand you've had a tough time of things lately, and some comments have reached my ears." Jerry looked uncomfortable now.

"I don't follow. I haven't had a tough time with things. They are honestly going pretty wonderful," I said carefully.

Jerry sighed and looked pained. "You were, um, attacked, right?"

"I don't see what that has to do with my job here," I answered without addressing his question.

"It doesn't, you are correct. I'm bringing it up because of the comments made, which, in my opinion, hold no water." Jerry shifted, his face pinkening a little.

"What comments?" I did my damn best to keep my tone even when all I wanted to do was shout. I didn't participate in the gossip mill here and wasn't happy I was getting talked about like this.

"There was an incident with another employee that they reported to HR. He said you made sexual advances, and when he turned you down, you got aggressive." Jerry's tone clearly told me he didn't believe that.

"Cory," I spat, then tried to cool my temper.

"First off, he hit on me in front of various people. I also cited company policy to Cory in front of those same people, turned him down, and requested that he stop the behavior, or I would report him to HR. He has a history of doing that with women here. Secondly, I'm seeing someone else, and I've never been aggressive."

"Lena, I didn't believe it was true, and I went to bat for you. I'm not accusing you; I'm aware of his behavior and pointed it out. However, none of the other women in the office will speak against him." Jerry rubbed his forehead. "Regardless, it isn't why I called you here, but I wanted you to know it in case HR requests a meeting."

"Then what is this about?" my words came out more clipped than I intended.

"You are wasted out there, plain and simple. I'm retiring in a few months and recommended you for my job. If I'm going to be entirely honest here, your talent is wasted here too. This job would come with a pay raise and better benefits and take you out of Cory's line of fire. You wouldn't have to interact with him daily like you do now." Jerry sighed again.

"You are offering me a promotion?" I asked, stunned.

"No. I recommended you. You must apply and go through the interview process; HR will post it tomorrow. I was hoping to convince you to apply. That's why I called you in here. It was hardly an appropriate conversation to have out there among people who have been here for twenty years and have not done the amount of work you've done in three. As I said, you are wasted here. I feel you could do all the jobs with your eyes closed."

"Won't applying for the job create tension among those who have been here so much longer than me?" I thought quickly about whether this was something that would interest me or not. Truthfully, I only took this job to put myself back in the workforce to gain employment, a paycheck, and experience until I could figure out what I wanted to do with my life.

"Most likely, it will, but that isn't your problem. These same people have been passed over for promotions many times. I've had lengthy discussions with HR and upper management about you already, first to dispel the rumors, which, to your credit, they didn't believe anyway, then to talk about you in this position. If you apply, they will seriously consider you; this isn't lip service, Lena. Your exemplary record speaks for itself. Where you fall short is in work experience, and I believe I've gotten them to look past that." Jerry gave me a small smile.

"How do I apply?" I asked him. I'd give it a shot. If anything, it would look great on my resume and my history with this company to let them know I was interested in advancement.

"Bring your resume in with you tomorrow, and I'll look over it, make suggestions on what to add or detract, and then give me the corrected copy with a cover letter. As ridiculous as it is, they treat internal openings as formally as they do external ones. From there, you wait for them to contact you," Jerry stated.

"What about the Cory thing?" I wondered if I'd have to bring Rowan in as counsel.

"I'm not sure about that. I hope human

resources drop it, but if they don't, then we take it from there. I'm fully in your corner on this," Jerry assured me.

"I'm not sure what to say right now," I admitted. "Thank you. I'll bring the resume in with me tomorrow." I stood up and went to shake his hand but thought better of it as people could see us.

As I opened the door, Jerry called out, "Lena, the time-off request for September received approval. I forgot to mention that." I smiled and nodded in response, knowing he'd already told me a month ago it was approved.

Again, I hurried back to my desk, ignoring the stares of everyone who became curious about what a closed-door meeting had been regarding. As expected, Marty popped her head over the cubicle wall when I sat down.

"Everything okay?" her nosy face squished up in fake concern and curiosity.

"Absolutely. Jerry needed to go over my time off in September when it's time to move Austin down to California," I replied. "I wasn't sure if I'd need more time." I'd taken a week initially but changed it to two last month. I wanted time to adjust to the empty nest mentally. I was even more glad I had upped it because it gave me extra time with Rowan.

"I forgot that was coming up soon," Marty feigned interest. "Is he excited?"

"He is, and I'm very proud of him." I looked down at my ringing phone, happy for the excuse to end the conversation. After Jerry's praise, I felt a little guilty for only giving it half my attention for the rest of the day.

Chapter 29

*O*h boy, my stomach was in knots. Austin had fallen silent after I got home and was waiting for Rowan outside. I had no idea what that meant because Austin had never really come out and told me he wanted me to move in with Rowan or what he thought I should do. He just wanted me to have a future with him.

Rowan had gone over my resume for me last night and sent it back with pointers, and we had talked about what the job could possibly mean for me and if I should do it. Rowan was all for it because he said it was an opportunity to grow and learn about myself. I could start looking for a new job if I didn't like it.

The whole open communication thing was new to me. Shane had told me he didn't want me working because I needed to raise Austin, and my place was at home, making sure they were both taken care of daily. I never argued with him because my time with Austin was something I treasured.

It was after Austin got older that I realized how unhappy I was despite Sasha, Lily, and Hope continually telling me to leave Shane because he was killing me. I never knew Shane like I knew Rowan. More than anything else, honestly, that has been a massive eye-opener for me. Not only that, Rowan knew me. He knew what I liked, my habits, and my moods and paid attention to what I had to say. Always.

I *wanted* him in my future; I was damn sure of that. I sighed; whatever Austin was going to do, he was going to do, and I would let him. I was still nervous about it, however. I was worried it would make Rowan upset or somehow damage this thing between us.

"Mom, Rowan's here," I heard Austin call from the front door and then shut it again. I checked the chicken in the oven for the twelfth time and started the vegetables. I heard the front door open again and then the sound of Demon's puppy feet scrabbling over the wood floors.

Smiling, I got down on the floor and waited until he barreled into the kitchen and jumped all over me. "Hi, baby, who's a good boy?" I crooned as he licked my face and shook his tail so hard the entire back half of his body was wiggling. "You are so excited! I love it."

I got up and got him a cookie, telling him to sit. We'd been working on this with him, and I laughed when he plopped down but was still wiggling. It counted. I tossed the cookie to him, and he caught it and flew out of the kitchen to drop it and bark at it.

I had just finished washing my hands and face of dog slobber when Rowan walked in. "I'm not sure what smells better, you or dinner." He wrapped his arms around me, hugging me. "Hi, beautiful."

I smiled up at him. "I get butterflies every time you say that."

"I plan on continuing to say it." Rowan dropped

a light kiss on my lips. "Can I help?"

"You can set the table," I told him. "I'm not used to being offered help."

"Hey! I help!" Austin frowned as he walked into the kitchen.

"I wasn't talking about you, kid." I gave him a hairy eyeball look.

"Oh. Yeah, Dad never did anything to help you." Austin pulled out the water pitcher and some glasses. "I think it's great that Rowan does it automatically."

"Do you think that because it means you have less to do?" I raised my eyebrow.

Austin laughed guiltily. "Only half the time. The other half is me thinking it's nice to see someone not expecting you to wait on them. Shit. I think there's something in that sentence that tells me there's a lesson to learn. Damn me and my wisdom."

"And your potty mouth," I chided him gently.

"I get that from you." Austin grinned back at me.

"He might have a point on that," I grudgingly admitted. Rowan laughed and carried the plates and silverware out to the table. I finished with the vegetables, and they both helped me bring it all to the dining room, and we sat down.

I smiled as Austin served us the chicken, carried the pan back into the kitchen, and ran water in it. He'd make a great partner to someone someday. When he sat back down, he cleared his throat. "I know this was my idea, and I've already asked Rowan the questions I wanted to ask him. The rest of it we can discuss as a group."

"What do you want to discuss?" Rowan asked

readily enough.

"Well, if my mom decides to move in with you, what should we do with this place?" Austin asked him.

Rowan shot me a surprised look. "Are you considering it?"

"I am," I admitted. The happy look that spread across Rowan's face warmed my heart. "That, right there," I said softly, "you can't fake that look."

"Nope. Sure can't," Austin agreed and continued eating.

"What would you like to happen to it?" Rowan turned back to Austin. "Are you emotionally attached to this house?"

"I used to think I wasn't because some ugly memories happened in this house. Then, more recently, like after Mom and I talked, I realized there are many more happy ones than bad ones. At the end of the day, it's just a house. If she needed to sell it, I'd understand," Austin told Rowan with a slight hesitation.

"But it would make you sad," Rowan filled in. "What if she were to leave it here for you? When you come back to visit, you could stay here, or if she does decide to move in with me, you'd always have a room there."

"I'm feeling torn on that." Austin piled some vegetables on his plate. "I think it would be cool to have my own place to return to; on the other hand, I'd have to take care of it. I won't lie and say I'd be great at that. The reality of the situation is, I'm young and still pretty stupid."

I wanted to argue with Austin because he was great at keeping his space clean and cleaning up after himself. Rowan touched my leg to quiet me, and I continued eating. He was right. Austin needed to talk it out for himself.

"In a perfect world," Rowan continued, "what would you like to have happen?"

"In a perfect world? I'd like to see my mom taken care of the way she deserves to be, and I'd like to have the house to use when in town and perhaps to move back into after college. I'm not naïve enough to believe this is a perfect world, and I'm well aware of the financial straits she's been in to keep us going. Her car is a piece of shit, but a well-maintained piece of shit. All her extra money goes into what I need. I'd like to see her do something for herself, and I need to learn how to make my way and be responsible in the way she has taught me to be. The bottom line is I want her happy, living for her, and not for me. It's time for me to live for me," Austin said bluntly.

My vision swam as tears filled my eyes. "Can you go back to being a little boy?" I asked, my voice rough.

"No, because then you'd still be married to that prick, and Rowan is a much better choice. Remember, I'll always need you; you are my mom." Austin caught my eye and smiled.

"There might be something about me selling the house in the divorce decree. I'd need to dig it up and look again," I replied quietly. "Regardless, if I do move in with Rowan, I can always rent this place until you decide if you want to move back here after college."

"If you know where your decree is, I'd be happy to look at it and see if there are any clauses about the house and ownership," Rowan offered.

"I figured you'd say that." Austin smiled mischievously and got up from the table.

"You're seriously considering it?" Rowan asked me softly.

"I am, and I'm pretty sure I'm decided," I returned slowly, stunned that I had no doubts about the move.

Austin walked back in and slid a folder to Rowan."Mom taught me to follow through on my decisions and see where they take me, or I'd never learn anything."

I almost choked as I looked to see my divorce papers in the folder. I glanced at Austin, who was back to eating his dinner with an innocent look on his face. I shook my head slowly as Rowan stifled a laugh and closed the folder, pushing it out of the way of the food on the table.

"The decision on this is fully up to your mother and you. I advise keeping the house, depending on what the decree says, and possibly renting it out. The housing market is incredibly hot, and at the very least, this is a guaranteed income. If you decide that you want a fresh start somewhere else, you can decide whether to sell, rent it out, or whatever you feel is best. I'd also suggest keeping it for the time being as a safety net. If you do move in with me and decide that I'm not right for you, there is somewhere for you to land," Rowan said this part more softly, but it was for the both of us.

"That's not putting faith in my decision if I were to keep it for that reason," I told Rowan. "I'd rather rent it out, bank that rental income for a nest egg for Austin, and then see what he wants to do after he graduates."

"Mom! Didn't you hear what I said about living for you? Why would you bank that income for me?" Austin blew up, irritated.

"Because you are my son, and no matter what, I will always try to take care of you," I informed him in my mother tone.

"It's a good plan, Austin," Rowan defended me. "Students getting out of college often find themselves in tough situations with debt, trying to find a job, and not having anything to fall back on. Her plan gives you a little breathing room not to be completely stressed out. It's also a way to not rely on anyone, mother or father, to help you."

I should have been irritated that Austin listened to Rowan's reason and not mine, but instead, I was grateful that he listened and that Rowan supported me. In fact, I was so stunned by the support that I dropped my fork, making food fall on the floor. The sound of Demon snorting it up broke the silence.

"It's things like that." Austin pointed at me but talked to Rowan. "Those reactions to someone backing her up make me wish my dad had been better. Don't ever surprise her that you support her, make her wonder how you feel about her, or make her so sad that her only happiness in life is me, and we'll be good."

"Don't talk about me like I'm not here," I snapped at Austin, irritated with myself for my welling emotions. I pushed away from the table and fled to the kitchen. The low murmur of voices told me they were discussing what I'd said.

Demon followed me, thinking there was food in it for him. I slid down the wall to sit on the floor and cried. Like the way dogs always do, he sensed I needed comfort, climbed in my lap, cuddled me, and stared with his big puppy eyes.

"Damn kid is going to be the death of me," I said into Demon's fur. "I'm going to miss him so much."

Demon whined and wiggled in my lap as I looked up to see Austin's remorseful face staring at me. Demon jumping between our laps, unsure of who needed him most.

"Sorry, Mom. I'm not trying to be a jerk. I want you to be happy. You've done so much for me, sacrificed and given me everything I could possibly need. Hannah has shown me things I never realized, and each time I learn something new and apply it to my life, and what I've gotten shown and how Dad treated you, it's like a little piece of me breaks. I hate how Dad hurt you, and I want to make sure it doesn't happen again." Austin started to cry with me.

"Aust, it's not your job to care for me or worry about things like that. I think it's amazing that you are thinking the way you are, and it tells me just how grown-up you are. It's your time right now. This age is where you discover who you are, what you want, and who you can be. That's what your focus needs to be, and that's what will make me happy. Seeing you succeed is my ultimate dream." I leaned forward to cup his cheeks. "Let Rowan and me worry about our relationship."

"Yeah, Rowan told me to leave that alone and do me. He loves you, Mom. I want so much to see you happy. Like you've been when you've been with Rowan. It gives me confidence that not everything will be like it was with Dad. Honestly, I think it's because I'm scared to leave you. I'm scared to fail and not have you there to tell me it's okay." Austin sniffled, making Demon lick his face.

"Oh, kid, you truly are going to be the death of me. You're going to fail at something. Everyone fails; it's a part of life. It's the failures that make you a success. I'm scared, too, Aust. I hate thinking you will be far away from me, but I'm also so proud of you. Let's do this: promise each other that we will be the best version of ourselves possible and never let anyone dictate how we should be. We follow our hearts." I held out my pinky to him.

"Pinky swear?" Austin gave me a teary smile. "We haven't done that since I was a kid." He held his pinky out and crossed it with mine. "I pinky swear it, Mom."

"Pinky swear it right back at you, kid." I let go. "Don't leave Rowan alone out there. Go back. I need to clean my face up again."

Chapter 30

Sasha was the first to arrive on Sunday, and she set up her recording equipment. "Is Austin at work?"

"He is. He's off at two," I told Sasha.

"You still struggling with him leaving?" she guessed by the look on my face.

"I am. Austin's not my baby anymore. He's this young man now and he keeps showing me that all the time." I'd told Sasha everything about our dinner after Rowan had gone home and Austin was watching TV.

"He's going to be fine, sugar. You've set him up in the best ways possible; don't borrow trouble." Sasha hugged me. "You're going to move in with Rowan, huh?"

"I haven't told Rowan that yet, but I think I will. I have a few lingering fears, but damn, I want to," I confessed.

"I don't have any fears about that man, which should tell you something right there, sugar. How many times did I try to talk you out of Shane? I'm doing all I can do not to wrap you in a bow and deliver you to Rowan, myself." Sasha rocked me back and forth, still hugging me. "I think not being in this house, you'll blossom."

"Oh! It's hug Lena time!" Lily exclaimed, walking in. "You okay?"

"I'm better now that you all are here," I told them while being squished in a group hug. "After we do this episode, you all can help me go through things and start packing and donating."

Hope and Lily gasped. "You're going to move out?" Hope shouted excitedly.

"After Austin moves, yeah," I told them, my belly fluttering like crazy. "I haven't told Rowan yet, so nothing about that on the show."

"Wait, does Austin know?" Lily stepped back and crossed her arms. "You aren't going to just spring this on him, are you?"

"Austin knows. He's the one who pushed me to do it. We decided to rent the house out while he's at college, and I'll bank that as a nest egg for him." I let Lily and Hope in on what Sasha and I had already talked about before they got there.

"That's a great idea!" Lily lost her protective stance.

"Let's get started then." Sasha led the way back to the living room, and we settled down while she did the opening.

"Okay, I've got a doozy," Hope started. "That guy I went out with a couple of times that I thought was great? Not great." She shook her head. "Total dick."

"Wait, aren't we waiting for Five?" Lily asked suddenly.

"Sorry, I forgot to tell you, she got called into work today," Sasha told us. "She texted me while I was on my way over here."

"Okay." Lily pursed her lips. "What happened, One?"

"We met to see a movie, and afterward, he took me to a strip club for dinner," Hope said dramatically. "A strip club. Not only that, but he also had a lap dance while we waited. He told me that I was so hot, I had him horny, and since he didn't want to put me in a position where I felt like I had to put out, this was a good alternative."

Sasha snorted, her tone derisive as she stated, "How kind of him."

"Who does that shit?" Hope declared, her voice going up an octave. "Gross."

"Which part is gross?" Lily asked for clarification. "The club or the so-called compliment?"

"The compliment," both Sasha and I answered.

"Think about my ex and his pastimes. It's an excuse to get what you want without putting any work into it." My voice held a tone of disgust. "If that's a thing for him, he should have done it on his own, not brought a date to it."

"Yep," Hope laughed bitterly, "he's done. I also had another date, and that one was slightly better, but not much. I don't think he'd showered in a week, and he took me to that fish shack on the water. The combined smells were nauseating. He was nice enough, but I don't think his nose works."

"Yuck!" Lily wrinkled her face up. "I had another date with the guy that Two set me up with, which was so much fun. We put-put golfed, went on a hike that didn't end like Two's, had dinner, and talked for hours about the influence of building style on interior style and vice versa."

"Well, I'm glad that worked for you," I quipped. "That would have bored me to death, the golf part, that is. With me in the mix, who knows what would have happened."

Sasha openly laughed at the expression on my face. "Don't jinx yourself, sugar. Did you have any dates?"

"Only with the lawyer. The guy who messaged me is still asking questions, which I'm fine with; he doesn't know he's on a deadline, and I'm not telling him. I took the lawyer and my son to a ghost town; we did a group thing with the three of us. Thankfully, no accidents happened, we learned history we didn't know, spent time outdoors and together, which was pretty great and had a fantastic time," I told them.

"Does it tell you something that you had no accidents with him?" Hope pointed out. "Universe is talking to you, Two."

"Okay, I had a date," Sasha started. I'd already heard about it when we talked, but I paid attention anyway. "He was a male underwear model type of hot, thought I was ten years younger than I am, and didn't complain when he found out I was old. We went dancing at that new place where the younger kids go."

"Oh, I've heard of that place. Is it fun?" Lily interrupted her.

"If you did what I was doing, then yup, sure was." Sasha grinned and waggled her eyebrows at us. "I did have a Two moment. I wasn't expecting him to put his hand up my skirt, and when he hit the right spot, my knees flat-out buckled. His big, muscly arms caught me, and we found a dark corner to occupy."

"Holy shit. You did not fuck someone in a dance club," Hope yelled.

"Oh, I did. It's my type of club." Sasha shot her a naughty look. "Three would love it."

Lily made a cat sound. "Cougar."

"I totally was, and it was so worth it!" Sasha crowed. "He was pierced too and had scrumptious ink. I do not regret that date at all. He even asked me out again. I told him I'd call."

I giggled at Sasha. "That poor guy probably didn't know what hit him."

"It's a good thing that the music was loud," Sasha agreed with a smirk. "I'm a little disappointed at the lack of ladies looking for another female on the site. I thought there would be more than there is. Maybe I'm just not appealing enough?"

"Unlikely," I told her. "You ooze appeal. You always have. You are the whole package, Four."

Sasha shot me a grateful look at the confidence boost. "Thanks. There's still time."

We spent another thirty minutes discussing the types of responses we've all gotten and then summarized it all up and signed off. "Was that a crappy episode?" I asked, standing and stretching.

"No, blessedly uneventful for once," Sasha answered quickly. "What room are we starting with?" She played with the equipment and then did the upload.

"I'd say the extra room. It's where all the miscellaneous stuff is at; you know, the crap we stash somewhere because we might need it one day but never look for again?" I picked up my water. "Who knows what's in that closet."

Hope moved and turned on the music. "Let's party!" She marched down the hall and into the extra room, throwing the closet open. A loud crashing sound came, and then a screech.

We all laughed but followed to see her standing on the bed and pointing at the closet. "Spider!"

"Oh, hell, no!" Sasha launched onto the bed next to Hope and clutched onto her. "Kill it, Lena!"

Lily doubled over laughing and stepped on it, squishing it into the carpet. "I can't believe you two." She grabbed a tissue and tried to scrape it up, carrying it out to the bathroom. "Sasha's only kryptonite. A tiny ass spider."

"No, not the only one. If a snake comes out of there, we both will burn this house to the ground," I told Lily. "Guaranteed."

"Oh my God, remember when that garter snake was in the playground when we were kids?" Sasha remembered. "It was halfway standing up, slithering across the grass while we were playing soccer, and we both cried and ran right smack into each other!"

Hope and Lily burst out laughing, "I'd have paid to see that."

"It's true. Our heads hit so hard into each other's we had matching goose eggs," I told them.

We found many childhood mementos stuffed in a box in that closet. By the time Austin had gotten home, we were a mess of dusty, tear-soaked faces from laughing so hard at some of it. We also had a gigantic pile of stuff to donate and another throwaway pile. Austin was so intrigued by our goofiness that he stayed there to help us. He listened to the countless stories of Sasha and me as kids.

When dinner time rolled around, we got through the entire room and found a little cubbyhole in the wall. I don't recall seeing it before, and Austin ran to get a flashlight. Hope moved back to the bed in case a spider came out, with Sasha somewhere between the halfway point, which Austin found hilarious.

"I'll beat your ass down, kid," Sasha warned him. "Kill anything that moves; I'm not joking."

Austin smirked at Sasha and pulled the door open. "It's filled with old boxes," he told them, shining the light inside.

"Donate pile then, or garbage. Obviously, it's not something you need, or you wouldn't have hidden back there," Lily surmised.

Austin had pulled a box out and pulled the lid back, grimacing and then dropping it with disgust. "Garbage. All of them. I'll take them out," he insisted, his face going rigid.

Sasha saw the look and pushed past Austin, grabbing another, huffing at the heaviness, and then sneezing at the cloud of dust that sprung up when she pried the cardboard open. Austin tried to stop her, but she leveled a look at him that froze him in his tracks.

"Porn. Looks like your ex forgot a large portion of it," Sasha sneered, "the fucking pig."

That made me want to burn the house down just as much as a snake would. My face must have expressed hurt because Austin slammed the cubby door, crawl space, more likely, and hugged me.

"I'll get rid of it all," Austin promised me.

Sasha yanked him away from me and hugged him. "Wrong, kid. *We*, meaning us girls, are going to get rid of it. You can be the muscle and get it all loaded in my car for me, please. Plus, I'm not crawling back in there because I did see a spider, and that's not okay."

Lily stifled a laugh but quickly agreed with Sasha, snatched the box from the floor, hefting it up, and promptly loaded it in Sasha's car. Hope followed suit, taking the one Sasha had opened. Austin looked at me for backup, but I just shrugged.

Chapter 31

$\mathcal{G}$ood morning, beautiful." Rowan kissed me sweetly as I exited my car. "How are you this morning?"

I filled him in on what we had found yesterday without telling him what we had been doing to discover it and what we had done with it. Which was, Sasha had decided to return them all to Shane, labeling the outside of the boxes with the type of porn it contained in big black letters on all sides of the boxes and leaving them on his front porch, in plain view of all his neighbors.

It was a better plan than her original idea of setting them all on fire on his lawn and watching it burn. Austin had been all for that one as well, but thankfully, the rest of us outnumbered them on that vote, and none of us wanted to have to call Rowan to bail us out of jail.

"Did we do anything illegal?" I asked him, hoping that I wouldn't get some sort of visit from the police.

"No. You didn't break and enter or vandalize anything. You didn't start any altercations. You just dropped it off on your ex's porch, right?" Rowan made sure.

"Correct. We didn't even knock on the door or anything," I confirmed.

"If he contacts you or you hear anything, let me know and refer it all to me," he told me. "I'll take care of it."

"I can fight my own battles, Rowan," I told him firmly. "Shane isn't one you need to concern yourself with."

"Did I overstep?" he frowned, and his eyes raked over my face. "I just want to take care of you."

"You didn't overstep, but you must remember that I've grown pretty independent, and I'm not used to someone ready to jump in and fight for me. In this case, I am well capable of handling this," I tried to assure Rowan.

He still looked worried but nodded his head. "I know you can take care of yourself. I'm saying that you don't have to do it alone. You know how much I care, right?" Rowan looked like he was going to say more but stopped himself.

I stood on tiptoe and brushed a kiss against his lips. "You show me how you feel all the time."

"I think I need to be better at saying it because it feels like I'm not doing enough." Shame colored his voice. "I'm in love with you. I love you, Lena."

My heart caught in my throat, and my voice wavered, "Rowan, I know. I feel the same; it just scares me to admit it."

We started walking into the building, moving at a slower pace. "Is it because this is happening too fast for you?"

Startled at that question, I looked back up at him and tripped, Rowan quickly catching my arm to keep me upright. "No. It scares me because you are perfect."

His rich laugh filled my ears, and the worry bled out of his face. "Far from it. I have a lunch meeting today, so I'll see you after work. Same time, the same place," he told me as the elevator stopped. People were standing there, so he gave me a small peck and a heart-stopping smile.

"I hope you put that man on lockdown," Marty told me as I put my purse on my desk.

"Excuse me?" I glanced up at her, peering over my drab cubicle wall.

"Lock him in, fast. He's a bit quiet but gorgeous," Marty said, giving me a catty smile and sitting back down. I wanted to smack her.

I texted Sasha quickly and dove into work, blocking everything else out. By the time lunch rolled around, I had grabbed my phone and headed outside. Away from the people at the office, and called Sasha.

I told her about my morning conversation with Rowan and Marty's remarks. "Ignore that bitch; she's jealous. He is gorgeous, and he's also totally into you. Is this insecurity talking?"

"A little. Marty made me feel like if I didn't do something to make Rowan commit, he would dump me because I'm ugly," I admitted in a rush.

"She'll eat her words when you're her boss," Sasha spat. "Don't dwell on it, sugar. There's always gonna be a hater."

Mollified, I grabbed a sandwich from the coffee shop and headed back to work, walking into the building in time to see a female putting her hands all over Rowan. I saw red. To his credit, he kept moving away from her, but she was persistent and stunning.

I had stopped moving when I spotted them, and as Rowan moved again, he saw me. His face morphed into fear and regret, and he made tracks for me, swinging me up in his arms as he repeatedly whispered apologies in my ear.

"I swear to you, I didn't touch her," Rowan promised as he set me back down. "I would never do that to you."

"I saw, Rowan. Calm down," I told him, my voice flat as those same insecurities reared their head that Marty had brought out. He clutched at my hand as I resumed walking, unfortunately right towards the stunning blonde in a power ensemble of a pencil skirt and business jacket with a low cut, see-through blouse, and push-up bra. "That was sexual harassment, and Rowan's taken. Hands-off," I growled at the woman as I walked by.

Fuck me, she followed behind us, her face filled with condescension as we got on the elevator. Jeez, I was insecure. It didn't matter that Rowan held my hand and stood as far away from her as possible; he still had to finish whatever meeting he had, and she was undoubtedly a part of it.

"I'll be up in a minute," I heard Rowan say, and he stepped off the elevator with me. "Sweetheart, can you look at me, please?"

I tried so damn hard to hide the sheen of tears that popped up, but he saw them. "Don't worry, Rowan, I'm fine. I'm feeling a tad insecure, but that's not your problem. It's mine. You did nothing wrong."

"The only hands I want on me are yours," Rowan whispered and kissed me with fire behind it. "We're talking about this later."

I nodded and waited until he returned to the elevator before turning into my office space and running right smack into my boss. "Lena? Are you okay?"

This day was complete shit. "I'm sorry, Jerry. I wasn't paying attention," I mumbled.

"I wasn't referring to the bumping into me; you look upset," Jerry said, ushering me into his office and closing the door. "I rarely see this kind of expression on your face."

"I apologize for being unprofessional. I think today is one of those off days," I replied lamely.

"They do happen to all of us. You aren't unprofessional unless you snap at someone needlessly. Do you feel like that is going to happen?" Jerry sat on the edge of his desk and looked at me.

"No, I can keep my cool. I'm an adult." I kept my tone neutral and hoped I could follow through. Why those insecurities were hitting me so hard today, I didn't understand.

"I've got about twenty-five years on you, Lena. I have a daughter close to your age, and I recognize that look. Would you like to duck out of here early today? Or perhaps sit here until you feel a little better?" Jerry offered kindly.

"What look?" I couldn't stop the words from leaving my mouth.

"Injured," Jerry said simply. "I'm not prying, and I'm not asking you to share your personal life. I'm letting you know it's okay to have feelings unrelated to this job. Life rarely keeps itself compartmentalized."

The kindness almost undid me, and after a

couple of deep breaths, I felt a little more stable. "I'd rather not take sick time for something like this. I still have a few things left to do and could use the distraction."

Jerry nodded his understanding. "You know yourself best. Shoot me an e-mail if something should change your mind."

"Thank you, Jerry. I appreciate the understanding," I said a little too formally and walked stiffly back to my desk. I hunched forward and shot Sasha a text telling her that I was having some sort of breakdown or something.

I tried to explain what had happened over a couple of texts as quickly, directly, and in as few words as possible. I set my phone on my desk, out of sight from anyone who would walk by and started in on my work while waiting for Sasha to reply. I knew she was probably with a client and could take time. After an hour, I got a response.

I'll meet you at your house after I'm off work. I was expecting this. Have another appt now.

I wasn't sure what to make of that statement, but I felt better knowing she would be there. I was nervous about facing Rowan after work and considered leaving a few minutes early to avoid him, but that wasn't really who I was anymore, and he didn't deserve that. Rowan hadn't done anything wrong.

The way a few women were looking toward the elevator, I guess leaving early from work wouldn't have mattered anyway. Rowan was already out there waiting for me. I needed to suck it up. I grabbed my purse and marched to the elevator. Rowan's worried face landed on mine, and I started to tear up.

He wrapped an arm around me and pulled me tight into his side, his warm body providing comfort without any words necessary. We walked out of the building in silence, and he opened my car door and sat me down, tipping my face to look at his.

"Without hearing from you, I can only guess what's going on, and it comes from experience in dealing with others who have had that same look. I won't push you to tell me, but I want you to understand that everything I have said today is true. I'm not an overly demonstrative person by nature, but I love you. I'll say it as many times as I need to and to whoever will listen to me." Rowan brushed his thumb under my eye. "Will you call me later?"

If I opened my mouth, I would bawl like a baby, so I simply nodded and hugged Rowan and then drove home as fast as possible before I crashed because I couldn't see through my tears. Maybe it was menopause.

Chapter 32

Sasha found me curled up on my bed, a soggy mess. Austin had hounded me about what was wrong until I threatened him with shutting off his cell phone and bodily harm. He finally relented, and I shut my door and fell on my bed, crying.

"Sugar, do you honestly have no idea why this is happening?" Sasha lay in front of me.

"No." I gulped air like I was suffocating.

"It's fallout, Lena. You decided to move out. You are moving on and ready to start great things, and in the midst, your past comes back to slap you across the face with ugly reminders. Then that cow you work with insinuated you shouldn't be able to hold on to your man, and then you see some woman putting her hands on Rowan. Your insecurities are because of that goddamn porn we found that reminded you of your shitty marriage that wasn't your fault." Sasha pushed my hair out of my face. "The rest just compounded it."

"Is that why you made us drop it off on Shane's porch?" I moved and rested my head on her shoulder.

"It is. I hoped confronting it and throwing it back would help you see that you are past it. I was probably wrong, seeing as you look like a hot mess. You never really crumbled after you filed for divorce; this isn't very surprising to me." Sasha stroked my back.

"I did, too," I argued, the tears slowing.

"No, you didn't, sugar. You had down days and angry moments but held it together so Austin didn't see you fall apart. Look where that got you," Sasha pointed out sarcastically. "Now he's eighteen, knows a lot more, and just saw his mom in the middle of a nervous breakdown. Heads are gonna roll."

"Oh God, did he call Shane?" I groaned.

"If he hasn't, he probably will. Austin's got your temper, sugar." Sasha laughed. "He probably also called Rowan and served him up a big helping of shit as well."

"This might just scare Rowan away," I muttered darkly.

"Not even close. Rowan called me to tell me that you could use a friend. He confessed everything to me, and I swear to God that man cried," Sasha told me. "He also correctly guessed what was wrong and asked me how to help you. I neither confirmed nor denied his guessing, but that is one intelligent man, and he is finely attuned to you."

"Rowan cried?" my tears stopped at that.

"Sounded like it to me. Rowan called himself an asshole for not stopping it immediately with his words. He told me he was trying to be diplomatic because she's a high-profile client. He said the woman had done the same thing with the other partners his age. Very similar situation to the good old boys club you experienced, except it's a woman flaunting her body and position to get a leg up and make herself feel more important,"

Sasha psychoanalyzed the woman.

"Rowan didn't do anything wrong," I said weakly. "I watched him trying to avoid the touches. He kept stepping out of the way, and she prowled after him."

"Are you understanding your feelings yet?" Sasha pushed me off her to look at me.

"Sort of," I grumbled. "I don't like that Shane is still interfering in my life. I should be over it."

"Bullshit. There's no timeline on trauma or grief." Sasha got angry with me. "Be gentle with yourself and be okay with the fact that it's okay to hurt. You gave up a lot of years for that asshole and withered and died inside because of him. You were putting your son before yourself, not for any other reason than you have a caring heart."

"I made a mess of things, didn't I?" I wiped my sleeve across my face, smearing the snot from my runny nose across my cheek.

"Well, that wasn't the classiest of moves there. Blow it, don't smear it across your face, sugar." Sasha bit back a laugh. "Rowan loves you. I've never been more sure of that than I am after his phone call. I think you needed to break down like that to move past it. It's healthy and a part of healing."

"I love you, Sash." I hugged her. "Thank you."

"Naturally, you love me. I'm amazing. Go, wash your face. I'm going to go make us some grilled cheese and try to calm that walking hormone down before Austin loses his shit completely." Sasha patted my non-snot-covered cheek. "Call him."

I grabbed my phone and sent Rowan a

text. *Busy?*

Not for you, Rowan replied so quickly I wondered if he'd been staring at his phone, waiting.

I called him. "I'm sorry," I softly said when he picked up. "I wasn't upset with you."

"I was upset with me, sweetheart. How are you feeling?" Rowan's voice was rough. Sasha was right; he'd cried.

"Like a wreck," I admitted. "Better than I was."

"Tell me what you need from me, and I'll make it happen," Rowan promised.

"Be you. That's all I need. Want to spend the night? I won't even try to get you to give in to sex," I vowed.

There was a light chuckle that took a little of the rawness from his voice. "I'd love to spend the night. Are you sure you want me there?"

"I'm sure. Give me at least an hour for Sasha to finish mothering me and make sure Austin hasn't lost his mind. I don't think he's ever seen me like that before." I was sure it was something he was going to remember, too.

"Want me to head over after a bit, or should I wait for you to give me the okay?" Rowan asked gently.

"You don't have to wait for the okay. Just give me at least an hour. Demon being here will soothe the rest of Austin's ruffled feathers," I assured him. "Having you close by will ease the rest of this."

I heard the choked sound Rowan made and knew my statement had an emotional response to him. "I'll see you soon, sweetheart."

I got up, washed my face, and took a moment to

change my clothes before heading to face the music. Austin was eating but looked distraught. He hadn't even noticed me walking in, poor kid. Maybe I should have let him see me fall apart before; hindsight smacked into me like a brick.

"Aust, honey, I'm sorry for that," I told him as I walked into the room.

He shot to his feet and hugged me, feeling like the little boy I remembered so fondly. "Mom," he sobbed, "are you okay?"

"I'm better. Sasha slapped me around a bit and helped me see things a little clearer." I kissed his cheek.

"I hate him, Mom. I hate how much of an asshole he is and how he hurt you," Austin cried. "He's not worth those tears."

"Austin, hate isn't a good thing to feel." I caressed his head. "It's okay if you don't like him. God knows I don't, but hate is ugly. There's enough of that in the world already. If you are going to hate, then hate actions, not people."

"How can you be so forgiving?" Austin let go and sat back down.

Sasha put a sandwich in front of me. "Finish eating," she told Austin.

"I'm not going to devalue my trauma, as Sasha puts it, because I don't think I could withstand a bashing from her about it. Your father hurt me, yes. The type of pain he inflicted is probably worse than physical violence, but I'm not the only one to suffer it." I heard Sasha start to protest, and I held my hand up to her. "However, I was probably wrong to hide from you the emotions I suffered for this very reason. Everyone gets hurt at some point, and seeing it might have helped you understand better when you see it again, whether it's in me or anyone else. I only wanted to protect you, and instead, I scared the shit out of you today. I'm sorry about that, Austin."

"Sasha explained triggers." Austin stuffed a bite of sandwich in his mouth and looked pointedly at mine until I picked it up to eat it. "No one is too good for you, Mom."

"Thank you, Austin." I smiled at him. "I called Rowan before coming out here and asked if he could spend the night. He'll be over in a bit."

"Good, Rowan was pretty worried," Austin replied, letting me know he had indeed called him. "Are you going to tell him you will move in with him?"

"I might. I need to have a candid talk with Rowan about these feelings, it looks like," I said glumly, eating my sandwich before Sasha yelled at me.

"Damn right, you do," Sasha agreed and sat down with a sandwich of her own. "Poor man was beside himself. Austin, you get clean-up duty," she told him.

Chapter 33

After the emotional night I had spent with Rowan, I thought I would be able to move into this last week with no dates. That hope got dashed when the guy who had been going back and forth with me on messages finally asked for a meet-up on Thursday.

It gave me a sense of relief that it would be the last one. Rowan had reminded me we would spend together with no outside dates and still no sex while the ladies finished the experiment. I was ready not to date anyone but him. I was ready for commitment, but only with him.

I told Jack I would meet him and suggested the martini bar unless he had somewhere else in mind. I scrolled back through his profile and looked closely at his pictures. Most of them were outdoors somewhere, and he liked wearing hats. His smile was great, and he looked friendly enough that I wasn't worried about meeting him elsewhere.

His questions were intuitive and showed me he was thoughtful and genuine. At least, that was the perception that had come across to me. The profile said he had a child, but he didn't specify what age and his occupation showed as an engineer; he didn't specify what type.

Aside from Todd, this guy would have real potential if I hadn't fallen hard for Rowan. I loved that in Jack's pictures, his eyes smiled with his mouth. Pretty blue eyes, too. My problem in deciding how handsome he was was that I kept comparing him to Rowan and finding Jack lacking. Regardless, per our agreement, I would go on this date.

Jack must have been online when I replied to his message because before I signed off, he had answered with the restaurant location near the martini bar. It was a steakhouse, one of the ones that cooked the meal in front of you. I replied that it sounded good, told him a time, and that I would meet him there.

I glanced at my watch and realized Austin would be home soon. It was too hot outside to cook anything for dinner, so I made a submarine sandwich with the meats we had in the fridge. By the time I finished, Austin was home and kissing me on the cheek.

"How was your day today?" he asked me, putting his stuff down.

"Not too bad, considering the mess I was yesterday. How about you?" I sliced the sandwich up and put it on a plate.

Austin grabbed a soda and my water, set them on the table, and then grinned at me. "I must have known you were making a sandwich because I got chips on my way home." He pulled the bag out and opened it, sitting down. "My day was fine. I had a phone call from Dad that I ignored."

"Are you going to call him back?" I sat down

across from Austin, putting the sandwich between us.

"Nope. I don't need to. Dad left a voicemail, telling me off for leaving that shit on his front porch and that he knows you put me up to it." Austin shook his head and grabbed a chunk of the sandwich. He took a big bite out of it and gave an appreciative nod. "These are always best when you overstuff it like this. Good call, Mom."

"If I'm behind it, why did he call you?" I knew Austin was trying to deflect away from talking about it.

"Because I'm the one who called Dad and bitched him out for leaving that shit here," Austin mumbled. "Sasha told you I called him," he said defensively.

"I'm not mad, Austin. He shouldn't have called you, though, since his problem is with me," I replied calmly.

"I texted Rowan about it. He asked me to let him know if I got any pushback from Dad. *Me*, not you," Austin said, emphasizing the me in that statement. "Are you two okay?"

I sighed and nodded. "Rowan and I are fine. We talked a lot, and I told him what was happening inside my head. I also told him that I would move in with him."

"You did?" Austin looked excited and scared about that. "Wow."

"I was right; a clause in the divorce decree says if we sell, he gets a portion of the sale. Rowan suggested I put the deed in your name after you graduate college. By doing that, the house becomes collateral if you need to take out a loan or money if you decide to sell. It's a loophole in the decree that our lawyers didn't spell out. I am gifting you the house, which isn't selling it. It specifies nothing about you selling it." I had rather enjoyed that news. Contract law was Rowan's specialty, and he found several loopholes that had been there from a not-very-careful attorney.

"Nice. That means I'll have to pay the taxes on the property, though, right?" Austin asked, concerned.

"If you keep it, yes. The tax bill will come with your name on it. If it's still getting rented out at that point, you can use the rental income to pay the taxes." I told him what Rowan had told me.

"Cool." He looked a little relieved by that. "What about repairs and upkeep? I'm assuming the rental income can cover that, too?"

"The rental income will get put in an account for you and will be stored there until you access it. It will just build and collect interest. For now, I'll take care of any necessary repairs or upkeep. Rowan will be writing the rental contract for us, and he will make it ironclad to make sure we stay protected," I replied as I grabbed another piece of sandwich and a handful of chips.

"Fun stuff now; Grandpa called me today. I leave to go down there in two weeks, remember?" his tone was so happy.

"I remember. Did Grandpa tell you what he had planned for you?" I smiled. I knew my dad would make an adventure for them.

"We talked a lot. I told him about Rowan, so you might get a call from Gram." He smirked, enjoying my moment of discomfort. "But yeah, we are going on an overnight trip to some caverns, and we are going to spelunk, he said. Sounds cool to me. I think he said the caves are in New Mexico, which means that's another state to mark off on my map. He also said Gram wants us to go up to Antelope Canyon. I had to look that one up, and holy crap, it looks amazing. It'll be fun, and I miss them."

"What exactly did you tell them about Rowan?" I narrowed my eyes at him, not missing the way he tried to distract me from it.

"That you will move in with Rowan and how awesome he is. I told them about our next week's concert, and Grandpa laughed. He asked if that was what tipped the scale in his favor." Austin laughed. "There's also the camping trip Rowan's been talking to me about, and I told Grandpa about that. I think they want to meet him."

"I'm sure they do now." I sighed. "Meddling little brat, you just had to rat me out, didn't you?"

"Were you trying to hide it from them?" Austin shot my narrowed eyes look back at me, his tone carrying an edge.

"No," I replied with finality to my tone. "I just don't want the barrage of questions I know will be coming at me either. You know how Gram is. You all but just ensured they will come out here for a visit now."

"I know, that's why I told them." Austin laughed.

"Evil child," I muttered. "Did you tell them about Hannah?"

Austin stilled and gave me a calculated look. "Well played. I'll stop about Rowan."

I chuckled at his sudden nervousness. "I wouldn't out you. Besides, Grandma would just get all snooty with me about it because I'm your mom, and I allowed it."

"Did you know Hannah is interested in Sasha?" Austin asked, a small smile on his lips.

"I did. You two talked about that?" I'm not sure why that surprised me, but it did.

"We talk about quite a lot of things, Mom. Isn't that what's supposed to happen when you date someone?" The look he gave me almost had me laughing out loud. "I think it's cool. Sasha would be good for her, but in my own opinion, I don't think it's a relationship that will last. It might last a couple of years or so, but they are a lot alike, and I think that would drive them both crazy."

Austin's insight stunned me. I had thought the same thing but kept my mouth shut because Sasha hated people meddling like that in her relationships. She only liked or appreciated it if we saw dangerous stuff she didn't notice.

"Since we are on the gossip train," Austin continued, "Patrick said his dad is totally into Lily. He hasn't met her yet, but he said she's all his dad is talking about now. Does Lily like him?"

"Yep, she sure does! I'm glad I made that introduction. It's working out well," I agreed. "On that topic, I accepted a date for Thursday at the steakhouse. This date will be my last one before the timeline that Rowan set and agreed to be exclusive with each other."

"Rowan's stubborn about that, isn't he?" Austin chuckled and shook his head.

"Incredibly," I groaned. "Remember to start packing everything that you will take to college, and pack whatever you are leaving behind and label it. I'll store those in Sasha's garage."

"Does Sasha know that you are going to store them there?" Austin took the last hunk of the sandwich.

"It was her idea, smart ass." I pushed the chips over to him and stood up, grabbing my plate and heading back into the kitchen.

With his mouth still full, Austin chased after me, snatched the plate from my hand, and rinsed them, putting them in the dishwasher. He swallowed his food and smirked at me. "I did the cleanup." I swatted at him with the towel as he ran out of the room, cackling.

Chapter 34

The last one, I told myself as I pulled into the parking lot of the steakhouse. The restaurant was busy and crowded, making it plausibly noisy inside. The air smelled of garlic and something spicy as I hopped out of the car, and my stomach growled.

It had been a long day at work, and I had barely eaten at lunchtime because I was trying to work on the project that had gotten dumped on me at the last minute. My stomach had also been a mess of nerves because I had gotten an e-mail from HR with an interview time for Jerry's position. The day of the concert, no less.

I trudged slowly inside, glancing at my watch. I was only five minutes early; Jack might be here already. I hoped he was, anyway. It might be unfair to want it over with already, but it was how I felt.

The noise was the first thing that hit me when I opened the doors to the restaurant; the second was the smell of the food. The third was how handsome Jack seriously was. His pictures didn't do him justice. He was sitting on the bench in front of the hostess station with a nervous smile.

"Hi, Lena! I'm Jack." He held his hand out to me, a very sexy British accent coming out of his mouth.

"Nice to meet you, Jack." I shook his hand. He had a lovely voice, too. He was taller than me, which was typical, but shorter than Rowan by a couple of inches. He had a nice build, was solid-looking, and dressed well.

"I didn't know it would be quite this loud in here. I'm sorry about that," Jack apologized as the waitress seated us in the back corner of the restaurant at one of the less populated grill tables. There was only one other couple there, and they were on opposite sides of us, intent on their own conversation.

"It's okay. It's a little quieter back here," I told Jack, sitting on the high stool. It was a little dark in the restaurant, at least where the seating was. The inside of the table where the chef worked was well-lit.

Jack had dark brown colored hair that wasn't visible in his photos because of the hats. For the last date, he wasn't a bad one to look at or listen to; I could deal. "Have you been here before?" he asked me, handing me a menu the hostess had left of our choices.

"No. A couple of my friends have been here, and they all said good things about it. I usually eat at home with my son," I said, scanning the menu. "I'm guessing you've been here?"

"I have. My daughter loves this place. If I may, I recommend the steak with the side of stir-fried noodles and vegetables." Jack pointed it out on the menu, smiling. "For an introduction to this place, you can't go wrong with that. You can choose which sauce, if any, you want on the side, and the vegetables are fresh and crisp."

The background noise of clinking silverware, talking voices, and the occasional grunts of the chefs filled the room, drowning out the sound of my growling stomach, thankfully. "Sounds good to me," I agreed. "Thanks for the recommendation."

We talked a bit before the chef showed up, took our orders, cooking for the other couple first, and put on a little show for them while we briefly watched and then resumed our conversation. Jack would have been a good contender if it had not been for Rowan. He piqued my interest in conversation, listened attentively, and had a wonderfully expressive face. He was a warm and genuine person.

I learned that his daughter had just turned sixteen, and I winced remembering how I was at that age and didn't envy him the next couple of years. I told him a few of the antics my friends and I had gotten up to, and he laughed and then mock prayed that his daughter didn't do the same things.

Finally, it was our turn for the chef to cook for us, and I watched in fascination as he flipped the utensils around and put on his show for us as he prepared our dinner. It was a lot of fun, and I found myself smiling and laughing right along with Jack.

The date was all happy times right up to the point that Jack's hair caught on fire. I didn't even know how it happened or how I hadn't noticed that it was a toupee. We were laughing and having a great time interacting with the chef when the flames whooshed, scaring the hell out of me.

I fell right off the stool with a violent shriek of fear; I jolted so hard. I went crashing into the couple behind me, who were in the process of being seated, knocking someone off their feet. That person then fell into a person at the table behind him. Their plate crashed into the floor, shattering, causing a cacophony of startled and furious shouts from the domino effect of the dating calamity I was driving.

I saw Jack fling his toupee off his head with a quick motion, which happened to be in the direction of the chef, who deftly knocked it out of the air with his utensil and a shout. The poor chef began dancing on it in a mad jig to put the flames out. The restaurant was in an uproar and pure chaos as the domino effect finally reached a screeching halt.

The man I had crashed into helped me up, and another chef was running around the table to see if those of us who fell were okay while another scurried to clean the spilled food and broken dishes up. Then, like magic, all the noise in the restaurant fell silent as everyone looked around them in amazement at what had just taken place.

Of course, I burst into uncontrollable laughter, drawing all the attention to us, the two who had started the disaster. Jack's eyes were wide with fright, and the pupils dilated so much he looked high. It wasn't until the chef bent over to retrieve the smoking toupee to hand to Jack that someone else started laughing.

I couldn't stop. I felt terrible because Jack felt mortified, and the chef repeatedly apologized, saying he must have used too much oil. I wiped my face of the tears caused by my laughter and righted my stool.

"Jack, are you hurt?" I managed to get out before another round of giggles hit.

"My pride sure is," Jack said gruffly. His face was flushed and he looked shamed.

"It shouldn't be," I tried to calm myself. "If you knew the crazy shit that has happened to me on my dates, you wouldn't be so embarrassed. Honestly, this could have been so much worse. Why wear a toupee at all? You look way more handsome without it," I told him truthfully, unable to stop. "It's that masculine, strong look."

Honestly, now that I looked at him, he was Hope's type to a T. Right down to the accent. If she had to describe her perfect man, you could insert Jack, and she'd be happy, which gave me the idea to set them up. After he got over his mortification, that is.

"I have never had something like this happen to me in my life," Jack muttered once the conversation around us picked back up.

"Might be the Lena effect trickling down. Here, let me show you this video of my last date, and then you won't feel so bad." I pulled out my phone, pulled up the video of the café, and played it for him.

"It shames me to admit that this does make me feel better." Jack let out a small laugh after he had watched it and tried to cover the amusement.

"Don't feel that way. One of my friends told me that the universe was telling me I was dating the wrong guy. With another one I've been seeing, the accidents all pushed me into him, hence her theory," I told him with a big smile. "She might not be wrong."

"Hearing that, she might not be." Jack relaxed a little. "This date will go in the record books for me as one to remember. Probably in my nightmares."

The chef resumed cooking, without the show this time, and cautiously set our food in front of us with a tiny bow. "My apologies for the rest. Your meal is on the house. The manager has offered to pay for a replacement for you." The chef nodded at the dead wig.

"Oh, please don't," I told Jack. "Truly, I'm not kidding or trying to placate you. You look a hundred times sexier without it."

Blushing, Jack nodded at the chef, who was most likely about to go into the backroom and lose his shit laughing. "You've been seeing someone else, then? I suppose that makes sense since you are on a dating site."

"I have been and feel pretty serious about him as well. Please don't feel discouraged. If you are open to it, one of my best friends is on a site and looking for a good man. You are perfect for her. Would you be interested in a setup?" I asked him, cutting into my steak.

"Do things like that happen on dates with her?" Jack's voice was meek. He was still smarting a bit, it seemed.

"No. I'm the only one lucky enough for that," I quipped with a laugh. "You can look Hope up; I think she's on the same site as I was on."

He pulled out his phone and brought up the site. I gave him Hope's name and city; he found her, looked over her profile, and then decided to send her a quick message. "She didn't come up as a match for me."

"Trust me, you are. I've known Hope for years. In fact, ask her to describe her perfect man," I suggested, taking a bite of dinner. Thankfully, it didn't taste like a flambe toupee. "You can even tell her you are out on a date with me right now, and I told you to do that."

He chuckled, put his phone back in his pocket and started eating. "Tell me about these other disasters you've been on?"

By the time we finished dinner, we were both sore from laughing, and Jack was genuinely interested in Hope. The thought that the two best dates I had from this experience would lead to happiness for two of my best friends made me stupidly giddy.

We finished the evening by walking a block down the road to an ice cream shop, where we continued our conversation. Hope had texted me.

"She's verifying you are actually on a date with me." I smiled at Jack and took his picture, sending it back to her with a message that she would seriously like this guy. I'd let him divulge the date information if he wanted; otherwise, she'd hear about it on Sunday.

We parted on good terms, and I told Jack I hoped I would see him again as Hope's date sometime in the future. When I returned to my car, I texted Rowan to see if he was home.

Not yet. I grabbed a pickup basketball game with a few friends. It should be over soon after this last break, Rowan replied.

Okay, then I'll talk to you later. Have fun. I'm on my way home.

The dots that told me he was typing reappeared, and I smiled, knowing he was struggling to say something. Finally, a kissy face emoji appeared, replacing whatever he had been trying to say. I laughed, put my phone away and headed home.

Chapter 35

Raucous laughter filled Sash's house as I described in vivid detail my date with Jack, finishing with me declaring the experiment's completion for the safety sake of everyone involved. The cursed dates had evolved to fire for crying out loud.

"I'm sad to see the comedy shows ending," Lily joked. Her eyes sparkled with happiness and life.

"Pictures would have been amazing," Sasha choked a little on a laugh.

"Okay, but really, this guy was seriously great. Obviously, just not for me," I told them, looking at Hope.

"I already saw him," Hope admitted. "I answered his message that night, and we talked back and forth before I gave him my cell number and he called. We talked for hours. Sheesh!" Hope exclaimed. "When you sent me that picture, I dropped my phone. He's hot!"

"You already went on a date with him?" I asked, shocked.

"Yesterday," Hope confirmed. "You are so right; he's perfect for me. I thought that about the other one, but this guy seems different. He already got the embarrassing stuff out of the way with you, and you vetted him for me. I think any other guy with a toupee caught on fire during a date would have run away screaming. He stuck it out and even went to ice cream with you."

"You sound smitten." Sasha studied Hope.

"I am kind of; man, that accent has me wanting to jump him as soon as he talks." Hope fanned herself theatrically. "You know what that means, right?" she waggled her eyebrows at Sasha. "It's just you left that we need to find someone for."

I zipped my lip at that, knowing she and Hannah were doing their back-and-forth thing until Austin left for school. I didn't understand why Lily and Hope hadn't caught on to that, but I wouldn't say anything since Sasha and Hannah weren't forthcoming with it.

"Now that Two is exclusive with her lawyer, there isn't much hope of her finding a connection for me," Sasha said with a light chuckle that I knew was fake.

Besides laughing, Hannah had remained mostly silent so far, which made me curious. She usually had some comment or another to throw in to keep the laughs going. I wondered if it was something with Austin. Even if it wasn't, that meant it was something with Sasha, which worried me just as much.

"I'd love to point out that things with the guy I've been seeing are fantastic. I've even learned he has some kink to him. We got kind of hot and heavy, and he had me pushed up against the wall and pinned. Before his son could catch us, he let me go but spanked me and growled one of those low, growly sounds that are such a turn-on," Lily gushed.

I snickered at the picture she painted. "Like a werewolf?"

"A less hairy one." Lily nodded, serious. I laughed because I had been kidding, but Lily was head over heels for Todd. "He liked it when I bit his nipple too."

"Talk to us when you bust out the butt plug on him and see what his reaction is," Sasha deadpanned.

"Oh, should I?" Lily asked, and we all laughed, confusing her. "What? He might like it. So far, he hasn't been a prude."

"Maybe you shouldn't tell us things. If we ever go on a group date, I'm going to be staring at your man, wondering how he feels about kinky sex and butt plugs. That could be an awkward conversation to have." I tried to keep my face straight.

Hope didn't even try. She howled out a laugh. "I'm with Two. I'd be looking at him and thinking about how I knew he likes butt plugs. God knows if we were drinking, one of us would probably say it, too."

"Oh, yeah, that probably wouldn't be good," Lily quickly agreed, looking at me. "I know it would be you. All sorts of things come out of your mouth when you drink."

Hannah finally spoke. "No, kidding. She asked me to kiss her."

"Only group dates, then without Two." Sasha raised her eyebrows and gave me a look out of the corner of her eye.

"Not fair," I protested weakly. I couldn't argue because it was true. I had zero filters if alcohol was at play.

"Aside from the dating experiment, many changes are coming up," Sasha changed the subject. "Two's son is leaving for college, and she's moving. She might even get laid at that point."

I coughed, choking on my water. "Gee, thanks."

"Practice, practice, practice," Lily advised with a wicked smile. "Purple alien penis should experience some good use."

"In conjunction with some of the others," Hannah added wisely.

"The look on Three's face makes me believe she should use all of them simultaneously," Sasha said quickly. Both Hope and I blushed.

"I think that's enough of that conversation," I declared, my face burning.

"Okay, we'll stop picking on you," Lily soothed me.

Sasha closed out the recording, got it uploaded and then disappeared into the kitchen, all of us frowning at her sudden departure. I motioned for them to stay in place and went to follow her. I found her bent over the kitchen sink, looking miserable.

"What's wrong, Sash? You aren't you today." I stroked her back in the way that usually calmed her until she turned and buried her face in my chest.

With a strangled-sounding sob, she asked, "Can you get rid of them all?"

I leaned her against the counter and kissed her temple. "Sure. Want me to go too?"

"No, I need you," Sasha whispered raggedly.

I left her in the kitchen and ushered the rest out, telling them Sasha didn't feel good and wanted to be alone. They all saw through me, but they didn't argue. I cleaned the napkins and water glasses and returned them to the kitchen.

Sasha was now sitting on the counter, looking absolutely miserable. Sasha contrasted her surroundings, more so than usual right now. Her house was a mix of whites and soft colors, while Sasha was bold, bright, and in your face. Except she looked like the color had drained out of her life completely.

"Want to talk here?" I put my hands on her knees and dipped down to look her in the eyes.

"No, we can go back out the living room." She slid down off the counter with a thump, none of her usual grace evident.

I followed behind, wondering if I needed to grab chocolate for this conversation, and before I made it out, I grabbed it out of the cupboard I was passing, just in case. It was rare to see Sasha this down; the few times it's happened, it hadn't been anything good.

Sasha curled up on her side on the couch, and I slid in next to her. She moved, putting her head on my lap. I wove my fingers through her hair, massaging her scalp while Sasha gulped in big breaths of air. I said nothing because I knew she would when she was ready.

We'd been through enough together to know when to push and simply sit silently in solidarity. It was silent time. Sasha just needed my presence for the time being, and I gave it to her. I'd already texted Austin and Rowan that I was here, and Sasha was going through something and needed me. I massaged and soothed.

She settled down after about an hour of silence, sniffles, and random bursts of crying. "One of my clients overdosed and died," she said into the silent room. "They think it was suicide. She went to school with Austin, and I think he'll find out soon. You should text him to come over here after he's off work."

"Austin's off today. I'll text him when you are finished talking. You think it will bother him?" I quietly asked, my heartbreaking for the girl's family, Sasha, and all her friends.

"They knew each other. I don't think Austin knew she saw me professionally, but they hung out while in school." Sasha pushed herself up to sit. "I was so attached to this kid. She reminded me of me when I was that age, and I saw her struggles, the warning signs, and everything I did couldn't get through to her. I failed her, and now her life is over."

Oh, shit. This Sasha was the Sasha that only I saw. That explains the tension with Hannah, the fake attitude earlier, and the weird glances. She never let Hope or Lily in on this part of her life. It was highly doubtful that Hannah even knew it existed.

"Why do you think you failed her?" I reached over and took her hand, trying to gauge where to tread. Sasha was on a delicate ledge right now, and if I pushed too hard to get her to see reason, she'd topple and fall into a giant tailspin of depression where she shut everyone out and resorted to what she would call risky behavior. It's what I called downright dangerous.

If I let Sasha fall into the trap of thinking she could have changed this, she'd go OCD style over the top to reach everyone Sasha thought was at risk and push them until she drove them crazy. Her heart was so soft under that tough shell she displayed. That layer of sarcasm she held to so tightly hid the vulnerabilities she was terrified to show anyone. When it cracked, her heart bled like crazy.

"We aren't allowed to divulge a lot of personal information when we talk with the kids. We must maintain this professional veneer and treat them and their issues without letting our personal feelings get involved. If I hadn't had you, that so easily could have been me back then when we were that age. She kept asking me questions about how I handled bullying, specifically me, because she considered herself bisexual too and was relentlessly getting bullied for it. She didn't want to hear the political line we have to say. She wanted me, Sasha, to talk to her. Every time I tried to put myself into an answer, we were interrupted by a supervisor or someone else. Like there was some bug in the room that picked up personal information," Sasha said sadly.

I wasn't sure what to say. I didn't believe this child's actions were the fault of Sasha, nor did I think that if suicide was what this girl intended, Sasha could have penetrated far enough to stop it. I didn't know a whole lot about this type of thing.

"I referred her to the right groups, even gave her names of people in the groups to talk to when she called. I noted her file and informed the school counselor that she was an at-risk teen. I did everything I was supposed to according to the job, and in my heart, I knew it wasn't enough. That's why I failed. I know I didn't make her do what she did, and if I had known her plans, I doubted I could have stopped her. When I say she was like me, I mean it. She was probably more stubborn than I was. I can't help but think that if I had just given her my story, maybe she wouldn't have gotten to where she found herself. If I had listened to my heart from the beginning, things might have been different." Sasha squeezed my hand.

I bit my lip, but the tears fell anyway. "What are you going to do?"

"Not follow the rules anymore," she said quietly. "I don't care if I get fired. My job is to help these kids, and if telling them I got beat up in a shower by mean girls helps them, why can't I say that? Why can't I tell them that I used to cut myself because I didn't know what else to do? They would know they aren't alone. God, she told me so many times that she was alone, and she wasn't! There are so many kids like her right now; it's ridiculous!"

"Use this to change the rules, Sash. Fight for policy change. Let those kids see you fighting for them in this way. You seeing us fight for you got you to stop hurting yourself. Start a support group of your own. Ask Rowan for tips; he volunteers his legal advice to a women's shelter, and he might know." I stroked her hand, keeping my voice low and soft.

"What if I could have saved her?" Sasha cried out.

"What if no matter what you did, it wouldn't change anything?" I answered automatically. "Don't play the what-if game, Sash. We both know how damaging that is. Use this to right the wrong."

"You know how I found out?" she asked suddenly, her eyes too large in her face. "That cop I dated for a while called me and told me because my name was in her file as her counselor. Hannah was here, heard me talking to her, and read into the situation all wrong. When I cried, she tried to help, and I pushed her away because I needed you. She snapped at me, saying that all I ever need is you."

"Oh, dear," I groaned, shaking my head. "She's young and has a few insecurities."

"Hannah's still attracted to you, too," Sasha told me flatly. "I feel like I'm competing with you, and I hate it. I know if we do evolve into a romantic relationship, it probably won't last, and that's hurting me, too, because I like her. I don't see it lasting, though."

"You aren't competing with me unless you set your sights on Rowan. If that were the case, we'd have a very different conversation. The age difference between you two isn't insurmountable, and you never know; it could last. You two are a lot alike and would need to learn how to compromise. Neither of you is very adept at that." I gave her a carefully crafted look of you know I'm right.

"Think Rowan will think I'm a giant pansy if he sees me like this? I mean, I do have a reputation to maintain." Sasha tried to joke, but it fell flat because it was something she was worried about on a deeply personal level.

"Rowan doesn't judge. Are you asking me to tell him to come over here?" I was confused.

"I am. Have Rowan bring Austin, too," she said tentatively. "I want him to look at my employment contract and the policies and ask for advice. I truly want to reach out to the girl's mom, but I'm unsure if I should."

Befuddled at the inexplicable response of my best friend, I reached out to Rowan and extended the invitation while watching Sasha closely for signs of regret. Life had kicked her in the teeth and she was clawing her way out.

I'm leaving to get Austin right now. See you soon, sweetheart.

"Rowan's on his way," I told her. "Big step for you, letting someone in like this."

"Yeah, well, I'm trying to be brave like you." She curled back into me. That explained some of the behavior.

"Hah! I'm not brave!" I snorted out. "You have us confused."

"No, I don't. You are the strongest person I know, sugar. Me, I'm all bravado until cornered. You, you push back and fight," Sasha murmured. "I'm working on it."

Stunned, I sat there in silence with her until Rowan and Austin showed up. By the ravaged look on Austin's face, I guessed he heard. He crumpled into me in a mess of tears, and then he and Sasha both snuggled and cried while I tried to explain it to Rowan.

Chapter 36

I thought I managed to get through the interview for Jerry's position pretty well. They did it panel style, which meant I was on one side of the table facing four different executives and HR. I answered their questions with intelligence and foresight. I gave suggestions on things I think need to improve and how I could help make that happen. When they asked about the situation with Cory, I told them the truth. Now I was racing home to get ready for the concert.

Rowan rented a limo to take us to the concert. Austin was so excited that he couldn't sit still. He talked in the loudest voice possible without getting told to stop yelling. It was so similar to me that I couldn't help but laugh. When Austin looked outside and saw the limo, it was over the top reaction time.

Seeing Rowan standing there in a well-worn pair of jeans, a band t-shirt and biker boots was drool-worthy for me. Sasha tapped my chin to get me to close my mouth and laughed at me, pushing me out the door past a bemused Rowan.

We stopped to pick up Hannah, who was still a little aloof towards Sasha, but she was here as Austin's date, so I didn't interfere. Austin talked the entire way to the venue, peppering Sasha and Hope with questions about concerts we had attended when we were young.

"Did Austin eat a bag full of candy?" Rowan whispered in my ear, chuckling.

"First concert and you got backstage passes. Austin's so excited he's probably going to puke when he sees the band," I responded. "I love it. I was like that when I was his age. If I had the energy, I probably still would be."

"Oh!" Hope exclaimed suddenly. "That reminds me! I found this!" she reached into her purse and pulled out a photo, handing it to Austin.

"Mom! Holy shit! This picture is so cool!" Austin bounced in his seat.

"What?" I asked, holding my hand out. Austin snickered and reached over to hand it to Rowan—a traitorous kid.

Rowan glanced down and laughed. "Priceless."

It was the picture of me pregnant with Austin and having my belly signed by the band after I got pulled from the mosh pit. They had stopped the concert to make sure I was okay, which I was. I honestly hadn't been in any danger.

Sasha laughed at the memory. "Man, those were the days. Look how young we were! Look at you, Lena. All glowing."

"That's sweat," I corrected her, laughing. "I miss those boobs, though."

"I happen to think the ones you have are pretty great," Rowan said in my ear, making me blush. He slid the photo into his jacket pocket. "I'm holding on to this."

Austin ignored the comment and asked Hope if she had more. "I have a ton of them," she told him. "I'll start going through and finding good ones for you," she promised Austin with a smirk at me.

Rowan hid a smile and turned back to whisper in my ear, "This is our official first date as a real couple."

"And you invited all my friends as moral support. That was so sweet of you." I fluttered my eyes rapidly at Rowan.

"After we told him of our shenanigans at concerts, can you seriously blame him for the backup?" Sasha retorted, much to Austin's amusement. "Between us, we should be able to keep you in line."

"After seeing that picture?" Austin burst out laughing. "Good luck with that." I smothered a laugh because it was true. At least back then, it had been. I wasn't so sure now that I was older. Mosh pits were fun, but I was sure my body wouldn't agree. I hoped that Austin would go in and experience it. There was nothing quite like that energy.

The excitement grew as we were given our VIP passes and led backstage. Austin looked like he was going to pee himself, and I was beyond happy I was here with him for his first concert. To see him this excited about something that we both shared a love of warmed my heart.

"Thank you for this." I stood on my toes to kiss Rowan quickly.

"My pleasure, sweetheart." Rowan gave me a dopey smile.

"Row! My man! It's been years!" A deep voice

bellowed out, and mine and Austin's eyes bugged out. The lead singer knew Rowan?

"It has! I was so glad to see that you were coming here. My girlfriend and her son are huge fans, and it gave me a chance to support the tour and see you." Rowan moved and did the man hug thing where they thump each other on the back.

"This is your girlfriend?" he smiled at me. Oh, shit. I felt a fangirl moment coming on and bit my tongue.

"Yes, this is Lena. She's not usually so tongue-tied. This man is her son Austin, and her friends, Hope, Sasha, and Hannah," Rowan introduced us. Sasha was even more tongue-tied than me, finally breaking my stupor enough for me to laugh.

"Sorry. I'm not used to meeting bands without being dragged over the gate by security," I blurted out stupidly.

Rowan threw his head back and laughed heartily at the confused expression on the poor guy's face. He pulled out the picture and showed it, causing the guy to smile and look back at me. "You are my kind of woman!" he threw his arm around me. "Good choice, Rowan. Come on, guys, let's meet the rest of the crew."

It was surreal and so much fun. We got to watch from backstage when the music started with the opening act. The magic of a live show hit me again, and when they finally went to take the stage, the security led us out to the front to watch. I grabbed Austin's hand and pulled him right into the mosh pit. He was stunned, but he went with it.

For the first ten minutes, it was like I was a

teenager again. At least until my old bones got tired of jumping up and down, then my ankle turned, dumping me on the floor. I only got jumped on twice before security pulled me back out again, a familiar feeling.

They brought me back slightly rumpled to a shocked Rowan and a hysterically laughing Sasha and Hope. Hannah was in the pit with Austin; it was perfect. I couldn't be happier. I stayed out of the mosh pit for the rest of the show. Afterward, we went backstage again and spent another few hours with the band.

When we finally left, my ears were ringing. Austin looked like he was about ready to crash now that his adrenaline wasn't racing anymore. Sasha and Hope were leaning against each other, half asleep, and I was smiling like an idiot at Rowan.

"So, you know him? Were you going to tell me that?" I asked, giving him a nudge with my elbow.

"We went to college together and were in the same frat." Rowan grinned at me. "He helped me get dates, and I helped him with his homework. When the band signed their first contract, he sent it to me to make sure he wasn't getting screwed over. I went over it and made suggestions, and he took them up. He offered me tickets and backstage passes to any show I wanted to attend afterward. It worked out well, I think."

"Holy shit," Hannah muttered. "Any more of those friends lying around you want to spring on us? That was fucking amazing."

"Hell yeah, it was!" Austin shouted. His ears must still be ringing, and he didn't know how loud he was talking. Sasha put her hand over his mouth until he got the hint. "I can't believe Mom pulled me into the mosh pit."

"Didn't surprise either of us," Hope said with a grin. "I am shocked she lasted as long as she did."

"Also, that she made it out without a broken bone," Sasha added sarcastically.

"Oh, kiss my ass, you two," I shot at them. "I was fine until my ankle turned. That's what took me down."

"Sugar, that statement didn't help your case." Sasha laughed, bending over to grab my leg and look at my swollen ankle. "Nope. Not even a little."

"She looked wild and adorable, though," Rowan told them. I wasn't sure that helped defend my actions, but he liked it, so I was good with it. I stuck my tongue out at Sasha.

"Let's see what he thinks after a weekend of camping with you, sugar." Sasha didn't even try to hold back a laugh.

"You are so evil. Thirty-four loyal years of friendship and you are plotting my downfall," I scolded Sasha. Secretly, I was slightly worried about camping. "You'll be there. I'm putting spiders in your tent."

Hannah snorted, spewing water across the seats at them. "Oh, ouch."

Austin looked between us nervously. "Now, I'm scared."

Hope shook her head and rolled her eyes. "Don't be. Your Mom might not be afraid to kill them, but she sure as shit isn't about to pick them up to screw with Sasha. For once, I'm happy I'm sitting this one out."

"Lily will protect me," Sasha declared, giving me a nervous look.

"Go ahead and tell yourself that. Lily's the only

one who will actually pick them up, and she's sharing a tent with you." I gave her my evil smile.

"I should be concerned, shouldn't I?" Rowan swiveled his head between us.

"Yes," both Hope and Austin answered.

"There's a reason their parents only let them camp in the backyard." Hope shook her head.

Chapter 37

One week remained until Austin left for Arizona. I was running out of time with him, and even though camping wasn't my thing, I was so happy that Rowan had planned a little camping trip that included him.

Austin was thrilled. Shane had never done anything like this with him. He never planned any of our vacations; it had always been me, and I had geared them towards things that would be fun for Austin. Half the time, Shane never even went.

I was standing in my mostly packed bedroom, trying to figure out which clothes to bring. Sasha had already called me twice to tell me to wear clothes that wouldn't allow a snake bite to penetrate my leg. I know she was messing with me, but I couldn't stop thinking about it.

"Sweetheart? Lena?" I heard Rowan call out from the front door.

"In my bedroom," I yelled back, listening to the sound of his footsteps coming towards me.

"Wow, what happened in here?" Rowan stepped into my room and looked at the clothes strewn all over.

"Sasha. She called twice, reminding me to pack

clothes a snake bite couldn't penetrate," I grumbled and crossed my arms, looking at him. "There are no snakes, right?"

Rowan chuckled. "Snakes are a fear, I take it?"

"Major one," I admitted, then leaned into him.

"Any of the ones we encounter will not be the type to bite. I can't say we won't see any because it's hot and dry out, but I'll do my best to make sure the area is snake-free," Rowan promised, kissing the top of my head.

"What do I pack then?" I said into his chest, unwilling to move.

"Shorts, swimsuit, t-shirts, leggings, a pair of sandals, and your hiking boots. Pajamas. It's only two nights, but if you get dirty clothes, pack two extra pairs—no scented lotions or soap. The mosquitos love that." Rowan stepped back to look down at me. "You okay?"

"Yeah, I'm fine. Nervous that you will see how ridiculously inept I am and break up with me over it, but fine." I looked back at the mess of clothes. "Two extra sets of everything?"

"No." Rowan laughed. "An extra set of shorts and shirts, a pair of leggings and a shirt. I won't break up with you over camping. I never want to break up with you over anything." He kissed me again.

"Maybe I should stay home," I said, nervous again.

"If you don't want to go, I'm not going to force you or guilt you into it." Rowan slid his arms around me. "If you do come with us, then I will do everything in my power to make sure that you have a pleasurable experience, and I will protect you from all the creepy things."

"You'll protect me from Sasha?" I hid a smile and looked up at him.

"Is Sasha creepy?" Rowan's answering grin made my insides flutter.

"Sasha's evil when it comes to practical jokes. We prank each other all the time. Not quite as much this summer since we've both been so busy, and I made a fool of myself plenty on my own," I told him. "We should totally go buy some plastic spiders."

Rowan laughed and kissed my head again. "Let's not. I'm sure we won't be the only campers in the area, and I don't want the rangers called on us when she screams bloody murder. Toss her in the river instead."

"What time are we leaving?" I sorted through the clothes on my bed and found some shorts.

"In the morning. I stopped by to see if there were any more boxes you wanted me to take home." Rowan grabbed some socks and set them by my shorts.

"Oh, yeah, they are the ones by the front door. Just pictures and stuff that I had up around here." I found some leggings under a mess of work shirts and pulled them out.

"I'll take them. I need to get home and let Demon out. It will be his first camping trip, too. I'm going to pick up the truck tonight." He kissed my forehead. "I'll call you later. Love you, sweetheart."

His look was soft and heated and did funny things to my heart. "Drive safe, love you too," I answered him, noticing the words didn't stick in my throat anymore. I was excited to start the next chapter of our lives and see what we created out of it.

I finished packing and went to set the duffle bag down by the front door. I looked at the sparsely furnished living room. All our personal belongings were packed up. It didn't even look like the same house.

"It's weird, isn't it?" a quiet voice asked from behind me.

"It is, but not in a bad way, Aust. Something has to end for new things to begin. Even if you decide to come back here and live, it will be a blank canvas to make into your place. Are you having second thoughts?" I turned and hugged him.

"Second, third, and fourth. What if Dad's right and I picked the wrong field? What if there are no jobs? What will happen to you if I work in a different state?" Questions flew out of Austin's mouth.

"No what-if game, remember? You do what feels right in your heart, and everything else will fall into place. No one can live your life for you; living your life should be what you are doing, following your dreams and making them happen. It's okay if the dream changes. It happens; just stay true to what makes you happy." I wiped a tear from my face before he saw it.

"What about you?" Austin squeezed me.

"What about me? You can't live my life; only I can. That's what I'm doing. This place, it's just a house, Austin. We've had happy and sad memories here, but it's still only a house. Home is where your heart is, with the people you love. It doesn't matter where you are; I'll always come to see you. You don't stop being my son just because you get older and grow up," I consoled him. "Did you pack for camping?"

"I did and made much less of a mess than you did. It looks like your room blew up." Austin gave me a snarky look. "Sasha?" he guessed.

"You know damn well it was," I snarled. "Damn woman is trying to give me a heart attack."

"Sasha's just as scared as you are." Austin laughed. "Come on, let's eat. I brought home some fried chicken, macaroni and cheese, biscuits, and corn."

"Wow. Worried you are going to starve over the weekend?" I poked at his belly.

"Rowan said we would fish for dinner. I've never fished; therefore, I don't have a lot of faith in my ability to catch enough dinner to survive. Stuffing myself now is my backup plan. I need food; I'm a growing boy," Austin rationalized.

"We are bringing food with us," I assured him. Nevertheless, we both gorged on comfort food and were in a food coma when Rowan called. I loved how he checked on me, tried to soothe my worries, and asked about my thoughts.

Rowan made me feel valued, respected, loved, and cherished. He had promised me always to make sure I never wondered how he felt about me, and he did. I hadn't once had a thought that doubted his feelings. He hadn't once done anything to make me think his feelings had changed.

While we weren't together on nights like this, I think a lot about how much I've changed from this experiment alone. I must admit that following through with it as much as I did was the right call on Rowan's part. I hadn't told him yet because I didn't know the words to say to convey what I genuinely meant. Merely telling Rowan that he was right seemed kind of understated and trite.

The flip side of it is that where Austin was coming from was right, too. A lot of change was about to happen for both of us, and it was scary in many ways. Exciting too. We would both struggle with it because we wouldn't be around each other every day anymore. I'd probably suffer more than he would.

I rolled over and punched my pillow, wishing for sleep. I reached for my phone. *I can't sleep,* I texted Rowan.

It took him a few minutes to respond, which told me I woke him up. I felt terrible about it, too. He'd put a lot of work into this weekend camping trip and was probably exhausted.

Are you worried about camping or Austin going to school? Rowan texted back.

Both. Change is scary, and there's so much of it coming. My brain won't stop.

If I was there, would you be asleep? Rowan wrote.

Probably. I swear this is not a guilt trip. I should have left you alone. Go back to sleep. I'll be fine.

I already packed the truck, sweetheart. All I need to do is get dressed, grab Demon, and come to get you in the morning. I'll be there in ten minutes, he replied.

I cried. I went and unlocked the front door and crawled back into bed. I was still crying when Rowan slipped under the sheets and pulled me to him. Like magic, the tears ceased, my mind quieted, and I fell asleep.

Chapter 38

*H*ow much work Rowan had put into this became evident when we loaded up in the morning. There was so much gear in the truck that I wondered if Rowan had time to do anything other than plan this camping trip. It was overwhelming.

Lily had a small SUV and was bringing Sasha, and we were picking up Hanna. Rowan had let me know that Lily had called him and said Todd and his son were interested in joining us, and they had their own gear, which Rowan had no problem with; the man was mostly unflappable.

"Do we have to hike to get to the camp spot?" I asked with an eye on all the stuff in the back of the truck.

Rowan shook his head. "We just pull up and unload. The spots are nicely separated, so space exists between us and whoever else is out there. This place isn't a busy campground, to begin with, so with luck, there won't be anyone else."

The farther we drove, the more isolated it felt to me. Lily was following behind us, and after about an hour and a half, we pulled down a gravel road I hadn't even known was there. We didn't see any other cars and drove quite a way back into a densely forested area. On Rowan's side, I saw several little dirt paths leading into the trees, which he told me were campsites.

Finally, he pulled off on one and drove back into it. I didn't see anything that marked it as a campsite and said so. My inexperience in this arena was evident to everyone.

"Mom, we are roughing it. Did you expect picnic tables and grills like a park." Austin scoffed.

I scowled at him, and Hannah elbowed him. "Chill. If all your mom ever did is backyard camping, this is a completely new experience for your mom."

Rowan led me out to relatively flat spots and showed me how they were suitable for tents, which, looking at the area, made the tents pretty well spaced apart as well. Someone built a fire pit at some point out from under the canopy of the trees. In front of that was a crystal-clear river you could see right through to the bottom—silt, sand, and rocks. The river was stunning.

The men all unloaded the tents and got them set up, grabbed some chairs to place around the fire pit, and the rest of us unpacked the sleeping bags and our bags and stowed them in our tents. Demon wasn't sure who to follow, but he stuck close to us.

"What are the yoga mats for?" Sasha asked Rowan, who stifled a laugh.

"Not yoga mats," he explained patiently. "These are sleeping pads to cushion you from rocks or sharp things."

Austin laughed and teased Sasha about it, his friend Patrick wanting to join in but being polite enough not to. Todd and Rowan got the food stored inside the vehicles so we didn't have to raise it off the ground, and then we carried fishing poles out to sit by the fire pit.

Lily was doing fine. She had been camping several times with her family when she was young, knew how to start a fire, what berries were safe to eat, and Lily even knew how to fish. Hannah was relaxed, and Sasha and I looked around for sticks that moved, fearing snakes and other creepy-crawly things.

Austin had a laughing fit when Sasha shrieked and jumped on my back because she walked into a spiderweb while we were gathering firewood. She followed behind Austin after that, so he walked into the spiderwebs first.

Rowan had brought some inner tubes that we inflated, walked up the river a bit, and floated back down to our campsite. We all enjoyed that, except Demon, who was tied up to a tree watching us have fun. We hadn't encountered any other people, but unfortunately, Patrick spotted a bear rambling around on the other side of the river.

Sasha just about walked on water to get on land. She climbed into the truck's bed as if that would keep her safe from bears. This time, we all laughed. The bear hadn't looked our way once and was doing its own thing. I had been excited to see one from a distance, of course.

We were having fun until Sasha and I realized we had to pee out in the woods. "What if a snake bites me in the ass?" I asked seriously. I couldn't hide the fear in my voice.

Rowan chuckled patiently. "The ones that would be out here don't bite, and I haven't seen any. If they are around, they will most likely be sunning themselves on rocks. Go back into the wooded area and try to find a fallen log; it would make it easier for you. You can hang over the back of it and keep your feet and shoes protected."

He handed us a roll of environmentally friendly toilet paper and pointed out a safe direction to head. We found a fallen tree not too far from camp but far enough that no one could see us, and we quickly peed and raced back to camp.

We finally began to relax as the guys went out to try their hand at fishing while we spaced ourselves around the campfire they had started for us. It was peaceful being out here. The smoke kept the bees away, and we had bug spray to keep the rest of the bugs from eating us alive.

Sasha and I went to get some snacks from the food in the truck, and we sat back down, happily munching on cheese and crackers while Lily told us stories of camping when she was a kid. After a while, we all napped, waking up when the empty-handed guys returned from fishing.

We made cold-cut sandwiches for dinner. Sasha entertained them with more stories of exploits she and I had, and we made s'mores. I was a little surprised at how much fun we were having, and the smile on Austin's face was worth it.

When the stars came out, it was so clear and unpolluted out here we could see the Milky Way, and that was a first for Sasha, Austin, and I. It was incredible. And boy, did it get dark out here fast. It was very dark. Then, all the sounds of the forest and whatever secrets it was hiding kicked in. Poor Demon wasn't sure what to do.

Sasha was practically in Lily's lap whenever a twig or something snapped, a tree creaked, or even when an owl hooted. When the first bat flew overhead, her scream pierced the darkness with the sound of pure crazy, and Demon went into a hysterical barking frenzy. Sasha might have had fun, but she was a city girl; there was no doubt about that.

She made Austin check the inside of her tent twice and then the interior of her sleeping bag to ensure no unwelcome guests were hiding there, and she went to bed. The rest of us drifted to our tents not too much later.

It was easy to stay up late, but sleeping in was a lot harder when the sun rose and shone through your tent like a beacon guiding a lost ship into shore. Rowan cooked us all oatmeal over the campfire and made coffee, which we sucked down faster than he could make it.

"I need a shower," Sasha griped. "I feel so icky."

"River bath," Lily told her. "Wear your swimsuit, grab a bar of soap, and wash up in the river."

"It's freezing." Sasha glared at Lily, offended at the suggestion.

"Go fast," Austin told Sasha. "I'll come with you. If I can do it, you can."

Sasha grumbled but went to change into her suit. I followed them down the river bank with Demon on his leash out of pure curiosity to see Sasha river bathing. I was having a tough time, not cracking up laughing. It would probably be less funny when I had to do it, but she was my current entertainment.

I almost fell over laughing when Austin couldn't walk in the water past his knees, and Sasha shoved him in, both of them shrieking like banshees as they toppled in the frigid water. They splashed around and played before quickly washing up.

Sasha was making her way out of the water when Austin let out a surprised yell. She turned and saw him following, but then she looked down in confusion at her leg. She reached down to brush something off and then screamed at top volume as she flung her hands right up, cascading water down over both of them, and something came flying out of the water at me.

I jumped backward, yanking on Demon, proud that I didn't fall over, but then gasped in surprise as a fish landed not too far in front of me, flopping around. This time, I let out a yell while Sasha and Austin flew from the water, her in fright over having touched a fish, and Austin because he didn't know why I was yelling. Demon was afraid of the fish and behind my legs, peering out at it.

Rowan and Lily came running. Both stopped in their tracks to gape at the spectacle of a terrified, soaking-wet Sasha and a freaked-out me, a confused Austin and the dying flopping around fish Sasha had single-handedly caught by flinging her hands up in the air, with Demon cowering behind my legs.

Lily was the first to break. She howled. Lily was leaning on Rowan for support; she was laughing so hard. I went next because, for once, it wasn't me. I wasn't the cause of this. True, if I hadn't moved, that fish would have probably smacked me right in the face and sent me sprawling, but it wasn't me. This show had been all Sasha.

She glared at me and then looked horrified that she had killed a fish and even worse, she had touched it. Sasha stomped past me, and I heard her holding back her laughter as she passed. "That's how you catch a fish, gentleman," she quipped and ducked into her tent.

Todd came up, chuckling, and grabbed the fish, clubbed it, and then gutted it. Gross. Cold-cut sandwiches for me it was. Rowan threw the guts in the water and cleaned off the blood so it didn't attract animals while Austin and I stood there.

"I still have no idea what just happened or how that fish flew through the air like that." Austin looked over at me, amazement written on his face. "I don't think Sasha will be going back in the water."

I giggled hard as the scene replayed in my head. "You might be right about that one. Lily will torture her for a long time about this, too."

"With good reason." Austin snorted. We headed back, and he went into his tent to change. Demon kept looking back as if trying to figure out what had happened and why everyone lost their minds.

Chapter 39

Rowan had decided to take us for a hike out to the waterfall. It wasn't far, but with the heat of the day, it felt like it was. Thankfully, we had all put our swimsuits back on or brought them, and standing in the waterfall's spray felt refreshing.

To my horror and disbelief as a mother, Patrick, Hannah, and Austin jumped off the cliff. But then Lily and Todd joined in, and unbelievably, Sasha. She shrugged at me from the top, which was only probably fifteen feet up, and cannonballed right in, dousing us and making Demon go nuts.

Rowan let him off-leash, and he barreled into the water and swam over to Austin, happily paddling around him and being part of the group. It was cute. It was cute until Sasha got out of the water and stood behind me, dripping all over me.

I scowled at her and pulled my top off. No sooner than I had done that when, she shoved me into the water and jumped back in next to me. Then it was on. There was the biggest dunking and splash war in history. Demon paddled back to shore, heaved himself out to lay on a rock, and watched us. He wasn't fond of the splashing. Rowan, however, got in and picked my side.

Sasha, who kept an eye on the clear water around her for any other fish that may try to bump into her, climbed up on Austin's shoulders and tried to battle Lily down off Todd's. You'd think we were in a beautiful warm pool with how we carried on.

Exhausted, I got out and sat near Demon on a warm rock. They were like little ovens. I saw movement out of the corner of my eye and expected another sneak attack from Sasha. But instead, I screamed as loud as possible and leaped into the water like a long-distance hurdler.

Sasha practically climbed Austin and was trying to stand on his shoulders. Her screams mixed with mine as I tried not to drown, clinging to Rowan as Demon grabbed the snake that had set this horror scene into motion with his mouth and jumped in the river as if he were playing fetch and bringing the snake to us.

Nope. I about had a heart attack. I used Rowan as a springboard, launched back to the rocks, and up them onto the ground without snakes. I checked thoroughly. I smacked my shirt with a stick to make sure no snakes were hiding in it. Once it was clear that my top was empty of the terrifying creatures, I put it on and gasped for air as Sasha had about twenty heart attacks while Patrick and Austin tried to get her safely back to land.

We were utterly pathetic and clung to each other as if life and death were laid out before us, demanding us to choose and choose now. Todd threw the snake to the other side of the shore, and Lily grabbed Demon, trying her best not to laugh.

Austin was grumbling about all the bruises he would have from Sasha battering him in fear, and Rowan, well, to his credit, didn't laugh at us. He simply exited the water, grabbed a towel from his backpack, and wrapped it around Sasha and me.

"Shit, Mom. Were you trying to kill us all with that stunt?" Austin growled, wrapping his towel around him. "The sound of you screaming had Sasha screaming, and now I think my ears are bleeding."

"Fuck off, you little shit. You pushed me into the water with a snake in it!" Sasha snarled at Austin, her lips blue and teeth chattering.

"You were drowning me!" Austin yelled back. Hannah stepped between them, biting her lips.

"So, that's a very potent, visceral fear that you two have," Hannah said mildly, making Lily lose it and crack up laughing. "I've never seen either of you move that fast before."

Patrick had his eyes glued to Sasha's very stiff nipples. "Yep, that was something to see."

I snorted but reached down to grab her shirt for her. "Might want to cover up."

Sasha looked down and then glared at Patrick. "Eyes up here, kid!" Todd smacked him on the back of the head, and Austin shoved him.

I couldn't help it. I dropped to the ground, laughing; Demon jumped on me excitedly. "How do you completely turn two independent women into bat-shit crazy banshees? Take them camping and have them see a snake."

"By the way, there will be several moments of

checking the tents and sleeping bags between now and bed," Sasha informed everyone gravely. "Or I will flat out go sleep in the truck. Jesus, tell me you brought alcohol, Rowan?"

Lily moved over to hug us. "I brought some whiskey. I know you, Sash. I planned accordingly."

Once we were dried off, we hiked back to camp, both Sasha and I having to pee after our breakdown. We went off-path a little while Lily scouted the area to make sure it was safe. We were almost back to our camp spot, but all the excitement, fear, and nerves had filled our bladders to the point of bursting.

We also felt safer peeing together. Confident that our combined volume would ward off the evilest of creatures, we dropped our shorts and leaned over the log we had found. Halfway done, Lily walked stealthily back into sight, holding something vaguely resembling a snake, and we lost it.

I gasped, which made Sasha look up and yelp, promptly releasing the rest of our bladders in a thick stream. And as she got closer, it moved like a snake, and we both fell backward over the log into some bushes and on top of our puddles of pee.

Lily started screaming frantically at us to get up, which we were trying to do anyway to escape from the crazy woman with a snake in her hands. She realized what had scared us and choked on a laugh while still demanding that we get up.

"It's a vine. It's not a snake. Get up! Now! You are in poison ivy!" she yelled at us.

Rowan and Todd came running over, Todd coming to a screeching halt at the sight of us bottomless, staring in horror at Lily as we tried to process the words she just said.

"Shit! Lena. The river. Both of you get to the river and wash!" Rowan shouted, bending over to yank my shorts up while Sasha finally pulled her own up.

We weren't runners, but we ran as my date had run at the sight of alcohol. We plunged right into the icy river while Lily ran over, bringing us soap. "Get those bottoms off and wash! Wash super good, and then wash some more!"

Hannah, Austin, and Patrick just lay down on the ground and laughed hysterically, with Demon bouncing excitedly between them. Rowan brought back clean clothes for us and fresh towels, his face a mask of concern, pity, and humor.

Sasha and I scrubbed our asses until they were raw. Lily grabbed our clothes and rinsed them out while shaking her head and sent the men back to camp. "Seriously, you two. Do you honestly think I'd be holding a snake? I don't like them any more than you do. I'm not afraid of them, but that doesn't mean I'd pick one up. And how the hell could you not know that was poison ivy? Oh my God. Sitting down will be very uncomfortable for you in a couple of days."

"Is that how long it takes to show up?" I asked, getting out of the water, my poor ass frozen, red, and sore.

"Typically." Lily chuckled. "I would have paid good money to have that on camera. Pretty much from the water freak out to now."

"I am never going camping again," Sasha growled as she brought herself out of the water and snatched up the towel Rowan had brought her. "Nature is trying to kill me."

"You both heard Rowan tell you that the snakes like the warm rocks," Lily reminded us, laughing. "Come on, let's start with the calamine lotion now."

Chapter 40

Austin left for Arizona, and we moved the rest of the stuff I could live without out of the house. It was a week of hell with red, itchy butt cheeks. I for sure knew what poison ivy looked like now. The image became seared into my memory for the rest of my life.

I wouldn't swear off camping because it had been fun, but I told Rowan I wanted one of those female pee-while-standing things. I was almost positive I would get a call from one of my parents after Austin told them all the stories he had, and when they did call, I promised to introduce them to Rowan soon.

By Friday, the worst of the rash was over, but I couldn't help wincing when I sat down in the hard plastic chair in Jerry's office. Not wanting to explain, I did my best to keep it to a minimum. That story didn't seem like a good one to share with your boss. Some things were better left unsaid.

"I just wanted to inform you that the selection process is down to you and one other person. I expect they will decide before you leave on vacation next Wednesday," Jerry informed me cheerily. "With that, have a good weekend."

I thanked him and returned to my desk, happy I was going home in a few minutes. Rowan had something to do for work and would stop by the women's shelter to speak to some clients. I had the night to myself. Well, myself and Demon. I grabbed a pizza to cook at home, went to pick up Demon, and then went home.

Demon and I enjoyed pizza and movies and fell asleep on the floor since the couch was gone. I woke up in bed and realized that Rowan must have brought me to bed at some point. There was no sign of him or Demon, so I went back to sleep.

Sunday was our last podcast about the experiment, and I showed up at Hope's, where she rolled around laughing at our tales of camping. We each concluded our feelings on online dating and what we learned through our experiences. That meant it was time for me to come clean.

"Okay, I must admit, I understand why the lawyer wanted me to see this through. I'm not going to lie and say I'm not looking forward to having sex. Believe me, that countdown is already happening in my mind. Because of this experiment, I've gotten to know the lawyer on a deeper level than I would have had we given in and just went at each other like animals." I gave them a small smile.

"Explain that," Sasha said gently, and I knew it wasn't just for the benefit of whoever would be listening. It was for her, too.

"I've learned that there needs to be something more between a couple in a relationship than sex. Yes, it's important, but it's not everything. My lawyer's shown me repeatedly how much I mean to him without the physical aspect of it. Simply lying next to me and holding me gave me the biggest feelings of comfort that I have ever had. We aren't two people lying in a bed trying to think of something to say after ten minutes of passion. I can talk to him for hours." I sighed. It felt understated and I couldn't find the correct words.

"What if the sex isn't great?" Hope asked quietly.

"Then, we learn how to make it better together. I have toys now. I sincerely don't think it will be an issue, but if it is, I know there's a foundation that we built that wasn't on sex to fall back on. I want to say my lawyer completes me, but he doesn't. He helped me see I was already complete before him. With him, it's just this huge bonus that adds more value to my already full life. We all look for someone to complete us when we need to focus on completing ourselves first. That was a big lesson for me." I took a sip of water because I felt emotional. The words weren't easy to say but were raw and honest.

"You make a good point." Sasha's tone was respectful. I could see the sentiment resonated with her.

"Is there more?" Hannah asked, riveted.

"So much more. Going on the dates helped me gain confidence, even though almost everything that happened while on them was a total disaster or misstep. The confidence helped me see that it doesn't matter what's thrown at me; it's how I react. The waiter at the restaurant where I went ass up helped me see that by telling me my attitude about the whole thing was sexy," I tried to explain but didn't feel like I was doing a good job. "I needed to change my perception."

"The lawyer was right, then, to push you to finish

it, even if you cut the deadline shorter." Lily smiled at me.

"He was. He was completely right. The concert, my dates with him, everything we've talked about, and even the bad moments where I fell apart showed me that under it all, I wasn't as lacking as I thought I was. I don't think that means I won't have struggles anymore, but I might not be as hard on myself as I used to be. Overall, I think many people, men and women, need to learn to forgive themselves. Not everything that happens to us in life is our fault," I said emphatically. "Even when it feels that way."

"That is a powerful truth," Hannah agreed with a soft look at Sasha.

"Are you ready to move in with him?" Hope cocked her head at me.

"More than ready. I need to get through getting my son settled in college first, then the next adventure begins. The nights I'm with the lawyer, the sheets feel silkier against my skin, the bed is more comfortable, the pillow softer, the air sweeter. I'm not trying to romanticize love, but it's that feeling of contentment when you know you are where you are supposed to be. That the person beside you adds value to your life, not detracts from it." I swiped at my eye.

"Do you see that you are beautiful?" Hannah threw in another one.

"I am not quite there, but I don't think I need to be. My lawyer thinks I am; he treats me as if I am. I think it's enough for me to understand that he believes it, and therefore, I believe in what he sees if that makes sense," I puzzled out. Self-image would always be something I needed to work on.

"Girl, you rock." Sasha sniffed. "Right here, ladies, we all need to experience this. Those are words we need to hear."

"I love him. I know you all know that, but I'm just outright saying it to the world. I love him with everything I have. He was within my sight all this time, and it took dates from hell for me to see it. I don't regret one bit of it," I told them, beaming. "I rolled the dice, fell when I didn't want to, among many other literal falls, and won. I'm still winning."

"It looks good on you," Sasha told me. She closed up the recording and uploaded it. "Now what?"

"Austin comes home tomorrow, he finishes his packing, and Wednesday, we leave," I told them. "He'll have his car down there with him, and I'll fly back and cry myself stupid that my baby is grown up and a man now. Then, I'm getting laid."

"Three days driving to get there," Sasha ticked off, "and you are staying there how many days?"

"Four. The parent thing is two days after we arrive, and Austin has orientation the next day. We'll go out to dinner that night, and the following night, I fly home. I think I'll go on a walk while I'm there, just to prove to myself that I can," I said with a small smile. The walk would be for me to center myself.

"If you need us, call," Lily reminded me.

"You know I will," I assured them. "Are you going to see Austin again?" I turned to Hannah.

"Tuesday, while you are at work, so he doesn't miss any time with you," Hannah told me. It was pretty thoughtful, and I appreciated it.

"Then why don't you all come for dinner on Tuesday?" I asked them all. "Austin would love it."

"I'm there," Hope said, getting teary already.

"Me too. We'll send Austin off in style," Lily promised. "But don't you make dinner. We'll all bring something that's a favorite of his. How about that?"

"Oh damn, I'm going to cry," I whispered and fell into Sasha.

"Hush, sugar, we've got this." She stroked my hair and then pushed me away. "Go home and relax a little. Let us figure this out."

Chapter 41

After weepy goodbyes and the dinner the ladies had planned, it was down to Rowan, Austin, and me, with Demon, who knew something was happening but didn't quite know what. Austin and Rowan got the car loaded up with all his stuff.

Austin sat on the floor with Demon, cuddling him and looking lost. It broke my heart, but I felt pride that he would miss being away from me. Rowan had spent some time talking with Austin, and all he wanted to do was watch movies with us.

We all fell asleep in the living room and woke up to the alarm to start getting ready to head out. I was going to do the driving, not because I didn't trust Austin, but because it would hold my attention and keep me from freaking out about leaving my baby in California without me.

Rowan gave me a lingering kiss goodbye, hugged Austin, and made him promise to keep in touch. Austin cried, saying goodbye to Demon, which was a front because he was really crying about leaving the only home he'd ever known. I don't know how I held it together, but I managed it.

I had planned out a few stops to lift Austin's spirits and get him excited about the changes and challenges he had coming, and when we got to the first one, he perked up. We spent an hour playing around the Sea Lion Caves and then hit the road again until we passed into California, our first scheduled night stay.

The next day, we stopped in San Francisco and played tourists. We sent goofy pictures to everyone back home, and his trepidation seemed to ease up slightly. We stopped for the night just outside of L.A., and as we were going to bed, he whispered a thank you to me.

"For what, kid?" I rolled on my side to face him.

"For everything, Mom. I thought I wasn't going to be scared, but I am. Not for you, for me. I never honestly realized how much I relied on you before now." His voice sounded small.

"You rely on me less than you think, Austin. It's just fears of change that's hitting you. It's getting me, too, and it's okay. It's pretty normal. You have a new life starting now. This adventure is what I've been preparing you for all this time. I'm proud to say I think you are going to smash it. Don't stress over the unknown." I was grabbing for anything I could think of so I didn't cry.

"You don't think I'll fall on my face?" Austin asked timidly.

"Nope. Those genes of mine missed you, thankfully. I'm sure you'll make a stupid decision here or there, but you have a good head on your shoulders. You'll get through it. Everyone makes mistakes, Austin. Everyone." I was glad the light was off, and he couldn't see me wiping my face. I heard him sniffling, but he said nothing else and went to sleep.

When we pulled into the campus the following day, he was a little nervous but seemed more sure of himself than he had been. We carried all his stuff to his dorm room and got him unpacked, moved in and settled. This was it, the moment I had been dreading.

I ordered an Uber to come and take me to the hotel while I surreptitiously glanced at Austin as he looked around his new living space. I hated leaving him here, but I needed to go. Austin had to adjust. We were going to meet tomorrow and go to Universal Studios as a last hurrah, but now was the moment I had to let him go. It was my first step.

"I'm going to wait for the car, Aust," I told him softly, tears stinging my eyes.

"Mom." Austin turned and had the same tears in his. "I love you."

"I love you, too, kid. You are the best thing I've ever done. Remember that. Settle in tonight. I'll see you tomorrow when you come to get me." I kissed his cheek and hugged him close. Then I reached into my purse to give him the tablet Rowan and I had gotten him and loaded it with all our favorite songs. "When you feel lonely, listen to that."

Austin's lips trembled, and he nodded. "See you in the morning."

I almost ran out of the dorm building. Thank God the car pulled up when it did, or I would have gone back in there and demanded a room next to his. I texted furiously to the ladies that I just ripped my heart out by walking away. They sent messages of love back to me.

I checked into the hotel room that Rowan had set up for me through some connections he had and found it super swanky. He'd even had flowers delivered to the room to cheer me up. I dropped my bag on the floor and called him, falling on the couch.

"Hi, sweetheart. You are in the hotel now, I take it," Rowan answered.

"Thanks for the flowers," I breathed out, my voice wobbly. "I miss Austin already."

"I can only imagine. Was Austin okay?" Rowan softened his tone, and I heard Demon bark at something.

"He cried. I miss you just as much as I miss him," I wailed. "This sucks."

"You'll be home soon, sweetheart. I miss you too. So does Demon; that's why he's barking," Rowan soothed me.

My phone chimed with a text message, and I put Rowan on speakerphone to check it. "Shit. We had the days wrong. The parent thing is tomorrow, and his orientation is on Monday, not Tuesday."

"That means you lose the Universal Studios day, and now, will be there in L.A. an extra day before you fly back?" Rowan asked. "Want me to change your flight?"

"No, I'll stay the day because it means I'm still near Austin. We'll lose out on Universal Studios, though. That's okay. I'll make it a point to come for a visit and take him then." I sighed and texted the same thing back to Austin.

"Are you going to sit in the hotel and be miserable all day on Tuesday?" Rowan correctly guessed.

"I might talk myself into a walk like you took me on. Make myself act brave," I mumbled. "Demon is going to end up one spoiled dog now."

Rowan's rich laugh filled my ears. "He already is."

"I can do this, right?" I asked quietly.

"There is not one shred of doubt in me that you can. You are a fantastic mother, and I can only imagine how hard this is. Austin loves and respects you, and most importantly, he will succeed because you gave him the tools needed to do so. I know you both are scared, but I've yet to see either of you back away from it," Rowan told me.

"Now, I miss you even more," I cried again. I was a mess. "Thank you. I love you."

"I can't tell you what hearing that does to me. I love you too, sweetheart. So much." Rowan's hoarse whisper came across the line. "We'll be together soon."

We talked a little more, and then I bathed in the giant pool-sized bathtub in this luxury room just because I could. I was emotionally wrung out and exhausted and collapsed into bed after setting my alarm for tomorrow. Austin promised to pick me up and bring me back to the campus.

It felt like the alarm was blaring in my ear only minutes later. I got up groggily and dressed, trying to make myself as presentable as possible and headed down to eat something since I hadn't eaten dinner the night before. I was nervous and felt off-kilter.

Austin showed up not long after, and we went back to the campus and did a parent orientation and a group meeting thing with other first-year students starting that year. They led us on a tour through the curriculums of various programs, the frat's and sororities, sports teams, everything. It was information overload, but I was happy that Austin looked excited.

The parents of the kids on scholarship broke off, and we went in a separate direction and went over the rules they had to follow, which didn't seem all that different from what the other rules they already went over were. They showed us how to check grades or inquire about costs and things that the scholarship didn't cover. They went over campus jobs that students could apply for and what expectations were on that.

I was happy Austin was as intelligent as he was and had already memorized practically all this information. When we finally broke, he introduced me to his dorm mate, and then we met up with his friends from when he was younger, and we all went out to dinner.

Surprisingly, he had Sunday free, so we revised our plans and decided to go to Universal Studios tomorrow, his friends coming with us. We had a blast. We hit every ride and attraction in that place and didn't return to the hotel until late. I only felt a little bad that Austin would be exhausted for tomorrow's orientation. I wouldn't trade that day with him for anything.

He'd get used to it with the schedule he had set for himself. We promised to meet for dinner again afterward. I used the free time to catch up on some sleep and then sat out at the pool for a little bit, doing absolutely nothing but reading a book. It was strangely cathartic, but I missed everyone. I was not too fond of the inactivity.

I wandered into the hotel and asked the concierge about local hikes that weren't insanely hard or dangerous. He suggested Santa Ynez Waterfall because it was short and not treacherous. A waterfall sounded beautiful to me. He printed out directions for me to follow along the hike and said there were many trail offshoots. He advised following the creek and told me to watch out for poison oak.

It sounded like I needed to pay attention while on this one, and the hike was precisely what I needed. It would get my mind off leaving Austin here and help me prove to myself that I could do things I've never done before. With my mind made up, I went to change for dinner and let Sasha know of my plans for the next day.

Chapter 42

I took a cab to the trailhead and noted that I still had a cell signal so I could call for a ride back to the hotel. That was excellent and I felt better about the situation. I was wearing pants because of the poison oak warning, and I looked at every green plant that was close to where I was walking.

I encountered several other people with children tromping all over, and it made me feel marginally better until I saw a sign warning of rattlesnakes. I took a deep breath; I could do this. Face the fear and do the damn hike, I told myself. For God's sake, there were kids out here.

I carefully made my way two and a half miles to the waterfall. It wasn't nearly as impressive as the ones at home, but it was still pretty, and this was a beautiful area. I turned around to head back down when a crack of thunder sounded overhead, and I looked up, surprised. I'd checked the weather and hadn't seen any storms in the forecast.

Naturally, it was going to rain. It was me. The hike wasn't enough of a challenge with rattlesnakes, a strange area, poison oak, and God only knows what else

I refused to let myself think about while out here. *Rain could only make it better, right?* I thought to myself.

Calling it rain might have been an understatement. The skies opened up and dropped a river on me. I moved to the tree line a bit, hoping for a tiny bit of dry space to wait the storm out because I saw a blue sky. This weather had to pass the same as all things did.

I kept moving with an eye on the sky and soon found myself in an area I didn't remember passing through before. Of course, it all looked different, with water streaming over everything and little mud rivers over the rocks. Crap, I'd somehow wandered away from the creek I was supposed to be following.

Downhill seemed a safe bet, so I kept heading that way. I found myself wishing for Rowan's cool head and calm manner because then I wouldn't be lost out here on a trail that I probably had no business being on, totally unprepared to boot.

"Goddamn it, Lena. Get your shit together. You just did a hike by yourself. You can get out of here. Find the creek," I scolded myself. I wasn't a child or an idiot. I needed to remind myself I could do this.

After another half an hour of wandering, the rain finally stopped. Mud coated everything and the ground was slippery as hell. I was trying to be as careful as possible not to fall and avoid the poison oak. I didn't need a repeat of that. I wished again for Rowan.

I took another step downhill, and my foot went right out from under me as I stepped into a thick patch of slick mud and went right over the side of the hill, careening out of control in a nice mudflow. I think I found every loose rock there was to see, and my hair was collecting a lovely assortment of loose twigs and shrubbery. I didn't even want to think about the bugs that were undoubtedly touching me.

I cried out several times as I tumbled downhill and then found myself stopped suddenly by the creek I had lost, right into a friendly little algae pool of standing water and mud and a tremendous splash with several people shouting in alarm. Several familiar voices, that is.

I tried to wipe the mud out of my eyes and smeared it even more. "Lena?" Rowan's shocked voice penetrated the mess that I was in. I finally dunked my face in the creek and looked back to see the mud-splattered group of my friends and my son staring at me.

"Rowan? Why are you wearing a muddy suit?" I tried to stand up and fell flat again. "Austin, why are you at school?"

"It wasn't muddy until your entrance." Rowan laughed and stretched out to give me a hand up. "I swear to all that's holy; I had just told them I wish I knew where you were when you landed."

"I don't have anything scheduled today, Mom." Austin grinned at me.

"Why are you here?" I asked, looking behind him to see the quietly laughing faces of my friends.

"Because you needed us, sugar." Sasha shoved Rowan forward.

"You need a shower," Hope corrected Sasha as she looked me over from head to toe.

"I'm so confused right now." I tried to wipe some of whatever was covering me off.

"This is not how I planned this, but it fits."

Rowan shook his head with laughter. "I asked them to come with me last week. I've had this planned for a while now. Austin and I discussed it right before you two left."

"Not exactly *that*." Lily waved her hand in my direction, and Hannah and Sasha laughed.

"Had what planned?" I felt like a broken record.

Rowan smiled his sweet smile and got down on one knee in front of me. "Lena, I've been in love with you for so long now. After these past months with you, I knew I couldn't see a future where you and I didn't exist together. My days are brighter, I laugh, and I love your friends and son. You are everything to me, and I know this is moving fast, but I know it's right. The universe just delivered you to me. Will you marry me?"

He held out a box to me. I took the box with a muddy hand and stared at the solitaire diamond presented prettily in the velvet lining. "You're proposing? Did I hit my head, and I'm lying unconscious somewhere dreaming this?"

"I'm sure you hit your head more than once; it's you, but you aren't dreaming, sugar." Sasha nudged me. "Answer the man. It's the least you can do after dousing him with mud and some weird green stuff."

"Snap out of it, Mom." Austin laughed. "Come on, answer him."

"Oh my God." I got down on my knees in front of Rowan. "Even knowing the disasters that follow me, you want to marry me?"

"More than anything." Rowan chuckled and kissed me despite the goo covering me. "Will you marry me, Lena?"

I threw my arms around his neck and sobbed. "Yes. I'll marry you." Rowan moved to slide that pristine and beautiful ring onto my not-so-clean finger. "It's funny because, at the top of wherever I just came from, I wished for you too, and here you are, right where I fell."